Lavender Beach

by

VICKIE McKEEHAN

beachdevils
PRESS

LAVENDER BEACH
A Pelican Pointe Novel

Published by Beachdevils Press
Copyright © 2015 Vickie McKeehan
All rights reserved.

Lavender Beach
A Pelican Pointe Novel
Copyright © 2015 Vickie McKeehan

This book is a work of fiction. The characters, incidents, and dialogue are drawn from the author's imagination and are not to be construed as real. Any resemblance to actual events or persons, living or dead, is entirely coincidental.

ISBN-10: 069249426X
ISBN-13: 978-0692494264

Published by
Beachdevils Press
Titles Available at Amazon

Cover design by Vanessa Mendozzi
Pelican Pointe map designed by Jess Johnson

You can visit the author at:
www.vickiemckeehan.com
www.facebook.com/VickieMcKeehan
http://vickiemckeehan.wordpress.com/
www.twitter.com/VickieMcKeehan

Don't miss these other exciting titles by bestselling author

Vickie McKeehan

The Pelican Pointe Series
PROMISE COVE
HIDDEN MOON BAY
DANCING TIDES
LIGHTHOUSE REEF
STARLIGHT DUNES
LAST CHANCE HARBOR
SEA GLASS COTTAGE
LAVENDER BEACH
SANDCASTLES UNDER THE CHRISTMAS MOON
BENEATH WINTER SAND
KEEPING CAPE SUMMER (2018)

The Evil Secrets Trilogy
JUST EVIL Book One
DEEPER EVIL Book Two
ENDING EVIL Book Three
EVIL SECRETS TRILOGY BOXED SET

The Skye Cree Novels
THE BONES OF OTHERS
THE BONES WILL TELL
THE BOX OF BONES
HIS GARDEN OF BONES
TRUTH IN THE BONES
SEA OF BONES (2018)

The Indigo Brothers Trilogy
INDIGO FIRE
INDIGO HEAT
INDIGO JUSTICE
INDIGO BROTHERS TRILOGY BOXED SET

Coyote Wells Mysteries
MYSTIC FALLS
SHADOW CANYON
SPIRIT LAKE (2018)

For Yvonne Branch
with the kind and generous spirit

And each man stands with his face in the light
Of his own drawn sword, ready to do what a hero can.

Elizabeth Barrett Browning

Lavender Beach

by

VICKIE McKEEHAN

beachdevils
PRESS

Welcome to Pelican Pointe

To see the complete **Cast of Characters** list go to my website:
www.vickiemckeehan.com
under the **Pelican Pointe Series** tab.

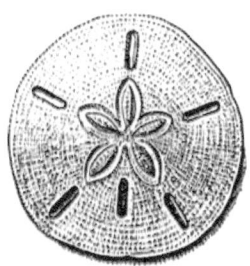

Prologue

Eight weeks earlier
Bakersfield, California

After making the six-hour drive from Pelican Pointe to Bakersfield, Nick Harris and Cord Bennett sat inside a coffee shop across the street from a shabby two-story smokehouse—their eyes glued on anyone coming in or going out of the building.

The two men had gotten their first good look at the place at two that afternoon. They'd already been waiting around for several hours. It was nearly dark now and still no sign of the reason they'd made the trip.

Parked at a table near the window, they nursed cups of coffee neither man wanted. But it was the best spot to keep an eye on the rooming house where Eastlyn Parker lived.

They already knew Eastlyn's no-nonsense landlady, a woman by the name of Clara Whitaker, owned the boarding house that sat two blocks north of the downtown area. It wasn't the best part of town.

Since entering the coffee shop, Nick had seen hustlers, panhandlers, and shady characters, many of whom were prostitutes, working the block.

Although Clara had promised to call Nick the minute Eastlyn walked in, the men were taking no chances. Both men were equally anxious to get this encounter over with. So far, their plan to stake out the house had been a bust. But giving up wasn't an option. They were too afraid they might somehow miss the former army helicopter pilot coming home.

"I don't see how I can drink another drop of coffee," Cord complained, pushing his cup away. "The stuff is making me sick."

With a growth of day-old beard beginning to itch on his face, Nick grumbled, "I'm right there with you. Every swallow is beginning to remind me of how burned beans must taste." He leveled a gaze at Cord and added, "Are you absolutely certain Ben Latham said this is where she lived?"

Cord nodded and glanced out the window. "Brent Cody verified the address with DMV. Plus, it's the last known address the VA has for her. It's also where she gets her disability checks. And it's the same address she gave the people at rehab when she checked out. Let's face it, Eastlyn Parker hasn't been doing well at all, Nick. You ever wonder what she'll say when she sees us?"

"I know exactly what she'll say and how she'll react. The same as you did when Jarrod Collins walked into that Houston jail several years back and bailed you out."

Cord gave him a sheepish grin. "The result of booze and a bad attitude. God. Am I ever glad you sent Jarrod to Texas to bring me back to California. Best thing that ever happened to me. If not for that, I probably would've ended up serving time for assault and battery."

"Yeah? But how long did it take you to figure that out? You weren't exactly thanking me those first three months you got dumped in Pelican Pointe. I doubt Eastlyn will be overjoyed we're planning this little intervention."

"Sure. I get it. Strangers show up on her doorstep threatening to cart her off. Eastlyn's bound to be pissed off."

Nick scratched the stubble on his chin. "Anyone would be. Is there a chance she may not recall that day in Iraq? A lot of water under the bridge since then."

"Who knows? It's been years. So how do we handle this little tactical operation? Do we have a backup plan for when she puts up major resistance? Which you know she will."

"We can't exactly kidnap her, if that's what you mean."

"Why not? We're here for her own good."

"Yeah, but convincing her of that is a monumental uphill battle. That day back in Houston, how exactly did Jarrod get you to come with him without you punching him out? You never did tell me that part."

Cord's eyes danced with mischief. "Jarrod refused to give me my truck keys, said he should do the driving to get us out of there and back to my apartment since I'd spent several restless nights in lockup. He suggested I get in the truck and catch some shuteye. I was so worn out I fell asleep. All I remember is leaning my head back on the headrest and Jarrod taking off around the loop heading back to my apartment. At least I thought that's what he planned to do. I trusted him to do what he said. Big mistake on my part. After spending three days in jail, my exhaustion took over and I conked out, slept like a baby. By the time I woke up, we were going down I-10 heading west, a hundred miles from El Paso, out in the middle of the Texas prairie. Since you and Ben had provided Jarrod his airplane ticket, he used my truck as his ride back to California, dragging me back with him."

Nick chuckled at the way the plan had come together. "So, in a sense, Jarrod did kidnap you?"

"Hell, yes. Why do you think I was so furious and resentful those first few months? The thing is, I didn't have any other place to go. So when Jarrod told me he was bringing me back to some town called Pelican Pointe, I thought I'd spend a couple days there and take off back down to San Diego. At least I'd be back where I started out. Problem is, I had no one there, either. Then once I met Keegan, my life completely changed. Now look at me, I'm an upstanding citizen, the town vet. Who would've believed *that* one-eighty turnaround, huh?"

Nick nodded. "I know what you mean. I admit I never imagined I'd end up there, either. Let alone happily married with two kids and a job at the bank."

"*President* of the bank no less. Funny how life has a way of throwing us a curveball when what we're expecting is a ninety-five-mile-per-hour heater down the middle. So how exactly do we get the captain to understand we're doing this for her own benefit?"

"We offer her a job. She's lost the last three."

"Spending multiple stints in rehab will tend to do that. So which one of us rides back with her so she doesn't try to bolt and lose us?"

"That would be you," Nick said evenly. "In fact, my strategy is to talk her into riding back with me and you driving her vehicle following behind."

Cord took a look out the plate glass window and sat up straighter. "Then get ready to test your scheme. There's her tan and red Ford Bronco pulling up at the curb now. She's getting out, so let's do this."

Nick pushed to his feet, tossed the tip on the table. "I've been working on my speech since learning about her. Let's get this over with."

The two men crossed the street, catching up with the former army captain before she stuck her key into the front door of the boarding house. As they reached the lawn Nick looked up at the front porch and called out, "Hey, Captain, you're the pilot who airlifted me out of that desert no man's land they called Iraq."

Nick stared at the thirty-two-year-old ex-pilot while waiting for a response.

Leggy Eastlyn Parker wore her golden-wheat hair in a bobbed but curly 'do. Her body was tan from all the work she picked up outdoors. Fit and in shape, she carried her shoulders back in a proud, resilient swagger. Her green eyes were sharp and clear despite another recent bout in rehab to kick a prescription drug addiction.

For the first time in seven years Nick got a look at the Black Hawk pilot who'd flown him out of harm's way.

Instead of what would've been certain death for him, he'd reached the hospital in time to undergo surgery. All because of Eastlyn Parker.

Nearly a year after his own rescue, she'd been flying another medevac mission—carrying another seriously injured soldier to the mobile hospital unit—when her chopper came under heavy fire.

Nick already knew that while at the controls she'd flown into a wall of surface-to-air missiles. As cannon fire hammered the chopper, she'd done her best to evade mortar after mortar to reach her destination.

While she skirted rocket fire, one penetrated the steel beneath her feet. It had cost her half of her left leg from the knee down. Though bleeding badly from her wound, Eastlyn had continued to fly her crew and the wounded serviceman out of the danger zone, landing the chopper miles away from enemy fire at the field hospital.

Her remarkable flying ability meant Eastlyn hadn't lost a man, not even the soldier who'd been slated for surgery.

Nick watched as she finally turned to stare down at him.

"I flew a lot of GIs out of that desert. Am I supposed to remember one in particular?"

"You ought to. I had a chest full of metal shrapnel and was bleeding out at the time. It was my good fortune that you were in the area and at the controls of the medevac chopper. You got me to the surgical unit in time for them to save my life."

"Sorry, but you'll have to narrow it down a little."

Moving closer to extend his hand, Nick accommodated. "Former Lieutenant Nick Harris, California National Guard. My Hummer hit an IED twenty miles east of Baghdad. The day it happened, the incident killed a friend of mine sitting right next to me."

Eastlyn politely reached out her hand to shake his, doing her best to think of something to say. After an awkward moment passed, she decided to fake it. "Ah, as I recall you went on and on about your buddy until they pumped you with enough morphine to shut you up." He didn't need to know that was a fairly accurate description of at least fifty of her missions. She went on, "Sorry about your friend. There was a lot of that going around back then, especially in those tin cans they called armored plating."

Nick tried not to let his emotions show. "I found out about you losing your leg after the fact. I'm sorry for it. But the day I got hit…you saved my life."

Eastlyn grimaced. With a wave of her hand she dismissed that notion. "I did my job." As she stood there eyeing the two men she began to suspect they had an ulterior motive for showing up. "Why is it you felt the need for a reunion, especially today, especially now?"

She spared a brief glance toward Cord but turned back to Nick, wanting an answer. "Why bring reinforcements with you? What is it you want from me?"

Cord stepped forward and reached out his hand, introduced himself. "I did tours in both Iraq and Afghanistan. I was there with Nick that day and…"

Eastlyn cut him off, eager to get rid of them and make her way inside the house. "Good for you. Well, it was real nice catching up and chatting like this. We'll do this again real soon. For future reference there's a bar around the corner. I haven't had a drink in six weeks but I'd be happy to meet you there for a beer…later." With no intentions of keeping that date, she turned to head inside.

But Nick's next words stopped her cold. "I understand you lost your pilot's license, which means you lost your job as a crop duster two years back. With it, you lost your ability to earn a living doing what you love."

Eastlyn spun around and narrowed a sharp gaze on Nick, sending out fiery daggers with one long glare. "FYI nobody calls it crop dusting anymore. It's known as *ag application*. It's a big deal around here in Kern County. It isn't all about spraying pesticides, you know. They use planes for seed sowing, especially where rice is grown in the Central Valley."

Undeterred, Nick went on, "Thanks for the lesson. Whatever it's called, the company fired you when you failed a drug test. They made sure the FAA yanked your pilot's license. After that, you were forced to get a job doing whatever you could to bring in a paycheck. You tried your hand as a machinist. But you lost that job, too. Two months ago you got your ass fired from a landscaping outfit for failing yet another drug test. In four years you've done four stints in rehab at four different locations. You're running out of money and friends and places to go that will have you."

"How the hell do you know all that? What are you—spying on me?" Eastlyn snapped. "And what business is it of yours anyway what I do? What do you care if I drop dead right here on the porch? What's it to you? Why the inquisition? What are you, DEA? Not that it's any of your damned business but the drugs I had in my system that day were painkillers for my leg injury, legally prescribed by a doctor."

"Nice story," Cord offered. "But the truth is you were flying under the influence the first time, running machinery under the influence of Vicodin the next. A big no-no when operating a commercial aircraft even for *ag application* and an expensive metal lathe. The company frowned on your using prescription drugs while putting together metal parts for an airplane engine."

Nick took one step toward her.

Eastlyn stepped back, put both hands on her hips in a show of defiance. "I got news for you, pal, don't come any closer. Just because I'm missing part of my leg, doesn't mean I'm less capable of taking care of myself. I can still kick your out-of-shape, soft, sorry ass any day of the week."

She shot a look at Nick's much taller sidekick, bobbed her head in his direction. "Yours too."

Cord raised his hands in peace. "These days I'm more of a lover than a fighter."

Nick fought the urge to smile at the exchange. But now was not the time to show a crack in the veneer. He knew he needed to keep a serious face. "You probably could kick my ass if you were motivated enough since I spend a lot of time these days sitting behind a desk, although I do have two active kids that keep me in pretty good shape running after them. Besides, I didn't say a thing about your lack of ability. Physically, you're fine. I'm sure you look the same as you did the day you saved my life," Nick asserted. "It's just…"

"Stop saying that! I flew your ass to the nearest mobile hospital and unloaded my cargo. That was my job. I made the same trip hundreds of times. That's it. You were the last pickup of the day. So what? How the hell did you find me, anyway? How the hell do you know about all that stuff?"

Her eyes, full of anger, darted from each man back to the other. "Who sent you here? And more importantly, after all these years, why bother looking me up now?"

Nick and Cord traded looks. Nick wasn't prepared to reveal anything just yet. He doubted she would believe that Scott Phillips had sent them. Since Scott died that day in the desert, thanks to an IED that had blown up their Humvee, Nick thought it best to leave Scott's name out of the mix.

Instead of any more disclosures, Nick went another way. "A guard buddy of mine named Ben Latham did an electrical job here in town a few months back. Your name came up then. Ben tried to look you up but discovered you were locked up—and not by choice."

"So? It was a misunderstanding about back pay. I wanted what they owed me and they didn't want to give it to me. I caused a fuss in a construction trailer and they called the cops for disturbing the peace. I spent one night in a holding cell. What do you plan to do about it at this late date? Go beat up the boss for old time's sake and get my money back?"

"Not exactly. We'd like to take you back to Pelican Pointe with us."

"You're both crazy if you think I'm going anywhere with you two."

Cord shifted his feet. "Just hear Nick out."

"Look, I don't care what catchy name you use for a treatment center, I'm not interested. I just spent the last six weeks cooped up in one sharing my thoughts and feelings with a bunch of strangers and a lot of other touchy-feely crap agreeing to their twelve-step requirements. So all things considered, I'm sure you already know I drove here from rehab so I won't waste time telling you what you can do with another recovery place. Are we clear?"

"Pelican Pointe isn't a hospital. It's a town five hours northwest of here along the coast. In fact, my wife Jordan and I own a bed and breakfast we call Promise Cove. Cord lives there too with his wife Keegan. That cop standing out by the curb is Brent Cody. He's our chief of police."

For the first time Eastlyn noticed the guy, dressed in khaki shirt and dark pants, a typical law enforcement getup, leaning against an official-looking Chevy Tahoe.

"You're kidding me, right? You brought a cop with you? What are you gonna do? Use him to muscle me into the car? Arrest me? For what exactly? I'm clean. I've been pill-free for six weeks. I haven't so much as taken an ibuprofen."

Nick expected her defiant attitude. He needed to bluff like hell. He hoped it rang true. "There's an arrest warrant out for you. It's either pack your things and come with us or that cop is ready to do his duty and escort you to County."

Eastlyn narrowed her eyes. "That's bullshit. I want all of you off the premises or *I'll* be the one calling the cops."

Nick shifted gears, prepared to play dirty. "Remember that night before you checked into rehab? Remember those pills you bought from the bartender, Durke Pedasco, at Hotshots? Your so-called friend turned you in to an undercover informant for buying a controlled substance.

You must've suspected something was up, otherwise you wouldn't have chosen that particular time to duck into rehab."

Nick could tell Eastlyn wasn't buying the story. He could also tell her bravado was starting to falter, so he embellished even more. "Brent Cody over there is happy to cooperate with the Kern County sheriff's department to let them know you're..."

"Available for arrest?"

"Look, you could face up to a year in County and a thousand dollar fine for buying illegal prescription drugs. It'd be in your best interests to come with us and start over in Pelican Pointe."

"And this threat endears you to me how exactly? Nice story, by the way. We both know that's what it is. Durke Pedasco is no more a drug informant than I am. I've known him since we sat beside each other in first grade. He never sold me, or anyone else for that matter, drugs. You'll have to do a little better than that."

Nick started to wonder if this trip had been a waste of time. "Cord and I want to help you. Personally, I want to help the pilot who was responsible for airlifting me to a hospital. Is that so difficult to understand?"

"Enough that you came all this way from Bird Pointe, California, to give me a bullshit story?" Eastlyn huffed out an angry breath and considered how fed up she was with Bakersfield. Maybe she *had* reached a dead end here. Maybe it was time to try someplace else. But she'd rather make that decision on her own without being forced into a corner. "You know what I'll do? Because I really am out of options in this town and because I'd like a trip to the beach on your dime, I'll go with you under two conditions."

"Okay. Let's hear it."

"I want to see some ID from all of you, especially from that guy on the street wearing that phony-looking cop uniform."

"Sure. ID is a reasonable request. What's the other condition?"

"I get to pack up my things *and* drive my own car there. I'll need wheels when I want to head back home to see my family."

Nick knew the only family she had left was a brother, and he was stationed overseas. "Okay, but Cord goes in the house with you and watches you gather up your stuff."

Cord glanced at Nick, nonplussed. "Hey man, why me?"

Nick stared at Cord's taller, bigger, six-foot-four frame and slapped him on the back. "Because, you, my friend, I think she'd have a tougher time taking down."

One

Present Day
Pelican Pointe, California

Even though she'd grown up there, Eastlyn Parker didn't miss a thing about dry, dusty Bakersfield.

Living along the coast, she could smell the sea every time she went outside.

Wherever she looked there was evidence of spring. April lilacs were in bloom. Flowerbeds burst with golden daffodils, red poppies, Shasta daisies, or grape-colored bee balm. Dormant winter lawns came alive with green patches of ryegrass and clover springing up alongside pesky dandelions and creeping Charlie.

She lifted her head to breathe in the soft ocean breezes that floated through birch and cypress and big leaf maple. The swaying branches reminded her she'd spent the first week along the coast in the country. She'd acclimated herself to the region while a guest at the bed and breakfast called Promise Cove, courtesy of Nick and his wife Jordan.

The second week she'd rented a little guesthouse in town that had belonged to Bran and Joy Sullivan before the couple retired and sold Bran's vet practice to Cord and Keegan Bennett.

Her only other option for housing had been a loft located over the town's flower shop owned by Drea

Jennings. Since Drea had moved in with her boyfriend Zach Dennison, the florist had been looking for a renter. The apartment had come fully furnished, which was an attractive incentive for a woman like Eastlyn who moved around a lot.

Too bad it was out of her price range.

Despite having to pass on Drea's digs, Eastlyn had settled into the clapboard cottage across the courtyard from the animal clinic.

Before selling the property, Joy Sullivan had spruced it up, painting the tiny bungalow a soft mint green with white and brown trim. It had an espresso front door with matching shutters that brought to mind dark chocolate wafers. To Eastlyn, the whole color scheme made the tiny house look like a yummy French petit-four sitting on a party tray.

The narrow porch out front held a wicker rocker, a little round table, and several clay pots filled with sweet-smelling alyssum. Joy had gone to the trouble to landscape the flowerbeds along the sidewalk. Red and white Americana "splash" geraniums fought for space next to dark blue sweet peas, presenting a patriotic theme up and down the footpath.

Eastlyn liked to sit outside and watch the sunset over the bay. Nightfall brought even more excitement when she'd wait patiently to watch the neighborhood kids dash home from the park down the street in time to eat supper. The occasional dog might wander by, hoping for a scratch or a rubdown.

She'd learned over the past few weeks to enjoy the slower pace, to take in the night sounds as the stars popped out overhead, to inhale the aroma of Mrs. McKay's cooking next door and know the old woman had fried up another batch of liver and onions.

All in all, Eastlyn had settled in without fanfare or notice. She found the little house practical and cheap—a detail she knew had been orchestrated by Nick and Jordan.

The place wasn't perfect, but then what in life was.

Finding a parking place for her Bronco had been a problem. What used to double as the Sullivans' main house and clinic was now used solely for the purpose of the Bennett veterinary practice. It seemed pet owners were forever showing up for scheduled office visits and dropping off sick animals for treatment at odd hours of the day and part of the night. Lack of street parking had proved the only annoying aspect of living in the five-hundred-square-foot house.

Eastlyn had fixed the place up, made it homey. At least, better looking than the room she'd rented back at the Bakersfield boarding house. By doing her furniture shopping at Reclaimed Treasures, she'd been able to furnish her three little rooms. For fifty bucks she'd found a bed frame made out of old doors. Another fifty got her a round pedestal farm table with two chairs. For seventy-five she'd scored an aqua-colored mid-century sofa still in good shape.

She'd picked up a good deal on dishes and the necessary kitchen items. But the things she treasured the most were those accessories she hadn't really needed at all, things she'd splurged on—like the wide Cape Cod bookcase made from salvaged lumber and old windows. The piece had been pricey at a hundred and fifty and took up an entire wall. It was her pride and joy because that's where she stored her collection of books and the old turntable along with the stack of classic record albums that went with it.

Which meant she had the basics—a bed, a place to eat, a place to sit and listen to her music, and her rows of books to pass the time. What more could a gypsy-at-heart want for a stay that would likely last a couple more months at best.

To cap it off, the bonus included the fact she could head to the beach for a walk any time she felt like it, even in the middle of the night when she couldn't sleep.

Day by day, little by little, her life in this coastal town began to look up.

She hadn't had a Vicodin in fourteen weeks. Oh, she still suffered bad dreams now and again, but for the most part she slept like a baby even without the vike. In part, because she worked sometimes seventy hours a week holding down three jobs. When she wasn't at Cord Bennett's vet clinic cleaning out cages—mostly for animals that had undergone surgery—she worked for the Delacourts. Thane and Isabella had given her a job up on the hilltop. From seven in the morning to noon, she put her farm skills to work along with her mechanical know-how helping Isabella get a project up and running.

Crazy as it sounded, she'd agreed to drive a John Deere tractor and plow up dirt at the lighthouse. Once the soil had been tilled, she intended to hang around to do whatever job Isabella had on hand that needed doing.

For five hours in the afternoon Eastlyn operated a forklift for Landon and Shelby Jennings at The Plant Habitat, unloading deliveries into the garden center's two warehouses.

After clocking out at six in the evening, Eastlyn often hung around to peruse the pallets of trees and shrubs and seedlings, picking out her favorites. She had a fondness for lavender. Maybe it was its purple color that popped for her, or maybe its fragrant blossoms. Whatever it was, she'd already bought several pots of the stuff to set around the porch.

She knew lavender wasn't exactly the most practical plant to grow if a family of four needed a basic food group. But she'd studied the herb's benefits online and learned it could be used in medicines and oils. The edible flowers of some varieties could even be used to make ice cream. Who didn't like lavender ice cream?

Not that she had much of a place to grow anything in large quantities, but it was nice to pretend she had her own plot of land for each row of rosemary or cherry tomato. Besides, Isabella often asked her advice on what to plant on the sprawling plot of land between the woods and the keeper's cottage. Isabella called it an agricultural co-op where the town's residents could pitch in to take care of the crops and share in its reward and harvest.

Eastlyn was skeptical that the townsfolk would live up to their promises. She doubted they understood what dedication was needed for an undertaking of this magnitude. In her opinion, most people could rarely be counted on to keep the pledges they'd made anyway. The past had taught her that.

Regardless of how Eastlyn felt, she'd spent hours conferring with Isabella on which vegetable plants were hardy enough to grow in the peaty soil.

Sitting atop the tractor that her boss had borrowed from Taggert Organic Farms, she watched the sun come up over the rolling hills to the east. The crimson and gold sky gave her pause. It reminded her of all the times she'd watched the sun come up from a cockpit.

She fought off the nostalgic walk down memory lane and focused on the goal at hand. With one last section of field to go, she'd be done with the plowing by Saturday. That's when the volunteers would show up to start planting the seedlings.

Irrigation would be a problem. In the midst of the worst drought in a hundred years, the state tipped on the verge of running dry. But unlike other parts of California, Pelican Pointe relied solely on groundwater—one main basin and several sub-basins—for their water source.

Still, they intended to seek out help from the professional growers at Taggert Farms, who had long ago come up with their own conservation system that relied on rainwater and roof runoff as the main water supply. So far, their collaborative effort had paid off.

This morning, while Eastlyn turned over the dirt, another crew installed a micro-drip system running from the water storage facility.

It was during the quiet times spent plowing she couldn't believe she'd resisted coming to this Mayberry-like little town. The fictional place had jumped to mind the minute she'd laid eyes on Main Street.

Those first few days at Promise Cove, she'd wasted her time resenting how Nick had manipulated her to get her here.

There had never been a warrant out for her arrest. She'd known that from the beginning. That fact hadn't lessened her anger. It took the end of the first week for her annoyance to slide into grudging acquiescence.

After those initial days, no matter how she'd tried, she couldn't find much to bitch about the place, certainly not with her room. The accommodations were first-rate. The innkeepers saw to that. Nick and Jordan routinely treated their guests like kings and queens however long their stay.

Her room came well stocked with toiletries she hadn't thought to pack, like luxurious body lotion and fancy soaps she rarely took the extra coin to splurge on, certainly not the fancy conditioners and shampoos.

Each night she'd slept on high-thread-count sheets, dried her body with super-plush towels, and headed down to a delicious home-cooked supper. Each morning a complimentary breakfast waited for her in the kitchen, and she could grab an apple or an orange for lunch from the bowl of fruit sitting out on the buffet in the dining room on her way out the door.

The congenial couple proved hard to dislike—which made her feel petty about trying. What was there not to adore about hardworking Nick and Jordan Harris or their two little kids? It was hard to knock the friendship they offered, the conversations they tried to start, or the family atmosphere she found herself longing for, not to mention their stellar dedication to guests.

Once upon a time, she'd considered trying their lifestyle—married with kids. But that had all changed by the time she'd celebrated her eighteenth birthday. She'd wanted to fly helicopters for the army more than wedded bliss. Both lofty plans seemed impossible now. Things had changed. Not many men wanted a woman whose ritual of getting dressed in the morning included strapping on a prosthesis.

No matter how many state-of-the-art improvements doctors hyped, no matter how much upgraded technology experts touted, the device was still a turnoff for most men, at least those she'd attempted to date.

So she'd followed Nick's lead and Jordan's advice and settled in at Promise Cove to give Pelican Pointe a shot. Try as she might she couldn't find a thing wrong with the stunning backdrop. Concealed from the two-lane road by towering cypress trees, the massive old Victorian the Harrises had renovated backed up to rocky cliffs.

Below the bluff was a pristine cove with sugar sand that stretched the length of the forty yards of beach. She'd been a frequent visitor there. She found it her favorite place to walk in the evening, to think about her life and contemplate how she'd so disappointed her father.

Kennan Parker had been the reason she'd learned to fly. Her dad had first taken her up over Bakersfield's farmlands while he sat at the controls of a Piper Super Cub. She'd spent years dusting acres of crops throughout Kern County, sitting beside him, often begging for him to touch the sky.

Once or twice, she almost had.

That's what flying meant to her—freedom.

It was that love of flying with her dad that had been the reason she'd pursued all the requirements to become a warrant officer, a rank necessary to get into army flight school. An eager seventeen-year-old had written her essay by herself and wheedled everyone she knew to draft letters of recommendation. From there, she'd aced the aptitude tests, cleared basic training, and gone on to complete classroom instruction at Fort Rucker.

Her father had been rooting for her on the day she graduated.

When she climbed into the cockpit of her first Black Hawk helicopter, no one had been prouder than Kennan Parker.

If only she'd been able to maintain that swell of pride. If only she'd had the opportunity to make it right before his death. That's what kept her on the straight and narrow now, the idea of trying to get her life back on track. Surely that had to count for something.

She should've known, though, her father wouldn't understand how she'd handled losing the ability to fly. She hadn't wanted to spend time in the army grounded, her ass parked behind a desk. If she couldn't fly, what was the point of becoming a desk jockey?

She'd proved over the years she could do just about any job. One good leg and a prosthetic didn't make her handicapped. The VA felt differently. Every month the government sent her a check. Since she wasn't considered full disability, the money wasn't all that much. Whatever she got, she banked, stuck it into a savings account hoping one day she'd have enough for a house, maybe even her own plane.

Yeah right, she thought now. She didn't even have her pilot's license.

But one thing Eastlyn Parker didn't do—she didn't take handouts.

And as long as she stayed busy, she could keep her mind off the past.

Less than a year earlier, Cooper Richmond had been living in Sausalito making his living as a photographer. He'd traveled all over the U.S. and abroad. No doubt with each move he'd been doing his best to run from his past.

Now, he'd relocated back to the town where it all started. He'd spent his first eighteen years of life here watching his parents verbally battle each other on a daily basis. He'd surprised a few longtime residents with his choice to come back. These days if he felt like it, Coop could have dinner with his brother, Caleb, or his sister, Drea, or his adoptive parents—who were really his aunt and uncle—Shelby and Landon Jennings.

He'd learned early on that family dynamics could be a minefield. Because history had taught him relationships were often mired in crazy, erratic behavior—most notably his mother. Over the years all three siblings had struggled mightily to put their dysfunctional early childhood behind them as much as possible.

But Cooper, by far, had the worst time of it.

Not everyone had a mother as sick or as mean as theirs had been. Not everyone could so easily get past Eleanor Jennings Richmond's misdeeds, certainly not her children. Not everyone had a mother who'd been arrested for taking two lives so violently—a double murder—one of whom had been his own father.

It might've taken twenty years after the fact to put Eleanor behind bars, but Cooper knew that his mother was exactly where she needed to be.

Cooper had lived a lifetime bogged down in the guilt of helping Eleanor dispose of the bodies. As a nine-year-old boy, he'd helped her dig the hole. He'd used a wagon belonging to his siblings to wheel the bodies to his uncle's landscape nursery. He'd had to make two trips. When the truth of it all had been exposed, Cooper had felt shame.

Even now he was surprised his uncle and siblings had forgiven him.

Since moving back he'd let his chestnut hair drape to his shoulders. His blue eyes didn't miss much despite his low-key approach to life. He preferred spending quiet times and turned to his books for solace.

He rarely went out. Even when he lived in the big city he hadn't dated all that much. He preferred spending his evenings repairing his trains, making frames for the photographs he'd taken over the years, or reading a good book—all the while listening to Rachmaninoff, Vivaldi, Tchaikovsky, or Bach.

Inside Layne's Trains, Cooper Richmond tinkered with the wheels on a Burlington Northern engine attempting to get it to roll again.

During the months his train shop had been opened, business had picked up. The Christmas season had been a boon. One thing about living in Pelican Pointe, residents supported local enterprises.

Thanks to his neighbors—Kinsey Donnelly, Julianne McLachlan, Bree Dayton—he could fall back on his photography skills. Occasionally he did weddings, passport photos, even took school shots. His services had been in such demand he'd dedicated one corner of his shop to taking portraits, much like others did at Sears, he mused.

Drea had talked him into creating a website so people could find his work online and purchase his landscape photographs. Sunsets proved his most popular item, but his pictures of rainforests and mountain ranges sold incredibly well. People even seemed interested in buying photos he'd taken around San Francisco.

He put the finishing touches on the frame he'd been working on and glanced out the window. The newcomer, Eastlyn Parker, caught his eye as she pulled up to his sister's flower shop across the street. The blonde often dropped off floral deliveries from his uncle's nursery to Drea's place, especially when Caleb got stuck somewhere else in the county.

It wasn't like he kept tabs on the woman. But since Eastlyn had settled into the guest cottage behind the animal clinic, he'd noticed her a time or two.

Like the times he'd seen her walking along the beach near the pier, or spotted her with a basket on her arm picking up a few items at Murphy's Market. He'd even bumped into her while browsing the literature section at Hidden Moon Bay Books.

As small town scuttlebutt went, he'd been told about Eastlyn's tour in Iraq, that she'd lost a leg in combat. He'd also heard rumors that she'd worked as a stripper or a drug informant back in Bakersfield depending on which conversation he caught at the drug store.

Cooper didn't believe half of what he heard. He liked to think when it came to a person's past very few people could top his. That's why he was in no position to judge anyone.

He was in the midst of those thoughts when the door to his shop opened and in walked the woman in question. He watched her look around at all the trains before settling her eyes on him.

"Hi. This is a toy store, right? I mean, you sell other stuff besides trains, right?"

"Uh, yeah."

"Great. Point me to your model airplane kits. You know, the kind that comes in pieces and you put them together with glue."

Coop finally got his feet to move. He swung around the counter, made his way to the back. "Kits are next to the balsa wood projects that kids use in school. A few in town make their own miniature buildings for their railroad sets. The thing is, I don't keep a lot of model kits in stock. Most kids these days don't have the patience to put them together and there aren't enough adults around anymore who do that kind of thing as a hobby. So it would depend on what you're looking for whether I'd have it on hand or not. Certain model kits are special order."

Eastlyn browsed the meager selections. "I don't see it on the shelf. The Huey AH-1 Cobra attack helicopter."

"Ah, the workhorse of the Vietnam War, the chopper that provided fire support for ground forces and additional aerial rocket artillery. Now they're used mostly for fighting forest fires. The army also used it to work in tandem with the light observation helicopter or LOH as hunter teams."

Eastlyn hooked a finger in the loop of her jeans. "I'm impressed. Most people know very little about the Huey Cobra's role in Southeast Asia, let alone how they worked in teams with the LOH."

"I should probably confess I'm a bit of a nerd when it comes to what I sell. For instance, I can tell you which types of trains run where and in what areas of the country, which planes were used in what war. I carry the most popular models. But I don't get much call for the helicopters. Tell you what. Let's look up Cobra in the catalogue from the manufacturer." Cooper reversed direction, turning on his heel to head back to the counter with Eastlyn trailing after him.

He grabbed the fat book, about an inch thick, and flipped it open, turned to the pages dealing with historic aviation. As soon as he found the right one, he pushed the listing toward Eastlyn for her to see. "It's pricey. And it'll take a couple days to get here. By the way, I'm Cooper Richmond and you are Eastlyn Parker. Ina Crawford said you used to fly Black Hawks in Iraq."

Eastlyn winced at the phrase "used to." But since it was true, she couldn't very well debunk some woman named Ina's assessment of her situation.

"Used to fly Black Hawks," she acknowledged. "My dad's the one who flew the Cobra."

"In Vietnam? Wow, that's amazing."

Eastlyn studied the photo of the ad in the catalogue, its description and its price. "I guess Kaeden's worth fifty bucks. Go ahead and order it. I hope you ship internationally because it would be great if you could send it to Germany for me. It's a birthday present for my brother."

"How soon does it need to get there?"

"Two weeks." She grinned. "I didn't wait til the last minute this year."

"Let me check shipping prices and how long it takes the manufacturer to ship overseas." Cooper went to his computer, logged into the website he needed. "By the way, if you like old choppers some of us in town recently uncovered one in a barn south of here."

He saw her eyes light up with interest and went on, "A junk collector by the name of Cleef Atkins died last year." He didn't want to mention the man had been murdered.

"Nick Harris found out that in Cleef's will he deeded the farmhouse and the land to the town. The property is filled with all kinds of odds and ends, lots of stuff just sitting there for decades collecting dust. So a few of us spent a couple weekends out there taking inventory. Imagine my surprise when I spotted the old movie marquee Thane and Isabella hoped to use to reopen the theater. But what sat behind it was even better, at least in my mind, an old helicopter with the glass bubble."

Eastlyn moved closer, leaned on the counter for support. "You can't be talking about the Bell H-13, that's the military version."

"I'm not sure. Let's look it up, too." Cooper shifted gears, opened up a new window on his computer and went to another website. He scanned through a lot of photos until he found the right one. "It looks similar to this."

She stepped around the counter to peer over his shoulder to get a better look. "Unbelievable. That's a Sioux three-seater, a single engine with a bubble canopy. It's also known as the *MASH* helicopter. You know, the one they used on the set of the TV show. What kind of shape is it in? Do you think it could be refurbished? Are you certain this is the aircraft you saw and not some replica? Because it could be the commercial version of the same model, the Bell-47."

Cooper smiled at her enthusiasm. "You could judge for yourself I could take you out there Sunday. It's the only day of the week I'm closed."

Getting a look at an actual Sioux chopper warred with the idea of starting up anything with one of the locals. There would be talk. Even a newcomer understood that in a small town one of the notable pastimes included a certain amount of leeway for gossip.

It wouldn't be a date, Eastlyn told herself after a few long seconds, more like an excursion to see a part of town she had yet to explore with someone who could show her the sights. "Okay. What about ten o'clock?"

"Works for me. The manufacturer will ship on Friday." Cooper handed her a sticky note. "Write down your brother's address for me, and an email address or phone number so I can send you the tracking information when the order ships."

"What's the damage?" Eastlyn asked, as she busied herself with writing down the details Cooper had requested.

He tossed out the amount as he keyed the address information into the website's order form.

Eastlyn dug out her Visa from her jeans pocket, handed it off. While he ran the credit card, she stared at the collection of photographs on the wall. "That's Redwood National Forest. My dad took my brother and me there the summer I turned ten. Kaeden was twelve. The three of us had such a great time on that trip exploring, camping, fishing."

Distracted ringing up the sale, Cooper asked, "Where was your mom?"

"My mom had died of breast cancer the previous winter, January eighteenth to be exact."

Cooper's head snapped up. He noticed the light had gone out of her eyes. "I'm so sorry."

"Me too." Uncomfortable now, she had to think of something else to say while she waited for Cooper to finish the transaction and her receipt to be printed. "Did you go to all these places? I mean, I recognize most of them. That one there is from the Grand Canyon. That one's fairly obvious. But then there's the third one from the left. That's Ireland, Leixlip in County Kildare, Castletown, if I'm not mistaken."

Cooper gaped. "Not a single person who's come into this store recognized that spot. Not one."

"Oh, come on, it has centuries-old Irish castle written all over it. The whole gothic design and rolling green hills in the background wasn't a dead giveaway?"

"I guess not." Cooper narrowed his eyes. "You've been there. You've been to Ireland."

"I had an Irish granny at one time and lots of cousins who call the place home. I've taken the tour around Leixlip a time or two just like thousands of other tourists. Funny though, my pictures never quite turned out the same way yours have, no blurry images."

Cooper did his best to keep a straight face, but failed. "Now that's just sad. Robert Capa would probably tell you to stand closer to your subject."

"Capa, the guy who covered the D-Day landing at Omaha Beach?"

"One and the same. What was your favorite room there, at Castletown?"

"If you're going for fancy then I'd have to say the red drawing room with all that damask. I mean, who uses damask on their walls anymore? But my favorite has to be the entrance hall with the brass balustrade staircase because it screams classy elegance. Wake up with that every day and you feel like you've stepped back into the nineteenth century. Let me guess, I bet your favorite was the little room where they kept all the maps."

Cooper's eyes lit with wonder. "How did you guess that? Although I did admit to being a geek, remember? And when it comes to stuff like maps and charts, I have a hard time resisting getting to spend several hours studying all those old atlases."

"I know the feeling. I felt that way about flying once. Oh, hell. I'm tired of looking at blank walls every night when I get home. How much do you want for the photograph? Knowing there's an empty place on my wall, how could I possibly leave without buying it?"

"That's what every store owner likes to hear. In my case, the photographer in me wants to help you fill up your walls." He named his price then added, "But since you're buying the model and have to wait for it to ship, I'll cut you a deal on the artwork."

"Do I get to keep the fancy frame it's in?"

He chuckled. "Absolutely. Want me to run the charge on the same credit card?"

"Might as well. I'm splurging."

She slid her receipt for the first purchase into the pocket of her jeans, rocked back on her heels to study him. "Even if only half of what you've told me about that chopper is true, I'm looking forward to seeing it for myself."

Cooper took down the wall art, began to wrap it in brown paper for her to carry with her. "Why would I exaggerate about the condition of an old helicopter?"

"It's been my experience that if a man's lips are moving, I'd say the percentage is sky high that he's embellishing the highlights."

He laughed again, shook his head. "You need to find new men."

"Now see, that's the tough part," Eastlyn noted as she tucked the package up under her arm and turned toward the door. Just before reaching for the handle, she tossed her head back and said with a wink, "You be sure to let me know where I can find one of those, will you? You've got my email address."

Two

Haunted, that's how Eastlyn felt tonight.

For the past few years she sometimes had to fight not to relive the way her father had died. Sometimes, like tonight, her lower leg hurt. Which was impossible since it wasn't there anymore. The doctors referred to it as phantom limb syndrome. Didn't matter what they called it. The tingling and shooting nerve pain felt real to her.

Between the blues and the aches, both gave her cause to crave the pills again.

Lying in bed, Eastlyn twitched and stirred and couldn't get comfortable. She'd been tossing and turning for an hour. It was time to throw in the towel and give in to defeat.

She rolled over, reached for the lamp on the nightstand. Instead of picking up the novel she'd tried to read before going to bed, she crawled out from under the covers, her one foot hitting the floor. Good thing she'd earned high marks in balancing on one leg during gait training. As a former pilot, she'd embraced stellar equilibrium a long time ago.

She hoped a walk on the beach would fix her insomnia, which meant she'd need her prosthetic. She reached for a sweater first before putting on her jeans. The prosthetic came next. After buckling up the strap top and bottom and clamping it down snug over her limb, she stood up.

Her gait looked normal if one didn't stare for too long. Since losing her lower limb she hadn't tried to hide it. She wore dresses if the occasion called for it. Okay, maybe she didn't go out of her way to put one on because wearing it made her prosthetic clearly visible. Sometimes it made other people uncomfortable or made them feel they needed to pay homage to it.

In warm weather, she even wore shorts like anybody else. She rarely wore high heels, though, but it wasn't because of her prosthetic foot. She'd never been into Louboutins or Jimmy Choos—too fancy for her taste even before when she had two perfectly good feet.

After tying the laces on her tennis shoes, she headed into the living room. Grabbing her jacket for the chilly April evening outside, she looked forward to the three-block walk to the beach.

She loved nights like this when the stars glinted overhead like diamonds poised to rain down in glittering clusters. The decorated night sky made the air pop like crystal glass.

She made her way down Crescent, crossed Ocean Street, and found the stairs down to the stretch of rocky shoreline. High tide told her it might be difficult to walk in the dark so she found one of the large boulders near the pier where she could sit and clear her mind.

It hit her then. She needed to have her head examined. What had she been thinking to blow so much money on a picture of an Irish landmark much like one she had taken herself some years back? If only she could remember where exactly that photo was now. Probably buried in the storage unit she paid for every month back in Bakersfield with the rest of her junk.

If she kept squandering her cash on stupid stuff she'd never save enough to buy her own place.

And agreeing to go see the old helicopter with the hunky Cooper? Another stupid move on her part.

"Why do you always question yourself like this?" Scott asked from his spot near the end of the wooden pylons as the water swirled around his legs.

Eastlyn jumped at the voice. "What the hell? You scared the crap out of me. Warn a person next time you're in the vicinity. Make some noise or something so I'll know you're there before sneaking up on me in the dark."

"Sorry. It's a nice night for being under the stars."

"Aren't you poetic? You look familiar." She tilted her head to study the man and decided the friendly approach was best, so she introduced herself. "Now it's your turn."

"You don't know who I am?"

"Should I? Oh wait. You're the guy I saw staying out at Promise Cove the same time I was there. Are you new in town, too?"

"Not exactly."

Alarm bells started to go off. How did he get in the water if the crunch of rocks on shore didn't alert her to his walking around? She'd heard no splash or splatter, just the hard waves battling the boulders.

It hit her then that she was sitting in the dark with a total stranger in close proximity who appeared to have an agenda. The hairs on the back of her neck stood up. "It's a little late to play twenty questions."

"I'm Scott Phillips."

"I've heard that name," Eastlyn admitted, wrinkling her brow in thought. Her shoulders relaxed a little. "There's a Phillips Park over on Main. One of your relatives?"

"Not exactly."

"Are you always this mysterious, Scott Phillips? Do you always wander around town in the middle of the night?"

"To tell you the truth, I find it's the best time to roam around and…check things out."

That creepy feeling returned. Her eyes darted to the right to quickly find the best escape route. She tried to judge how long it would take her to get down from the rock and take off running. Maybe it was best to keep him talking while she prepared to do that. "Really? What are you checking out exactly?"

Scott smiled. "There's no need to be afraid of me. Your father's death wasn't on you. Sometimes it's a person's time to go and there's nothing you can do about it."

"What are you talking about? How do you know anything about my father?"

Scott went on, unfazed at the questions. "You didn't start taking pills or drinking because you lost your leg even though it was a painful experience. No one knows you got hooked on the Vicodin after your father died. You'd had an argument with him because he didn't understand why you couldn't stay in the army. If you couldn't have your old job flying Black Hawks for the army, you didn't want a desk job. He called you a wuss because of it. You said things you regretted. But then so did he. I have news for you, Eastlyn Parker. You're not the first strong person who's come unglued because of guilt."

"How do you know all this shit about me? Have you been talking to Kaeden?"

Scott shook his head, stuck his hands in the pockets of his khaki shorts. "Do you know why you're here? In Pelican Pointe?"

"Yeah, to get Nick and Cord off my back."

"No. You're here for an entirely different reason. Something big is about to happen and you're part of it."

"Get real."

"You're not in Pelican Pointe to heal yourself, Eastlyn. You're here to help someone else. Life isn't always about you."

When she started to object to that and rise off the rock, she watched the man vanish out of the water and into the night.

In a matter of seconds, he'd gone poof.

"Son of a bitch. What just happened? No pills. I haven't taken a single pill. I didn't even drink a beer before I went to bed." She scrubbed her hands over her face. "Now you're hallucinating. You're talking to yourself. Sheesh, no wonder they won't let you fly anymore."

Seven blocks from the beach Cooper had fallen asleep in the leather recliner in his living room, his nose stuck in a book. This time it was a hardcover delving into the history of the Black Hawk helicopter that he'd picked up after learning the attractive blonde had flown that type of aircraft.

At two-thirty something woke him and made him abruptly sit up. As he tried to get the kinks out of a stiff neck, the book on his lap fell to the tile floor with a thud.

To retrieve it, he had to get to his feet. He stretched his back and took a few steps before realizing he was no longer alone.

He snatched up the book and glanced toward the Kiva fireplace on the other side of the room, only to see Scott Phillips standing in front of it.

"In the months you've lived here, you've done wonders with this place. I used to know the Ashford family who lived here. They had a daughter named Jane Ellen, gorgeous brown eyes."

Cooper rubbed the sleep out of his eyes. "This is what you woke me up for, to listen to your nostalgic ramblings about your teen lust? I knew Jane Ellen. But when I knew her she was ten years older and married to an asshole, the town bully."

"We aren't all lucky in love. God knows Jane Ellen wasn't."

"Whatever happened to Bolton Waters anyway?"

"You mean after Ethan Cody stopped him from beating on his wife the fourth time?"

"Let me guess, Jane Ellen refused to press charges."

"Sadly, that's often the case. It's difficult to figure out why that is. But ol' Bolton eventually ended up getting arrested for cooking meth. Luckily, Ethan and Brent's combined efforts put him behind bars for ten years. That was after you headed out of town for greener pastures though. There's still a meth problem outside of town."

"And? Why wake me up to have this conversation now?"

Unfazed by his defensive posture, Scott went on, "Did you know that government research shows female veterans commit suicide at six times the national average of other women? Since the Iraq War the numbers have skyrocketed with servicemen in general, but the statistics reveal women veterans have now surpassed their male counterparts in one distinctive category—they take their own life in greater numbers."

Cooper ran a hand through his hair. "I suppose it's no coincidence that the only female veteran we know in town is Eastlyn Parker. Which means you think Eastlyn is suicidal."

"She's a lot like you are—riddled with guilt."

"You already know she came into my shop this afternoon. She didn't give off any suicidal vibes to me. Besides, the woman's entitled to her own troubled past. That's what a lot of people don't understand. You get to this stage in life, early thirties, and each of us carries around our own set of heavy, useless baggage. You should know that better than most."

"Just because I know it, doesn't mean I'll let good people spiral down a destructive path without trying to do something to stop it. Eastlyn's had it tough enough already without me, or you, sitting on the sidelines and watching it happen. Why shouldn't we try to help her?"

Cooper rolled his eyes. The two had gone back and forth on this for weeks, ever since Scott had appeared to him in the train store wanting to discuss this same topic. "I still have no idea how you got her to come to Pelican Pointe in the first place. She doesn't exactly seem like the type of person who'd settle for farming a strip of land up at the lighthouse or working part-time driving a forklift for my uncle."

"I got you to come back, didn't I? And look how that's turned out."

"It's annoying the way you think you're never wrong. You know that? The know-it-all Scott Phillips, who drives a person over the edge."

Scott bobbed his head in affirmation. "I know. It must be annoying because I'm always right. I just wish I didn't have to go through this tap dance every time to convince the parties involved."

"What makes you think you can save everyone?"

"What makes you want to give up before we try?" Scott shot back.

"That's another annoying habit you have of answering a question with a question. I'm going to bed."

Cooper shoved the book toward him. "Meanwhile study up on Black Hawks. Something tells me it'll be important down the road if you want to get through to her."

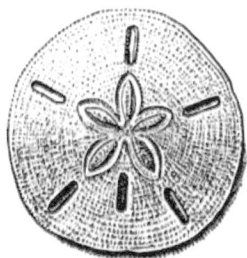

Three

It wasn't until later that night when Eastlyn couldn't get back to sleep that she remembered where she'd seen the name Scott Phillips. Her faculties might not have been at their best when she checked into Promise Cove initially, but there was nothing wrong with them now. Scott Phillips' name had been right there on the sign at the bed and breakfast—something about how he founded the inn in 2009.

"An interesting story there," Eastlyn muttered.

But it had been a flesh and blood man she'd seen on the beach. What did that mean?

She mulled that over most of the night until she finally got dressed for work and made her way across the courtyard to the clinic. She let herself in at five-thirty and went directly back to the post-op area to check on the Delacourt dogs, Jax and Jazz. The pooches had undergone a spaying procedure the day before.

Eastlyn opened the enclosure, noticed the two were livelier than they'd been when she checked on them at ten o'clock last night. Both doggies came over to lick her fingers.

She used both hands to scratch ears and rub backs. "Well, girls, how are we doing this morning?" Eastlyn took hold of Jax's snout and gazed into her big brown eyes. She did the same with Jazz. "Hmm, you both still look a little wobbly to me. Let's put off breakfast until the doc gets here and gives his okay. Drink some water instead. You're bound to have dry throats from the anesthetic."

She filled the water bowls and checked on the other animals—Jill and Ross Campbell's reddish brown cat they called Milkdud, and a silky Siamese named Felicia belonging to Emma Colter.

After spreading out food for Milkdud and Felicia, she made a point to wait around so she could corner Cord as soon as he got to work.

At six-forty-five, she got her chance when she heard his truck pull into the driveway. As soon as his feet hit the cement, she was right there with questions.

"Who is Scott Phillips exactly? I need to know what's going on around here."

"Good morning to you, too," Cord mumbled, picking up on her agitated state. Reaching back to grab his laptop bag, he added, "Don't tell me, let me guess. You had your first encounter with Scott. That took a few weeks longer than we expected."

"Now see, that's what I mean. Encounter? Is that code or something? And what exactly took longer? I couldn't sleep last night so I went for a walk on the beach. There the guy was just standing in the water."

"He wasn't walking on the water, was he?" Cord cracked. "Because that would be a new one."

She gave him a fake smile. "Very funny. What the man did was go *poof* right in front of me." She snapped her fingers for emphasis in front of Cord's face. "Just like that, the man disappeared. And before you accuse me of using again, I most certainly was not. No pills in over three months. I've had the occasional beer but I haven't been drunk, not once. I've been working my ass off…"

Cord made his way to the front door of the clinic and stopped. "Calm down. I'm not accusing you of anything. I've been there." He tilted his head, stared at the bags under her eyes. "You look like you had a rough night."

"Gee, just what every female longs to hear. Your wife must be such a lucky woman to have you to sweet-talk your way into a romantic situation."

"Typical pilot smartass. Do you want my help or not?"

"You know I do."

"Then you really should go talk to Nick and Jordan about this. They're the experts on Scott. They could explain it to you a lot better than I ever could."

Not willing to be put off until she could do that, she pushed him. "How would this guy know personal stuff about me though? How? Did you or Nick tell him shit about me? Have Nick and that Ben person been talking about me?"

Cord shook his head. "Look, you're working yourself up into a snit again. Wrong move. I don't know any easy way to say this so I'll just be blunt. Scott Phillips died in Iraq the same day you flew Nick out of that hell zone."

"Okay, so he has a brother. The guy I saw must've been Scott's brother."

Cord shook his head again. "No. Scott was an only child who lost his parents at the age of five. After that he came to Pelican Pointe to live with his grandparents. He grew up in the house where Promise Cove is now. Once his grandparents died, Scott never had any family until Jordan and Hutton came along."

That gave Eastlyn pause. "Hutton's his? Interesting. Then what I saw last night had to be a figment of my imagination, a hallucination of some kind brought on by withdrawal. Sure, that's it. I must've seen his pictures out at the inn and just banked the photos in my head…" When she saw the look on Cord's face, she protested, "What I saw last night isn't possible."

"You justify it any way you want. But the same thing's happened to a lot of other people around here, including me."

"You see Scott?"

"All the time."

"But he's dead."

"Next time you see him, be sure to bring that up. Sometimes he forgets that little nugget. I'm sure that info will get a laugh out of him."

"I've landed in the *Twilight Zone*," Eastlyn said, running her hand through the unruly waves of hair she hadn't bothered to brush.

"More like *The Sixth Sense*. You know, a bunch of ghosts who don't know they're already dead. I always loved that movie."

"How can you joke about this?"

"I'm used to it. Him. I'm used to seeing Scott around town. He's the reason Nick and I drove to Bakersfield."

"What? Why?"

"He urged us to go to there and see if we could talk you into coming here to start your life over."

"You mean you do everything Scott tells you to do?"

"Mostly. It's easier that way than to bump heads with him in the middle of the night when he shows up, unannounced, scares the bejesus out of you and refuses to leave you in peace. Plus, Scott has this annoying habit of being right all the time."

Cord ignored the look on her face and shifted gears. "By the way, I meant to mention this earlier, thought I'd let you settle in a little bit first. There's an AA meeting every Sunday afternoon at the church. It's such a small group that we've managed to merge into a get-together for both recovering alcoholics and those with substance abuse problems, a place to pour your heart out if need be. Most Sundays I manage to make it over there before they finish up. That is, if I'm not tending to an emergency. You're welcome to join us."

"You? Had a problem?"

"Me. Have. I'll always be an alcoholic who takes antidepressants every single morning. My dad says it runs in the family."

"I had no idea. Look, I appreciate you thinking of me. But it hasn't been all that long for me out of rehab and I'm still managing to follow the program pretty well on my own without outsiders listening to my heartfelt story. So I think I'm good to go."

"Suit yourself. Just remember the group is there, if or when, you need to talk."

Eastlyn left it at that. But on her way to work, she decided to swing by Phillips Park just to reaffirm to herself that the whole thing was real, that Scott was really dead and she couldn't possibly have talked to him on the beach.

When she pulled up at the curb, she didn't even bother getting out of the Bronco. Instead, she stared at the entrance where a plain wooden sign with the words, *Phillips Park*, hung between two stone pillars, metal lanterns on top of each post. It was a simple, yet powerful memorial from the town to a war veteran.

As she sat there on Main Street, she began to think back to her first week at the inn. There had been little things she'd been unable to explain while staying there, especially at night. She recalled the first time she'd taken a walk on the beach at the cove, hidden below the cliffs. While there, she remembered feeling as though someone had been watching her. At the time, she'd chalked it up to a deep-seated anxiety at starting over in a new place, in new surroundings. Then, there was the night she'd heard whispering outside her door. When she got up to investigate the sound, the hallway had been empty. She considered the fact that she might be headed for the loony bin when she'd misplaced her dad's army dog tags, which she carried with her wherever she went. Strangely, they had turned up the morning she checked out.

It might not add up to much. But then she included the incidents where she'd actually spotted Scott Phillips. Not knowing his name, he'd looked as real then as he had last night.

After some thought, she took out her phone, dialed the number for Promise Cove, decided Cord was right. It was best to ask the source.

Eastlyn didn't make it to the bed and breakfast until six-thirty that evening, a good twelve hours after her conversation with Cord.

When she made the turn down the narrow lane toward the inn, she slowed her speed past the apple-green sign where Scott's name appeared.

As soon as the house came into view, Eastlyn saw Jordan waiting on the porch.

"Thanks for making time to talk," Eastlyn said getting out of the truck. "I know this is your busy season so I appreciate it."

"Don't be silly. I always have time to talk about Scott. Come on inside, Nick's on kitchen duty. Have you eaten?"

Eastlyn sent her a wide smile. "I didn't come to impose like that. But I wouldn't turn down a plate of anything you have on hand. You're a genius in the kitchen."

"Tonight it was buttermilk fried chicken with mashed potatoes and fried okra. The meal was in honor of the couple from Nashville staying here on their honeymoon. They're due to check out tomorrow. They're down at the cove taking pictures before they head back home." In a casual tone, Jordan added, "So you've seen Scott."

"Last night. And a couple times while I was here but I thought it was a real person, you know, walking the hallways, out in the courtyard, down at the cove. I just assumed…"

Jordan hooted with laughter. "That's our Scott. He gets around."

"How can you laugh about it? When I got to work this morning Isabella did the same thing. She wanted to know what was bothering me. When I told her, she said Scott appeared to her like it was no big deal. She told me the whole story. How you were married to Scott when he left for Iraq. How you're now married to his best friend. Isabella was the first one of you who actually used the word 'ghost' to describe Scott. You should know, I don't believe in this kind of stuff."

Eastlyn followed Jordan into the kitchen where Nick, was indeed cleaning up the dishes. He caught the last bit of the conversation. "Then how do you explain what you saw with your own eyes? Tell me that."

"I need glasses? My vision's always been twenty/twenty but I guess now that I'm getting older…" Her voice trailed off knowing she could still see just fine. "I don't know."

"Scott brought me here, to this town, to this place, to this woman," Nick said. "Without Scott's interference in my life I wouldn't have all this."

"What does that have to do with me? I've never even met Scott."

"But neither had Isabella," Jordan pointed out. "Want something to drink?"

"Iced tea would be fine." Eastlyn stuck her hands in her back pockets, wandered around the room in a nervous stride designed to buy her some time to think. "Maybe you guys should start at the beginning. Cord said that the reason you made the drive to Bakersfield in the first place is to bring me back—at Scott's request."

"I'll fix you a plate and Nick will tell you everything."

Over savory chicken and mashed potatoes Nick explained what happened. "I used to see Scott all the time. These days, not so much, unless he has something specific to say. Having said that, about two months ago I got up at two a.m. to let the dog out, and there he was standing right over there in the corner of the kitchen. We stayed up until four a.m. talking about you."

"Me? That doesn't make sense."

"I admit in all these years I hadn't bothered to give the pilot who flew me to a hospital that day, a second thought. After all, if it wasn't for you…" Nick's voice trailed off giving him time to compose his thoughts and emotions. "I was kept alive during what the medics call the 'golden hour,' that dangerous period after a life-threatening injury when they can't stop the bleeding and shock sets in."

She'd certainly heard of the golden hour. She'd lost her share of soldiers during the ride, those whose injuries were so severe they hadn't made it through that window to reach the hospital in time to get treatment.

"You were lucky," Eastlyn finally uttered.

"I won't argue with that assessment. But when the stars align and you live through something like that, you better pay attention, correct the things in your life that have gone wrong. You realize that same luck needs to be spread around to others. Scott told me you were in trouble. Ben did the recon. We cooked up this idea that he would go to Bakersfield to scout out a job. While he was there, he found out that what Scott said was true. I had to make a decision. Drive there myself to bring you back or let you spiral further downward."

"Why bring Cord along?"

"Because we did the exact same thing with Cord. And this time Cord wanted to be a part of it. It was his choice, despite what he told you. Scott didn't have to twist his arm or haunt him by rattling around chains until we got to Bakersfield."

Eastlyn smiled. "I see. So Scott likes to save people from themselves."

"Something like that."

"Last night Scott knew things about me most people wouldn't know. In fact, he said I was here to help someone else. Bringing me here wasn't about me. Any clue what he meant?"

Nick shook his head. "Get used to Scott's vagueness."

"That'll get annoying real quick," Eastlyn proclaimed. "Scott also said something big was about to happen. You're the town banker. You have your pipeline into everything that happens in this town. So what do you think Scott's talking about?"

"I honestly have no idea." Nick tossed a glance at Jordan. "What about you?"

Jordan frowned. "I guess Scott wouldn't be referring to the fact that the Memorial Day parade is coming together or that his daughter is about to complete her first year of school."

Jordan tilted her head to study Eastlyn. "No doubt you fit into the grand scheme of things. You're here so that you'll be a critical part of whatever it is that's about to happen."

Eastlyn's face showed her disappointment with that assessment and Jordan added, "Sorry. But you already know that none of us have the kind of prescient ability Scott does."

"No offense but Cord says you guys are supposed to be the experts."

Nick chuckled. "That's news to us. We're usually as much in the dark as the rest of the town, although you could go talk to Wade Hawkins, the retired history professor. He's done so much research that he's written a book about Scott."

Jordan chortled with laughter. "Everyone in town bought a copy when it came out last January. Wade even held a book signing at Hayden's bookstore last month. If you don't have the time to look him up I'll let you have my copy. It's actually informative."

Jordan scooted around the table and disappeared into the dining room. While she was out of the room, Eastlyn stared at Nick and held up her index finger. "Don't even suggest I should thank you for dragging me to the *Outer Limits* otherwise known as Pelican Pointe."

Undaunted with her outlook, Nick deadpanned, "Tsk, tsk, such an attitude. And to think, you haven't even seen the plot twist at the end yet."

"Yeah. Exactly. That's what I'm afraid of."

Four

It was never a good thing when the cops showed up at your door at six a.m., especially on a Saturday.

Eastlyn peered through the peephole to see Brent Cody standing on her little stoop. She glanced down at what she wore. She hadn't even had time to dress for work yet. Coffee in hand, still wearing a tank top and pajamas, she flung open the door.

"If this is a raid you'll be mighty disappointed in what you find inside. The strongest drug in this house is ibuprofen, and maybe a shot of espresso."

Her attitude made Brent grin. "Not a morning person. I'll definitely log that into my book. I wouldn't mind the espresso, though. Sorry to stop by so early but I needed to catch you before you headed out to the lighthouse."

"Half a day for me today."

"Still grinding away at the dirt?"

"Almost got it done. What's up?"

"The authorities in Kern County wanted me to ask you about Durke Pedasco."

"Oh, for God's sakes. Come on in. Durke was never an informant if that's what this is about."

"Durke's gone missing, Eastlyn."

Eastlyn lowered her cup. "Define missing?"

"I mean, he left a bar called Hotshots four weeks ago and hasn't been seen since. His employer said he didn't pick up his last paycheck and that Durke's not at his apartment. The landlord says Durke disappeared without paying the rent. In fact, Durke's belongings were boxed up, things like his cell phone, clothes, personal items. His boss checked with his parents, discovered they'd filed a missing persons report. What can you tell me about Durke Pedasco that might help the police locate him? Do you have any idea where he might be?"

She lifted a shoulder in a shrug. But she was far from unconcerned. Gathering her thoughts, she finally thought of something that might help. "Durke's parents own a cabin about an hour and a half outside Bakersfield off Highway 178. He's been known to go up there to get away. But his parents surely checked the cabin for themselves. And if Durke had gone there, he'd definitely call them so they wouldn't worry."

Brent took out a small notebook where he'd jotted down what the Kern County sheriff had shared with him. "His parents are Shirleen and Dale Novack."

"That's not quite true. Shirleen, yes, but Dale Novack is Durke's stepfather."

"Problems there?"

"Not really. Shirleen waited years to remarry. Durke gets along well enough with Dale as far as I know."

"Are you sure you haven't been in touch with him since you got out of rehab?"

"The last text message I got from him was just before that, maybe a few days. After that, I've heard nothing. It occurred to me that Durke might be upset because I left without saying goodbye. Come to think of it, I did send him an email but never got a reply."

"What exactly is your relationship to him?" Brent asked, sending her a determined look.

She gave him a long stare.

He dropped the cop angle. "I have to ask these questions, Eastlyn. It could be the difference in locating him or not."

She let out an extended sigh and plopped on the couch. "Okay. You're right. Durke's a lifelong friend. We grew up together. He lived one block over from me. His dad walked out when he was eight, my mom died when I was nine. So we helped each other through some really rough times over the years. I guess I'd describe him as my best friend."

"Boyfriend?"

Eastlyn ran a hand through her rumpled hair. "It's too early to walk down memory lane like this. But, if Durke's gone missing… I want to help find him. Look, we tried the boyfriend girlfriend thing. High school stuff. So yes, Durke's a former lover, an ex, many years in the past." She stood up, rubbed her hands on her thighs. "If I'm under the gun here, answering questions like this, I'll need another cup of coffee. Want some?"

"Sure. Did Durke have a drug problem, too?"

Eastlyn scowled into her cup on the way into her tiny kitchen. "You mean like I did? Durke's problems happened ten years ago when I was squeaky clean and in the military. Mine was…well, you know, more recent. I helped him fight his demons, he helped me through mine."

"By selling you prescription drugs?"

She whirled on the cop. "That's not what happened at all. Durke was no dealer or informant. I don't how that rumor ever got started. I should know. I went to Durke the night before I headed to rehab. I went there to plead for anything Durke might have on hand, not as a dealer, but from his own personal medicine cabinet, not to buy it, but to beg. Do you understand what I mean?"

Brent nodded. "I think I get the picture."

"I was desperate. Durke had been to the oral surgeon a couple weeks before to get a root canal done. I knew the dentist had given him Vicodin for the pain. But Durke refused to give me anything at all. I left Hotshots empty-handed and decided I'd reached one more low point in my life. I needed to do something about it. When Durke called it a night at the bar, he showed up at the rooming house where I lived to help me get through the night so that I could check into rehab the next day."

She caught the look on Brent's face, took it for disdain, and added, "As a friend. Our relationship had been strictly platonic for years. The next morning I drove myself to a treatment facility called Caliente Hills at the base of the Sequoia National Forest—beautiful spot, but it was no weekend spa. The counselors were tough, tougher than the other places I'd tried, different than all the rest I'd been to. They forced me to face all the hows and whys of my life so I could better focus on the main goal—getting myself off the pills. I think they might've given me that kick in the ass I needed to stay clean. Then when I got out that day, I went back to the boarding house, and there you guys were—standing there to drag me back here. That's the truth of it."

"Did Durke have a significant other?"

"He'd recently broken up with a woman. They'd only been dating for about six months though." She rattled off a name.

"Could you give me directions on how to get to this cabin?"

"Sure. And Brent? Could you keep me posted with updates?"

"Absolutely."

Layne's Trains shared a dumpster and an alleyway directly across from the animal clinic.

That night when Cooper took the trash out after closing up his shop, he spotted Eastlyn outside sitting on her little porch. She looked so forlorn that he decided to wander over and see what was wrong.

On approach, he heard Shostakovich's Symphony No. 5 soaring from inside the bungalow. Well into the movement on the track known as Largo, Cooper recognized the familiar weeping violin and cello in harmony with the flutes and piccolos.

"From your choice of music, you look like you just lost your best friend," he said as he took a seat on the steps.

"I just may have," she muttered before telling him about Durke's disappearance.

Cooper's face showed immediate empathy. "I'm sorry. I had no idea."

"Not your problem. So you're no fan of Shostakovich?"

"On the contrary, this is one of the most moving and brilliant pieces. From the peppered rhythm to the burst of finish that says he's mocking the politics of his time, Shostakovich slams you straight into the despair and hopelessness of the Soviet people."

Eastlyn lifted a brow. "Despair? You picked up on that as though it's something you've known firsthand."

"We could start a club. But I doubt we could charge admission. I get listening to classical music but why Shostakovich?"

"It's usually the one piece that matches up with all my different moods at one time or another. Did you know Northwestern University did a study that said Shostakovich was the one composer whose music helped get patients suffering from depression through their ordeal the best?"

"I wouldn't be at all surprised. His music has a way of reaching into the soul and pulling out a hunger and a desire to overcome whatever anguish is there. Never underestimate the power of music."

She tilted her head to study him. "I like the way you think."

"Mind if I ask you something?"

Her study turned into an irritated stare. "I guess. As long as it isn't some silly notion that I worked as an exotic dancer back in Bakersfield."

"Ah, I was wondering if you'd heard that rumor."

"Abby Anderson asked me about it two seconds after I rented this place. For a marine biologist Abby's not shy about sharing what she knows. She said she heard it from some woman named Myrtle Pettibone. Imagine that picture, me as a stripper. The strip joint would have to be pretty hard up to hire a woman who wears a prosthetic. Not to mention the fact that I'm way too old for such a ridiculous job."

"That's bullshit and you know it. If you're old then so am I."

"When men age they're viewed as distinguished. They grow old gracefully, women, not so much. Some days I already feel like the good days are behind me and I'm facing down middle age with a pitchfork in my hand."

That brought a chuckle out of him. "I'd planned to warn you to watch out for Myrtle, the woman's a pistol. In fact, she often packs one, so beware. But now I'm thinking we should all watch out for the newcomer with the lethal pitchfork."

Eastlyn's temperament morphed into a teasing tone. "Anyway, she has a crush on you."

"Myrtle or Abby?"

"No, silly. Abby." Eastlyn cracked a grin. "Hmm, for all I know maybe Myrtle has one, too. You're a popular guy, Cooper Richmond."

"Ah. No wonder Abby's forever coming into the shop. Did she tell you she has a crush on me?"

"She didn't have to. The first time I met her, Abby went on and on about Cooper Richmond for a solid fifteen minutes."

Cooper looked as though lightning had come down from the heavens and struck him in the head. "I've never once encouraged her. She's a nice girl, but... I have no interest in Abby."

"Why not? She's blonde, beautiful, has a sunny disposition, and loves animals. Cord tells me when she finished her grad school she stayed in Pelican Pointe even though she could've had her pick of places to work. She passed on San Diego's Sea World *and* the Monterey Bay Aquarium. Maybe you're the reason."

"But she's what? Ten years younger than I am?"

"Age is merely a state of mind. Anyway, I promised Abby, the girl with the major crush on you, that I'd make it over to the Fanning Marine Rescue Center so she could give me the tour. So who's nosier, Myrtle or Abby?"

"Now that I think about it, both. Between the two, they cover one end of the generation gap to the other. Although, I think Myrtle must have special radar that Abby lacks." He paused as if he wanted to change the subject.

"You did say you wanted to ask me something."

"I'm curious. When you flew for the army what was your call sign?"

"Well, that came from left field." She cracked a smile at the memory. "Zerker." When she noticed his face contorted in confusion, she added, "It's short for berserker."

The bafflement disappeared replaced by a wide curve of lips. "You mean like the fierce Viking warrior? Those berserkers?"

She looked down to gape at him sitting on the step. "Not many people would know that. Ah, I get it. The nerd surfaces, once again, the guy who loves to read."

"Ancient Norse history speaks of a fighter known to plunge headlong into the heart of battle without a thought to his own personal welfare and unwilling to back down to the enemy. It's where the word berserk originated."

"The guys I trained with picked up on the Norse blonde hair and fair skin. Not to mention my mom and dad started out in Minnesota. My mom could trace her roots back to Scandinavia."

"Zerker," Cooper repeated. "I can see how the tag might fit. You're tall, probably five-eleven or so with a pilot's daredevil personality."

"I was never careless with my crew," Eastlyn pointed out.

"I couldn't imagine you'd be careless at flying. You carry yourself with confidence, have a warrior legacy, what with your dad's service in Vietnam, not to mention your Irish granny."

"On my dad's side, never underestimate my Irish granny."

"On your dad's side and you probably hate to lose a fight."

She burst out in laughter. "You just met me yesterday. Unless you're psychic you don't really know me all that well."

"Nick and Cord consider you a hero."

"Believe me, I'm not. Besides, I'm sure some in town still feel that I'm a druggie who hasn't yet fully reformed."

"You don't strike me as the type who cares much about what other people think."

Eastlyn winked and pointed a finger at him. "Again, perceptive. Want a beer?"

"You're allowed to drink?" With that one question Coop realized he'd stepped over the line. "Sorry. I'd love a beer."

She rose out of the rocker and turned to go into the house, but stopped. "Now it's my turn. What can you tell me about Scott Phillips?"

"He's our local legend, the guardian of the town, watching over the people he loves. That's the urban myth."

Cooper followed her into the cottage, watched as she turned down the volume on the stereo. His eyes landed on the Cape Cod bookcase. He ran his hand over the wood. "I wondered where this beauty ended up. I went back to buy it the other day and it was gone."

She handed off a bottle of Blue Moon. "Hope you like honey wheat."

"That's fine." He started flicking through the stack of vinyl record albums.

She took a seat on the sofa and studied him. She liked the look of him, the way he moved, the way he made his point with savvy and smarts. "Why do you have a different last name than Caleb and Drea? I know Landon and Shelby adopted you, which made you a Jennings. Drea told me the story."

He continued perusing her music selections until he turned to face her. "I've always been a Jennings in some form or another. Cooper Jennings Richmond. That's the name on my birth certificate. For a time after the adoption, I dropped the Richmond part hoping it'd make me feel that I fit in. But using Jennings wasn't the problem. In my heart I knew my father deserved to have a son who was proud of the Richmond name. If Drea told you the story then you know my mother, Eleanor, killed our father."

Eastlyn gave an uncomfortable nod of assent. "She killed your dad and your dad's girlfriend while the two sat under the pier making plans to leave Pelican Pointe. It's a tragic story about a man who was locked into a situation. Both victims never got a chance at real happiness. Drea knows now your father didn't want to leave his children with such a twisted woman."

The words were difficult to get out. But Cooper stared at her and did just that. "And did Drea tell you that I helped Eleanor bury the bodies that night?"

Eastlyn sucked in a tense breath, swallowed hard. "She left that part out."

"Little wonder. Not many sisters want to believe a brother could do such a disgusting thing."

"Cooper, what were you, ten maybe? Drea and Caleb even younger?"

"Nine. Fourth grade. I was never the same after that, not in school, not in town, not anywhere. My grandfather owned the same train store I run now. Getting to escape through the doors for a couple hours was my refuge. *If* my mother had chosen to allow me more access to him, I'd have spent my entire day there, working on the trains with my grandpop, wishing I could be somewhere else other than home, anywhere else. It kept me from going off the deep end. To this day, I can still see my father's body lying in the sand, what his face looked like, how grayish white Miss Caldwell's skin appeared."

"We've both seen horrific things. No one blames you for something you were forced to do by an adult who should've known better, certainly your family doesn't blame you. Everyone understands that you were a small child following directions from a warped female."

"Eleanor Richmond was most certainly twisted. Even before she picked up a gun, she'd been poisoning her own husband using arsenic. The coroner found the stuff in his hair and bones. The murders were premeditated and vile. The night she jumped in the water and left us was the best thing that could have happened to all of us."

Eastlyn decided to let him talk because he looked as though he needed to get it all out in the open.

"Did Drea mention the little side note about how Eleanor took off?"

Eastlyn shook her head. "Why don't you tell me?"

Cooper roamed the little living room in a distracted pace. "One night she barged into our bedrooms, shook us all awake, ranting and raving, and marched us across the street and then over to the dock. She loaded us into a boat tied up at the end of the pier. Of course it wasn't her boat. It never occurred to Eleanor she didn't own it. Those kinds of details went right over her head. Once she got us in there, she rowed us out into the middle of the harbor. We sat there like survivors on the Titanic wondering what she planned to do until we watched her jump into the water. She left us there—alone and scared. Drea and I knew how to swim but not little Caleb. We'd never seen so much water or blackness. Everywhere we looked we couldn't see anything but night. All we could hear was the waves lapping against that little boat."

Cooper took a breath before going on, "There were no emotional goodbyes on mommy's part, no concern about how we'd get back safely to shore, no care about whether we'd make it on our own or whether someone would come for us—another detail she didn't think about too much. By chance, hours later, a fisherman going out to sea to snag his catch for the day found us. By that time, Caleb and Drea had fallen asleep."

"But not you."

"No, not me. I'd done my best to take us back in, but the current was too strong. I eventually had to give up. But I sat there for hours listening to Drea and Caleb crying, screaming, until they just…cried themselves dry. Ever seen anyone do that before? Cry, but no tears are left. It was gut wrenching to the core, especially for a little kid. I never admitted this to anyone but the entire time we sat there, I was scared to death myself. And yet, Eleanor didn't even think twice about leaving her kids in the middle of the ocean without a way back in. As far as she knew, we could've floated out further into the water. What if the fisherman hadn't come along when he did?"

Eastlyn got up and went to him then, wrapped him up in her arms. "It wasn't your fault, Cooper. There's no need for all this guilt you have stored up. You're tormented by something you had no part in, no control over. No child is able to stand up to the will of a sick parent."

"God, I didn't mean to come off as self-pitying. Sorry. It must be the weeping strings of Shostakovich." Cooper took her by the shoulders. "Look, have you eaten? How about if I go home, put a couple steaks on the grill, and shake this mood we're both in?"

She wouldn't have said no to him now for anything in the world. "Sounds like a plan."

"I'm just down Tradewinds on Sandy Pointe. The house is at the end of the street on the left. You can't miss it. It's the only hacienda on the block."

Without warning, he leaned in, smelling like orange spice. The minute he took her head in his hands and crushed his mouth over hers, she felt like a goner. This was no get-to-know-you kiss but a whirl of heat that spread like an uncontrolled fire through tangled, neglected vines. He tasted as sweet as creamy liqueur, packing as much of a kick as hot Jamaican rum.

Eastlyn gave back as good as she got until he suddenly let her go.

"There, I had to get that out of my system. I've been wanting to do that since you walked into my shop."

Amused, she gripped his shirt and laid another one on him. They ate at each other's mouths for several long seconds. Just as suddenly as he had, she broke the kiss and let him go, patted his chest. "Right back atcha."

Cooper's hacienda had the style of Pueblo revival mixed with Spanish eclectic. Painted in a subtle ginger color, the festive bungalow stood out from the other architecture on the block. It was the only one with a low adobe wall surrounding the yard and a set of wooden double doors at the gated center point.

Eastlyn pushed open the latch and went through the gateway that opened up to a stone-tiled courtyard. Plants in bright containers filled the sunny open space. She went up steps that led to a narrow veranda, a castle-like turret forming the entryway.

Cooper had left the front door open in invitation.

"This is amazing," Eastlyn noted as she got her first look inside the atrium.

Cooper had made the best use of brick and stone and Creamsicle-colored tile. The indoor garden setting popped with tall windmill palms, dracaenas, and aromatic bay laurel. Towering schefflera adorned the rounded hallway.

The sound of trickling water had her head turning toward a small fountain on one wall. Underneath sat rows of clay containers filled with pink and orange camellias.

Several more colorful ceramic planters decorated the entryway.

"Come on back," he yelled from the kitchen.

"Now I know where most of The Plant Habitat inventory ended up," she said and followed the sound of his voice to the other half circle at the rear of the house that formed the kitchen.

He stood at the counter marinating two big steaks for the grill. Behind him, she took in the backyard.

Through open double doors, the terrace was home to a forest of lush foliage. Sturdy yucca thrived with an abundance of gold and red kangaroo paws. Pots of pink foxtail and fountain grass adorned the flagstone patio. Chairs formed a circle in front of a cozy fire pit. A teak table with an umbrella provided a place for outdoor dining. He'd set up a telescope and aimed it eastward toward the low retaining wall that helped cordon off the garden piazza from the next property line.

She threw him a look. "So you snoop on your neighbors. Shame on you, Cooper Richmond."

He chuckled. "How else do I get to know that family of sandpipers nesting twenty-five feet from the Trotters' fence line? See. There on the ground tucked under the dune buckwheat."

She peered over the rock wall.

He studied her shapely form draped over the barrier before taking her by the arm and directing her to stand in front of the telescope. "See mama bird and her four speckled eggs about ready to add to the family."

Through the lens, she focused in on the sight and grinned. She leaned back into him before spinning away. "The train man and the nature lover. Now I see why you call this place the hacienda. Love the Spanish influence in the archways and the tile. And just look at all these plants…"

He gripped her hand and pulled her back inside to the kitchen. "Never underestimate the benefits of knowing the owner of a landscape nursery. Between Drea and Shelby, they just kept bringing over some of Landon's hybrid experiments and adding all kinds of color to the mix. I'm sure they wanted to make sure the renter had a nice place to hang his hat."

"It works. So this is a lease?"

"Was. Logan Donnelly started out renting it to me."

"Because you weren't convinced you intended to stay."

He smiled at the way she got it. "Exactly. I thought maybe I'd hang out for a while with Drea and Caleb, maybe take Landon and Shelby out to dinner once a week, shore up the family ties I'd missed over the years. Then I'd get the train shop up and running for an income down the road, and then hand it off to a manager to take care of the daily headaches. But…"

"You found you couldn't bolt after all."

Coop nodded. "Within a few weeks of being back, living here, I realized I'd found the spot where I wanted to stay. This house was it. Imagine coming back to the town where I spent those first hellish nine years of my life and finding I actually love it here. Anyway, after closing at the bank, I got to work on renovating the kitchen right off." He spread his arms out wide. "This is the result. It isn't beach living, but it's within walking distance and that's just fine by me."

Eastlyn got the gist. It was as far away as Cooper could get from where his father had been murdered under the pier. She turned in a circle, continuing to take it all in. "Airy and open. And you can never go wrong with stainless steel appliances and plenty of cabinets."

He took two wine glasses out of the cupboard and poured from the bottle of merlot, half a glass for each. "I know we started out with beer, but a little red with our porterhouse couldn't hurt."

She took the goblet, sipped the vino. When he took off back outside to put the meat on the grill, she followed with questions running through her head. "You truly don't miss San Francisco? At all? You're happy living in this little town?" She watched as he arranged the steaks on the fire and the confident way his body moved to handle the simple chore.

"Honestly, I thought I would. But the hectic pace I kept up—maybe because I was trying to run from my past—was often too physically exhausting for me to see many of the sights. I didn't dare put down real roots anywhere, and now, I think I know why."

"Because this is where you wanted to be all along."

"You got it. And even though this house needs more upgrading—you haven't seen the outdated plumbing in the bathrooms yet—I've discovered that each night when I close up shop, I look forward to coming home. Home. Now that's a word I never thought I'd associate with myself, let alone here in Pelican Pointe where it all started. At least anything that leaned toward permanent anyway."

"Well, you've done a beautiful job on the hacienda so far."

"Ever think about putting down roots yourself?"

"My roots are back in Bakersfield."

"So you don't intend to stay here?"

"I didn't say that. I realize there's not much for me back in Kern County, especially now that my dad died. I'm just…"

"Keeping your options open?" he prompted.

"I guess I am."

"I'm sorry about your father." When she didn't elaborate or even respond, he studied her eyes, her body language. Even though he recognized a block of hardheaded female, he decided to take a gentler approach. "You're entitled to your grief. How long has it been?"

"Two years. And I don't want to talk about it."

He already knew that. "You put up that same wall enough times you'll find all that anger slowly builds up to rage. I ought to know."

"Is that what happened to you?"

Coop acknowledged the question with a nod. "Two decades of it, beginning at nine. I don't recommend it."

"Then I guess two years is nothing."

"Just make sure it doesn't boil over into how you treat people or else it becomes a habit that's hard to break," he reasoned as he moved to flip the meat on the grill.

Eastlyn sent him a wry smile. "Duly noted. So when do we eat?"

"Depends. How do you like your steak?"

She peered over his shoulder. "That looks about done to me. Want me to throw together a salad?"

"Sure. While I babysit the steaks why don't you throw together some greens? Fixins are already sitting on the counter. By the time you're done we should be ready to eat."

She wandered into the kitchen, found all the veggies she needed and took out the chopping block. She washed and drained the spinach, sliced red and yellow bell peppers, cut an avocado into two halves, spooned out the pit. She dumped the chunks on top, and finished it off by tossing plump cherry tomatoes into the mix.

Perusing the fridge, she grabbed the bottle of store-bought dressing from the shelf and carried it all over to the table. That's when her eyes homed in on the book about Black Hawk helicopters she hadn't noticed before.

Cooper came back in at that moment to get a plate for the steaks. His attention turned to Eastlyn, flipping through the pages of the hardcover. A little embarrassed that he hadn't thought to put the book away out of sight, he said, "I decided to see what the fuss was all about."

She gave him a dour look. "Hmm, the fuss. There are things you'll definitely never get from a book. Let me see if I can sum it up for you. The night missions were the toughest—those that occurred around midnight when you're flying with night-vision goggles."

"Really? I'd think they would help see."

"That's the general opinion. However it isn't the whole story. During bad weather they've been known to hamper depth perception, cause blurry eyesight and prevent a pilot from picking up cloud formations, or blowing dust and sand. They make already tough flying conditions even tougher."

"I had no idea."

"Most people don't."

"So go on."

"Well, like I said, it's nighttime, you're sitting at the flight controls in the lead chopper. You suddenly start taking enemy fire from multiple sources. Door gunners yell, six o'clock, six o'clock, because the fire is coming from directly below our position. You cut left, then right, hoping to evade because your mission is to pick up several wounded GIs in a particular hot zone. So you continue on to get them out of a dangerous situation. You focus on doing your job because there are soldiers out there having a worse day than you are. The job is to get them to a doctor quick. So you keep trying to dodge the fire and work your way to the pick up point."

His admiration for her doubled. "Good flying on your part," Coop pointed out.

She grinned. "Yeah, that too. And then after it's all over and you've dropped off your cargo, you celebrate because your team made it out of there and back to base in one piece."

He could only picture that swagger multiplied whenever she crawled out of a cockpit. He'd seen it before, even while she was delivering and unloading flowers to Drea's place. He took her hand, touched her cheek. "You have so many layers in there. It makes me want to strip off each one to get to know them all."

The room got warmer fast when he leaned in, touched his lips to hers. This time it wasn't urgent take like before, but rather a slow build of greedy need and lusty want. Her arms went around his shoulders. His hands wandered to her back bringing her up against his chest.

Inside, she felt like steam bursting from a hidden volcano she didn't know existed. She sank into the heat until the kiss played out and they broke apart.

"We should eat outside," she announced, just to slam the brakes on the moment. "It's too pretty a night to stay inside."

"I like making you nervous. It gives me a certain thrill."

"Who's nervous? I'm just starving."

He cracked a grin. "Working up an appetite with you is certainly one of my priorities."

He sailed over to the cabinet, got down a plate for the meat and snagged the bottle of wine, took both to the patio.

With darkness descending and for ambiance, Coop lit several candles sitting out on the patio table. Over juicy steaks and healthy greens, they ate in companionable silence until Eastlyn leaned back and picked up her glass. "You cook a good porterhouse."

"Fischer's been giving me pointers."

"At the pizza place?"

"Yep. Since I never really dabbled in the whole barbeque thing, he was able to give me all kinds of tips to cook the perfect steak. I think Fischer might be sweet on Sydney Reed."

Eastlyn lifted one eyebrow. "Interesting. That's not what I heard. Your sister, Drea, told me Sydney had gone out with Malachi Rafferty, the guy who owns the T-shirt shop."

"Yeah, but I have it from a reliable source that two weekends ago Sydney went over to Santa Cruz with Archer Gates to catch a movie. It came from Sydney's own sister, Hayden, at the bookstore."

Eastlyn hooted with laughter. "Sounds like Sydney's playing the field, scoping out her choices. I love the dynamics in this little town."

She suddenly got to her feet, went over to look through the telescope tilting it toward the stars. "So you're a fan of astronomy?"

Cooper joined her at the telescope, took his turn to peer through the powerful eyepiece. He adjusted the magnification, sharpening the image. "I'm a fan of all the exoplanets that orbit something other than the sun, constellations like Draco and Lyra tend to pull me in, and the meteor showers that light up the sky are a joy to watch."

His nearness made her heart do a quick double beat in her chest. Her pulse picked up. Her knees wanted to buckle. Who knew she'd find such a guy so easy on the eyes just six blocks from her front door? "Your nerd is showing. But it's an adorable trait."

"How adorable?"

She grabbed his shirt, pulled him up close so she could nibble at his lips before planting a kiss on his mouth. As soon as she let go, she muttered, "Right about now your adorable quotient is off the charts."

"Lucky me," he said yanking her up against him in return.

They fed off each other's mouths as the heat ratcheted to a frenzy before settling into silky layers. They fused together, the kiss becoming a molten mass of want.

Eastlyn suddenly came to her senses and pushed him back. "I've got to get home."

"We're still on for tomorrow, right? You still want to see the old chopper though, right?"

"Of course."

"Then I'll walk you home."

"That isn't necessary."

He captured her hand in his. "There's an attraction here, Eastlyn. It won't do one bit of good to deny it."

"I know that. But, when you get to know me, there are things you won't like about me."

"Like what?"

"For starters I'm missing half my leg. It's an ugly stump that turns most people off, especially guys, sometimes young and old alike."

"I'm not most people."

"I've heard that same song before." Turning toward the front door, she pivoted back. "What are you saying? That my stump wouldn't be a turnoff for you, seeing me without my jeans?"

"Now there's a picture."

"You'll excuse me if I think you're full of shit."

Cooper met her hazel eyes with a stony glare. "What kind of guys have you been dating anyway?"

"Hmm, that would be mostly assholes," she mumbled as she sailed out the door.

He followed her out into the courtyard, caught up to her at the gate. "You move pretty fast."

"I've had plenty of practice."

Under a creamy moon that floated on a sea of hazy clouds overhead, they headed along the sidewalk toward her little bungalow.

She filled her lungs with fresh air. "Sorry I didn't stay to clean up the dishes, usually I offer to help."

"Don't worry about it."

"You should know, spending the evening with you put me in a much better frame of mind. Thanks for that. I'm still worried about Durke but…"

"I got you to focus on something else. Making out usually does the trick."

She cracked a smile. "Making out is something I haven't done for a good long while. You have a knack."

He busted out in a roar of laughter. "I try."

By the time they reached her front door, she turned to him with a glint in her eye. "Thanks for taking my mind off everything."

Coop took her chin. They were standing eye-to-eye when he touched his lips to hers. "Sure, any time, after all, what are neighbors for?"

She touched his cheek. "I'm thinking certain neighbors offer a lot more perks than others."

Five

In the dream, she'd gone back in time six years earlier to Southeastern Iraq, and a rural, dusty combat post out in the middle of nowhere.

At the controls of her army Black Hawk helicopter, twenty-five-year-old Eastlyn Parker pushed the engine to the max knowing they were battling time. Somewhere in the distance a soldier's life hung in the balance.

As a matter of routine she flew with a crew of six, which included her co-pilot, two seasoned flight medics along with a paramedic, crew chief, and enough medical equipment and supplies to make sure any wounded soldier had a chance at surviving an injury.

Once they received a call, it would normally take the "Dustoff" crew a quick eight minutes to get airborne. From that moment on, every precious second counted. That's why Eastlyn flew like the hounds of hell were chasing them now.

She and her crew had already made four medevac runs that day, pulling the wounded out of several other combat zones, flying them to the field hospital located in Central Iraq.

Coming up on the designated site, she saw a wave of thick, black smoke and located the best spot to touch down. On this, her fifth run of the day, Eastlyn eased the aircraft onto the rocky desert sand in the midst of enemy fire.

A burning rubber smell hit her nose. Gunfire broke out around them.

Amid the hostile welcome, she looked out the window, spotted the chaotic scene, a Humvee on fire, and a bleeding soldier lying on the ground a few feet away from the still burning vehicle.

Members of her team jumped out and immediately went to work on the man. Even through her sunglasses she could tell his injuries were severe. Blood covered his chest because shrapnel had eaten through the flesh.

Another Jeep exploded to their left, the result of more rocket fire.

The co-pilot, Moe Turner, shouted over the din of the chopper blades, "What's taking so long? We need to load up and get the hell out of here. Now!"

Used to Turner's outlook in messy situations like this one, she replied, "We just got here. Relax. We're not going anywhere until they stabilize that soldier for transport."

Another round pinged the metal on Turner's side.

"We're taking fire!" said the jumpy co-pilot, who peered over her form to give his own diagnosis of the wounded man lying on the ground. "He looks like he's a goner already. He isn't even on the stretcher yet. We can't wait forever."

"We'll wait," Eastlyn commanded. "We're not moving an inch until they've loaded him up."

"One day you're gonna get us all killed, Zerker. You know that?"

"We're not budging until they get that guy's IV started and get him on board. You got that?" Eastlyn snapped.

"Sure, I got it. Even though we're about to get our asses handed to us by a bunch more lob bombs, I got it."

To emphasize Turner's point, a rocket-assisted-mortar exploded nearby. The ground shook when it made contact with another Humvee, sending metal shards shooting out in all directions.

Eastlyn directed her crew chief to radio HQ. "We're getting shelled here. Have them send in air cover."

"Roger that."

Another several long, anxious moments ticked by while they waited for the crew to load up the GI. When they finally had him on board, Turner yelled, "Let's get out of here."

Eastlyn felt the jolt of fire as she lifted the helicopter into the sky. The bird rattled and shook, the vibration making the aircraft sway under a combination of heavy wind gusts and more rounds of rocket fire. Maneuvering the chopper through the storm of sweltering air and up to ten thousand feet, she dipped over the dry, dusty terrain, desert that seemed to go on and on. She headed for cover behind the stretch of mountain slopes.

Her eyes shot open as she came out of the dream like a fog lifting and dragging her over the edge of a cliff.

She'd lied to Nick Harris about not remembering him. She recalled that particular day, that specific soldier, mainly because he'd been in so much pain, so much distress. On the flight to the hospital, the paramedic had warned everyone he might not survive the seriousness of his injuries.

But Nick had made it. Not only that, he'd done his best to pull her out of her own patch of quicksand.

For the first time in a long while, Eastlyn realized she needed to put the past where it belonged. She closed her eyes, dropped back into her pillow.

And this time, she clung to the hope of better days.

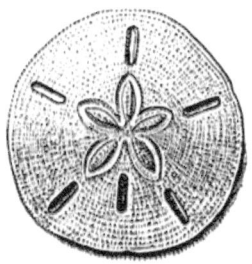

Six

Army training didn't go away when a person mustered out.

Eastlyn's habit of rising early didn't change on weekends. So Sunday morning while drinking her second cup of coffee, she stood in front of her tiny closet and pondered what to wear.

She hadn't packed a lot of clothes when she left Bakersfield. Nick and Cord hadn't exactly given her a lot of time. Who was she kidding? She'd never kept that much at the boarding house, preferring instead to store most of her stuff at a storage facility a couple blocks away.

Staring at her meager wardrobe choices, she gave up. "To hell with it. This isn't a date. I'm headed to an old barn to inspect a hunk of junk. Who in their right mind thinks about dressing up for that?"

"If you're worried about it, Cooper's already seen you in your work clothes," Scott pointed out from the other side of the room.

"Would you stop sneaking up on people?" Eastlyn shouted when she was finally able to catch her breath enough to speak. "That Peeping Tom thing you do is unnerving."

"Hey, I'm just trying to help out. You're obviously going off the deep end about this. No one's gonna notice that you always wear the same thing—over and over again. Jeans and a shirt are perfectly acceptable attire for hanging out. And that's what you're doing with Cooper, just hanging out. No need to change things up when your primary concern is making sure no one sees your prosthetic."

"I am not." Her forehead creased in deep lines. "Is it that obvious?"

Scott cocked a brow. "You can deny it all you want but look at what's hanging in your closet. It's either boring pants near the same color or sturdy work jeans."

"What are you the fashion police? Go away."

"I'm just saying you should wear what's comfortable. Pay no mind to what people say. Who cares if people think you dress like a guy most of the time? No jewelry, no frills, that's Eastlyn Parker."

"What people?"

Scott ignored the question and went on, "No, you definitely have the right idea. Stick to what works for you. Keep wearing your work clothes wherever you go, no matter where it is. A trip to an old barn deserves a practical outfit. I wouldn't even bother to accessorize or put earrings on, plain works for you."

"What is this, reverse psychology? Why should I care about what I wear?"

"That one's easy to figure out. Since losing your foot, the prosthesis makes you self-conscious about wearing anything other than pants or jeans. Putting on a dress might test the limits of Cooper's attraction to you. You're not prepared for the disappointment in his eyes when he sees your leg uncovered for the first time."

"Oh, go to hell. Leave me alone."

Scott held up his hands in a sign of concession. "I'm out of here. But don't say I didn't try."

After his disappearing act, she plopped down on the edge of the bed.

She decided today wasn't the day for pushing the envelope. What would it hurt if she kept the fantasy for a little while longer that he'd find her attractive regardless of what her leg looked like?

Having made that decision, she tapped her prosthesis before tugging on her jeans. She found a bright red blouse in the back of her closet and snubbed her nose at Scott while she buttoned it up.

She started out of the room and spotted her little ceramic jewelry box. Digging around the few pieces, she found what she wanted, a pair of earrings made from carnelian gemstones. The jewelry had been a gift from her father for her sixteenth birthday.

She looked at herself in the mirror, and with some reluctance, had to admit the orangey-red jewels made the blouse pop. The stones also set off her hair and eyes.

"Okay, Scott, you win. Satisfied now?" she asked as she made her way into the kitchen.

After cramming down toast and jam, Eastlyn cleaned up the mess, drank the last bit of coffee and went outside on the stoop to wait for Cooper to show up.

Prepared for a late arrival, she was surprised to see Cooper show up at ten on the dot.

It shouldn't have surprised him that she was waiting outside, pacing back and forth on the concrete.

At the wheel of his 1967, fully restored Ford Mustang, he swung into the driveway, and watched her jaw drop at the sight.

Eastlyn stared at the two-door vintage forest green convertible. "Holy crap... That's one nice pony you have there. This ride rocks."

She ran her hand over the hood, felt the heat of the engine. "What have you got under the hood?"

Cooper grinned at her reaction. "Two-eighty-nine."

"Dual muffler," she muttered in approval, as she climbed into the passenger seat. She rubbed a hand over the dash in appreciation. "Restored to factory condition. You have good taste."

He slanted her a look. "I certainly do." He picked up her hand, kissed the palm before shoving the gear into reverse and taking off down the street.

She noted he hadn't let go of her hand until he'd shifted out of the driveway. A tad uncomfortable in the close quarters, she made small talk. "Where is this place we're headed? Will we get to let this baby run on the open road so I can see what she's got?"

"Cleef's place is a few miles south of town and about five miles after the cutoff. I think that'll be enough distance to show you what she's got."

"Where'd you get the wheels? This car suits you."

"It belonged to my father, Layne Richmond. After my dad disappeared—and before anyone knew he'd been murdered under the pier—my grandfather kept his car in the garage. All that time, I don't think grandpop had the heart to take it for a spin, not even to keep it in running order. When grandpop died, about ten years back, he left the Mustang to me in his will. He left Drea the loft space over the florist shop and Caleb inherited his house on Cape May. After such a long time parked, however, the car needed a major overhaul to get it on the road. The good part about that was it didn't have many miles on it. Grandpop had kept it out of the elements and the damp weather we have around here."

"Your grandfather must've known you didn't want to live in town. So he left you something other than property."

"Oh, he did. I'm sure that's the reason for it. I feel bad about that now."

She ran a hand up his arm. "Don't. The guilt is a waste of energy. Believe me, I know."

"What about yours? The guilt, I mean."

"I deal with it every single day," Eastlyn said with a bite to each word, shutting down any further discussion. But then she realized he was staring at her. "How do you know? What makes you think I'm dealing with guilt?"

"Simple. Scott mentioned it…several times as a matter of fact."

She rolled her eyes, exasperated. "You too? Scott's been bugging you about me? Who does this guy think he is anyway?"

"I'm pretty sure if they live in Pelican Pointe, they're on Scott's radar. After all, he bugs everyone."

As soon as they reached the Coast Highway, Eastlyn prompted, "Punch it. Show me what this pony can do."

Coop didn't need any more encouragement than that since there wasn't much traffic. He gunned the engine for a burst in power and speed. They hugged curves and zipped along flat stretches of roadway, eating up pavement. With the ocean on the right and rolling hills to the left, they cruised with the wind in their faces.

Eastlyn looked over and studied the driver. He seemed relaxed and carefree, his long hair blowing back, his face exuding a calm peacefulness that she'd rarely experienced for herself in the last two years.

It wasn't long before Cooper slowed so he could take the cutoff east toward San Sebastian. The Mustang forged along the countryside dotted with patches of spring wildflowers. The blooming fields laden with golden fennel and wild lavender sloped and curved into pretty pastureland.

It was two more miles before Cooper pulled onto the rutted pavement that led to the Atkins farmhouse. They hiccupped along the lane, dodged a rabbit hopping from pathway to tall brush.

Even months after Cleef's death, a jumble of odds and ends still lined both sides of the roadway. Rusted-out metal tractors, the shells of two old Chevys, a mass of broken discarded furniture sat among knee-high weeds.

It seemed the Mustang hit every pothole in the road before Cooper stopped in front of a frame house. "Believe it or not we've tried to clean up some of the old tires, sold off most of the corroded barrels for scrap metal, as well as a few of the chunks of concrete that were real eyesores."

Eastlyn got out of the car, took in the acres and acres of junk and wondered how long it had taken the farmer to carve out this much space for the castoff landmarks no one else wanted. "I think you might've missed the faded, decades-old Coke machine rusting away next to that carob tree over there. This place is a graveyard of trash or a goldmine of treasure depending on one's point of view."

"Each time I come out here I expect to see Cleef come walking out to the car."

She walked around the Mustang, patted him on the back. "I'm sorry about your friend. It hurts to lose someone." In one swoop, she stopped to snap off a pink buttercup pushing its way between a patch of thistle and milkweed.

"I wouldn't exactly call Cleef a friend of mine but more like a mainstay. I came out here as a kid with my dad. Walked through the junk while Dad held onto my hand. Cleef sold us a train table on one of those trips. It's another cherished memory I have of my father, at a time when there aren't enough good ones in the back of my mind because I didn't have him for very long. My mother's meanness saw to that."

Eastlyn handed the bloom off to him in an expression of concern and added, "This won't help much, but it's a reminder that all things in life circle around."

"Why thank you," he said, taking the stem and sniffing the bud, a little embarrassed that he hadn't been the one to make the gesture. It wasn't the first time at the farm that he'd been caught up in a wave of nostalgia. "Sometimes this place has a creepy feel to it."

"How so?"

"Before Isabella married Thane they had some trouble out here with her ex. I'm not completely certain about all the facts involved but since…"

She grabbed his arm in the middle of his tale. "Wait. Am I to understand that something happened in this town and you don't know all the gritty details? That's pathetic.

Sounds to me like you don't have access to intel the same way Myrtle Pettibone does."

"No one possesses intel like Myrtle. Although I should point out that she got the stripper story totally wrong about you. You should deduct points for that. It shows there's a chink somewhere in her system."

"Good point," Eastlyn conceded with a laugh. "Myrtle could've at least pegged the source before starting those rumors."

"Do you want to hear the story about Cleef's murder or not?"

"Sorry. Absolutely."

"Okay then. One night the ex showed up in town and abducted Isabella right off the street as she headed home from working at the pizza place."

Eastlyn's mouth dropped open. "*Abducted*? As in against her will? She never said a word to me about that. But then come to think of it, most of our convos have been centered around the planting project. So how does Isabella's kidnapping relate to what happened out here to Mr. Atkins?"

"It was Isabella's ex, a man by the name of Henry Navarro who killed Cleef." Cooper left out the gory details and went on, "The sad thing is, if Isabella hadn't been kidnapped and if her ex hadn't brought her back out here to Cleef's farm that night, the old man's death might've gone unnoticed for days—since the guy lived alone, so far away from town—his body might not have been discovered for weeks. If Isabella hadn't overpowered Navarro that night, if Scott hadn't directed them out here…"

"Scott? Ah, I'm beginning to get the picture."

"Anyone ever tell you that you interrupt a lot? Anyway, if it all hadn't come down the way it did, Brent might've thought that Cleef's death had something to do with the meth labs out here."

Eastlyn shot a look around the line of trees in the distance. "Here? In Pelican Pointe?"

"Not in town, no. But back to the east of Cleef's farm sits a compound along with a dangerous element that prefers to be left alone, prefers to keep their illegal enterprises from becoming public knowledge."

"But you already got wind of these 'enterprises' and you've been in town for what...? Less than a year?"

"I should emphasize the word 'prefers' more because the people involved fail miserably at keeping their activities quiet. When I first heard about Cleef's death that's who I thought was responsible for killing him. Then of course the news slowly trickled out about Isabella's ex and the real story behind it all."

"So the town cop knows about the meth activity around here and does nothing about it? No wonder he acted as though he didn't really want to do much to look for Durke."

Coop shook his head. "I think that's unfair. I don't know about looking for your friend Durke, but I do know Brent Cody. I know he keeps a close eye on the situation. The meth problem has been common knowledge in these parts for years. One family used to head up the entire operation. Harley Edgecombe pretty much ran the whole set-up. But while Brent was sheriff, he cleaned up the area as much as he could, more than anyone else ever did who held that office. Brent even sent Harley to San Quentin for twenty years and put away his sons, Rodney and Bruno, in Corcoran for fifteen. It's one of the reasons the Edgecombe family steers clear of Brent and Pelican Pointe. Which means it can't be easy catching the rest of the scum in the act of running meth. That part requires some cooperation from the current county sheriff. Richardson is his name. That's the tricky part for Brent. From what I gather there's no love lost between Richardson and Brent Cody."

"And all this time I thought I'd landed in Mayberry."

"For the most part you have. But hey, we live in a real world scenario that is by no means perfect. Even Andy

Taylor sometimes had to crack down on moonshiners and bank robbers."

She hooted with laughter. "Yeah, but Andy Taylor had help from his trusted sidekick, Barney Fife."

"Maybe Brent needs his own Barney Fife."

She ignored that last bit of sarcasm, suggesting instead, "Let's see this chopper."

They made their way into the barn through a minefield of outdated hubcaps and old rims. Filled to the brim with all kinds of furniture and equipment long sitting idle, the ramshackle building reeked of musty smells. Everything contained layers on layers of dirt and dust.

"Here it is," Cooper declared, pulling a filthy cover off the dated aircraft.

Eastlyn whistled through her teeth. "Wow, you weren't kidding. This is really old."

But despite its age, she stepped forward to run her hand over the discolored metal like a familiar lover. Peering into the cockpit, she rattled off what she knew about the model. "The army used these little babies starting out in 1948 all the way up to 1969, mostly in a general purpose, all-around role. They used the Sioux H-13 to perform medevac missions, strapping two litters on either side. Or in the event they needed reconnaissance, they could fasten thirty caliber machine guns to the skids. In its time this chopper probably saw a lot of service. Wonder who the old farmer picked it up from? I wonder how long it's sat here gathering cobwebs."

Cooper leaned over, inspected the rusted mounts. "This one doesn't look like it ever had litters or weapons attached to it."

"Might've ended up in a civilian role. Aren't there papers on it somewhere?"

"If there are papers among Cleef's possessions, we haven't found them yet."

"I venture there's a story about how this chopper ended up here."

"The only guy who knows for sure is dead. But could you fly it?"

She sent him a withering stare. "Is the sky blue? The controls in this thing are straight forward, I'd even say simple." Her hand roamed to the bubble. "And look at this, no cracks in the cockpit, not one. In her time, she provided an excellent view for reconnaissance or search and rescue."

"So what do you think? Is it worth fixing up?"

"Oh yeah, I'm in. You get a price for me and I'll see if I can raise the cash."

They started for the car and Eastlyn looked around at the rest of the junk. She stopped to stare at the broken parts of a marquee. "So when does this movie theater reopen in town? I thought you said they planned to use the sign from the old theater?"

"That was the plan. It's scheduled to open the end of summer. June through August the town has what they call movie nights in the park. Thane thought it best if they didn't compete with that and let the people enjoy their summer evenings in an old-fashioned venue, sitting on the grass. They've already gutted the insides though and begun the refurbishing. The project's pretty far along. It put a lot of the locals back to work, which I'm thinking was part of the idea."

"But they didn't use the old sign?"

"They couldn't. They tried to salvage the signboard but found it was in no shape to repurpose. Some months back Thane and Isabella started scratching their heads to figure out what to do. They decided to tear the sign apart, rewire it with new lighting and rename it using all new neon."

"Well, I've seen the sign in town, passed by it five dozen times, hoping it would be open by now. You know, for someplace to hang out. I like movies. I kind of like the name they settled on."

"Yeah, The Driftwood works. I think everyone is disappointed it hasn't opened yet. I'm told that even though Thane and Isabella opted for a new sign, they still intend to keep the retro look, inside and out. We're all waiting for the grand unveiling."

By the time she reached the Mustang, she'd thought of something she wanted to clear up. "So Coop, who owns all this stuff? Where does the money go exactly? Who gets the profits from the sales?"

"Technically the town owns the place. And actually the city council voted to set aside any proceeds to go solely to the school fund with the hope that one day we'll be able to expand and open up a middle school."

Eastlyn smiled. "I like that about this town, optimistic enough that they can sell a bunch of junk sitting around a barn gathering cobwebs and seven layers of dust to benefit the kids."

"Those who knew Cleef think he'd be pleased knowing all this stuff out here might help keep the school going, maybe even get enough to support opening a junior high."

"Ever thought about holding an auction for the big ticket items? Although I'd appreciate it if you'd keep from making that particular suggestion until I get my hands on the Bell helicopter."

Coop grinned. "Someone already came up with that idea. But look around you. It would take a massive amount of organization, someone would have to go through every single piece of machinery and catalogue it. Maybe one day, the right person will come along with enough time to do that. But for now, I don't see it happening."

"It's a shame the old guy had to die." She spread her arms out wide, turned a circle. "Just look, after years of collecting all this, probably driving for miles to pick it up and going to the trouble of hauling it back here, this is his legacy. It makes you wonder about things."

"It often makes me wonder how I'll be remembered, what legacy I'll leave. Makes me want to do better."

"Good point. Because I guess we could all do so much better."

To break the melancholy atmosphere, Cooper asked, "So what would you like to do now?"

"What are my choices?"

"We could take a tour of the local Chumash Museum. It's something River's worked really hard getting open, something the town's really proud of."

"Okay. I'd also like to take a look at the mammals inside the Fanning Marine Rescue Center. Cord's been bugging me to do that since I got here. After that, I'll show you around the lighthouse."

It never occurred to Coop to mention that he'd already been up to the cliff at least a dozen times already. But the truth was, he'd never been up there with her.

At the moment, that was all that mattered.

For the rest of that day, Cooper showed off all that Pelican Pointe had to offer in the way of things to do.

Their first stop was the museum where they spent two hours picking their way past glass cases that held cultural artifacts—hunting tools, assorted beaded necklaces, cookware. They studied exhibits, even watched a video demonstration, a vivid depiction that showed how the Chumash had lived for thousands of years along the same stretch of beach they all enjoyed now.

"Brent's wife dug all this stuff up out of the ground?" Eastlyn asked as she examined a series of rudimentary bowls and eating utensils. "What a fascinating job to have, uncovering all these old things."

"The dig in town is what originally brought her to the area," Cooper explained. "All this is what River's team excavated from the site."

She stared at the large canoe called a tomol that hung from the rafters down to eye level. "They used these things to paddle across the bay and into the ocean to fish."

"Which reminds me I'm getting hungry. How about we go across the street to Perry Altman's restaurant for lunch?"

She looked down at her jeans, still grimy from their excursion at Cleef's. "The fancy place with a view of the water? That'd be great but I'm not really dressed for anything so formal."

She looped her arm through his. "Instead of eating inside, it's a pretty day, why don't we take advantage of that and pick up food and eat at the lighthouse?"

"Now you're talking. We could buy sandwich fixins at Murphy's, grab a nice bottle of wine if you don't consider it too early in the day."

"Soft drinks might be the way to go."

"Soda it is. So what will it be? Greasy cheeseburgers-to-go at the diner, or head to Murphy's for ham and cheese? What's your pleasure?"

Arm in arm, they strolled out of the museum and headed toward the car.

After sniffing the air, Eastlyn decided, "I'm in the mood for that greasy hamburger and a chocolate malt."

"Looks like it's the Hilltop Diner then. We should really get pie. Margie makes a mighty fine apple pie. And it is Sunday."

"What does Sunday have to do with pie?"

"No Sunday should pass without indulging in fruit-filled pastry."

"Words to live by."

They drove the two blocks to Main Street to find the diner almost empty. Despite the lack of customers, Tim McGraw's sexy voice spun from the Wurlitzer jukebox singing his praises for southern girls.

The place looked exactly like what it was—a retro malt shop that had been part of the town for almost five decades. It had a stained black-and-white-checkered linoleum floor, a black marble-looking counter, red barstools that had seen better days, but not since Kennedy had been in office.

The owner, Margie Rosterman, greeted them with menus but Cooper waved her off. "We know what we want. Give us two of Max's biggest cheeseburgers with all the trimmings and a basket of fries. Throw in two chocolate malts and two slices of your apple pie to go and a couple of Cokes."

"Sounds like you two kids worked up an appetite," Margie said with a wink. She stood almost six feet tall with flaming red hair she'd recently tinted, pale skin with a ton of freckles, and big blue eyes. Margie did her best to make people believe she was tough as nails. But everyone in town knew the woman had a heart of gold. She often took a chance on hiring waitresses with little experience and would give them multiple chances until they proved her wrong. It was common knowledge she and her cook, Max Bingham, had been together for years but had never bothered to make it official.

"We decided to take our food and eat up on the cliff," Eastlyn explained, not knowing why she felt the need to set the scene for anyone else.

"You picked a pretty day for it." Margie yelled out the order to Max and turned back to the counter to take Cooper's money. Margie counted out his change and turned to Eastlyn. "Pacific storm's predicted for the middle of the week. Hope you're done with the plowing by then. Max and I are chomping at the bit to get that call that tells us it's time to plant the seeds. Haven't been this excited about anything since we went to Sissy Carr's funeral just so we could make sure she was dead."

Cooper glanced at Eastlyn and winked. "By way of explanation, Sissy Carr was the small town hussy who finally got her comeuppance when they found her drowned in the bay."

"Ah. Translation appreciated for the benefit of the newcomer." Eastlyn turned to Margie, snaked out a laugh. "Isabella is in charge of eager volunteers. So any day now you should expect the call."

"That's us, we're ready and willing. Isabella just has to say the word. Imagine, coming up with the idea to grow our own food out of that piece of land that's sat vacant for years before Logan came to fix it up. That's one renovation that's been good for the whole town."

"I agree," Eastlyn said, noting Margie's type of excitement seemed to prevail throughout town. "I'd also like to go on record as saying Max makes the best burgers. I've been all over and his are, by far, cooked to perfection every time."

Margie beamed, relayed the praise to her significant other by hollering it at the top of her voice. "Hear that, Max. You have a fan."

From the long window into the kitchen, Max waved his spatula in Eastlyn's direction and yelled just as loud as Margie had, "The girl knows good food."

"I never got that kind of reaction when I heaped compliments on Max for his meatloaf," Cooper pointed out. "I've traveled all over, too, you know. And I've been here a hundred times more than Eastlyn."

Margie waved a hand in Cooper's direction. "We're used to you. I've come to appreciate the newcomers. They breathe new life into this town. Just look at what Nick's done. New ideas, new business, and new people, add in the school reopening and it does wonders for my bank account."

"As long as it helps your bottom line." Eastlyn gave the owner a strange look before trading glances with Cooper.

After Margie bagged up their food order, they left for the lighthouse. But when Cooper started to take a blanket out of the trunk of the car, Eastlyn stopped him.

"I think I'll forego sitting on the ground and…"

"I'm sorry. I wasn't thinking."

"It's no big deal." Carrying the sack with the burgers, she pointed to a bench near the cliff. "I'll opt for the view over the water." She started toward what she thought of as the scenic observation point and said over her shoulder, "By the way, do you have any idea what this inscription means?"

"What inscription?"

Eastlyn stood in front of a raised base made from the same stone that matched the keeper's cottage. On top of the platform sat a five-foot-long garden bench with a black and gold plaque screwed into the back.

She stepped up on the six-inch high foundation to read the words out loud: "In memory of Isabella Rialto, whose spirit lives on within those who loved her."

"Beats me. But how can it read 'in memory' when Isabella is alive and married to Thane Delacourt?"

Eastlyn took out a burger, handed one off to Cooper. Peeling back the wrapper on hers, she dug in but she couldn't let go of her curiosity. "That's the same thing I thought the first time I read it. Why would you erect a memorial to yourself, especially since you're alive? I didn't want to ask and make it appear like I was a nosy busybody, but…it's odd, don't you think?"

Cooper reached in the bag and dug out a French fry. "It's gotta be another Isabella."

"What are the odds of that? That a woman we know as Isabella puts a bench here dedicated to someone else with the same name? I wonder… You did say Isabella had a run-in with an ex. Maybe it has something to do with that?"

"We should find out. Only way to know for sure is to ask the source. That's your department."

"Why me? You've been in town longer. Why couldn't you utilize the handy rumor mill in town and dig deeper?"

"Because whatever we found out would probably be more speculation than fact. And I don't really know Isabella that well to open up a dialogue about why she put the bench here. You work for her, see her every day. You're the logical choice."

"How do I bring it up in conversation?"

"You'll find a way. I do know Isabella special-ordered this thing from Ferguson's Hardware. I just thought she chose to place it here because of the scenic overhang. You know, so people could sit and look out to sea like we are now. I didn't even know about the inscription."

Eastlyn looked out over the water. "It's a pretty spot, maybe my favorite in the entire town. This is where I'd like to plant lavender. I have to run it by Isabella first though. What I'd do is spread the seedlings along here to set this section apart from the rest. And over there by the lighthouse, I'd like to make that the strawberry patch, a pick-your-own-basket type deal."

"Both plants should do well here along the coast."

Abruptly she pivoted on her hip to face Coop. "There's something that's been bothering me since we left the farm. Why do you suppose that old chopper was covered up the way it was, like it was purposely hidden from view? You say there's no paper on it that you've been able to locate."

"Hey, I just helped with inventory. Lots of us turned out for that. Murphy might know the whereabouts of the title, or at least the bird's history. Nick might be another one who'd know. I'll find out for you."

"Good, because I think I want it."

"You think? When will you know?"

"As soon as I work out a few logistics."

"Like what?"

"I hate to beat this drum to a dull bang but getting my license back will likely be an uphill battle. It's a very big deal to me. If things go south in that area and I find I'm the owner of a refurbished bird that I can't fly, selling it to a collector might be the only option I have down the road."

"Tell you what, let's get your mind off this decision." He offered his hand to help her step down off the platform. "Come on, I hear the seals from here. They're calling our name. If we hurry we'll make it before the Fanning Center closes its doors."

They spent the rest of the afternoon watching the playful sea otters and stayed until Pete Alden, the caretaker, locked the gate.

"I feel like I've been to the circus and the zoo all in one day," Eastlyn said as they walked back to the car.

He slid his hand into hers. "How do you feel about trains?"

She sent him a quizzical look, then decided she knew where he was going with the question. "Freight or passenger? Doesn't matter. Why don't you show me your trains, Cooper?"

"I thought you'd never ask."

After ten minutes inside the store, Eastlyn felt the draw of his model railway sets. Another playful side to him emerged as they fiddled with different configurations and layouts until Eastlyn was as captivated with him as she was the trains. They spent two hours, putting sets together that didn't match and coming up with city designs they'd seen in their travels.

By the time he pulled up in front of her house it was almost eleven o'clock. They'd spent more than twelve hours together. It had been a long time since that had happened for either one of them.

But when they reached the front door, Eastlyn could tell he wanted to come inside. She wasn't ready for more. "Look, I appreciate you taking me out to Cleef's and letting me know about the chopper. I appreciate the hot make-out kisses since it's been a while for me."

She thought back to a boozy night around Christmastime of last year. The memory didn't exactly bring to mind candy canes and tinsel. It wasn't sugar plums she'd had dancing in her head, more like shots of tequila mixed with painkillers. That night, Durke had refused to serve her after ten o'clock so she'd moved on to another bar around the corner where she'd met an oilfield worker named Tex. Or was it Rex?

Cooper's voice, tinged with irritation, brought her back to the present. "I'm not shoving you into the sack, am I? I just thought we could watch a little TV together. My mistake."

He turned to go but Eastlyn latched onto his shirtsleeve. "Don't go away mad and ruin what a great day we had together. Give me some time, okay? Right now, I'm in the middle of working out a lot of things about myself that I need to fix. I'm doing the best I know how to do. Every day is a struggle."

Coop knew about inner demons taking hold and not wanting to let go. "You want to sleep with me," he stated matter-of-factly. "There's no point denying it. I can tell each time I kiss you."

"Okay, I'm attracted to you. We already agreed on that. So what?"

As he started for the car, he turned back. "I'm not in the habit of rushing women. But I don't play games, either. As long as you know where we're headed, and that we're on the same page, I'm okay with waiting for you to get your head on straight."

Seven

After a good night's sleep, that's the first thing that popped into her head when she stood under the shower trying to wake up.

Was she on the same page as Cooper? That was the thousand-dollar question.

She liked his no-nonsense manner, the way he delivered a punch line, his easygoing nature. She had a feeling there was more to this hunk than she'd had a chance to wrap her arms around.

As she hopped out of the shower to dry off and get dressed, she found herself annoyed with her thought process. She should've been focused solely getting her license back and moving toward what she wanted. Instead, she wasted her time like some schoolgirl thinking all mushy thoughts over a boy.

She knew better. Her track record with men—especially since the loss of her leg—was doomed to failure. The sooner she put Cooper Richmond on the backburner, the better off she'd be.

Eastlyn took that attitude to work with her as she walked the newly turned rows of dirt she'd fashioned for the co-op's planting project.

She stood in the middle of the spot designated for growing spinach and Swiss chard, feeling skeptical about the whole venture.

When she heard a car door slam shut she glanced toward the keeper's cottage, only to see Isabella bounding toward her in an energetic state.

Eastlyn searched the woman's eyes for the reason. But the smile on her boss's face said it couldn't be that serious, certainly not bad news.

"I'm pregnant," Isabella announced, slightly out of breath. "Due in seven months. Thane is about to burst wide open with the news. By noon when he opens the doors at Longboard Pizza he'll no doubt spread the word one customer at a time."

Eastlyn chuckled. "Congrats. He's not the only one. I guess that explains why you look as though you're about to burst wide open too," Eastlyn noted, reaching out to give her a hug. "How is Jonah taking the news?"

Jonah, Isabella's stepson, had recently turned seven. Eastlyn knew from seeing the boy around town that the kid considered Isabella his mom.

"Jonah is thrilled to have a baby brother. We've tried to explain to him, numerous times since yesterday when I found out for certain, that the baby might possibly be a sister. But Jonah's got it into his head it'll be a boy. And no matter how many times or how many ways we explain it to him, he won't think of having a sister."

"Uh-oh. You know what that means?"

"Yep, I sure do. It's bound to be a little girl. Thane and I don't care which though as long as we have a healthy baby. You know Jonah had medical problems when he was born because of his mother's drug addiction." Isabella's olive complexion turned to gray as if she'd put her foot in her mouth. "I'm sorry, I didn't mean to bring up drug addiction…"

Eastlyn patted her arm. "Relax. It's okay. I'm well aware of the problems I've had, brought on by myself without any help from anyone else. So there's no need to tippy-toe around the subject."

"At least you sought treatment. Alyson, Jonah's mother, never had the foresight to do that. Look, there's something I want to talk to you about. Thane and I discussed this in detail last night. I think because of the pregnancy, I'll have to find someone to take over for me here at the co-op. Even though I decided not to use toxins on the crops, the blowing dust from the plowing is beginning to bother my allergies, a lot. I found that out weeks ago. Now that I'm pregnant, I don't think it's a good idea to be around all the blowing dust as much. Don't worry. I'll still manage the day-to-day operations, ordering and paperwork, getting the specifics ironed out, stuff like that. But as far as the hands-on role goes… I'm afraid it takes a backseat to everything else. Thane's way too busy at Longboard Pizza to add to his schedule. The bottom line is, Thane and I believe you're the person to oversee things on site."

"Me? Why me? Okay, so I'm the only regular here, except for Silas and Ben. And they have jobs back at Taggert Farms. It's just that I told you when I took this job that I'm hoping to eventually get my pilot's license back. And when that happens…"

Isabella laid a hand on her arm. "Don't worry. Thane and I know it's just until you do. Your hours won't change all that much. I promise it won't interfere one bit with your other jobs, in fact, think of it as a pay raise. You take away a chunk of my daily responsibilities here and it frees up all kinds of time for me to handle all the other things at home."

That had Eastlyn wondering about how she'd handle all the work on the helicopter *and* find the time to work on getting her license back.

But the hopeful look on Isabella's face and the reminder that the woman had given her a job when she needed one had Eastlyn blurting out, "Okay. Sure. I'll do it. What else have I got to do?"

"Great. I'll make sure you're caught up to speed on all the week's plans, all the ordering, all the details on the volunteers I have lined up."

Eastlyn saw an opening. "Can I ask you something?"

"Sure."

"What's with the bench?"

"What do you mean?"

"The plaque says it's in memory of Isabella. It doesn't make sense that it would be you."

Eastlyn noticed the topic had taken the happy glint out of Isabella's eyes. "I'm sorry. I didn't mean to be so nosy and upset you."

"No, it's okay. Ever since I donated this land back to the town, it's a public place. That includes the bench. But to answer your question, in a way, *that* Isabella and I, are definitely one and the same. You see, she and I shared a kindred spirit and a horrible taste in men. I was lucky enough to escape my situation. That Isabella was not. But there are many other Isabellas out there. Most wonder whether they'll ever be fast enough or fortunate enough to get out of their miserable relationships and live a decent life. That bench is one way to always remember there's hope, even if it's only a fifty-fifty shot."

"I'm so sorry you lost your friend," Eastlyn said again, not knowing what else to say. "I..."

"Surprisingly not all that many in town ever asked me about the bench. I think most people consider me a little eccentric. I'm just the weird newcomer who stuck a bench near the cliff and put my own name on it. I appreciate you asking. It gives me the chance to talk about her. Someday when we have more time, I'll tell you the whole story."

"I'd love to hear it. That kind of statement only heightens my curiosity."

"Now I'm the one sorry. But today isn't the day for stories."

"Then I'll get back to work. Do you still want me to get Landon's input on whether eggplant is doable?"

Isabella laughed at the abrupt change in subject matter. "Oh yeah. Eggplant *and* cilantro."

"I spoke with Shelby in detail and she agrees with me that we should try growing at least five different herbs. I'd like to make it six and include lavender on that list."

Eastlyn noted the grimace on Isabella's face and quickly added, "Yes, I'm fully aware that lavender's more decorative than practical. But Hayden Cody, who runs the bookstore, said she could extract oil from it to make fragrant candles."

"That sounds promising."

"And the other day when I picked up a pizza from Longboard's, I asked the man there who makes the pies…"

"Fischer Robbins."

"That's the guy. Anyway, I asked him about its practical uses in cooking and he said that he'd buy whatever we have on hand to use it to make lavender ice cream."

Eastlyn saw the concern drain of Isabella's eyes and turn to amusement.

"Now see, that's another reason you'll be perfect at supervising the planting and everything else out here. So we'll add lavender to the rosemary, chives, mint, sage, and basil plot we already picked out."

"Thanks. But… I thought we could spread the lavender seedlings out near the overhang, that area near the bench where people tend to sit and look out over the water. They use it as a scenic observation point. That area will look amazing when the plants get big enough to bloom and spread."

Eastlyn noticed Isabella dabbing at her watery eyes. She didn't think it was allergy related.

Isabella sniffed and said, "That's a wonderful idea. I can picture it now. Has anyone ever told you that you have a knack for this sort of thing?"

"My father was an avid gardener. Since getting here I'm finding I like playing around in the dirt." Eastlyn lifted a shoulder. "Who knew?"

Eastlyn decided to get Isabella's mind going in a different direction. "For example, if we put raised beds up near that patch of open space at the corner of the lighthouse where the sun is practically an all-day thing, it would serve as an ideal spot for growing strawberries. We could offer a pick-your-own-basket day. Which brings me to another question? How does all this get divvied up?"

"Whenever they sign up to volunteer their time, they're asked to list which crops they're interested in taking care of and then receiving?"

"I'm impressed. So you're still getting plenty of volunteers to help us out with the planting?"

"You bet. The list gets longer every day. People are enthusiastic and eager. So it's our job to see their excitement stays at a fever pitch during planting and keeps going until it's time to harvest. You say the word and I'll have thirty people willing to sow the seeds by this afternoon."

"Then you should probably know there's been considerable lack of interest toward butter beans," Eastlyn quipped.

Isabella grinned again. "Ah, well, Fischer and Jonah predicted that might be the case. We'd better scratch that crop."

"We could always add more tomatoes, they grow vertical and it would free up space to plant a patch of red and yellow peppers."

Isabella patted her on the back. "I love the way we're always on the same page."

"At least with vegetables."

The boss smiled again as if she knew a secret. "We have good taste in men, too. Cooper Richmond's a real hottie."

Eastlyn sighed. "I knew it. I suppose if I'm willing to dish out dirt on Sydney Reed, I ought to be able to take it when it comes back around to me. I knew it would be a matter of hours before the tongues started wagging. The thing is, how did word spread so fast? This is Monday."

"Comes with the excellent Pelican Pointe gossip trough, otherwise known as Myrtle Pettibone."

"That name keeps popping up. I've seen her around town. She's the one who brings her own shopping basket to the market. She has to be pushing eighty?"

"That's Myrtle."

"Then Myrtle needs to get a life."

"Since she's a staple here, I doubt there's much chance of her changing the way she obtains intel," Isabella explained, her voice dripping with mischief and merriment.

"How on earth did Myrtle know Cooper and I spent Saturday night *and* Sunday together?"

Isabella lifted a brow. "I saw Myrtle Pettibone at Murphy's Market buying cat food. But she didn't say a word about you two spending Saturday *night* together."

"We had dinner. Nothing happened." Except for the electrifying sexual heat between them, enough to melt the ice within the Arctic Circle.

"Well, that's a darn shame," Isabella lamented. "I was hoping for some tidbit to throw into the gossip pot."

Eastlyn sent her a sidelong glance. "Oh brother. Since it's pointless to stand here and try to battle the rumor mill, I'm going back to work."

An hour later, Eastlyn was still replaying that underlying current she'd felt as she drove the tractor over the section of land she'd dubbed the "back forty." Located at the corner of the property where the edge of the cliff met up with the copse of trees at a ninety-degree angle, the back forty had so far been the roughest to plow. So when she felt an exceptionally large bump, it wasn't that unusual.

Once she looked down at the ground and to the side, a flash of something white caught her eye. The white stood out in the black dirt, enough that she thought she'd hit one of the newly installed sprinklers. Engaging the clutch, she shifted into Park and stomped on the brake. She shut off the engine and set the parking brake before hopping to the ground. She walked around the machinery, ducked her head underneath to inspect the area around the wheels. There beneath the rubber a white blob stood out in the black dirt. This was no sprinkler head she'd unearthed. The mass looked like bones.

"Probably animal," she muttered. But that was before she saw the unmistakable shape of a human skull a few feet away.

She dug in her pocket for her cell to call Brent Cody. As she stared down at the ground, she replayed the grisly scene for the town cop.

Less than eight minutes ticked by before she spotted Brent's Chevy Tahoe screeching to a stop at the entrance to the lighthouse where she waited with the owners.

Isabella and Thane were as shaken as she was. They were all visibly distraught. But it was Logan who pulled up behind Brent and seemed even more upset and angrier than the rest. Eastlyn wasn't sure why.

When Brent walked up, he nodded in their direction. "You guys stay put until I make sure the bones are human."

"They're human," Eastlyn stated. "Thane and Isabella tried to calm me down because I know those bones belong to a person. I've been in combat. I've seen all kinds of bodies in various stages of injury and death. They're human bones."

Brent bobbed his head again and took off in toward the tractor. "Most likely they are, since we had us a serial killer working the area here for probably twenty years or more." He went on to explain how the pharmacist, Carl Knudsen, had killed a string of young girls.

Eastlyn's mouth fell open. She decided that might explain Logan's presence. "Holy crap. That means I'm definitely taking this town out of the running for Mayberry runner-up."

"Mayberry it's not," Logan murmured as he got back in his truck in a huff.

Thane spoke up. "Don't be so hard on us. That Knudsen fellow was always a creepy guy. I remember him as a kid. No one around here will admit to missing him. Not that Ross and Jill Campbell took over Knudsen's business, the town's never looked back."

Eastlyn decided to follow Brent as he began stepping off the distance to where the bones had been spread out over a ten-foot plot of ground. She listened as he went into detail about the eerie past. "Part of Knudsen's burial ground was those woods over there. Logan Donnelly's sister was one of his early victims."

"That explains his attitude. That's why you don't seem at all surprised I uncovered this set of bones."

"That's because I've been expecting something like this ever since Isabella announced her plans to farm this land."

"So I guess the fact that I discovered this disturbing piece of history on my own is my fault. You might've mentioned it in passing. Someone could have warned me, you know, anyone at all, that I might unearth bones."

"You're right. Sorry. We should've told you as soon as you turned the first bit of dirt," Brent admitted as he walked around the tractor.

She watched as the police chief slapped on latex gloves and studied the path of bones.

Eastlyn tried patience as long as she could. It didn't work for long. "I hate to point this out, but as you can see, there's not a shred of clothing near the bones, which might mean the unfortunate victim was buried without them."

Brent squatted on his haunches, stared at the remains. "You're perceptive. I have a list of girls who disappeared, three probable victims whose bodies were never found. They went missing, last sighting was less than twenty miles from here near the freeway."

"That's…probably not a coincidence."

"I'll call the county medical examiner and the crime scene techs, give them a heads up. It won't be their first trip out here. If I were you I'd plan to take the next couple days off."

"They should plan to fan out from this spot and see if there are any others."

Brent gave her a knowing look. "That's the plan. If we're lucky we can give another family a measure of closure."

When she looked up, she saw Cooper running up to the lighthouse at a jog. She chewed her lip. "Pretty soon the entire town will come up here for a look-see."

Brent sighed. "Then I guess we'd better start heading them back down the hill."

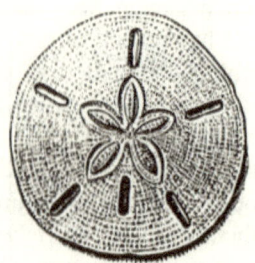

Eight

Inside Layne's Trains, Cooper was eating a tuna fish sandwich he'd brought from home when Eastlyn walked through the door carrying her own brown paper bag.

She jiggled it in the air and said, "Hey, want some company? I've got an hour before I have to clock in at your uncle's."

"Sure. What's on the menu?" Coop asked, eyeing the sack. "If it's better than what I have, how about we trade?"

"Pimento cheese I made from scratch and potato chips. What's your offering?"

Cooper eyed his paper plate. "Tuna fish salad with walnuts and apples."

"Hmm, sounds better than mine. Half and half?"

"Deal. Have a seat. Want something to drink?"

"Whatcha got?"

"The fresh coffee I made ten minutes ago, a bottle of Orangina or cream soda."

Eastlyn pulled up a stool to sit at the counter. "Cream soda. I've had enough coffee to keep me floating down a river, especially after the surreal portion of the morning at the lighthouse."

"That was like a scene from a horror movie. I'd heard about the Knudsen thing but…seeing it from thirty yards away was a different matter entirely. It stirred memories inside me I don't like to think about." Cooper went to a small fridge in the rear of the store and brought back two sodas. "I never expected to see that in such a picturesque setting."

"Me either. Especially since I made out the set of eye sockets and teeth. I'd even say by getting a good look at the rest of the remains, Brent Cody's dealing with a female buried there for quite some time."

"You okay?"

"I will be. It isn't the first time I've seen human remains."

"Are you really happy working at all these jobs? I mean, come on, be honest, you have to miss flying."

"Sure I miss it. But there isn't much I can do until I'm able to get recertified. It may take me another six months, especially with the missing limb / disability / handicap thing the FAA has a tendency to focus on. I'll need to be medically evaluated again, from head to toe, literally, orthopedically and neurologically and—"

"Are there any modifications you need because of your…leg?"

"You mean because of my polymer-coated foot?" she quipped. "I'm not without a sense of humor about it. There's this guy in Britain, a former Royal Air Force pilot, who came up with a device called the HeliLeg to use to fly rotorcraft."

"You made that up?"

"No, I didn't. His name's McQuillan and his HeliLeg device is designed to let pilots with disabilities fly helicopters and operate the leg controls using a portable device, approved by the FAA. There's a flight school that teaches how to use it in Colorado. I've already checked it out and contacted them."

"Good for you."

"Hey, I want back in the air. And when you consider that the FAA finally cleared Tammy Duckworth to fly after years of her trying, there's hope for all disabled vets who want to get back in the cockpit again. And Tammy's a double amputee. Of course, they only cleared her to fly fixed wing and not rotorcraft, but that's beside the point. If a pilot can operate her aircraft safely and perform the duties of flight, then why shouldn't a disabled person be able to get back in the air? The fact is I'm willing to do whatever it takes to get airborne again. I've already been through the FAA's rigorous medical process once before to prove I'm fly-worthy after I came back stateside and again when I got back to Bakersfield. Believe me, by now I know the drill backwards and forwards. I understand exactly what I'm up against to get it back. I was an idiot for losing my license in the first place."

"How'd that happen anyway?"

"I failed a drug test."

"Oh."

She tipped her head back, met his eyes with her jaw jutted out in defiance. "Just so you know, I offer no excuses. I had a rough couple years adjusting and was in a bad place when my dad died. I should've held it together better. But I didn't. Simple as that. The good news is my flying record is clean and clear other than that one incident."

"So no drug convictions?"

"Nope, which goes a long way with the FAA."

He laid his hand over hers. "So after veering off course that one time, you're back on the right path now. If you're interested, I think I can swing you a sweet deal on that Sioux chopper."

"Really? How sweet?" She let out a loud sigh. "Who am I kidding? It would take massive hours of restoration. And where would I put it? I don't have a place to work on it at my current address."

"What if you worked on it out at Cleef's place? In addition to all those other buildings he had a nice little workshop next to his garage. It'd be a perfect place for the renovation."

"I could do that? Keep it there on the premises? That'd work." Again, she shook her head. "Let's say I get it up and running. What would I do with the chopper if I don't get my license back? It is a distinct possibility. And if I do get it back, it may only be for fixed wing aircraft."

"Ah. Which would rule out the chopper. That is a problem. Or...you could think of it this way. It'd be a good investment. In the event the FAA turns you down, then sell it for a profit. There has to be a collector out there somewhere who would pay dearly to have it."

"Let's not get carried away. We need to find out the price before I start making big plans." Or get her hopes up, she decided. Without overthinking it, she blurted out, "Why don't you come to my house for dinner Friday night? I can't promise steaks on the grill but it'll be home-cooked."

"It's a date."

That afternoon Cooper wandered over to the bank to have a talk with Nick. The man wore many hats around town—the loan officer, innkeeper, town councilman, husband, and father. But at the end of the day, the guy was primarily known for being a fair man when dealing with his neighbors.

Cooper found himself envying certain portions of Nick's life. Even though, he'd never seen himself in the role of father, he'd often wondered about it. His own had been a good man. Layne Richmond had been cheated out of all that life offered. Cooper didn't realize until now how much bitterness and resentment he'd built up toward Eleanor for taking away the only father he'd ever have.

As he stood outside Nick's office waiting to get a free minute, a feeling of déjà vu hit him. He remembered another day when Eleanor had dragged him into the bank to confront one of the tellers because her checks had been bouncing all over town. Eleanor had yelled at the teller for fifteen minutes before Milton Carr, the then bank president, had emerged from his office to put a stop to the commotion. But Mr. Carr's presence had given Eleanor another person at whom to direct her venom. As the embarrassing scene played out, Cooper remembered as a kid how he'd wished to have a sane person for a mother. Just that one thing seemed so simple, yet would've been such a gift at the time.

If only TV mom, Carol Brady, had heard his pleas. If only Carol had decided to abandon her *Brady Bunch* family to come rescue him in Pelican Pointe and take him away to the coveted fantasy world of television where all disputes ended in a hug. If only…

Cooper was still daydreaming when Nick's admin showed him into the office.

He moved through the doorway and said, "If the price is right I think I have a buyer for that old helicopter out at Cleef's place."

Nick eyed Cooper with open interest. "Are you suggesting Eastlyn wants to try and fix that thing up and actually fly it? Uh, did she mention she doesn't have her pilot's license?"

"It came up in conversation. But hey, that woman has the skills to do just about anything she sets her mind to do."

"No argument from me."

"I'm blown away that Eastlyn's able to go through everything she's seen and still keeps at it. I doubt most people could deal with losing part of a leg the way she has. In my book, she's a true hero."

Nick sent him a curious look and leaned back in his chair. "I'm sure you mean that as a compliment, but…the Eastlyn I know I doubt would view that statement as a positive."

"Why not? It was meant as a compliment."

"Because she's like most veterans who've seen war. While the mention of their military service is both laudable *and* noteworthy, it's also something they don't like to dwell on very often, especially if they're suffering from self-doubt, or self-consciousness due to some type of loss. In Eastlyn's case, a limb."

Cooper dropped his chin. "I've noticed that. She has this amazing personality, the ability to laugh even at herself. She has so much history to offer, but then just when you think it's all coming together, she puts up this wall and shuts you down. What do you suggest I do about it? You know, if I want to get to know her better."

Nick chewed the inside of his jaw. "I'll be blunt. It has very little to do with you. Eastlyn has to come to terms with it herself. Until she does, she'll be prickly whenever you push her toward any kind of intimacy. For me, it was inside my head. Not to mention I have these ugly scars across my chest. Not a very attractive look if you want to take the right woman to bed."

"It sounds like you know what she's going through."

"Yeah. I wouldn't even suggest that I know what goes on in the mind of a woman. But as far as the veteran side of her, I understand exactly how her self-consciousness affects the way she deals with social settings. She'll likely try your patience until you want to wring her neck. And she'll continue to do it until she feels she's able to trust you. Right now, she's convinced herself she's not that attractive. You'll have to find a way to get her to believe that her disability is insubstantial to how you feel. Either that, or you'll get fed up with her touchiness and walk away."

"I'm not sure I could do that. Walk away, that is."

"I hope you mean that. I do. I hope you have the fortitude to stick it out. Because Eastlyn is one of the few people I think would be worth fighting for."

Later Coop stood at the counter in his kitchen whipping together scrambled eggs and frying hash browns for supper—his mind on Nick's words—when Caleb came sauntering in.

Caleb had the same looks as his older brother. They were almost the same height and build, same coloring. Although Caleb wore his hair shorter and his eyes were flaked with more green than blue, anyone could tell they were related.

"You always did love eating breakfast for dinner. Why is that?" Caleb noted.

"Maybe because our mother never bothered feeding her kids a regular supper and I got stuck with meal prep for two little hungry mouths that usually had to eat what I put in front of them," Cooper returned easily.

"Yeah, there was that. Why didn't you tell me you were seeing the hot new arrival in town? Why do I have to hear everything secondhand from Drea? I mean, you're my older brother. You're supposed to share the important stuff like that with a bro'. When you get a woman in your life, you share the deets."

Cooper shot him a grin. "Sorry about that, I must be out of practice about the rules between bros."

"That's okay. I'll cut you some slack this time. Just don't let it happen again. Have you asked her out yet? And no, I'm not talking about taking her out to some junkyard to clomp around a bunch of rusted metal."

"Why? She enjoyed clomping around all that rusted metal, especially what she found in the barn." Cooper told him about the Sioux helicopter with the bubble canopy and how Eastlyn's eyes had bugged out at the find.

"What kind of woman wants to fix up an old bird like that?"

"The kind that knows how to fly it."

"Cool. But I thought she was having…you know, problems on that score. I thought her flying days were ancient history, what with her foot gone and all. Which makes me wonder, have you seen it? Her stump?"

"Geez, Caleb. Grow up. The woman's been to war. That's one of the casualties of combat, or haven't you heard? Soldiers lose limbs, come back stateside with massive burns, and a whole slew of PTSD problems to deal with. Eastlyn's no different than a hundred thousand other wounded vets."

Caleb held up his hands. "Okay, okay. I was just curious. Most people around here are."

"They can get over it then. Are you staying for supper or what?"

"Got enough to feed your little brother?"

"If not, I'll stuff a cheese sandwich down you like I used to do. Want a beer?"

"Absolutely. How about we watch the Giants take on the Cardinals sitting in front of the tube?" Before Cooper could answer, Caleb ambled over to the living room and picked up the remote to the TV, found the local channel that carried the baseball game. "I'm hoping Buster pulls ahead of Yadier Molina in the all-star vote for catcher."

Cooper brought plates piled high with food and set them down on the coffee table for easy access. "Buster's stats are impressive, but everybody knows Molina's got the rocket arm."

That statement brought a round of good-natured brotherly discord as they disagreed on each catcher's abilities. But both took the time to dig into the potatoes and eggs with a vengeance as the start of the game overshadowed the debate.

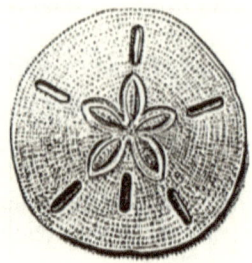

Nine

Before heading home for the day, Eastlyn pulled up in front of the police station on Main. She swung through the glass door thinking she'd see a deputy or sergeant parked on duty stopping her progress. Instead, she was surprised to see an empty workstation.

It didn't take long for her to realize this was a one-man police force. Beyond an inside window she saw into Brent's office. The guy sat preoccupied behind his desk. He'd shed the khaki uniform and opted instead for jeans and a button-down light blue shirt.

When he glanced up from his paperwork and spotted her, Eastlyn rounded the corner, stuck her head in the small room. "So you just wear the uniform when you need to intimidate people?"

"You're living in town, aren't you?" There was a sparkle in his eyes when he said it.

Her tension fell away. She stifled a laugh, but felt the need to point out, "I'm here by my own choice. Any word yet on Durke Pedasco?"

"No. However I did talk to the Feds this morning and finally got someone there to confirm none of their agencies had ever approached your friend to work as an informant."

Satisfaction brought Eastlyn all the way into the room. "You're thorough. I told you Durke wasn't an informant for anyone."

"That's if they were telling me the truth. That look on your face tells me you really have no idea what your friend could've been up to. I'm convinced, however, Pedasco is in trouble, that he felt the need for some reason to go on the run, to get out of the area...and fast...without taking anything with him."

"If you're right, that means Durke could be...dead."

"Maybe, or Durke knew something and had to slip away because of it. Either way, as a bartender Pedasco could successfully pick up on conversations. Think about it. Maybe he caught wind of something he wasn't supposed to know about. The options are endless. Let's face it, during those last few weeks before you entered rehab, you were..."

"Out of it? Thinking of myself? Yeah, I guess I was. So you're saying you still think there's a possibility Durke could be an informant?"

"I'm saying I'm keeping an open mind. Any good cop knows a reliable informant is necessary to overcome certain obstacles in proving a drug case."

"Did anyone think to double back to check the cabin a second time to see if he eventually made his way there?"

"They did. No sign of him anywhere. Any other ideas where to look?"

"If Durke's on the run he might find a way to contact his parents, or me."

"I was hoping you'd say that. If he should get in touch with you, let me know."

"And you'll do what? If he's a drug informant, will you put him under protection? Unless I have your assurance that Durke will be safe I won't hang my friend out to dry, not for anyone. I may have my faults, but I'm loyal."

"Loyalty is admirable. Now let me ask you something. Is there any way you're involved in the same thing he is?"

Eastlyn sank down in the chair in front of his desk. "I'm no dealer. I'm a lowly recovering pill addict. What exactly do you want from me to convince you?"

"That isn't what I meant at all. Is there any way that someone might *think* you know something vital, some key piece of information about the drug trade in Bakersfield and come after you? If there's a chance of that, tell me now."

"You mean by association? My friendship with Durke was never about drugs or his bartending job. We talked about... This is embarrassing. We talked about the same things friends talk about. I bitched about the assholes I dated. Durke bitched about the women he hooked up with. We talked about why we didn't have the same kinds of luck in relationships other people had. There's no mystery to our friendship. None at all. I don't have many longtime friends from my military days. When I got back to Bakersfield my prosthetic made a lot of people uncomfortable. But Durke accepted it, just as he had always accepted me with all the other quirks I had. Friends like that are hard to find. Even now, I'm worried about him."

Eastlyn narrowed her eyes, stared at the man in front of her. For the first time, she noticed the dark circles under his eyes. "You look like you haven't slept. Is anything wrong?"

He scrubbed his hands over his face. "Other than the fact that my two-month-old son was fussy last night? Not a thing."

She softened her face, sending him a wide grin, "I've heard babies like the motion of a car. Ever consider putting the kid into your cruiser and going for a ride at two in the morning? Or get a noise machine."

He lifted his face out of his hands. "Hmm, not a bad idea. After four hours of walking the floor, why didn't my wife come up with those suggestions? This is my first newborn and her second."

"Uh, maybe your wife's so exhausted she can't think straight."

"You got me there. How is it you know about cranky babies?"

"I don't, not really. In the army you pick up the occasional tidbits from crewmembers. Some things turn out to be useful information and you pass it on. I overheard one of my medics, whose wife had given birth while he was in Iraq, suggest a string of things to deal with his daughter's colic. To get the kid to sleep, the ride in the car thing worked the best."

She hesitated, collecting her thoughts before dealing with a sticky subject. "There's something bothering me. What exactly are you doing about the drug trade going on in your own backyard?"

Eastlyn saw the cop's warm brown eyes go stone cold. She quickly added, "There's no need to get your back up like that. Cooper told me about what happened with Edgecombe and his two sons, the ones you put away from the east part of the county during the time you were sheriff. Your arrest was commendable. But if someone is still running meth out there it needs to stop."

Brent sat back in his chair, fascinated at her outrage. "I've communicated that to the guy who took over for me at the helm back in Santa Cruz. I've tried to get Jim Richardson to listen, on numerous occasions. Got nowhere. The area you're talking about is out of my jurisdiction. Not only that, Richardson's made it clear to me a long time ago that the county's fight, their time *and* county money designated to fight the war on drugs, is elsewhere. It doesn't include that part of the county, or for that matter, Pelican Pointe."

"That's nuts."

"It's called politics and payback. Richardson claims he has more important drug traffickers to go after than a few meth cookers holed up between Pelican Pointe and San Sebastian."

"And you accept that?"

"Accept it? No. But I'm a stickler for things like enforcing the laws in my own jurisdiction. Now if the people in that compound were to bring their dirty business to my doorstep within my city limits, I'd be able to do something about it. Until then…"

"Good. Because I've recently become a hardworking, tax-paying resident and I take exception to having drug traffickers muddying up my new turf."

"Interesting."

"What?"

"That you know the difference between two-bit dealing and trafficking. Most people don't."

"Dealing is small time. Trafficking, on the other hand, is a major source of income and a disgusting way to make a buck."

Brent took a deep breath, let out a tired sigh. "What part of 'it's out of my jurisdiction' don't you get? Which part of 'I'm no longer the county sheriff' don't you understand? I'm now the chief of police for Pelican Pointe. My jurisdiction ends at the city limits. The area we're talking about is…"

"Someone else's problem? I get that. There's gotta be a way around that though."

Brent shook his head but finally cracked a grin. "I admit I usually don't have many of the town folk walk through my door volunteering to help me kick a little ass. Although sometimes I can count on Ethan in a pinch for backup."

"It's commendable your brother helps out like that but…"

Brent didn't let her finish. "Look, I'm grateful for your newly-minted loyalty to the town but until something pops within my precinct I suggest you let this go." He eyed the stubborn bent to her spine and added, "Nick told me you were a helluva pilot in Iraq."

"I loved flying. But that's in the past. Who exactly is left in that compound?"

Brent folded his hands behind his head willing to indulge her curiosity. "Edgecombe's wife and her in-laws, several members of the Thorwald family, and the usual bunch of hangers-on."

"How many would you say altogether?"

"More than a dozen or so. Why do you ask?"

"Cooper mentioned you had former army training."

Brent eyed her with open curiosity. After a few long seconds, he began to catch on. "What exactly did you have in mind?"

"Want me to do a little recon? We'd need to know the enemy before taking any kind of action. That means going inside that compound to see the layout and setup to know just what we'd be dealing with. If I got enough intel for you to take to this Richardson guy, he wouldn't be able to ignore it. What kind of top cop ignores drug activity? Unless… Are you sure this Richardson isn't getting cash to look the other way?"

Brent had often wondered about that as a possibility. But what good would it do to speculate about such a serious offense now when he was no longer part of that good old boys' club. "I'd be lying if I said I haven't considered the possibility."

"So we could nose around out there and see…"

"No. You're a civilian. That area is very gray when it comes to me going out there and sticking my nose into someone else's jurisdiction. I hate to say this, but it's Richardson's problem."

"That's why I'm volunteering."

"It's far too dangerous."

"I saw combat. I think I can handle a bunch of meth cookers."

"In case it's escaped you, you're not a soldier anymore. You've been out of the army for quite some time. Plus, the few Edgecombes who are still out there and the Thorwalds have armed that compound to the teeth. Not only would you be walking into uncharted territory, you'd be surrounded by a very unfriendly mob. And make no mistake, that's what they are." He pointed a finger at her. "Don't even try it."

Eastlyn stood up, blew out a breath in defeat. "Okay, but if you ever change your mind, you know where to find me."

That night Eastlyn used her smartphone to Skype with her brother, Kaeden, for more than forty-five minutes.

Kaeden was an army pilot flying a Kiowa Warrior chopper, assigned to a task force that gathered intelligence information and provided reconnaissance for all types of different ops overseas.

During that call she did her best to assure him she was doing a lot better.

From long distance it was a tough sale.

"I worry about you."

"I know you do. But there's no need. I'm doing okay. Really I am. In fact, when you get time off I want you to come visit me here. I don't have much room, but you can bunk on my couch."

"Hey, that's a step up. Last time I slept in a sleeping bag on the floor. I could probably take leave around Labor Day."

"That's perfect."

"How small is this place?"

"My rental or the town? The house is tiny and Pelican Pointe is a tad larger than that. Less than three thousand people."

"I'm having a hard time wrapping my mind around the fact that you left Bakersfield for good."

"For good remains to be seen."

"You're able to pick up enough work there in this little town? Do I need to send you some…?"

"Don't do that. You're not lending me money. I stay busy enough. Now stop worrying about me, big brother. I can take care of myself."

"Doesn't mean I can't worry about my little sister."

"Do you remember Durke Pedasco? He went missing several weeks back and hasn't been seen since."

"I never did understand what you saw in that guy."

"Don't start. Durke and I are friends. Besides, you know very well that I don't have a lot of my army pals who stayed in touch after I mustered out. They didn't know how to handle being around me, didn't know what to say. But I could always rely on Durke. He's been a good friend to me."

"Okay, okay. You're right. But do me a favor. Try to stay out of trouble for longer than five minutes, will you?"

"You always did say that same thing to me when we were kids."

Kaeden laughed. "Yeah, I wonder why? Trouble always seems to find you one way or another."

When she hung up she realized a text message had come in from Cooper. *What are you wearing?*

It had been a long time since Eastlyn had flirted, let alone flirted via phone, but she texted back anyway. *A smile. How about you?*

Nothing sexier than your smile.

Those kinds of texts went back and forth for the remainder of the evening until both of them agreed it was time to call it a night.

Even then, Eastlyn closed her eyes feeling like a teenager again. She found herself eagerly anticipating dinner with him on Friday night. Drifting off to sleep, her thoughts turned to lustful images. But then reality took over. If only she had the same body she'd had at sixteen there wouldn't be all this second-guessing. But as she floated into slumber everything seemed perfect. At the sheer joy of being whole again, she smiled—her dreams taking over.

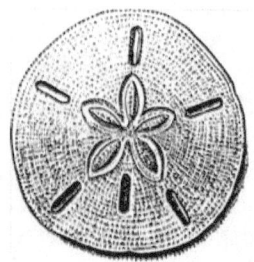

Ten

Margie had been right about the storm. By the end of the week it had dumped three inches of rain in a twenty-four-hour period. Wind gusts had wreaked havoc and ripped off tiles from rooftops, knocked out power, and uprooted a swath of trees.

The weather and the forensic team's lockdown at the lighthouse had put the planting behind schedule. Isabella had told Eastlyn not to worry about it. No one else seemed to mind too much, either. Such was the mindset in a small town where laidback ruled. A happy-go-lucky attitude might conflict with Eastlyn's military training, but she had no intentions of rocking the boat.

Good thing Landon Jennings had found plenty for her to do in the slack time, moving supplies around the warehouse at the garden center.

But today was a rare day off that came with a list of chores a mile long. She intended to get to all of them and leave behind the daily grind of all her jobs. Even Cord had sensed she needed a break and made arrangements for Abby Anderson to take care of all the animals slated for surgery this weekend.

Plus, she had a dinner guest coming. Tonight Cooper was headed to her house for a home cooked meal, which meant she'd have to go to the market.

As she indulged in a third cup of coffee, she decided it was time to touch base with Durke's parents back in Bakersfield. She'd known Shirleen and Dale Novack for more than two decades. She'd corresponded with them once via email while she'd been in rehab, but now she needed to do more.

Shirleen was probably wondering if Eastlyn had fallen off the face of the earth right along with Durke.

Eastlyn let the phone ring until Dale picked up.

"Hi, Mr. Novack, this is Eastlyn Parker. Any word at all from Durke?"

"Not a thing. We're worried sick. It's not like him to do this. You know Durke would never let his mother worry herself sick like this."

"I do know that. Durke's always been one to call his mom."

"The local cops say there's been no activity on his credit cards, no ATM withdrawals. Shirleen and I watch our share of crime shows. Even we know that's not a good sign. We're worried, Eastlyn."

"Look, I know you guys are going out of your mind. But remember, Durke is smart and savvy. He also knows Kern County like the back of his hand. If he went on the run for any reason at all, he has a plan. I feel it in my heart he'll turn up."

"Thanks for that. I hope you're right. I hope you have a few minutes because Shirleen wants to talk to you."

"Sure. I'll try to keep her mind from…" Eastlyn's voice trailed off. She sighed into the phone. "Okay, I know that's impossible, but I'll do my best to put her mind at ease."

Later, as Eastlyn walked through the produce section at Murphy's Market, she had to admit her attempt had failed. Shirleen had started crying halfway through their conversation, which had caused Eastlyn to tear up as well. The whole phone call had ended up an emotional rollercoaster along with a stroll down memory lane. In the absence of her own mother, Shirleen had played a key role during the teen years, giving Eastlyn plenty of tips on applying makeup and buying clothes.

In the process of replaying her chat with Shirleen, Eastlyn wasn't paying attention and bumped her shopping cart into someone else's. The woman pushing the other basket was a sleek, longhaired beauty, who brought to mind Native American royalty. Her cart was filled to the brim with groceries and kids—a sleeping infant tucked into a carrier and a little boy demanding to be set free.

Eastlyn immediately began to apologize. "I'm sorry about that. I wasn't watching where I was going. I was a million miles away, thinking of something else."

The woman sent her a disarming smile. "That's okay. I'm often distracted myself. I'm River Cody, Brent's wife."

River scooped up the toddler before he got restless and set his feet down on the floor. The exotic eyes zeroed in on the child and she pointed a stern finger in the air. "No running off. You stay beside me or back in the cart you go."

Eastlyn lifted a brow in surprise and introduced herself. "You're the noted archaeologist? You look more like a model."

River snorted with laughter. "Ah, words to inspire a woman who's recently given birth and feels like a fat cow."

"Not a thing wrong with the way you look. I met your husband early on."

River slapped Eastlyn on the arm in a friendly gesture. "If it's any consolation I tried my best to discourage Brent's trip to Bakersfield and dissuade him from taking part in dragging you back here. But it's difficult to derail the Scott power train whenever it gets going in one direction. Besides, we're glad you're in town now. And look at you, settling in, becoming a part of the community so fast."

"Scott seems to have a hold on the people in this town," Eastlyn grumbled. But peering at the baby softened her mood."

"That's Seth," River explained.

"He's beautiful." Eastlyn noticed the little boy at River's side growing bored with the conversation so she bent at the waist to the tot's eye level. "And who are you?"

"Luke Cody. I'm four, and I go to school. My dad's chief."

River rubbed a hand over her son's hair. "Luke goes to preschool three days a week at the Community Church to get him ready for kindergarten next year. Brent's working today and I have grocery duty. We switch off chores to keep it fair. And I'm rambling. Another sign I've been caged up in the house too long without having another adult to talk to."

Eastlyn stood up, grinned. "I'm not at home much but if you ever want to spend time away from the kids and Brent agrees to babysit…"

"I'd love to," River said quickly. "Whatever it is, I'd love to do it. As long as we aren't robbing a convenience store, I'm in. Now that I think about it, Jordan holds this 'mother's day out' event once a month. The husbands are required to take the kids for an entire afternoon so we meet for lunch at Promise Cove. It's four hours of no crying, no diaper changing or wiping snotty noses. We'd love for you to join us."

"But I don't have kids."

"Doesn't matter. Julianne McLachlan doesn't have kids either. It's girls only. You'll fit in perfectly."

"There's Scott," Luke announced, sticking one finger in his mouth and waving toward the dairy section. "Hi, Scott."

"Where?" Eastlyn asked.

"Over there." The little boy pointed to where the milk and cheese were kept. "Scott gave me a firetwuck for Cwistmas. It's my favorite twuck."

Eastlyn's eyes roamed the store. Sure enough, Scott stood by the refrigerated section. "Your son actually sees Scott? Doesn't that alarm you? Is everyone around here used to the Scott Phillips bandwagon?"

River turned to stick Seth's pacifier back in his mouth. "Why would it alarm me? Scott isn't malevolent or anything close, if that's what you're thinking."

"It's just that…reasonable people don't see ghosts."

"Are you saying my son isn't reasonable?" River teased with a glint in her eye. "Who says any of us around here fit into the reasonable column?" The archaeologist leaned in and asked in a low voice, "So you aren't a fan of living in a real life ghost story? Understandable."

Eastlyn resisted the urge to take a step back. "But reasonable people should be able to think on their own."

"If only we could find reasonable people most of the time, who always do the right thing," River cracked. "That's the problem."

Eastlyn wasn't exactly sure what River meant by that. But since Scott seemed to have everyone under his spell, she tried to change the subject. "I stopped by your museum last Sunday, spent several hours getting to know the history of the Chumash. As docent, you've done a tremendous job there."

"Thanks. It's been both a dream and a nightmare rolled into one. But now that tourists and school groups are streaming through the doors, all the hard work is behind us, for the most part anyway. You say you went through the entire gallery from top to bottom? Then you should know Native Americans are big on spirit guides. It's evident in the museum. Since you're caught up in Scott's role here, maybe it's best if you think of it this way. It isn't voodoo or witchcraft or ghostly interference. The hold Scott has stems from how he feels about his hometown. He helps people through their life choices, helps them make the right decisions. Scott's nothing to fear. You may accept him for what he is or not. No one will force you to do either one. Scott wouldn't want it that way."

"You talk as though he's a real person."

River tilted her head to make a point. "You were a pilot, right? Pilots depend on their instruments to land or an air traffic controller telling them the best flight path to take to avoid bad weather. You'll fare better if you think of Scott as the one who'll make sure you have a smooth flight."

The tiny baby boy in the infant seat began to squirm. "Uh-oh. That's my signal to wrap this up, Seth's getting hungry. Come by and see me and we'll finish this Scott thing. Better still, next Saturday plan to make it to Promise Cove for lunch."

Eastlyn stood there and watched River take off down the aisle feeling as though a Mack truck had whizzed by her doing ninety-five.

While finishing up her shopping, it occurred to Eastlyn that a scientist like River who dealt in facts could so easily believe and readily accept Scott's existence. It made her wonder what was in the Pelican Pointe water.

Eastlyn's idea of throwing a meal together meant making the best use of her go-to kitchen appliance—the ever-reliable Crock-Pot. For a girl who'd lost her mother at the age of nine, she'd perfected the art of cooking the four basic food groups all in one pot. Whether it was beans, a hearty winter soup with vegetables, or a simmering stew, if it couldn't be dumped into a slow cooker, she didn't bother fixing it.

She'd long ago come up with creative ways to spice up taco meat and make it tasty. She even found ways to fix eggs by tossing all sorts of breakfast ingredients in and serving them up like casseroles. Her Crock-Pot acted as her source for making just about any meal edible.

Her father used to say that when he turned the corner coming in from work, he could always smell Eastlyn's special dishes from the end of the driveway. But he never knew what was in store for him until he walked through the door.

So tonight for a sit-down supper with Cooper, she'd taken extra care to tenderize brisket, slow-roasted it all day smothered in the homemade barbeque sauce she'd created at fourteen from scratch. The meal had been a family favorite, with her dad and brother always filling their plates with seconds. That's one reason she trusted that the food would melt in Cooper's mouth without complaint.

From her tiny kitchen, she heard footsteps on the porch. She moved toward the door where Coop greeted her holding a huge cluster of snowy gerbera daisies mixed with plum-colored lavender. The flowers were already in a stunning turquoise-colored vase.

Like most females, her nose went straight into the blossoms. "They're beautiful. Thank you."

"No problem. Shelby told me you had a fondness for them. And the other day I saw that you'd spread out the same ones all across your stoop."

She'd never known a man who noticed such things. "I love the color of the container. You had to know I probably wouldn't have anything to put them in."

"It crossed my mind. Something smells good."

"What would you like to drink? I picked up an inexpensive bottle of red at Murphy's. Or I have beer."

"The red's fine. I talked to Nick the other day. He thinks there'll be no problem swinging the deal for the chopper."

"Wow, that was quick. So how much are we talking about?"

Cooper tossed out an extremely low number.

"You're kidding? This thing might really happen? I'd be the owner of my own bird." She hooted with laughter and went over to set the flowers down in the center of the table. "Now that's some major irony—me without my pilot's license."

"While making it air-worthy, you'll deal with that little detail."

"I should go back out there and examine it more carefully first before taking that giant step. It truly might be more of a headache than I can handle right now."

Cooper looked puzzled. What had happened to turn her excitement into hesitation, or more like indecision? "You're having second thoughts."

"I'm cautious, there's a difference."

"No, it's more than that."

"Does it look like I'm rolling in dough? That I have cash to waste on what will likely be nothing more than a hobby?"

"So we'll find a use for it. You could start a charter service, carry tourists out to sightseeing locations along the coast."

"Doesn't Bree Dayton already do that for Promise Cove?"

"A variation. She hauls guests back and forth to Treasure Island."

Eastlyn began to fuss with dinner, setting the main dish out along with a huge bowl of salad. "I hope you like brisket."

"I'm a carnivore. What's not to like about barbeque?"

Eastlyn got down glasses, poured the wine. When she noticed he was still standing in her little living room, she said, "Go ahead and take a seat. I don't bite."

"That's a shame. I bet I could sweet-talk you into changing your mind."

She actually blushed and tried to maintain a measure of poise and control. "I don't usually need much coaxing," she fired back.

"That's good to know," he said with a grin, taking his first bite of tasty beef. "This is good."

Feeling as though she'd regained the balance of power, she went on, "I bumped into River Cody at the market today. Believe it or not, her little boy actually spotted Scott hanging around the dairy section, which led us into an interesting conversation. River's premise is that Scott acts as a spirit guide for the whole town, or at least those who believe in such things."

"That's not far from the truth. Throughout various cultures people have believed in protectors of sorts, like the gatekeeper whose role is to drive away evil spirits. Then there are the message bearers. Think of them in the same vein as the three wise men. Then you have the Native American shamans, who act as the spiritual backbone of the tribe. The monks of olden times were thought of in much the same way. The Irish believed in the fairies, the magical creatures that spread merriment and joy wherever they went. As you can see, Scott is a little bit of all of those things."

"I'm guessing I haven't experienced any of Scott's merriment and joy yet," Eastlyn quipped. "Considering his irritating habit of springing up during inappropriate times."

"Or in the middle of the night. Those will cause a few gray hairs to pop up. I believe he's in that category of spirits who've crossed over, yet choose to come back. No one knows why."

"That's fairly easy. He's under the mistaken impression he's helping people.

She leaned back in her chair, picked up her wine and studied Cooper's face. "Has anyone ever told you that with all your theories you'd make a good teacher?"

He cracked a grin. "When I was younger Landon and Shelby encouraged me to pursue that as a career. But it meant being cooped up in a classroom all day. That's not me."

"No, it isn't you. You're at home in your store because it makes you happy being there. It's a solitary environment." When he sent her a curious look, she added, "There's not a thing wrong with a solo workplace."

"And you're at home in the air," Coop said matter-of-factly. "That could be construed as a solo endeavor.

"It could. It certainly applied to my dad."

"Tell me about him."

Cooper noticed the soft look that came into her eyes at the mention of her father.

"Dad didn't settle down and get married until late in life. He was thirty-eight when he met my mom. Had my brother at forty, and me two years later at forty-two. There were times he wasn't sure what to do with us. But after my mom got sick, it was up to him to see we got fed, had clean clothes, and went to bed at a decent hour. It was a difficult time for him. I've never seen a man more devastated at losing a mate. Even then, I knew how much he must've loved her."

"Love like that doesn't come along very often."

"No, it doesn't."

To lighten the mood, he recited the latest gossip. "Drea tells me she's getting serious about Zach Dennison, but she doesn't think he feels the same way."

"See, love is a tricky slope that causes heartache more often than not."

When Cooper pushed back from the table indicating he was done with his meal, she couldn't resist showing him that the newcomer had her own direct line to a measure of gossip. She told him about her conversation with Brent.

"What? I told you that stuff about the Edgecombes and their compound so you'd know more about the area and know which part of the county to stay out of, not so you'd go after the lowlifes still living there."

She took a calming breath, prepared to butt heads with him.

"You need to realize that area for what it is—a dangerous place. Those people are merciless. They'll do anything to keep their activities from becoming common knowledge. Anyone who cooks up crystal meth lives a ruthless life. Besides…"

She pushed her once-tasty barbeque around her plate, her appetite gone. "You're overreacting. Offering to help doesn't mean I'd go looking for trouble inside someone's meth compound willy-nilly. I'm not stupid. There are other ways to do that effectively."

He cut her a disbelieving glower. "Do you know what that bunch would do to you if they found you spying on them, on their own property? You just said you and Brent cooked up this scheme to go snooping around."

"It wasn't Brent's idea. I'm the one who approached him about it."

"I know you mean well, but not everyone who lives in that area has put out the welcome mat. They don't appreciate unwanted visitors. You need to be aware that the Edgecombes' place is less than two miles from that barn. You start working on that chopper and you might cross paths with them. That's the reason I brought it up. If you're planning to buy that thing, you'd obviously be hanging around the farm a lot." Cooper ran a hand through his long hair. "I was trying to…"

"Protect me?" She laid a hand on his arm. "That's sweet. I didn't mean to snap at you. There's no point in arguing about this or getting upset because Brent thought it was a stupid idea. He told me to drop it."

Cooper's eyebrows knitted together in a frown. He linked his fingers with hers squeezing her hand. He tugged her closer. His voice grew quiet. "It might've been a good idea if you'd thought to lead with that little nugget first. I'm sorry I reacted the way I did."

On impulse, Cooper nipped her up out of her chair, moved in to close his mouth over hers. He teased and coaxed a smile out of her lips. With a playful tongue he worked on getting more, until finally she began to loosen her hold on the string of knots around her set jaw.

Her pulse quickened. Her belly quivered. Desire poked its way through the tangle of tension over the argument.

They slid into the kiss, as soft as velvet and satin, a slow meeting of lips laced with lust. When they finally broke apart, he took a measured breath. "Who knew this meal would be so special? It marks our first major disagreement."

"Our first? Who knew a nerdy train store owner packed such a punch."

"I'm just warming up. Besides, a geek has to start somewhere."

After Cooper left for home she cleaned up the dishes and got ready for bed. While brushing her teeth, Eastlyn began to wonder what was truly bothering her about the discussion at supper. She'd felt edgy all evening. It was more than sexual tension. Now as bedtime approached, she faced another night of going to sleep without having her crutch to help her nod off. Vicodin had been her prop for two years.

Indecision warred with her insides. Did she really want to go on the hook for an old helicopter?

Why did Cooper feel she needed a protector? She could take care of herself. But she'd kept quiet on that score. Had she simply talked him down to keep the argument from escalating?

Edgy, she felt it building up, the jitters coming. Nights like these were tougher than others.

"You're scared and doubting yourself, afraid of trying new things."

Eastlyn recognized the voice and turned to see Scott sitting on the windowsill.

"You're either in or out," Eastlyn snarled. "Which is it?"

The ghost didn't hang around.

"Damn. When will I learn to keep my mouth shut?"

She tried to get off to sleep but each time she tried to close her eyes Scott's words kept coming back to her.

Was she scared of trying new things? Was she in the habit of doubting herself? She'd had plenty of self-confidence in the army. You couldn't become a pilot without a heavy chunk of swagger.

But having to leave her dream behind along with the military life she'd planned in exchange for civilian life hadn't been easy. With a life-altering disability there had been adjustments to make. She and her father had butted heads about it.

It was tough living with the fact that their last words had been so ugly.

Eleven

Eastlyn started her day on the road. She heading south out of town to Cleef's farm as the sunrise tried to push its way through a May gray haze.

Making her way past rolling terrain that dropped its curves into fertile emerald hills, she wanted to get a second look at the Bell chopper. Alone. The plan was to watch the sun finish its climb in the morning sky, drink the coffee from the Thermos she'd brought along, and maybe, just maybe, see if she could dig that old bird out of the muck it had sat in for decades. In the process, maybe she'd rub off a few layers of rust.

As she drove, she realized now she should have kept the confab with Brent to herself. That was the tricky part about getting close to someone. At some point they always felt the need to tell you what you should do and how you should do it.

When would she learn that she was just too independent for a relationship to work the way it did with normal people?

Since her disability, a part of her understood how people might believe she was incapable of doing the same things others took for granted. But she had never considered that Cooper might be one of them.

Maybe that's why she hadn't seen him in two days. Correction, she'd avoided him for two days.

"After all his talk about my military service, about how proud he was, it turns out Cooper's just like all the rest," she mumbled to herself as she made the turn toward San Sebastian.

"You know that isn't true," Scott pointed out from the passenger seat of the Bronco.

Eastlyn stomped on the brake. The Ford skidded onto the shoulder to an abrupt stop sending gravel pinging into the underbelly.

She turned in her seat and shot a deadly look at Scott. "What the hell? Why do you do that to people? Can't a body have a conversation by themselves without you horning in? I could've wrecked the car. I could've rolled into the ditch. What's the matter with you?"

Scott sent her a sideways glance. "Did you ever consider that maybe life as a civilian is what you were meant to do? Making plans is great and all. Everybody gets that you wanted a life in the army. It's time to face facts. Life doesn't always turn out the way you plan."

"You know what? Cord and Cooper and Nick are right about you. You're a know-it-all, an annoying worm that gets inside a person's skin and won't go away. Don't you get it? Why are men so stubborn anyway? I wanted to make a life flying choppers. Now I can't." Eastlyn's frustration bubbled to the surface and she hit the steering wheel with both fists. "I didn't want to sit behind a desk! What about that is so difficult to understand? I want to fly again!"

"Who's stopping you?" Scott shouted right back. "You have a chance to fly here. Try not to fuck it up this time."

"Get out. Get out of my car! Now! You don't know shit about me."

"Oh, poor Captain Parker," Scott drawled. "She got her leg blown off. In case you haven't noticed, Eastlyn, I'm dead, as in not able to go on with the life *I'd* planned *with* the wife I loved and the daughter I never got to hold. I didn't make it back. You did. Try doing something with your life instead of crawling into a bottle of pills or boo-hooing about what you don't get to do. Try standing on your own two feet again. Yes, I said your *feet*. Be grateful you can walk. You're able to live. Stop feeling sorry for yourself. Where's that pride you used to have?" With that final parting shot, Scott disappeared into thin air.

Once he was gone, a void hung in the air. The confined space started closing in on her. It took her several minutes to calm down enough so she could drive.

When she did manage to get back on the road, her hands started to shake. She rolled down the window to breathe in fresh air.

After another two miles of slow, careful driving, she recognized the rutted lane that led to the farmhouse. Pulling to a stop in front of the barn, she cut the engine, reached for the Thermos. With her hands still trembling, she pulled out the stopper, slopped coffee into the plastic cup.

She hated to admit it but Scott was right.

The day that had cost her a leg, her crew had come under attack. Despite her injury, she'd flown her team out of harm's way. After getting hit, she'd had to listen to Moe Turner demand that she let him take over the stick. But she'd stuck it out. She'd stayed conscious long enough to orchestrate touch down at the hospital before passing out. It's the last thing she remembered until waking up in post-op after surgery.

She'd survived.

Dazed at the memory, she leaned back in the seat sipping her coffee. She decided then and there she needed to stop letting the past rule the present. As Scott had pointed out, there were worse things than wearing a prosthetic.

If only she'd been able to square things with her dad before he'd died.

"Let it go," Eastlyn muttered to herself as she ran a hand through her hair.

"What good does it do to keep blaming yourself for your father's death? It was a car accident." Scott's voice echoed through the Bronco's interior.

But when she looked over at the passenger seat it was empty.

Tears wanted to come but she fought them back. "Dad left the house that day angry with me. You were right before. We'd had an argument, an ugly one, two stubborn heads butting up against each other. He insisted I should let the army stick me behind a desk. 'Think of the retirement you're giving up, the pension. You're crazy if you give up the military.' That's what he said to put a wedge between us," Eastlyn said, remembering her dad's stinging words. "It seems ridiculously insignificant now. I couldn't see his point of view and he couldn't see mine."

She stared out the windshield of the Ford. "That was the basis for the argument. He refused to listen when I told him I'd rather do anything other than sit surrounded by four walls. Flying was what I wanted to do. Dad called me immature. He said I was an idiot for choosing to muster out of the military and lose all the hard work I'd put into getting there. I couldn't do what he wanted. In a dozen years, he'd never have understood the way I felt. Never."

"Then let it go," Scott stressed. "It's eating you up inside. Do you think he'd want you struggling like this? Turning to pills to get by?"

She shook her head.

"Then it's best for you, for your future, to move past this."

"Don't go yet. Do you see him, my father?"

"No. It doesn't work that way. Kennan Parker was a good father. Remember those times. Honor him by living your life in happiness instead of bitter resentment and disappointment."

She didn't need to see Scott go, she felt the air go cold in his absence.

It took her several long minutes to get out of the car.

When she finally slid on work gloves, she made her way into the barn and went straight to the rusted heap. She began to tug weeds from around the helicopter's base to get a better look at its sad condition.

She patted the old, bubbled metal. "We have something in common, you and me. We both need a second chance."

While she dug out the dirt from around the skids, she kept picturing the chopper painted a sleek silver and white. And with each layer of dirt that fell away, she made her decision. She'd go see Nick herself.

Eastlyn worked for another hour before she heard a car pull up outside. She stretched her back and went to see who the visitor was out and about so early.

She spotted a woman in her late sixties getting out of the passenger seat of a pickup truck. A man about the same age got out on the driver's side. They were dressed in jeans and matching shirts.

"Yoohoo, anyone here?" the woman shouted from the pothole-laden driveway about the time Eastlyn emerged from the barn and sent up a wave.

"Just me. I'm Eastlyn Parker."

"Hi there. I'm Joy Sullivan and this is my husband, Bran."

"Ah, you guys are the vets Cord bought his business from. You used to own the cottage I'm living in. Just so you know, I love the little house."

"Oh, I loved every minute fixing up that place, picking out the paint. We moved out here so we could enjoy our horses. But, out here alone, we've come to miss everything about town, especially the people we saw every day. We miss keeping up with what's going on. There was always a steady stream of people we got to see and talk to, in the office. Now, we live way out here away from Pelican Pointe, down the road about a mile or so, and no one bothers coming to see us. So you're thinking of buying some of Cleef's old junk?" Joy asked.

Bran sent his wife an annoyed look for chatting up a virtual stranger. "We were passing by on our way to a flea market in San Sebastian when we saw your truck. What brings you out here so early?" he asked.

To Eastlyn's mind the question bordered a tad on the nosy side. Instead of taking offense though, she tried for an amused demeanor. "I'm interested in the old Bell chopper inside. You caught me trying to dig it out of its mound of dirt in the barn to get a better gauge on whether or not it's worth fixing up. So far, I've been able to determine the engine's shot, beyond an overhaul, and will need a new one. After the last couple hours, I'm not even sure it's worth my time."

Eastlyn eyed the two busybodies and fired back with a question of her own. "How about you guys? What brings you two out this time of day other than heading to a swap meet?"

"We promised Brent we'd do our best to keep an eye on the place," Bran explained. "Truth is, ever since Cleef's murder we've been a little spooked living this far out."

"We sure never bargained for murder," Joy noted. "Almost right in our own backyard, too."

Eastlyn immediately felt bad about her initial assessment. These two were clearly bummed about the area. They didn't even look that happy about their current retirement situation. "I heard about Cleef, but at least the scumbag who did it is locked away."

"Doesn't mean we still don't have problems," Joy said.

"What does that mean?" Eastlyn asked.

"She means that since moving here we've discovered it's not exactly the great place we'd hoped it would be."

"We bought our spread about three years ago. At the time, it seemed like the perfect area. But now that we've been out here on a regular basis, we've found it's not as idyllic as we thought it was."

Something in Joy's words struck a chord. "By any chance, have you shared how you feel about the area with Brent?"

Bran gave her a sheepish look. "We're no longer Brent's concern. Living this far out of town we knew we'd be leaving behind that safety net. That's why I called the sheriff's department to report what I thought was suspicious drug activity next to our place. They didn't even send a deputy out to investigate our complaint. Joy wanted me to kick it back over to Brent, but I told her that maybe we shouldn't make waves. Somebody already tried to scare us by leaving graffiti near our mailbox."

Joy shook her head. "And my response to that was if these lowlifes are running meth labs they ought to be stopped."

So there it was, out in the open. Eastlyn chewed the inside of her jaw, now steamed that the couple in retirement had to put up with that type of intimidation. "What kind of graffiti?"

"Warnings to stay out of their business, that's what."

"You really should come clean with Brent about being on the receiving end of these bullies. Call him. Report it. Make it official. Maybe one cop to another will have better luck at the county level."

Joy laid a hand on her arm. "That's what we'll do then."

As soon as she got back to town, she drove to Cooper's house. The surprised look on his face said it all.

"I wanted to apologize for avoiding you for the last couple of days."

"Is that what you were doing? So I take it you've decided we should pick up where we left off the other night? I'm all for it."

She let him slide an arm around her waist and nuzzle her neck.

"Down, boy." She pushed him back a step. "I'd love nothing better, but I'm helping Caleb make deliveries today. I'm running late as it is."

"Then why are you here?"

She replayed the scene at the barn and the conversation with the Sullivans. "So it seems the drug traffickers in the area are upping their activity. Add to that, they've taken to menacing their neighbors. I think Brent should know."

"Stay out of it, Eastlyn. They're dangerous people. I didn't mention this before but I'm pretty sure Harley Edgecombe is the one who supplied Eleanor with her drugs all those years ago. The woman wouldn't take her prescribed antidepressants but she never missed an opportunity to snort cocaine."

"Cocaine? I'm not surprised. Did anyone ever find out where the Edgecombes got their supply?"

"Who cares where it came from? I don't want you going near those scumbags."

"I'm sorry about your mother, Cooper. I am. But I can take care of myself. It's best you know that upfront. I came by here to share with you what the Sullivans told me so you'd know my intent hasn't changed."

"I'm not saying you can't take care of yourself. I'd be disappointed in your army training if you couldn't. But you're only one person."

"How about this? I suggest we table this discussion for later. Right now, I have to get to work."

"Then come over tonight. We'll watch a movie and settle this once and for all."

With an itch to scratch but not completely ready to get naked with Cooper yet, Eastlyn wondered how much longer she could hold out. She wasn't even sure she wanted to. Putting him off seemed rude when she so wanted to give in and sleep with him.

Although she couldn't make her self-consciousness disappear overnight, she also couldn't grow back a limb. Her fear that he wouldn't be able to handle the sight of her stump might be unreasonable to some. But she'd lived through it several times before.

After the last time, she vowed to guard her heart from the embarrassment of that ever happening again. But those men weren't Cooper Richmond. She had to admit he wasn't like any of the others. She could only trust her instincts and go where her heart took her.

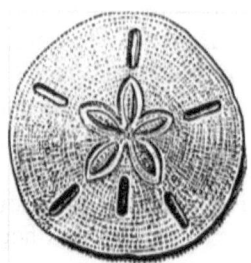

Twelve

Brent spent so much time mulling over Eastlyn's suggestion that after almost a week, he finally sought out advice on the matter from his brother Ethan, who'd been a deputy sheriff before following his passion into writing.

On a weekday morning Brent caught up with the writer pushing a lawnmower around the front yard of his home on Landings Bay.

Brent stared at his younger brother, who'd hit the big time with his first novel, a thriller about the hunt for treasure off the coast of California.

Today, the sweaty job had Ethan looking more like a handyman with his raven hair pulled back in a tight ponytail and a bandana wrapped around his head.

The brothers shared Native American roots along with a penchant for "picking up on things" from other people. They shared an intuitive nature with their father, Marcus Cody. It was common knowledge Marcus had solved a number of missing persons cases all over the West coast. The knack for it seemed to run from father to sons, which might be the reason Brent and Ethan were so adept at law enforcement.

As soon as Ethan spotted Brent, he cut the engine on the mower. "Hey, what brings you out so early? How's the new little Cody doing? Is Seth sleeping any better?"

"Some, last night anyway. Look, there's something I need to run by you. Got a minute?"

"Sure. Want coffee?"

He trailed after Ethan into the kitchen. "I never turn down caffeine these days. Although what I really need is a nap that lasts longer than two hours."

"Lots of luck with that."

"The house is awful quiet. Where's Hayden?"

"She took the kids over to her sister's place for a couple hours so they could play with their auntie. I think Hayden was hoping I'd spend the free time jotting down a few ideas for my latest manuscript. I'm behind deadline. But the truth is, I'm having trouble with this one scene in particular. For the life of me I can't get it to pop."

"So you thought you'd mow the grass for inspiration?"

Ethan filled two mugs with steaming brew and set them on the counter. "It's happened before. What's the latest word on the bones Eastlyn uncovered?"

"Too early to tell. But you know as well as I do what those remains were doing there. I've already contacted prison officials to request an interview with Carl Knudsen."

"Let me know when approval comes in. I'd like to go with you. I've been kicking around doing a book about the murders."

Brent sipped his coffee and sent Ethan a grim look over the rim. "Are you sure you want to travel into the mind of a sadistic killer, one you knew as a kid? That's a dark path you'll more than likely regret. I've watched interviews from writers who tackled other serials. They all say the same thing. The process was difficult and time-consuming. The journey took them to a dark place they had a hard time crawling out of."

"That's just it. If I don't do it, who will? Who better to write this book than me?"

"Okay. As long as you're prepared for the hits it will take in your personal life and all the fame and fortune that goes with it."

Ethan chuckled. "I imagine fame and fortune all the time. Did you know, according to Sydney, Doc Prescott is thinking about retiring at the end of the year?"

"River mentioned it when she took Seth and Luke in for their checkups last month. No one's blaming Doc for wanting to call it quits after all these years. But I'd hate to see this town lose its only doctor."

"Nick and Murphy are already putting out feelers for help on that score. They've sent inquiries to Seattle and as far away as Chicago. Word is that the pharmacist, Ross Campbell, has a friend, a general practitioner, who runs a private practice in Portland, Oregon. Ross is hoping to talk him into relocating."

Ethan took a seat on one of the barstools and gawked at his brother noting the bags under his eyes. "What's troubling you other than lack of sleep that comes with having a newborn in the house?"

Brent took his coffee over to the kitchen table, laced it with plenty of sugar to boost his outlook. "You remember when we finally nailed the meth dealers Harley Edgecombe and his sons, sent them away for a long time?"

"You bet, hard to forget the way I felt taking down that whole compound near San Sebastian. It's one of the highlights of my brief stint in law enforcement. Why? Has Richardson finally decided to go after them and now's begging your cooperation?"

"I wish." Brent told him about how the Thorwalds had now taken over the lucrative enterprise and Eastlyn's offer to scope it out. "Trouble is, the first time we went in there, I was sheriff. Here in Pelican Pointe as police chief I have no reason to officially be in that area. Yet, knowing that compound is still out there, knowing what crystal meth does to kids, or anyone else for that matter, how can I sit on my butt and do nothing?"

Ethan knew his brother. "I can see the war going on in your head from here. Especially when a private citizen offers to put her ass on the line to make it go away and you stymied."

"Exactly. It makes me question why I took this job if all I plan to do is write speeding tickets and hassle the occasional transient trying to catch a few winks on the bench along the pier."

"It isn't like you to question yourself. So don't hand me that hangdog attitude by selling yourself short. You do a helluva lot more around here than that. Do I have to list everything so you'll quit feeling sorry for yourself?"

Brent lifted his cup and said as only a brother could, "Screw you. With kids I'd think you'd be as concerned as I am with the idea we didn't completely put an end to the drugs coming out of that compound."

"Okay, now that you've opened that door, there's been an ugly rumor floating around for several years now that the drug trade in the area has managed to infiltrate our own quaint city limit borders."

Brent sent him a knowing look. "I've heard that before. For some time I've had my eye on McCready's, maybe because I live practically across the street from the place. Rowdy weekend crowds are becoming more and more routine and there's something about Flynn's clientele I find…questionable."

"I know you've been suspicious of that place for a long time because of the seedy crowd."

"When it's the only local watering hole for miles around that tends to be the norm. Up to now, I've given Flynn some leeway, or tried to, often times cutting him some major slack with the noise ordinance."

"Hey, during the time the town was my turf, we managed to drive many of the criminal types away for good. No one gave us a medal for it, but then, we weren't looking for one either. "

"Those were the days." Brent sat back, sipped his coffee. "So if I could find a link here in town to that compound, I'd be justified in going after the Thorwalds?"

"I'm no legal eagle, but I'd say if you made a connection like that, you'd be able to justify following any suspect. If that suspect just happened to lead you to

Thorwald's front door, you'd have plenty of reason to kick it down and see if the operation has been revitalized. But having a civilian do your intel is risky and dangerous. This woman wouldn't do it on her own, would she?"

"Nah, I don't think she's that wound up. I'm pretty sure I discouraged her from going near that place on her own."

"You know, big brother, if you ever need backup, I still keep my .45 locked and loaded."

"I can see it now at the family barbeque, Hayden giving me hell because I dragged you into that role and back into the danger zone."

Ethan let out a whoop of laughter. "Chances are if I went charging out the door to help you in a firefight, she'd definitely have something to say about it. But I can still handle my wife."

Brent found humor in Ethan's bravado. "Yeah, right. As far as Hayden's concerned, I've seen you cave at the slightest little thing. But you're entitled to keep your 'king of the castle' delusions."

Ethan raised his middle finger toward his brother in response. "You're as prone to caving in to River as I am to Hayden. Don't pretend otherwise. So what do you intend to do about the ex-pilot?"

Brent rubbed the stubble on his chin. "I'm not sure exactly. Maybe emphasize again that she should avoid the area. Make sure she understands how dangerous it is."

"What prompted her to make such an offer?"

"Honestly, I think she's bored. She reminds me of when I left the army. Do you remember how long it took me to get comfortable in civilian life? I think it's hard for her to leave behind that search for an adrenaline rush. I think she's going through several kinds of withdrawal other than the pills."

"Sounds like a tough place to be. Have you thought of bringing her on as a police officer, at least part-time?"

Brent's eyes widened. He started to speak but then sat back and thought about that. "I could, couldn't I?"

"There's your built-in backup." Switching topics, Ethan wanted to know, "Are you babysitting the kids next Saturday when our wives take the mother's day out excursion to Promise Cove?"

"Who else? The nanny?" He squirmed in his chair. "We should start a father's day out."

"Yeah, you be sure to mention that to River when you get home."

"Only if you'll bring it up to Hayden."

"I'm not stupid. Hayden already believes she has it tough stuck at the store all day with the kids while I try my damnedest to write."

"Who are we kidding? Marriage is complicated. We've been ruled by our wives since the day we said 'I do.' Women are sneaky. They've brought allies into the mix—our own kids."

Ethan snorted out a laugh. "Ain't that the truth? It's a foregone conclusion we've been domesticated by sexy females who invaded the town and took us by storm."

Brent peered at him over the rim of his cup. "Do you use that kind of crap in your books?"

"Not until now, but I'm desperate enough to try to work it into the storyline somewhere."

"Lots of luck with that."

Landon Jennings, owner of The Plant Habitat, studied the hard-working Eastlyn Parker as she zipped the forklift around the warehouse, moving empty pallets from the dock to where the stacks were stored overnight.

After an exhausting day spent landscaping Ina Crawford's front yard, Caleb came up to him, wiping the sweat off his forehead. "It's a hot one today. Despite the heat I finished the job in three days as planned." He handed Landon an invoice, all the while tracking his uncle's line of vision. When they landed on Eastlyn, Caleb added, "You know, Cooper's been out with her a couple times."

"Yeah, word gets out. The other day I stopped by the store and caught Coop humming along to a tune by James Taylor."

"No way. Are you sure it was our Cooper? Maybe aliens took over his body."

A smile formed at the corners of Landon's mouth. "It gave me hope that he's finally in a place where he can put the past behind him. It's significant, too, because he's right back in the town where it all started."

Caleb rested his hand on Landon's shoulder. "Sometimes I wish I had memories of my father like Cooper has. But all I remember is you being there for me in that role. What I recall most is how you and Shelby would always show up at assorted school events for all three of us, right on time, never late. Whether you were swamped at the nursery or not, you'd take the time for us. Those first few months had to be a confusing, awful time for Coop and Drea. I was younger. It didn't affect me the way it did them. I only remember you and Shelby as my mom and dad."

Landon's eyes misted up. He laid a hand on Caleb's shoulder. "It's good to hear you say that. You're my son and that's the truth of it. Shelby and I thought of all three of you as our own from day one. I don't know. Maybe it was from guilt because we didn't see Eleanor's mental illness as that serious, certainly had no idea she was ever capable of murder. Poor Layne and Brooke, trying to turn to each other for a little happiness in life and getting killed for it."

"It's amazing that you'd see it like that."

Landon swallowed hard. "It wasn't easy. But you don't remember how cruel and vicious Eleanor could be. The woman used her tongue like a weapon. She's my sister but I swear after she left her kids out in the middle of the water that night, I was done with her."

"But everyone thought she'd committed suicide."

"I'll be honest. I never thought she did. Eleanor was too narcissistic to take her own life. Anyway, I never mentioned your mother to any of you kids after that and you guys never really asked. It was as if all of you were happy to be rid of her. I know I was."

"No one would blame you for that."

"Doesn't matter. I blame myself for what you guys went through. I should've intervened long before I let it get that far. I didn't. I have to live with that every time I see the sadness in Cooper's eyes, the way he's wary of connecting with anyone on a deep emotional level."

"You've noticed that, too. I thought I was the only one who picked up on that in him."

Landon shook his head. "That's why if Eastlyn Parker can bring Coop some level of happiness, I'm all for it."

Not knowing the seriousness of the conversation between her brother and uncle, Drea glided into the warehouse with problems of her own. All she saw were two men lazing on the job, staring off into space. "What are you guys doing? Why are you standing around watching Eastlyn work?"

"What does it look like we're doing? We're standing here working on world peace," Caleb said good-naturedly.

In response, Drea gave him a light punch to the shoulder.

"Is that all you got?" Caleb teased in challenge.

"What is it with men these days?" Drea sighed. "I'm fed up with all of them."

Caleb exchanged a look with Landon before holding up his hands in surrender. "Uh oh, that sounds like there's trouble in paradise. Is that statement meant for men in general or Zach in particular? What did he do this time?"

"I'll tell you what he did. He forgot our one-year anniversary. He's been acting strange now for some time.

But when a guy you've been dating for a year doesn't even bother to remember the dinner I'd planned to celebrate the occasion, I'd say it's time to take a serious look at what's not working. When I moved into his house I expected a little attention. Is that too much to ask? I knew how busy he was at the time with his business so for months and months, I cut him some slack. But I draw the line at completely forgetting the reason we made dinner plans."

"He didn't even think to bring the florist a flower?" Landon asked.

"No. Not a card. Not an email. Not a text message. No lunch date. No dinner date. He didn't even plan a movie at home. In fact, he went off by himself. God knows where."

"He went off by himself? Is Zach having an affair?" Caleb asked.

"Maybe. Who knows?" Drea grumbled.

Ever the practical cynic when it came to affairs of the heart, Caleb reasoned, "Then I guess it's a good thing you didn't find a renter for your loft."

Drea's face went white at the prospect of that. "I packed my things up already and slept there last night. So I hope Coop and Eastlyn have a lot better luck at love than I did, because I've decided to break things off with Zach for good."

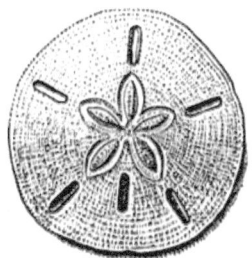

Thirteen

Once the county forensic team finished digging in the dirt, it was Eastlyn's turn to get back to the plowing. It took two more days before she deemed the ground ready for planting. When that happened, she helped Isabella and Thane make at least four dozen calls to spread the word.

The next morning people began showing up at six a.m., so many volunteers that the mass arrival created a parking problem.

After Brent and Ethan solved that issue they realized two shifts were needed to accommodate all the troops willing to help. No one was turned away. Children of various ages were assigned to a grownup to act as helper. The kids, depending on their ages, either toted the seed bags or handled the scattering of seeds.

Sure the process could've been done a lot faster and far less labor intensive. But that had never been Isabella's intent. The Lighthouse Project as folks around town now called it, was supposed to show kids and adults there was joy and personal satisfaction in the art of gardening.

"Your hard work's finally paid off," Thane noted as he came up to stand next to Eastlyn. "A job well done all around."

Eastlyn surveyed all the workers in the field. "There was a time I thought your wife might be delusional.

Whenever she went on about how many people she expected to show up, I had my doubts. Now, I see she that was the heart and soul of this project."

"She believed in the townspeople every step of the way," Thane said with pride. "I admit there were times I thought she might be exaggerating the extent of everyone's participation."

"I hear congrats are in order. Jonah's been telling anyone who's willing to listen that he's getting a baby brother for Christmas."

Thane took off his ball cap to wipe the sweat from his brow. "Oh geez, that boy is likely setting himself up for a big disappointment."

From a few feet away Coop overheard the exchange. Standing at the back of a Plant Habitat delivery van, he added, "Think of it this way, Jonah's simply playing the percentages."

Coop slid a crate of tomato plants off the back, handed them off to Thane in assembly-line fashion. "There's a fifty-fifty shot the boy's right and he'll be able to strut around telling everyone he's the one who knew it from the start."

Thane hefted the carton from Coop, handed it off to one of the volunteers waiting in line for another pallet of seedlings. "We'll know for sure in a couple weeks, around the middle of June. That's when Isabella goes in for the first sonogram."

Dressed in a pair of overalls, hair pulled back in a ponytail, Shelby Jennings came up to them looking far younger than her fifty years. "When we finish the planting, all the volunteers have already decided we should stay put and have ourselves a cookout on the grounds to celebrate. Murphy and Nick went to round up as many barbeque grills as they could find."

It warmed Eastlyn to be part of such camaraderie again. Since leaving the army, she'd missed that feeling of teamwork, that pulling together toward a single, common objective.

Right now, Isabella's vision for the co-op was coming together nicely.

"So you're saying the first shift will hang around till the second one gets done?" Coop asked, amazed at that kind of enthusiasm.

Shelby's voice cracked with emotion. "Coop, you were away a long time. But the truth is, this place has a lot of good people in it who come together like nothing I've ever seen. Murph and Nick and Jordan turned this town around. So to answer your question, they're all planning to chip in for the food and stay to make it a party."

Landon came up, tossed in his two cents. "Plus, they don't want this beautiful place overshadowed by death. The negative stamp Carl Knudsen tried to leave, they want it erased for good, replaced by a positive."

That sounded like a plan to Eastlyn. "We could make a bonfire over near the edge of the cliff."

Thane nodded. "Good idea. I'll round up some of the kids and get them busy gathering firewood."

For the next hour or so the first wave set up folding tables in a common area to use for the food. They unloaded lawn chairs and coolers packed with soft drinks and beer.

As soon as Nick and Murphy returned, the men fired up the grills. Because everyone had worked up an appetite and wanted their food fast, they kept the menu to meat that would cook quickly. They broke open packages of hot dogs for the kids, bratwurst and links for the grownups.

Margie and Max dished out buckets of old-fashioned potato salad while Fischer Robbins served up helpings of his pre-prepared macaroni and cheese.

When the work in the field began to wind down, Eastlyn stood back and watched the contented faces on the volunteers as they lined up to get their food. So much community spirit made her wonder how long it had been since she'd felt such satisfaction in a job well done.

The Lighthouse Project had come to an end—at least a good portion of it. Sure, Isabella planned to keep her on as an overseer, but how much time would the job really take to line up the volunteers needed to water and tend the place? No, she'd need to start looking for something else. She'd need to stretch every dollar from the garden center if she intended to buy that old chopper.

She was staring off into the horizon when Cooper walked up with his camera in hand. "What are you fretting about? Where were you just now? You didn't even see me come up."

Without answering him, her eyes immediately went to the camera. "I hope you don't aim that thing at me."

He took her chin in his hand, moved her head from side to side. "Why are you so camera shy? You of all people."

"What does that mean?"

"It means, why would such a beautiful woman object to having her picture taken?"

"You need glasses," she grumbled as she moved away. "Come on, there's something I want to show you." She led him over to an area away from the others where she'd already decided this was her favorite spot.

She plopped down on the bench among the newly planted lavender seedlings, some already laden with fragrant buds. "By July this spot will be blooming with fragrant buds."

Instinctively, Cooper raised his lens and zoomed in on her. He started clicking off shots one after the other.

For those brief few minutes, he made her feel like a runway model. If only she'd been better dressed and wasn't wearing tattered jeans and a top leftover from the nineties.

Cooper looked around and adjusted the lens again taking snapshots of the cliff and the surrounding landscape.

She watched him zero in on his target like a trained sniper. But instead of a weapon, he used the camera as a natural extension, capturing this one special moment in time, documenting the project like no one else had thought to do.

Eastlyn spread her arms out wide. "The train store owner slash photographer in his element."

That brought him back to where he'd started. One more time, he aimed the lens at her sitting on the bench among the plentiful lavender. "What to know what I think? This is your element right here. That smile on your face says Pelican Pointe agrees with you."

He sat down next to her, stretched out his long legs. "Drea tells me she plans a big kick off-to-summer bash at her place this Friday night. She'd hoped it would be her engagement party to Zach. My guess is she's trying to put on a brave face after the split."

"Really? Those two broke up? How long had they been dating?"

"About a year. I want you to go with me."

How could she possibly get out of going to his sister's first party after a bad breakup with her boyfriend? "Of course," she heard herself say.

"Do me a favor."

"Okay."

"Do you own a dress?"

She tilted her head, considered his motives. "Is that a snotty way of saying you don't like what I wear?"

"I'm saying I'd like to see you in a dress. There's no need to be self-conscious about your prosthesis, none at all. You're beautiful exactly the way you are. I wouldn't change a thing."

"Except what I wear," she pointed out in a huff.

"My motives are entirely selfish. I'd like to get you out of your clothes. There, I admitted it, honestly and without malice."

She chewed her lip. "What you're really saying is you want to see my leg."

"Okay, that, too."

She turned in his arms. "You think you're ready but I guarantee you won't be. No one is."

"I'm fairly certain I'm ready to see all of you. It's you who I haven't convinced. You're still not quite ready to trust me yet. I've made it clear I want to take you to bed, Eastlyn, and that's a little hard to do if you're constantly afraid I'll somehow act differently the minute I see your prosthetic. And since I don't intend to make love to you in the dark…"

"Ever? What do you have against the dark?"

"Not a thing. But when we make love for the first time I'll want to explore every inch of you."

"Cooper…"

When she tried to protest, he simply cut her off with a soft press of his lips to hers. It was as if they were the only two people who existed, right then and there, looking out to sea. At that moment, they shut out the hum of conversation behind them. All the people gathering to eat nearby didn't exist. That left them alone to drop into the kiss. In their own world, nothing else mattered but the two of them.

A flock of squawky seagulls broke the moment.

His eyes danced as he stood up and held out a hand to help her up. "Let's go get something to eat before I strip your clothes off right here."

"That would definitely headline Myrtle's newsletter," Eastlyn quipped.

"The woman's smarter than that. Myrtle's learned to utilize email. It's faster than waiting for a newsletter to print." He glanced up to where the grills were going. "The line's thinned out quite a bit. You must be starving."

Eastlyn got to her feet, ran a seductive finger down his throat. The gesture had nothing to do with food. "You know what? I just realized I'm a lot hungrier than I thought I was. You make me hungry, Cooper."

His smile curved wide, showing a pair of dimples in his cheeks. "I knew I'd eventually beat down your resistance."

Before they could make it over to the buffet of food, Cooper's cell phone suddenly came to life on vibrate. Out of habit, he glanced down at the digital readout and set his jaw. His face became a mask of disappointment mired in anger.

Sliding the arrow to the right to take the call, he listened to what turned out to be a recording. But he put an end to the spiel before it had time to finish and crammed the device back into his jeans pocket. To reassure himself, he reached out to touch Eastlyn's hand.

"Who was that?" she wanted to know.

"No one important."

But Eastlyn wasn't buying it. "Don't give me that. You look like you could break someone in half without even trying. I know what frustration looks like."

He shook his head, lifted his shoulder in a shrug. "Some telemarketer who won't take no for an answer."

And with each step he did his best to push the rage he felt back where it belonged—deep into his past.

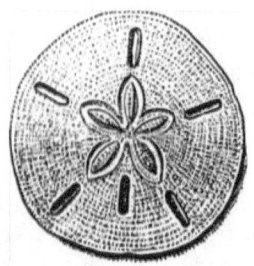

Fourteen

For Eastlyn, the luncheon at Promise Cove proved a true eye opener, a window into the female mindset that made up the town.

She'd been there only a few minutes when she scanned the dining room where most of the women in town gathered around Jordan's long dining table. Young and old, women of all ages snatched up delicate little finger sandwiches from fancy trays lined with lacy paper doilies and drank tea poured from sterling silver pots.

Eastlyn had heard of such things but never once had she ever gone to an afternoon tea. She stood in the entryway in her bland gray pantsuit feeling about as frumpy as a Muppet while everyone else around her wore spring dresses in bright colors or stylish skirts and tops. Her drab wardrobe made her feel out of place and awkward.

"There's plenty to eat and drink," Jordan sang out in cheerful greeting, giving her reticent guest a little nudge toward the action.

Eastlyn took the hint and moved toward the buffet.

"Try the quiche," Emma Colter suggested. "Personally, I never make the stuff, but Jordan's got it down to an art."

A skeptical Eastlyn nodded and surveyed the other tasty-looking appetizers. But after perusing the table, she came back to the mini spinach quiche. Nibbling the crusty edges, she decided this tea thing might have its own merits.

The fact that for most of her life Eastlyn had struggled to make girlfriends tended to affect the way she looked at social events like this. She'd found out at an early age she had little in common with most of her girly classmates. They seemed to want different things out of life than she did. They wanted to become wives and mothers, or ballet dancers, or beauty queens, or bankers. At sleepovers her friends often preoccupied themselves with Barbie dolls, played dress up, experimented with makeup. Later, during the awkward teen years, it would become girl talk that bordered on obsession with getting dates out of boys and planning future weddings.

Not Eastlyn Parker.

Even as a kid, Eastlyn had wanted to fly. Her daydreams, more often than not, consisted of trips to the moon and back. Somewhere around the age of thirteen she realized becoming an astronaut might not be practical, so she aimed her sights on something closer to reality, something more attainable—flying for the army, just as her father had, became her goal.

So while this coffee klatch might not be something she would have ever put at the top of her must-do list, today she was enjoying herself. The party allowed her the opportunity to talk to some of the women in town she had yet to meet on her own.

Women like Cord's wife, Keegan Bennett, the other veterinarian in town. Eastlyn decided that Keegan, with her long red hair tied back in a sleek ponytail, looked far younger than Cord and told her so.

Keegan roared with laughter. "Oh, I can't wait to tell him that. I'm surprised you're even speaking to Cord after the way he and Nick dragged you here."

"It's strange but I don't hold that against him, at least not like I did when I first got here."

Keegan patted her arm. "Oh, I'm so glad to hear it. I know he appreciates the way you've taken such good care of our furry patients at the clinic undergoing surgery. You'd be surprised how difficult it is to find people who care enough about the animals to go the extra mile for them the way you do."

"I adore the animals. By the way, we spent an amazing three hours walking through your rescue center on Sunday. It's a wonderful thing you do for the animals."

Pleased with the praise, Keegan's mouth curved up. "It's a testament to my grandparents and their devotion to saving marine life. I just try to keep it going, with Cord's help, of course. What was your favorite part?"

"We loved the sea otters."

"Who's *we*?"

"Uh, Cooper Richmond showed me around the place."

"Cooper's a sweetheart. Last fall he donated giveaways, a slew of toys, to our annual fundraising effort. The event gets bigger every year. And the philanthropy from the town makes me proud to call this place home."

"I've noticed the businesses here are very supportive that way."

"Oh, they are. From the bank to the florist we take care of our own. And now that the old tightwad Joe Ferguson's left town, his son Tucker seems to have finally gotten the message. Even Tucker's stepped up his game."

When Kinsey Donnelly, the legal eagle, walked up, Keegan nodded to the lawyer. "And if you ever find yourself in a situation where you need an attorney, don't hesitate to call this one. Kinsey's a whiz at drawing up estates, trusts, wills, that sort of thing."

"You're making me blush," Kinsey said faking a southern drawl. "Although there's an element of truth in what you say."

"Do you handle divorce?" Eastlyn asked with a serious face.

That question all but stopped Kinsey's clowning around. She became all business-like. "Uh…sure I can… I represented Greg Prather and Archer Gates with theirs. But I thought… Um, Cooper told Logan you two were… I didn't know… I had no idea you were married and needed a divorce attorney."

Eastlyn bumped the lawyer's shoulder in a playful gesture and grinned. "Gotcha. I don't. I'm not. Never have been. Married, that is. I just wanted to see the look on your face."

Kinsey snorted out a belly laugh then bumped Eastlyn's shoulder right back. "Well, you certainly had me going. You're all right. I like a woman who isn't afraid to show she has an offbeat sense of humor."

"In the army, you learn to develop thick skin, or the ability to laugh at yourself. If you can't take a joke, you might as well put a sign around your neck that you're ripe for all the punksters in the unit."

Bree Dayton overheard the comment and leaned over to grab a helping of crab salad. "I can't even imagine being in a combat zone. If Troy were somehow shipped off to war, I'd worry myself sick. Nick says you saved his life."

Eastlyn had crossed paths with Bree Dayton a time or two while she'd been a guest at the bed and breakfast. But she had yet to talk to Bree one-on-one. "I just did my job and flew him out of the hot zone. The medics on my team were the true heroes. They're the ones who started the IVs that probably saved his life. They're the ones who patched him up enough before I dropped him off at the field unit."

Principal Julianne McLachlan sat across the table and recognized a reluctance to accept credit for saving a life. She'd seen it before. "I'm sure all that's true. But you flew the chopper that got him there. My husband, Ryder, was in Afghanistan with Cord. Ryder is like you. He refuses to talk about his time over there."

When Eastlyn remained silent, Julianne studied the ex-pilot. "I just had a brilliant idea. I'd love it if you'd agree to speak to the kids at school during our year-end assembly. I'd be able to offer you punch and cookies in return."

Eastlyn was too dumbfounded to get the humor. "Me? Why me?"

"You're a hero."

A pained look crossed Eastlyn's face. "I don't know where you got that impression but…"

"Oh, that idea rocks," River chimed in with an amused look on her face as she got up to help herself to the dessert tray.

When Eastlyn tried to object, Julianne rolled right over the attempt to protest. "That way, you could talk to the various grades all at the same time as one of the motivational speakers, a headliner."

"Wait. Slow down a minute. How would I be able to motivate anyone? I'm not a hero."

"Nick and Cord think differently," Julianne stated.

"Yeah, well, did they mention I had to spend six weeks in rehab before getting to town? I went to detox for six weeks." Eastlyn noted the look on Julianne's face. "They left that part out, didn't they? It's okay. I won't hold you to the invite."

Unmoved, Julianne dug in, determined. She waved off the protest. "Rehab's pretty common these days."

Panic started to knot in Eastlyn's stomach at the idea of standing up in front of the whole school. She turned to their hostess, sent Jordan a pleading look to say something. "If you don't believe me, ask Jordan. She'll tell you the circumstances in which Nick and Cord brought me back here. Go ahead, tell them, I don't mind. Tell them I couldn't possibly be a role model for kids."

While pouring more tea into one of the fancy teapots, Jordan stopped long enough to lay a hand on Eastlyn's arm. "Don't be silly. When Nick first came here, he felt just like you do. He didn't want to talk about the war. You'll see, it'll be fine."

Sympathetic, Julianne came around to pat Eastlyn's shoulder. "Don't worry you won't be up on the dais alone. I drafted Ryder to show up and give a little talk, too. And just so you know, the school district in Santa Cruz features former drug addicts as speakers all the time as a deterrent. Talking to the older students, fifth graders and above, we're hopeful by doing that we prevent kids from starting drugs in the first place. But what I'm really hoping for is that you'll say a few words about your recovery time from the serious injury that took your leg."

Eastlyn's face turned ashen at the thought. She was so upset she stood up to pace. "But I… I wouldn't know what to say. How long do I have to prepare?"

"It's nothing to be alarmed about. The assembly is next week, the last day of school. I'm sure you'll come up with something brilliant to talk about."

"Don't count on it," Eastlyn muttered before chugging down an entire cup of Darjeeling tea. Or for all she knew, it might've been Oolong.

River came up to her then, gave her a little hug. "I once gave a lecture at a seminar in Minneapolis. I was so nervous I didn't sleep a wink the night before."

"What happened?"

"I got up there on stage and went blank, forgot everything I wanted to say."

"Gee thanks. That really cheers me up."

River let out a deep laugh. "No problem. You strike me as a woman who has the ability to think on her feet. You'll be fine."

Eastlyn looked around at the faces of the guests. "You guys act like this is a foregone conclusion."

Understanding moved through Lilly Pierce. "I'm not sure I've met anyone able to say no to Julianne. You're not the only one she's roped into doing this type of thing. Wally made an appearance early last fall to talk to the kids about surfing. Even though it's been months, kids still show up on our doorstep at seven o'clock Saturday mornings wearing wetsuits hoping he'll give them lessons."

Eastlyn had seen Lilly around town, especially whenever she'd filled up her car at the gas station. This was the first time she'd had a chance to do more than passing chitchat. Her mind whirled with the prospect. But before she could slide into another topic, she realized River still had something to add.

"Brent's slated to appear at that same end-of-school event. He got drafted some months back into saying yes. His little presentation is meant to elevate law enforcement as a career choice."

Eastlyn frowned. "But that means he's had plenty of time to prepare. That's exactly my point, there's not enough time for me to adequately..."

River cut in. "You have a week, that's seven days to work on your speech. Piece of cake."

Eastlyn wasn't so sure. But she realized she needed to let this go for now and stop freaking out. Lilly provided that distraction, the break she needed. "Since you and Wally own the Pump N Go, is it true your husband has a way with engines?"

Lilly beamed with pride. "Absolutely. Wally's a genius with a motor."

"I've heard there's really no engine he hasn't tackled."

"He's had a wrench in his hand since he was old enough to walk. If you're having trouble with that Bronco, bring it in on Monday and I'll see that he fits you in."

"That's sweet. Other than the occasional carburetor issue now and again where I have to jam a screwdriver into the butterfly valve to keep it open, it's running fine. I was thinking more along the lines of having him give me his opinion about a Bell helicopter, specifically the Sioux model H-13, military version." Eastlyn went into the details about its sad shape. "I might need some help locating a new engine for it. And if Wally found one, do you think he could help me install it?"

Lilly chuckled. "That's a new one. But I'm sure Wally would give it his best shot. That man loves to tinker with anything mechanical."

"Great. I'll run it by him the next time I fill up."

"If you don't mind me asking, where did you get your name?" Lilly asked. "You're so tall and gorgeous."

Eastlyn let out a little laugh. "I was just thinking the same thing about you minus the tall part. How is it tall women most often prefer to be short and short women prefer tall?"

"It's the way of life I suppose. The grass is always greener thing. Did you ever want to be petite?"

"All the time. But I grew out of it. Having height in the army proved a plus. As for my name, Eastlyn was my mother's maiden name. Elizabeth Eastlyn Parker."

"It's lovely." Lilly leaned in to where no one else could hear and in a whisper added, "Don't tell anyone, but Wally and I are thinking of having a baby. Now that things have smoothed out for us, we're thinking of giving Kyra and Joey a sibling."

"And if it's a girl, you'd name her Eastlyn?"

"I love the name. Do you think it'd work for a boy as well?"

"I don't see why not."

"I need a little advice," Drea announced to the room, getting everyone to turn their eyes on her. "Since I have all of you ladies present, I need to know if you think I'm being too hard on Zach. As you may have heard, I recently broke up with him because he's so busy at work he forgot our anniversary. At least that's what he claims. Lately, he's been very absentminded. He thinks I'm being unreasonable though, that I should understand how slammed he is at work, how much pressure he's under. I need your input."

"Cooper was convinced you guys were on the brink of getting engaged," Eastlyn pointed out.

Drea let out a sad little sigh. "We were definitely on the brink of something. None of it good."

Everyone in the room seemed to have an opinion and didn't mind sharing it. They all began talking at once.

Jordan intervened to try and get the clamor under control. "It sounds like forgetfulness isn't the only issue at play here."

Bree did her best to defend her brother Zach. "Look, any guy who works as hard as Zach does gets distracted from time to time. It's a natural thing."

"Oh really," Kinsey charged. "So if Troy did that, you'd give him a pass?"

Bree backtracked. "Troy's always been a sweetheart while Zach is more…prickly about things."

Kinsey had known Troy a lot longer than Zach. "That's just it. I don't see Troy ever forgetting important dates like the day you two got together. The thing is Troy works alongside Zach at literally the same job. Everyone knows Zach's had his share of trouble around town. Nothing major but still…"

Across the room, Isabella took in Drea's demeanor. There was something about the pleading look in the woman's eyes that sent red flags soaring.

After going through an abusive and manipulative relationship of her own, Isabella couldn't stay quiet. "I, for one, think Drea should hang tough and stick to her guns. Especially if the breakup encompasses other problem areas, which I think it does. If you ever want to talk, call me."

"Thanks. I really needed a sympathetic ear. This isn't really about forgetfulness," Drea admitted.

Jordan exchanged looks with Isabella. "I didn't think so."

From that serious theme, the talk switched to ideas for the Memorial Day parade in town.

But Eastlyn's mind was someplace else. She began mentally making her own plans that had nothing to do with the holiday. She wasn't absolutely certain what she'd do with the chopper. All she knew was she'd never wanted anything more.

Cooper sat in the middle of his courtyard, smoking a cigar. It was one of the few vices he allowed himself, and then only one a day. There was something about sitting outside under the stars and drinking a beer in solitude that gave a man a sense of peace.

But when he heard a car pull up at the curb and he spotted Drea getting out, he knew the serene moment had all but ended. Just like Ripley opened the hatch of her spacecraft and sucked the alien out into the darkness of space, he could feel his joy headed to the same place.

Drea looked mad as a hornet as she stormed into the courtyard and dropped her bag onto the concrete before slipping into one of the chairs next to him. "You heard about me breaking up with Zach, right?"

Cooper sent his sister an amused look. "You sent everybody on your contact list a detailed email about it the morning after it happened. I'm sure it's just a spat. All couples have…"

Drea cut him off. "No, it isn't a spat. I'm done. I broke up with him for a reason."

He puffed out a sigh. "Because he forgot your anniversary. I know."

"Would you just listen for a minute? I broke it off, but now I have this problem with Zach wanting to get back together because he won't leave me alone. I need advice."

"Do you want to get back together?"

She shook her head. "No."

"Really? A year ago, you said you were sure this was *the* guy."

"So I did. I thought we'd get married, you know. But it's a lot different living with Zach than I thought it'd be."

"I thought he made you happy. I thought you two were about to plan a wedding."

"I don't think Zach's at a place where that's ever going to happen. Sometimes he does make me happy. But then there are the other times when he mostly drives me crazy with his surly attitude. All the late work hours don't help. We spend almost zero time together doing couple stuff other than watching TV. The last thing we truly did as a couple was sex two weeks ago, the first time in almost a month."

"If you're about to tell your older brother a comprehensive account of your sex life, I beg you, please don't."

"Come on, Coop, don't be like that. After asking for advice at the luncheon just now, I need my older brother to weigh in on what you think I should do."

"Is it really over?"

"I'm pretty sure it is."

"Then tell him you're done and that he needs to stop bugging you and move on. Breakups happen. Relationships come to an end." He saw the look in her eye and picked up on the reason for the visit. "You want me to tell him to knock it off? Is that why you're here?"

"Would you? He showed up at the loft last night and wouldn't leave. That's the second night in a row. I had this flashback to when we were kids and the arguments were so loud and…scary."

Cooper frowned. "Has he ever hit you?" When Drea turned her eyes away and wouldn't look at him he had his answer. "When? Why didn't you say something?"

"Last Christmas. We got into an argument and he slapped me. I thought it was my fault for egging him on."

He reached over and squeezed her hand. "You know better than that. I'll stop by his house in the morning and talk to him. The last thing you need is a relationship that resembles the one our parents had."

"Thanks, Cooper. I knew I could count on you."

Cooper was still sitting in the same chair, drinking his beer that had now turned warm, when Eastlyn drove up and parked in exactly the same spot where Drea's car had been earlier.

He took one look at Eastlyn and decided fancy afternoon teas took a lot out of women.

"You look like you've been through the wringer," he noted. "I thought this tea business was supposed to be a relaxing afternoon."

Eastlyn sent him a worried look. "Julianne wants me to speak at her school."

"Leave it to Julianne to come up with a great idea."

"What? No. It's not a good idea at all. I'm totally unprepared. This is too last minute."

He could see the worry lines already forming on her forehead, the muscles tightening along her neck. "For someone who spent their afternoon lunching with a roomful of women, you seem really tense."

"Cooper, I'm out of my element here. I'm a terrible speaker. And Julianne wants me to talk about my recovery, some motivational crap about overcoming adversity."

"What's wrong with that?"

"Okay, then you do it. Stand up in front of a roomful of kids and talk about how you feel about your childhood. Dredge up all those awful old memories. Relive all the times you felt like shit because you realized there was no way you would ever get your old life back again."

"I didn't want my old life back," he stated flatly. "My old life never worked as a kid. In fact, it pretty much sucked."

"There you go. So did mine after I lost my leg."

He stood up, came around the chair to rub the tension out of her shoulders. "You're overthinking this. Just get up on stage and tell them one significant fact about your life. Tell them something heartfelt. All Julianne expects is honesty."

Leaning down, he kissed the top of her hair before moving to her ear then her throat. "I know a sure-fire way to relax you."

He tugged a kiss out of her. Somehow that fusing of lips lit a passion. Restless longing ignited a fire inside.

Her mouth was impatient but so was his. He discovered one taste, one touch would never be enough.

When she drew away, he realized that if he didn't change the scenery right this minute and get out of there, he'd end up rushing her into the bedroom. He didn't want that.

On impulse, he snatched her hand and tugged her out of the courtyard to the sidewalk.

"Where are we going?"

"Somewhere there's a spectacular view and a new perspective."

Hand in hand, they strolled down Pacific Street until it dead-ended in front of the pier. Knowing this place had bad memories for him, Eastlyn focused on getting his mind on something else. "My brother and I used to catch fireflies this time of night. We'd go outside in the evening, sit in my dad's garden and wait for them to light up the backyard."

She laughed. "I remember times my dad would send me out there to pick tomatoes for supper and I'd end up sitting in the grass under the trees watching the fireflies. I'd take so long lollygagging that he'd start wondering where his tomatoes were."

"Do you know your voice changes whenever you talk about him?"

"It does?"

"It changes octaves to a much softer tone."

"That's because I have warm memories of him. After my mother died he became our world. Kaeden and I had no idea how much pressure he was under. As far back as I can remember he never even talked about dating anyone or getting remarried or moving past my mom. It never occurred to us back then what he must've given up to raise us."

"Maybe he just wasn't interested in dating. He'd already found the right woman and that was it for him." Cooper thought about Drea and Zach. "Who knows why some relationships work for life and others fail miserably before they get off the launching pad?"

"I'm pretty sure it has everything to do with the two people involved." She looked out over the water, contemplated full disclosure. "Maybe now would be a good time to tell you that I've started the process to take my medical flight exam. I contacted an aviation medical examiner."

"That's great. What does it entail?"

"The aviation medical examiner sends the results to the Aerospace Certification Division in OKC. Someone there will determine if I need a medical flight test. This is where it gets tricky. With my military flight experience I shouldn't have to take one. But if I do, they'll forward the information on to the FAA Flight Standards District Office here in the Central Valley. If they deem it necessary that's when I'll need to set up an appointment to take the test and get my SODA, or Statement of Demonstrated Ability. It's a shame I have to go through that all over again, but it's my own fault."

"What are your chances?"

"If you'd asked me that question a week ago, I'd have said not very good. Mainly because I'm battling the nasty fact that I got my license yanked for failing a drug test. But I've reached out to several other pilots with disabilities and they were surprisingly very encouraging. Besides, if it doesn't go my way this round, I'll just keep trying until I prove I've kicked the pills. I won't give up."

Cooper put his arms around her. "I'd be shocked if you did. Somehow I get the impression giving up isn't in your DNA."

"I love it when you do that."

"Do what?"

"When you make me feel a whole lot better about everything."

Fifteen

Cooper woke the next morning with one goal in mind. His brotherly duty was to hunt down Zach and have a talk with him, man-to-man. He wasn't sure what he'd do if it spiked up into more than a discussion. He'd never been one to turn to his fists to solve a problem. Yet, he knew going in that he needed to get through to the guy to leave his sister the hell alone.

But he was in for a surprise when he went out to get into his car and saw Caleb sitting in the courtyard, waiting for him.

"What are you doing out here? Why didn't you come in? You want some coffee?"

"No. I'm too upset. Right now I'm trying to keep from getting in my car and going over to Dennison's house and beating him to a pulp."

Ah, the difference in brothers, Cooper mused. "I'm on my way there now. Has something happened I should know about first?"

"You're not going without me. Drea didn't tell you?"

"Tell me what? She was here last night."

"That bastard sat outside her door again causing a scene for hours and refused to leave."

"Did she call Brent?"

"I asked her that very thing and her response was so typical. She didn't want to get Zach in trouble with the cops. And she didn't want to call either one of us because she knew what we'd do to him."

"That's nuts. What's wrong with this guy anyway? I don't really know him all that well. Do you?"

"He's had some anger issues before but I can't figure the guy out. When a person breaks off a relationship and you refuse to take the message, it borders on stalking."

"We're on the same page there. Let me handle it, okay? If we both show up it won't be one-on-one anymore but two against one."

"Who cares about having him outnumbered? Not me. I'm going with you and that's final. I want to beat him into the next county."

"Nice, Caleb, real grownup. Is he still at Drea's?"

"No, he left to go get ready for work and that's when she called me. She said she called you first but there was no answer. At least she thinks Zach went home. Who the hell knows?"

"I must've been in the shower when she called. We'll start at his house. If he's not there then we'll work our way to the boatyard."

But when they pulled up in front of the house where Zach had grown up, his truck was still parked in the driveway. After they had knocked on the door for almost five minutes, Zach finally appeared wearing a bathrobe. He looked disheveled and confused. His eyes seemed glassy from staying up all night.

To Cooper, it looked as though the man had gone off the deep end some time ago and they were about six months too late.

Instead of the confrontational speech Cooper had been prepared to deliver, he took one look at Zach and decided another strategy might be the way to go. "Is there something you're keeping from Drea, some medical reason you're behaving the way you are?"

"What? No. Why? No. I don't think so. Drea just doesn't understand that I'm under a lot of pressure at work."

Cooper went into his condensed pitch. "If there isn't some medical reason, then why not let her move past the time you two had together. It's not working for her anymore. Things like this happen sometimes. Two people come together. It works for a while, but then one person wants to go another way. You have to let Drea go another way and let her move on."

"I don't want her to move on. I love her. We talked about getting married. That's why I spent the night sitting on the stairs. I want her back."

Coop shook his head. "But most people would leave when they're asked to leave. Don't you see how crazy it is that you wouldn't go away? It's almost like you're stalking her. She's made it clear she doesn't want things to remain the same between you two. Change is hard for some people. But breakups happen all the time. You have to move on, Zach."

It was Caleb's turn to emphasize that. "You're scaring her the way you've been behaving."

"Drea's afraid of me?"

Cooper struggled to maintain his composure. "Why wouldn't she be? You beat down her door the other night then you refused to leave last night. If it happens again, I'm instructing her to call Brent. Is that what you want?"

"I thought I could talk to her, talk her into coming back."

Losing patience with him, Caleb's voice rose. "It's over, Zach, as in done. Leave her alone. We've all experienced relationships that went south. This is no different."

"Do you want us to call Bree? Do you need to talk to your sister about this?" Cooper offered.

Zach bristled. "Everyone in town knows Drea dumped me."

Cooper began to suspect this dialogue would get them nowhere. Were they dealing with something other than ego here? "So she dumped you? Everyone's been in your shoes a time or two. It's no big deal. But the way you've been behaving lately there are people worried about you. When was the last time you had a physical?"

"I don't know. Five years maybe."

"How long have you been having anger issues?"

Caleb's patience evaporated. He turned to stare at his brother. "Who cares? Our job is to get him to stay away from Drea."

Cooper sent Caleb a lethal stare. "Zach, will you stop bothering Drea?"

"Hey, if she doesn't want to be with me, that's fine. Tell her I got the message." With that, Zach slammed the door shut.

"What the hell was that about?" Caleb complained when they started for the car. "Get him to see a doctor? What were you thinking?"

"That man is suffering from major depression. I have no idea for how long but he's exhibiting all the signs."

"That's not our problem."

"Sure it is. I don't want him around Drea any more than you do. But neither do I want another domestic issue leading to a violent end on my hands because of mental issues. If Zach's spiraling downward, and all the signs say he is, I'm getting him some help."

As soon as they'd settled inside the Mustang, Cooper began the quest to find Bree's contact info. The perks of a small town didn't take too many tries before he landed the right person. Jordan not only had the number he needed, the innkeeper said Bree was there at Promise Cove about to take out a boatload of tourists on a sightseeing trip. Jordan simply handed the phone to Bree.

"This is Cooper Richmond. I need to talk to you about your brother Zach."

Cooper had agreed to wait around until Bree got there, which irritated Caleb.

"I don't see why we had to sit here and babysit the guy. I don't know why we had to get involved like this. It wasn't part of the equation," Caleb groused.

Cooper snapped back. "I didn't drag you over here. In fact, I suggested that you not to come. But since you insisted, you're stuck unless you want to walk to work, which you could just as easily do as sit here and bitch. So shut up."

It took thirty minutes sitting in stony silence before Bree showed up. She'd brought reinforcements—Troy and Zach's other business partner, Ryder McLachlan.

Bree stood outside the car wringing her hands. "Thanks, Cooper for calling me. I'm sorry it took so long but I had to round up the troops and rearrange the tour schedule for this afternoon. Do you really think Zach's having a mental breakdown?"

"I don't know. If I'm wrong, what's the worst that could happen? He gets an office visit with Doc Prescott and a complete checkup. But if I'm right…"

Ryder spoke up. "For what it's worth, I think Cooper's on to something. Over the past several months there've been signs that Zach might be coming unglued. Troy and I have seen him freaking out at work more than usual."

Troy nodded in agreement. "Zach's always been a stickler for things clicking, but when they don't, he's been losing it over the least little thing."

Ryder went on, "Then when Drea blew up at him about forgetting their anniversary, it just him over the edge when she packed up."

Troy boosted that incident with another example. "There was that week before Christmas last year when we had this big job to finish. Zach couldn't concentrate. He kept messing up with the router, the sander. He's usually a perfectionist with his work, takes pride in a job well done, but not lately."

Bree had heard enough. "Okay, okay, I'll give Doc a call. Hopefully, he can work us in today." She turned to Troy. "I don't think I should leave him alone. Just yesterday I tried defending him at the luncheon because I love him so much. There have been times in the last two years I don't want to concede that my only brother has his faults."

When Bree and Troy disappeared inside the house, Cooper said to Ryder, "They may not be faults. It's possible Zach might be experiencing undiagnosed clinical depression. It usually takes years to get to this point to completely unravel."

"There's medication for that, right?" Ryder asked. "I mean he isn't so far gone that he's about to go postal or climb up on a tower, right?"

"There are meds. It takes time to fiddle with the right dosage before it kicks in and it won't happen overnight. Plus, he has to take the stuff for it to work."

Ryder nodded. "Then I'll stick around, too. Bree and Troy may need help talking him into seeing Doc."

Once Cooper started the Mustang and got underway, Caleb turned to eye his brother. "I'm sorry I said those things to you. Obviously, you've seen mental illness firsthand. At least your recollections are better than mine are. Which means you know more about it than I do."

"Be glad. I wouldn't wish those memories on anyone."

With days yet to go to the school assembly, Eastlyn's jobs kept her busy. But her mind kept circling back to the helicopter. She'd decided there were many things she could with it. She could start a charter service as Cooper had suggested, or she could start her own private search and rescue outfit. There was a third option. She could offer life flight services, including medical runs, up and down the California coast.

The prospects were actually endless.

At the end of her workday one afternoon, she stopped by the Pump N Go to meet Wally Pierce. When she entered the garage he owned, she spotted the mechanic—a guy with brown hair down to his shoulders standing under a shiny red SS Chevelle changing the oil.

Now that she got a better look at Wally's surfer looks, Lilly's story about his topic at school made a lot more sense.

The love of a classic muscle car had Eastlyn appreciating the machine. Letting out a loud whistle, she stepped under the car, peered at the engine. "Whoever owns this baby is one lucky dude."

"It's mine. Refurbished it from scratch," Wally said proudly.

"Looks like it has the small engine block three-fifty."

Impressed with her knowledge, Wally abandoned his task, more than willing to discuss his pride and joy. "Only kind you could buy in California from '68 through '71 because of the state's standards back then."

"Any heat soak problems?"

Wally eyed her with fascination. "Used to. But that was before I installed a new starter with a heat shield buffering the exhaust. You know your cars."

"And engines. I had a father who tinkered with his El Camino and an older brother who loved muscle cars. Both let me hang around the driveway enough to pick up a few things whenever they labored over a '69 Dodge Charger."

"My dad and I looked at the six-cylinder Charger. But it was our second choice." Wally stuffed a rag into his back pocket and turned to face her. "Lilly mentioned you had your eye on an old chopper Cooper found out at Cleef's place."

"Your wife sings your praises. But the truth is everyone around here does the same. They say you know more about engines than anybody else. And that's why I need your input before I put my hard-earned cash into what could be a money pit."

"You know, I've spent hours out there at that old junkyard going through the stuff and I don't ever remember seeing that chopper in the barn."

"Probably because it was buried under a mound of hay and dirt. I gotta tell you the same thing I told Cooper. I think that chopper was hidden for a reason."

Wally lifted a brow in surprise. "Stolen? That doesn't sound like Cleef."

She winced at the word. "I'm not saying that or accusing anyone. But I had to dig the thing out of at least three feet of muck just to get a better look at the skids. It was as if someone had buried it to keep it out of sight. Anyway, could you take a trip out there with me sometime, at your convenience, of course, and tell me what you think?"

"I'd be glad to. When do you want to go?"

"You pick."

"How about now?"

"What about finishing your oil change?"

"I can do that anytime. Let's go see this mysterious bird."

They made one stop at Layne's Trains before getting on the road.

Cooper had already made plans for his evening. In fact, he'd spent the better part of the day looking forward to nothing more than getting home, making himself a quick sandwich to eat in front of the tube, grabbing an ice cold beer, and watching the Giants take on the Mets back east. Because of the three-hour time difference, the game was due to start in less than an hour.

So when Eastlyn came into his shop, he knew right away by that brooding look she had an ulterior motive.

"Come on, Cooper. It's almost closing time anyway. Ride out to Cleef's with us. It won't take that long. I'll have you back home in time to catch the last five innings. I promise. I need both of you there to make sure I'm not making a huge mistake. What if I sink all my money into it and…?"

He wanted to stand steadfast and firm and stick to his plans. But the way her eyes lit up at the prospect and the pleading look on her face… It wasn't like Eastlyn to wheedle. And when she gave him that last parting shot about the money, he decided to cave.

Cooper sighed. "I'll do it, but not because of that pouty, dejected look on your face. I've been stuck in here all day and need to get outside. I wouldn't mind getting some sun. But you're driving."

She gave him a quick hug and a kiss, pumped her fist in the air and sailed out the door in front of him.

As he turned the sign around and flipped the lock, it occurred to him that some women could talk a body into spending an afternoon doing anything and everything other than what he'd intended to do.

Behind the wheel, Eastlyn took the men through the string of ideas she'd earmarked as the best options for the chopper.

Cooper was impressed. "The charter service takes a backseat to the life flight option. This area could use that kind of deal. The nearest major hospital is fifty plus miles from here. Getting a patient with a major injury to treatment quicker than by ambulance would be a huge bonus for the town."

Eastlyn chewed her lip and pointed out, "The only drawback with that idea is the H-13 is so small on the inside. It isn't equipped with a way to transport the injured other than the litters attached to the skids."

Sitting in the backseat, Wally had his own thoughts. "As a parent, either the life flight idea or the search and rescue would be the way to go. I know Lilly and I worry a lot that if the kids ever need emergency medical care other than what Doc offers at the clinic, we're looking at a long trip to Santa Cruz."

Once they reached the barn, Eastlyn ushered them to where she'd dug the trench around the base.

"It was buried in layers. The only way to get a better look at the condition of the bottom was to burrow down until I'd seen all of it. The skids were stuck in so much dirt it made me wonder if they'd rusted out. But as you can see, the metal isn't even damaged all that much, certainly not like all the rest that was exposed to the elements. And look at this, there's not a single crack in the bubble canopy, not one."

Cooper gave her a little smile. "Sounds to me like you've already figured things out for yourself without any help from us."

Wally bobbed his head in agreement. "It's good you've determined for yourself what kind of shape it's in. Otherwise, when you're deep into the work, you'd be kicking yourself at finding an unexpected surprise waiting for you. Did you try to crank her up, see if she'll start?"

She grinned back. "I did, but no luck. The thing is, if I go for it, I need to figure out which to work on first, the ugly exterior or the engine."

"Definitely focus on mechanical. Every time," Wally urged. "The cosmetic stuff will come later. Right now you need to concentrate on getting the engine in prime condition to fly. I can help you with that."

She leaned back on the dusty chopper and looked at both men. "Okay then, I'll talk to Nick and get the paperwork started for the purchase. Because I can't wait to see this bird in the air."

She made time to meet with Nick the next morning at the bank and got a surprise. The man sat behind his desk and seemed downright elated that she'd already taken steps to getting her license back.

"Are we talking six weeks?"

"More like six months. After all, we're talking about the FAA. But I'm not complaining. Six months will give me time to work on the chopper."

"Do you have any idea how long it'll take to get it up and running?"

"If you're talking airborne ready, Wally thought it could be done in ninety days. That's if I could dedicate eight hours a day to it, which I can't. I have other responsibilities, other jobs. Nights and weekends are the only time I could spare. Then there's the time it will take to rewire the instrument panel in the cockpit. The bright spot is that Wally's already agreed to help me find an engine. As soon as he locates one, we'll go pick it up or have it shipped here, depending on where it is."

Nick leaned back in his chair. "What if I could get you some help? Logan Donnelly works with metal all the time. He could offer his expertise on finishing the outside."

"Why would a sculptor want to work on an old aircraft out in a dusty barn?"

"Are you kidding? Logan loves that kind of stuff. Besides, it's what we do around here."

"But why? Why would he want to help me?"

"You still don't get it, do you? We all want you to get your license back and be able to fly this thing. You do that, and you'll not only help yourself but the town as well."

"As long as you know I want to be the one who flies it, I have no problem sharing the load though. Since you're giving me such a good deal on it, I'd be crazy to complain."

"We'll help you finance the engine if it comes to that."

"Some days I wake up and think about that scene in *Field of Dreams*. You know the one, where Shoeless Joe asks Ray Kinsella, 'Is this heaven?' Are you sure I'm not in heaven?"

"No, it's Pelican Pointe," Nick said with a grin. "And Iowa is about two thousand miles in the opposite direction."

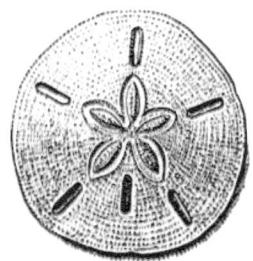

Sixteen

Eastlyn sat on her front porch and listened as the Memorial Day parade got underway. The marching band started with a blast of *You're a Grand Ol' Flag*. At least she assumed the song signaled the start of the festivities by the roar of cheers that reverberated all the way to her little bungalow.

Despite the holiday she wasn't in the same frame of mind as everyone else. It wasn't like her to mope around the house in a sulky mood and then wonder why she felt this way.

She had the day off. She'd slept late. Later tonight she had a date with Cooper. But in the face of all that, she wasn't in a celebratory mood. She didn't think a line of cars driving down the street disguised as corny floats, rolling past a bunch of flag-wavers, would do much to lift her spirits.

"They mean well," Scott said from the end of the stoop. "Parades are a big deal around here—for the kids."

By this time, Eastlyn had grown accustomed to Scott's habit of popping in at intrusive times. "I know they do. But I'm no kid. I don't feel much like partying, not the way they do. I don't really understand why."

"You need cheering up. But today you're thinking about Corporal Alan Silvestre, one of your early medics who one day hopped out of the chopper like normal to render aid to a wounded soldier and took a barrage of enemy fire to the chest."

She narrowed her gaze on him. "So what if I am? Alan was twenty-one years old with the rest of his life ahead of him, nicest guy you'd ever want to meet. He left a pregnant wife behind in Brooklyn, two parents who loved him, a couple of younger brothers and a slew of cousins. I watched Silvestre die right in front of me. The damage to his chest was… We couldn't save him."

She hung her head, rubbed her eyes. "All those months we brought wounded onboard, some of them bleeding out, you don't forget the iron smell of blood. It stays with you long after you wash the chopper down for the day. Sometimes the bird reeked of the stuff."

She glanced up to look into Scott's face. "I'm sorry. I didn't mean to snap at you. It's just that… I told you upfront I didn't feel particularly festive today."

"You ordered members of your crew to get out and pull Silvestre back into the chopper in the middle of a hot zone. You did everything you could to save him."

"And failed. It isn't just Silvestre. There were others along the way."

"Yeah, I know."

Scott understood all too well the guilt she felt. "There isn't a soldier alive who went through combat who doesn't remember guys like Silvestre, who had potential, everything to live for, but it was all snatched away in one moment of war."

"You were one of those who had everything waiting back here at home. I think I get it now. Cooper's right. You've passed on but you came back because you don't want to leave this place."

"If you give this town a chance, you'll like it here. One day you'll wake up and won't want to live anywhere else."

As she sat there pondering that, teens Sonnet and Sonoma Rafferty skated by on their rollerblades.

"That looks like fun," Scott offered.

"Is that your subtle way of telling me I should get up off my butt and stop feeling sorry for myself?"

"You know the answer to that."

"You're a man of many riddles, Scott Phillips. But you're not as clever as you think."

"Why's that?"

"Because you're about as subtle as a brick through a window."

Several blocks away, Cooper wasn't having any better day off than Eastlyn.

Because the store was closed today, he'd slept late. Then he'd stumbled into the kitchen at nine o'clock and found his illustrious coffeemaker—the pricey one still under warranty—had quit working. Instead of grabbing his keys and heading for the diner like any sane man would've done, he settled for a jar of instant he discovered in the back of his pantry.

While trying to get the foul-tasting stuff past his throat, he'd had the brilliant idea to go ahead and shave. Half awake, he'd cut himself, not the little nick that comes with wielding a razor but a nasty angled cut along his chin that refused to stop bleeding.

So when the phone on the nightstand rang at ten-twenty he wasn't cheery, not even nice.

"What?" he barked.

That's when the recorded message kicked in saying that an inmate, named Eleanor Jennings Richmond, from the California Correctional Facility in Chowchilla, requested that he accept her collect call.

It took him several seconds of realization before he felt like he'd been hit with a stun gun. He held the phone to his ear until the message ended and then he promptly slammed it back on the hook without accepting the charge.

After all, if Eleanor Richmond was that pigheaded to keep calling, then he could damn well be just as obstinate in refusing to take her calls.

What he couldn't figure out was why she bothered with him now. God knows, she hadn't done it when he was a kid.

By afternoon, Eastlyn had forced herself to shake off the sullen attitude and get ready for her date.

But something else nagged at her.

Cooper's comment about her wearing a dress had weighed on her for more than a week. And she still had the problem of what to wear at the school assembly. Appearing on stage wearing a stuffy suit didn't appeal to her. Maybe it was time to think about sprucing up her appearance. Everywhere she went in town every other adult female seemed to already be wearing something summery.

She decided that tonight, she'd girl it up. It was time to stop hiding her leg behind ugly denim and outdated pantsuits. Today was the day she unveiled a new confidence, one left over from her military days.

But going through her closet and the limited selections it held ended in utter disappointment. Chewing her lip, she knew Reclaimed Treasures sold cute clothes but was closed up tight for the holiday. Thinking back to the luncheon at Promise Cove she decided to call in a favor.

She dug out a business card, picked up her cell phone and keyed in the number.

A half hour later, Julianne met her in front of Reclaimed Treasures. The shop held an assortment of used furniture that Julianne and her manager, Greg Prather, had repurposed from other old wood and refurbished antiques. There were rows and rows of handy household items. But one section stood out in Eastlyn's memory. She remembered from her very first visit a corner with a mix of trendy eclectic clothes and vintage pieces.

"I'm sorry to bother you today. I know you were probably gearing up for a relaxing day…"

"I told you over the phone not to worry about that. One favor deserves another. You promised to make an appearance at the assembly and I'm helping you keep it."

"I'm so nervous."

"Come Friday, don't let it show. Besides, I know a little something about wardrobe emergencies. As principal, I live for crisis situations like having a change of clothes on hand for accidents. I'm usually ready for anything. I'm so pleased that you called me. I love being a part of helping you prepare for your big day."

"Which one? Tonight or Friday?"

"Both."

"You're a lifesaver for opening up like this. I should've taken care of my wardrobe issues a long time ago."

Diplomatically, Julianne patted her arm. "You're here now and that's what matters. I've been hailed a time or two for coming through in the 'lifesaver' department with six-year-olds so I'm happy you feel that way today."

"You saw the pantsuit I wore at the luncheon. I'd planned to repeat that look at the school rally. So you know how critical it is I do something about my apparel. Plus, it occurred to me I need an attitude adjustment when it comes to how I look. I used to dress better than this. For once, I'd like to put on something fashionable that promises to wow Cooper. Is that even possible?"

"Of course it is. With your figure, your height, you'll look sensational."

Julianne watched as Eastlyn made a beeline straight for the corner where the clothes were hanging as if she'd already made up her mind and knew exactly what she was looking for. Sure enough she picked out several items in record time—a summery pastel sundress with a surplice neckline, a silky, flowing skirt, a couple of tops, and a lightweight jersey cardigan.

She pulled out a few others and held them up for Julianne's appraisal. "On second thought, this transformation isn't just for Cooper, but for me."

"Glad to hear it. Want to try those on?"

"It's been so long since I've worn a dress I probably should. But I know you're in a hurry to get back home."

"Nonsense. When I left, Ryder was watching the Indy 500. You take your time. The dressing room is back here. Follow me."

Julianne ushered Eastlyn into a little room in the back and said, "If you need help, I'll be out here waiting for you to make your grand entrance."

"It might take a while to undress. I usually have to allow an extra twenty minutes every morning," Eastlyn explained as she disappeared into the dressing room.

Julianne was left to consider all the adjustments Eastlyn must have to face every day in order to deal with her disability. Her respect for the woman grew twofold.

Several minutes went by before Eastlyn reappeared in the hallway to stand in front of the mirror.

Julianne stood back and gaped. "Oh my God, that color is you. You knew exactly what would work for you."

"You think so?"

"I know so. With your hair and skin tone it's fabulous. Trust me, Cooper will think so, too. What about shoes?"

Eastlyn chewed her lip. "I think I'll stick with flats for now, even though I have this adjustable foot at home that's supposed to let me set the heel height. I think it's still in the carton. I haven't had a reason to use it yet."

"Uh, now might be an excellent time to drag it out of the box. Do you need to practice walking with it?"

"Probably. I'll have to work with adjusting the heel height. Heel height is important. Otherwise it throws my whole balance off. If I remember the sales pitch it's supposed to be a matter of pushing a button."

"Let's hope it's that easy. You amaze me," Julianne admitted.

Eastlyn smiled. "Why? Because I had to relearn to walk using an inflatable, weight-bearing walking aid?" She snickered at the memory. "You should've seen me stumble and fall the first couple times like a fifteen-month-old toddler. It's humiliating. But you learn to deal. Thank goodness prosthetics have come a long way since the days of wooden legs. They now have this robotic ankle that makes it possible to move from side to side. I'm hoping the FAA sees the possibilities of it and keeps an open mind."

Eastlyn turned to go back into the dressing room and stopped, reconsidered the pair of sandals. "You know what? On second thought, I think I'll give the wedges a try. I can use the rest of the afternoon to practice the adjustable foot thing. I might be able to pull it off. If not, I can always order the right one from my supplier back in Bakersfield."

Eastlyn picked up a bottle of perfume, spritzed the fumes into the air and sniffed. "Oh, I like this. Add this to my bill."

"You buy the clothes and the shoes, and it's yours, on the house."

"Thanks. I'm beginning to really like this place more and more."

Loaded down with bags, Eastlyn left Reclaimed Treasures over four hundred dollars lighter in the pocketbook. But she felt elated at the prospect of getting back her former self—that part she'd tried to bury. The woman inside finally wanted out. She hoped her old self was still there somewhere because she was determined to bring her into the light again for all to see, prosthetic and all. The afternoon's shopping trip was a good launching pad for it.

As soon as she got home, she dug out the adjustable foot from the bottom of her closet. The Runway® design used a slider mechanism with different notches. She tested several settings before finding the right one and making sure the flex was there in both front and back. She even walked up and down the driveway a dozen times or so to make sure the sandals worked.

Turns out, from now on, wearing heels would be a piece of cake.

Why had she waited so long to try it out? That one was easy, she thought. Before Cooper, there had been no one she'd truly wanted to impress.

With one problem solved, she fussed with her hair, settled on a wild tangle of waves and curls. She put the finishing touches on her outfit and turned in front of the mirror. Pleased with the image she saw staring back at her, she hoped the titanium rod—clearly visible with the length of the dress—didn't repulse him.

Eager for Cooper to arrive, she had this insane notion to go wait for him on the porch. But she tamped down that idea and realized that might send the wrong signal.

As soon as Cooper knocked on the door she flung it open before he'd had time to adjust the expression on his face.

One look at Eastlyn decked out in a pale orchid sundress with the plunging neckline, and a clingy little cardigan that accentuated her breasts, and Cooper took a step back to get a better look.

"Wow, you take my breath away."

"I do?"

It suddenly hit him that this was a side to her she'd kept purposely hidden.

She wore strappy wedges that made her even taller. But then, he loved her height. To complete the girly look, a lavender quartz necklace dangled from her throat.

He let out a loud whistle. "I knew it. Just as I suspected you've been covering up a pair of sexy stems under all that denim."

How did he always manage to make her feel like a schoolgirl. "Who knew you'd be a fan of titanium," she pointed out.

He whistled through his teeth again. "Not that there's anything wrong with jeans, but man, do you make a sexy picture, or what?"

"It was your reaction to the 'or what' that I was afraid of. I'm sure the prosthetic is a real turn-on."

"Would you stop that? Take a look in the mirror." He spun her around to stand in front of her reflection. He ran a hand across her silky throat, fingered the necklace. "We should all be as fortunate in the looks department. You're blessed with flawless skin. You have beautiful eyes. You're a natural blonde without having to bleach your hair dry. You've got a quick wit. You're so gorgeous every man will want to dance with you tonight."

"Dance? You didn't say anything about dancing."

"Didn't I? Huh. I guess I left that part out."

She elbowed him in the ribs as they sailed out the door. "Listen pal, I don't think I can two-step in these wedges. I just learned to walk in them about two seconds ago. I'll probably have enough trouble trekking down to the bay as it is."

"Somehow I feel we're wading in bullshit here," he teased. "I didn't think you'd go for the sympathy angle this quick. As long as I can stand still on the dance floor with my arms wrapped around you, I'll die a happy man."

She tilted her head, reached over and took his chin. "You get a ten for a perfect comeback."

"I always did do well on tests," he proclaimed.

She inhaled his aftershave, eyed his pressed shirt and jeans. She took hold of his chin. "Maybe I should be the one ogling you. You make my mouth water."

"Let's just stay in. Who needs a dance floor when we can burn up the sheets here?"

She dragged him along the driveway. "Oh no you don't. I paid a week's pay for this outfit and I want someone to see it."

"I'm someone."

"Clarification. Bunches of someones."

"Showoff. I've created a monster," Cooper complained as they made their way to the wharf.

They heard the band already on stage building up to a crescendo of bull fiddle and guitar.

To handle the crowds, the town council had decided to close off traffic on Ocean Street, which made for more room and made the place look like a rock fest. As they got closer they could see the throng of people gathering at the food booths, the lines snaking around for half a block.

She tugged him along behind her and followed the smell of funnel cake. "Feed me. I haven't eaten since my bowl of Raisin Bran at breakfast. I'm so hungry I could eat a small horse. You'll have to get your own, though."

"Who knew you'd be so greedy at splitting a side of meat?" Cooper quipped as he studied the menu. "I'm ordering a cheeseburger."

"Make it two and a basket of fries."

They found a table and dug into their meal while the Raffertys—Sonnet and Sonoma and their father, Malachi—took the stage carrying violins. The trio entertained with Bach and Mozart until they switched gears and wound into a wild rendition of *Honky Tonk Man*.

Eastlyn spotted Drea. "Cooper, there's your sister over there sitting by herself. She looks so down. Why don't you ask *her* to dance?"

He dipped one of his French fries into a glob of ketchup. "Let's see, I haven't danced with my sister since I was twelve. Landon and Shelby insisted that we take lessons. At six, Caleb was too young, so the lucky little so-and-so got out of it."

Eastlyn put down her burger long enough to sip from her soda, used the cup to make a point. "But you didn't. I find you more and more fascinating with each layer I peel back. Cooper Richmond, a true Renaissance man, and a connoisseur of books, a world traveler, a photographer, and all-around train nerd. Now I discover you can dance."

"What can I say? I'm a faceted man of many talents. Anyway, you know that vacant house next to the bookstore? It used to be a dance studio. A lady by the name of Dora Lee Spangler opened it up in 1975. By the time I knew her, Dora Lee was already in her sixties. But they say, in her heyday Dora Lee used to dance with the Rockettes. She even appeared in several of those old black and white films in Hollywood."

"Whatever happened to her?"

"What usually happens to loners and gypsies? Dora Lee died alone, had no family, no heirs. With no one to pick up where Dora Lee left off, the studio shut its doors and everyone in town went on without a dance instructor."

"That's sad. And one more reason you should go ask Drea to join us."

Cooper looked around for his sister. "There, see, Drea's fine. She's already dancing with Tucker Ferguson." His mouth formed into a little scowl. "That's moving on past Zach pretty fast. I hope she knows what she's doing."

"Why is it that people are so negative when they talk about Tucker?"

"Maybe because his father lived here for decades and was a genuine asshole."

There was a break in performers as the group Ninth Dog took to the stage. All the young people in the crowd went wild. This was far from classical or country. Ninth Dog offered up bold guitar riffs, killer drums and crazy keyboard sounds. These musicians relied on a synthesizer that hit somewhere between punk and acid.

Eastlyn turned her attention back to Cooper. "I thought you wanted to dance?"

"Not to this. I'm waiting for something slow and soulful."

They endured the synthesizer until the pharmacist, Ross Campbell, stepped up on stage and sat down at the piano. Ross's brown face showed concentration as his lean fingers sailed over the ivory and black keys. Showing off a knack for the sweet sound of rhythm and blues, his varied song list ran the gamut from Bill Withers to Stevie

Wonder, sending the adults of a certain age on a journey back through the '70s.

"Who knew?" Cooper whispered as he leaned in, swaying to the beat in his chair. "Ross never said a word about his talent when I bought a box of condoms from him at the drug store."

Eastlyn's hand muffled a laugh. "You didn't?"

"Last week. What's so funny?"

"I bought a box, too. Yesterday."

"I'm sensing a united front here," Cooper said, his voice full of hope at the prospect.

They sat under a canopy of Japanese lanterns strung from one end of the pier to the other. The lights rocked in the breeze, overhead, illuminating their way to the dance floor. In invitation, he held out his hand. "It's time you danced with me."

If there were stares from the curious gawkers as the two took to the dance floor, Eastlyn paid no mind. Once his arms circled her waist, she was lost in the rhythm of their bodies, their gypsy souls swaying to saxophone and keyboard.

His arms went around her as they moved to Ross's soul rendering voice. Cooper decided her hair smelled like silk and summer, a mix of burnished sea and sweet-smelling lavender.

They weren't even aware when Ross left the stage. Nor did they notice that the music had changed to more patriotic flare at the first pop of fireworks over the water. As the fireballs rocketed up in clusters of red, white, and blue, they kept moving to their own beat. While the flashes lit up the deep purple night sky and spread out in a dazzling display above them, they were lost in each other. As the colorful bursts fizzled out and trailed down in glittery brocade, their minds drifted to another kind of celebration.

Eastlyn lifted her head skyward, took in the roof full of stars above them. After everything that had transpired over the course of the last two months, she figured she was due. No more putting off Cooper.

"Your place or mine?" she asked as he nibbled her neck.

"Your house is closer, but I've got a bigger bed," he said, pulling her down the pier and along the boardwalk.

"Is that a euphemism?"

"You'll find out soon enough."

They crossed the street. High on the moment, Eastlyn teased, "We should take the car."

"That'd be a little difficult to do since we hotfooted it here."

She looked out at the line of parked cars slotted in tight spaces at the curb. A laugh escaped. "Let's just borrow one of these. People in town are so friendly. I'm sure they won't mind."

Coop chuckled. "No way do I want Brent showing up in the morning putting a damper on the mood after a perfectly good night of sweaty sex."

Her heart thudded at the idea. "You're pretty sure of yourself."

"Right now, you wouldn't have it any other way."

The rest of the walk home was a blur until they reached Cooper's courtyard. They stumbled their way into the atrium in a whirl of growing lust. That need to mate unleashed an impatient wave to get each other naked. They stumbled into the umbrella tree almost snapping off one of the delicate branches.

Hot tastes and flurried kisses had her yanking him by the shirt for a lot more.

They bounced along the wall into the living room.

"I have to get you out of this dress before I rip it to shreds."

She spun to give him access. He gladly slid the zipper down. The dress puddled to the floor around her feet.

In the dark, his eyes flicked sharp and hot. "You're not wearing a bra."

"I didn't see the need since I'm the A cup variety."

He whirled her around to judge for himself. All that was left was a thin strip of pink scalloped lace, slung low, hugging her hips. He ran one finger around the trim, moved up, filled his hands with those perfect breasts. "Every part of you I uncover is so damned beautiful."

Before she could worry about him seeing her stump, he grabbed her hips, hoisted her up. She threw her legs around his waist. Impatience had him taking off down the hall, carrying her to his bed.

From the moment she'd relinquished control to him, Coop wanted to show her all the magic he possessed, all the finesse he could gather. He was by no means a ladies' man or an accomplished lover. But with Eastlyn, he was determined to take his time no matter what.

One toss on the mattress and her wedge sandal thudded to the floor. He bent down, tried to get the other one out of the foot thing. "How do I get you out of this?"

"Are you sure you're ready?"

He looked down at himself, picked up her hand, ran it across the front of his jeans. "Does that answer your question?"

"I believe it does. I'll leave my liner on...for now anyway." She reached down, pressed the pin release causing the prosthetic to drop to the floor with a clunk.

He shoved her back on the bed, roamed his hands over her breasts. "You let me know if I do anything that hurts."

His touch made her feel alive, like he'd found her in the desert, thirsting for water. "So far you're doing just fine," she said as she arched her back, offered herself up.

Taking the hint, he ran the tip of his tongue along each pebbled nipple, licked the perfume off one bare shoulder, used his teeth to graze, and sampled skin from throat to belly.

She tried to get his shirt unbuttoned but her hands were far from steady. She gave up when his head moved between her legs. Her pulse skidded. Her blood pumped like fire.

On the race to that higher peak, she willed him not to stop. Frenzy followed the line of pleasure as it burst like a thundercloud, bringing with it the lightning that rolled through her.

Rising up, she reached for him, undoing buttons so she could get down to skin.

He tried to shuck out of his jeans as she nipped at his throat, scraped her nails down his chest. When she decided he was taking too long, she urged him on. "Hurry."

His body rocked above hers until she bucked up and rolled, reversing their positions. She felt him grip her hips. That one touch had her picking up the pace. She felt him tighten around her so she rode him, fast and hard.

Lightning did strike twice. It lit up the sky in purple and silver before thinning out to a slow, satisfied peak sending them crashing back down to earth.

Out of breath, damp and sweaty, she floated over him and then slid down, dropped onto his chest.

He flicked a finger over a pebbled nipple. "I…that was…I think we broke something."

"I hope it wasn't something important that we'll need for later."

His laugh bellowed out as he wondered how to persuade her to spend the night. But in the end, he didn't have to coax her at all. She cozied up, dropped her head to rest on his shoulder.

Cooper ran a hand over her thigh, did a slow perusal of her body. That's when he noticed the ink on her right shoulder—a hawk with wings fully spread in flight positioned over a full, glowing, fiery sun.

"You're a wonder, Eastlyn Parker. I've never met anyone quite like you before and I've traveled all over the world once or twice."

"If I get my license back I'd like to take you flying sometime."

"It felt like you just did."

"I did, didn't I?"

"Any higher and we'd have both flown off the bed."

Her laugh, generous and warm, rolled out in waves. "Oh, I like the idea of that. I see us flying over Pelican Pointe, a bed sailing through the air. There's a news crew standing on the ground waiting to capture the moment when we land, a mix of *Mary Poppins* and *Sex and the City*."

"You've got a warped streak in you."

"I thought you'd never notice." She ran a hand past his stomach and felt him come to life.

"Oh, I noticed."

"Okay. Then let's see just how warped we can get."

They made love again with all the zest and zeal of new lovers. Later, they drifted into lazy slumber as the soft night breeze from the ocean flowed in through the open windows, lulling them into eventual exhaustion.

Seventeen

The week building up to the end-of-school event was a nerve-racking one for Eastlyn.

There were nights Cooper did his best to alleviate her fears. But his soothing words often fell on deaf ears. She was like a prickly pear—try to pluck off the fruit and you risked getting poked by the needles causing a sting that lasted for hours.

One night they were watching a baseball game together on TV, a pastime they both enjoyed. Suddenly Eastlyn picked up the remote, flicked off the screen and declared, "God, how do you stand being around me? I'm making you crazy. I'm making myself crazy. The only thing to do is to go to Julianne, make her listen to reason, and get her to take me off the list. Surely there's someone in town—Nick or Cord maybe—who could offer more in the way of motivation than I would."

While Cooper felt a measure of sympathy for her angst at getting up before a crowd and talking about herself, he chose a more realistic path.

Keeping his voice level and calm, he proposed what he thought was a better solution. "Or, you could come up with a heartfelt, five-minute talk that reflects the time you spent flying Black Hawks. Focus on what you love about flying. The kids are eager to hear about adventure. You don't necessarily have to hit them over the head by talking about your disability. Bring them into your army exploits—as a pilot you must have a hundred of them—minus the death and destruction of war. Get them to hang on every word that comes out of your mouth. Inspire the girls in the audience to learn to fly. Be the motivation behind them. Be the instrument of inspiration like your dad was for you."

Eastlyn turned to gape at the man sitting next to her on the sofa. She looked at him as if he'd fallen down to earth from another galaxy wearing a Wookiee suit. At that moment, it felt like her heart melted in her chest.

Not since the last time she'd been in a cockpit had she felt such euphoria. The joy tried to bond together with the security and trust that welled up inside. She sat back, suddenly realized the importance of the moment. "All this time you've been trying to tell me and I wouldn't listen. I've made your life miserable for the past week and yet, you hung in there with me. Why?"

Cooper lifted a shoulder. "It's simple. I care what happens to you. Besides, I bet after tomorrow they give you a commendation for your oratory skills."

"Bite me."

He moved closer. "Where should I start?" He held a finger to her lips. "No, the choice should be mine."

She gave him a playful little push. "See, that's what I mean. You keep me laughing. You're easy to talk to, so unassuming and patient after I've spent the last week freaking out. I've never known a man like you before."

He took her chin. "You know what you need?"

She leaned in. Her hand cupped his neck. "I do. And I sense you're gearing up to give it to me."

"Maybe you should give it to me first." To show her he meant business, he boosted her up to straddle his lap. "Since you turned off my ballgame, you owe me."

"And I always pay my debts."

Clothes began to fly while he ravaged her mouth.

The scrape of teeth, the way his tongue tagged hers, caused pleasure to curl through her, the knots and tension fading away. Arching her back, she offered herself up. Her hips rocked as glorious waves, jagged and urgent, rippled hot and hard. She called out his name.

"Say it again," he demanded.

"Cooper. Now, Cooper."

Their eyes locked. His hands went around her hips. They came together, quickened the rhythm. The pace was on to satisfy lust and greed. Sensations punched like a sea between angry riptides and undertow as he dragged them up and over.

Out of breath, Eastlyn dropped her forehead onto his.

He framed her face between his hands. "There's a joy in getting naked with you."

She burst out laughing. "I second that."

Later, they sprawled out on the bed with a bottle of fingernail polish nearby as Cooper helped Eastlyn paint the toenails on her adjustable foot, a nice purple shade that would go with the outfit she'd chosen for tomorrow.

"I've never bothered to do this before," Eastlyn admitted. "I feel kinda silly. It seems like a waste of time, or maybe overkill."

"No, you'll see, your toes will rock along with the rest of you. You're not nervous anymore, are you?"

"Maybe a little. Not nearly as much though, not since I settled on a clear-cut topic. Thanks to you."

"Shelby's pestering me to invite you over for Sunday dinner."

"What's wrong with that? Working with Shelby and Landon, I've discovered that as bosses go they're two of the best, fair, even funny at times. You don't slack off with Landon though. He spends most of his time in the greenhouse fiddling with propagation. But when he wants that warehouse organized, watch out. He sort of reminds me of my own dad that way."

"I'm sure I disappointed Landon by not taking to digging in the dirt the way he wanted me to. I'm glad Caleb was around to follow in those footsteps."

She ran a hand over his. "That must be why Landon and Shelby have your photographs plastered from one end of the office to the other. Obviously, I've never been inside their house, but tell me I'm wrong to think it's the same way there."

"You're not wrong. But they are my family. They wouldn't want to hurt my feelings by hiding them in the closet, especially after the boxes full of my pictures I sent them, it would be rude not to display my work."

"Please. They're so proud of you they could bust." She caught the worry on his face. "What's eating at you? Don't deny it," she warned. "You helped me earlier when I needed it. Now tell me what's troubling you."

"Eleanor keeps calling me. She won't leave me alone."

"From prison?"

"She calls collect."

A memory flicked through her brain from that day on the cliff. She'd seen for herself how upset the calls made him. "We'll call the prison. Even if it means getting some of her privileges taken away. She shouldn't be allowed to harass you. That's wrong. If calling the warden or whoever, if that doesn't work, then we'll go to Kinsey and get her to go through legal channels to get Eleanor to stop."

He rolled on top of her, pinned her under him. "I didn't even think of doing that. You're more than beautiful. You're savvy and smart. The kind that makes me want to do all manner of things to you."

She tilted her head, sizing him up. "Then you'd better show me whatcha got, Renaissance boy. I have a big day tomorrow."

Walking through the doors at Pelican Pointe Elementary, Eastlyn thought back to her own last days of school; lots of them popped into mind. That breath of summer waiting beyond those double doors, waiting for you to fling them open and run as far away from routine lessons as you could get, a chance to let yourself go for three whole months.

Today there were echoes of laughing children. Voices of conversations whirred around her. The buzz droned in her ear as she strutted into the hallway wearing a summery silk dress in blue and gold, the wedge sandals on her feet decidedly making a statement, and her prosthetic prominently displayed for all to see.

The outfit was more than a splash of color. It made her feel feminine, even powerful.

But the feeling was short-lived when she took a look at the size of the crowd. It seemed everyone in town had decided to show up.

A jumble of nerves warred in her stomach and made her regret forcing down one of the blueberry muffins Jordan had included in the gift basket she'd sent over the day before. The coffee she'd consumed wanted to make its own reappearance.

Outside the auditorium, Lilly Pierce greeted her with a smile and a stunned look on her face. "I've only seen you in jeans and pants. You look amazing in that dress, like a different person."

"That's the idea," Eastlyn said with a grin. "But it doesn't help if I'm unable to form a thought."

"You'll be fine. Wally was nervous before going through his spiel, too. Don't worry. These kids will love you."

She recognized most of the other speakers lined up on the dais. When it came her turn she walked to the center of the stage, adjusted the microphone for her height and stood with her spine straight and proud. She looked out into the sea of young, fresh faces, took a deep breath and thought of her father right before catching sight of Cooper standing in the back of the auditorium.

Maybe it was seeing his face that caused a calm to move over her. Whatever it was, she began in simple fashion.

"Hello. My name's Eastlyn Parker and I used to fly Black Hawk helicopters, specifically medevac missions for the army. The first time I flew, though, was in the cockpit of a Piper Super Cub, a lowly crop duster. My father sat at the controls. It was so noisy we could barely hear each other talk. But every time I went up with him and settled into that seat next to him, I'd beg him to let me take over. I wanted to fly so high I could touch the clouds. I must've pleaded two dozen times to no avail until one day he let me handle the stick. Or maybe he simply pretended to turn the controls over to me. Whichever it was, I made the most of it. I was thirteen. From that moment on I knew what I wanted to do. I wanted to fly more than anything else. While other girls went the beauty queen route, I kept to my goal. I so wanted to take that trip to the moon and back. I never made it there. But you can. Anyone in this room can set their sights on becoming an astronaut, a pilot, whatever you choose. Because, if I can fly, anyone here can achieve their dream."

Cooper stood at the back watching her body language. The joy on her face practically lit up the room as she talked about doing what she loved. It occurred to him then that it had been stripped away without warning.

The invitation to have dinner at Landon and Shelby's didn't wait for Sunday.

Friday afternoon Eastlyn had been running the forklift inside the warehouse when Shelby waved her to a stop.

"There's been a change in plans. Could you guys make it Saturday night instead of Sunday? Caleb and Drea are both free then and I'd like to make it a family event."

"Did you run it by Cooper?" Eastlyn asked.

"I did and he said to check with you."

"Sure. No problem."

Her quick response proved to be the first in a series of events that came back to haunt Eastlyn later. But then Cooper had warned her that family dynamics could change into a minefield in a heartbeat.

The evening started out well enough on Saturday night when at precisely seven on the dot they pulled into the circular driveway in front of the Jennings home at the northwest corner of Landings Bay. It was the last house at the end of the block.

Four fluted Greek-style columns welcomed them onto a long porch with all the charm of a grand southern colonial. The place looked so much like an antebellum estate that Eastlyn thought she even smelled magnolias from the walled garden next to the portico.

Without ringing the bell, Cooper lifted the handle on the front door and ushered her into an entry hall with a parlor on one side and a dining room across from that. The furnishings were an odd mix of old world charm and country comfortable.

Caleb met them at the door to the living room. He tugged on Cooper's sleeve to hold him back for a minute longer while Shelby latched onto Eastlyn. While Eastlyn was pulled into the living room where Drea already sat with a glass of wine in her hand, Caleb kept a hold on Cooper's arm.

Once the women had drifted deeper into the interior of the room, Caleb leaned in, whispered into Cooper's ear, "Why didn't you let me know that you were getting calls from the prison?"

Cooper stared at his brother. "How do you know that?"

"Because Eleanor calls me at least three times every day. I figure she's bound to be calling you as well."

"Damn it, why won't she get the message and leave us alone? Have you taken her calls?"

Caleb shot a look back at Cooper. "Are you nuts? I have nothing to say to the woman. I can't figure out how she got my number though."

"Look, we'll talk about this later. I don't want to ruin Shelby's dinner by bringing up Eleanor's crazy stuff."

"Okay, fine, but Eleanor's crazy shit has to stop. So you promise me that we talk about this tonight before you leave."

Across the room, Shelby handed Eastlyn a glass of white wine. "I hear that you hit the ball out of the park with your speech at school."

Eastlyn scowled, but then her face broke out into a wide smile, beginning to relax. "I wouldn't say I rocked it exactly, but I did manage to move my mouth enough that coherent words flowed out without freezing up. So, all in all, I guess it was a win on my part."

Landon entered the room with a tray of cheesy stuffed mushrooms. "Try these. They're delicious. My own recipe."

Cooper walked to the bar, poured a shot of bourbon, doing his best to act nonchalant.

But Eastlyn could tell whatever Caleb had said to him upon entering, had sent his good mood south.

Thank goodness Drea transformed the charged air into another topic. "I'm starting to feel guilty about ending things with Zach in the middle of all his issues."

Cooper popped one of Landon's appetizers in his mouth, roamed the room. "Guilt is never a good reason to keep a relationship going."

"Was it working out, Drea?" Eastlyn asked her. "Because unless it was a relationship worth saving…"

Drea twisted her hands together. "No, you're right. It wasn't working. Not even a little bit. By the time I packed up and left, it had been bad for six months or more before I actually got the nerve to leave."

Cooper raised his glass of whiskey. "Then you shouldn't question the decision. How is Zach doing anyway?"

"Not good. You were right, by the way. I talked to Bree and Doc Prescott says he's suffering from clinical depression, probably has been for years. Zach ended up in Santa Cruz for an evaluation. The doctors there agreed with his diagnosis and put him on a drug called lurasidone. But Bree says he doesn't like taking it."

Cooper set his drink down. "That's the problem with people diagnosed with depressive disorders. They start feeling better in a short amount of time and decide the meds aren't really necessary. So they stop taking them and go right back into the paranoid delusional state they were in."

Drea got to her feet, went to the window to look out on the side garden. "That sounds like a terrible state for Zach to be in. It sounds like a vicious cycle. You have to believe that there was a time I truly cared for him, even thought I loved him. We'd talked about…"

Eastlyn went to her, put an arm around her shoulder. "No one's blaming you. What Zach needs right now is his family. From what Cooper says, Bree and Troy are there for him. Zach has his. You have yours. You have to stop beating yourself up because it didn't work out."

Shelby picked up that refrain. "We're all here for you, honey. You know that. You're not to take the breakup so hard. You and that Tucker Ferguson even went out after the Memorial Day festivities. You told us you had a nice time with him."

"I did have a nice time. We went to dinner at The Pointe but…"

Caleb cut in. "What's the deal with Tucker anyway? Does he take after his old man?"

Cooper noticed Drea bristle and her defensiveness kick in. The fireworks at the pier were lame compared to Drea's temper.

"There's no reason to treat him like that. I happen to like Tucker. I don't understand why people are so hard on him just because his father had a reputation for being the town cheapskate."

"More like the resident asshole," Caleb intoned. "Don't believe me. Ask Landon. Joe Ferguson used to try to raise the price of our lumber order every other month. The only reason the old man didn't was because Landon threatened to take his business elsewhere."

Sensing an argument brewing between siblings, Shelby put her foot down. "No squabbling allowed before dinner."

"Who's squabbling?" Caleb asked. "Has anyone else been getting calls from the prison?"

Cooper glowered at his younger brother. "I thought we agreed to table this discussion until later after we ate." He glanced over at Shelby. "I told him to wait."

"I knew something was causing tension between all of you tonight," Shelby admitted. "I'm going to check on dinner."

When she'd left the room, Cooper turned on Caleb. "Couldn't you have waited? Couldn't you tell that Shelby was looking forward having us all here this evening? Sometimes you really are a jerk."

Caleb looked contrite. "I'll go apologize. But we need to bring this thing with Eleanor front and center and deal with it," he suggested as he disappeared toward the kitchen.

"Eleanor called me, too," Drea said quietly.

"Did you take the call? Because Caleb and I have been ignoring them." Cooper noticed his sister wouldn't look him in the eye. "Drea, did you talk to her?"

Drea frowned into her wine glass. "She called me about a week ago at the shop."

"And you talked to her?" Cooper barked.

"There's no need to be upset with me. I spoke with her for maybe ten minutes. I was polite but distant. I didn't really know what to say to her anyway. She was too pushy so I just mostly listened."

Caleb came back in and glared at his sister. "But we all agreed that day at the courthouse after Eleanor pled guilty that we wouldn't have anything more to do with her. We took an oath, the three of us."

Drea glared right back, first at Caleb, then Cooper. "That's the point I tried to make earlier about Tucker and his father. We don't get to pick our family, now do we? I can't exactly pass judgment on Tucker's dad when my own mother is in prison for killing our father. It doesn't work for me that way. I wasn't the one who got in touch with her. She called me. I picked up the phone. I was cordial and that was it. There's no need to act like I betrayed my vow that day in Santa Cruz."

"Has she called back?" Cooper asked.

"A couple of times, but there were other calls, times I caught the number that popped up and let it go to voicemail. Now did I make my point about Tucker or not? Because he should be given a chance like…" Drea glanced at Eastlyn. "Just like giving Eastlyn a chance at a new start, in a new town. Eastlyn's had problems but I don't see anyone passing judgment on her."

Across the room Eastlyn nodded. "Drea has a point. Tucker deserves a chance. He shouldn't be lumped into the same category as his father. Dislike him if and when he exhibits those 'asshole' character flaws that made his dad the talk of the town. But until then, Tucker should be on equal footing with everyone else."

"Fair enough," Caleb said, announcing it was time to eat. "But, I for one, am not taking Eleanor's calls. I have nothing to say to the woman."

Just thinking about actually speaking to her on the phone or by any other method made Cooper lose his appetite for whatever Shelby had fixed. "That makes two of us."

As they made their way into the dining room, Cooper went on to recommend what Eastlyn had suggested. "We could always try to force her to stop calling us through legal channels. Kinsey could handle that for us."

Caleb held up his beer. "Let's give it a shot. I vote we talk to Kinsey and let her loose on Eleanor and see what results we get."

Cooper looked around the table. "If it's unanimous, then I'll set up the appointment."

Later after dinner, Eastlyn walked out onto the terrace to get fresh air. The garden setting provided a backdrop of Grecian walkways lit up in twinkling lights. She spotted Shelby sitting on one of the benches surrounded by flowing vines of purple clematis. The look on her face told Eastlyn she'd been crying.

"Has it always been like this?" Eastlyn asked.

Shelby smiled and dabbed at her eyes. "Not always. I try to tell myself that you don't take in three damaged children suffering from what could only be described as post traumatic stress and think you can bake cookies and make everything all right overnight."

"Doesn't stop a person who cares deeply from trying."

"No, it didn't stop me from trying or Landon for that matter. I hear Drea talk about guilt over her relationship with Zach and it concerns me. Landon and I have so much guilt where Eleanor is concerned. We knew she had major problems. But we kept hoping those issues would go away. I guess you must think that sounds like we were pretty naïve to think that way. But when you're so close to a situation and caught up in all the drama, you reach a point that you just want it all to go away. So you ignore a few things and hope for the best."

"You and Landon couldn't possibly have predicted Eleanor would take a gun and murder two people."

Shelby looked at her with sad eyes. "You're wrong about that. You'd think differently if you'd ever met Eleanor. She's exactly where she needs to be."

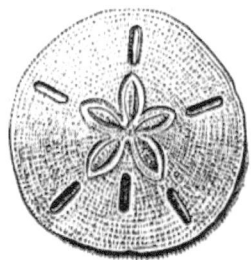

Eighteen

Since the Memorial Day weekend, Cooper and Eastlyn had spent every night together. They either bunked at her little bungalow or his place.

It might've taken a considerable amount of trust on both sides to get to that point, but once they had, they seemed determine to bust down all barriers.

During that time they mostly stayed bunched between the sheets, especially on weekends. They'd listened to Rachmaninoff in front of the Kiva fireplace, or strutted around the room to Chuck Berry's rocking guitar, or stretched out on the sofa to unwind to the music of Tchaikovsky.

On weekdays they'd lounge in bed until the very last second before having to jump up and start their workday.

Eastlyn had never thought she could ever be as happy as she was at this point in her life. If anyone had suggested such a thing six months earlier, she would've probably hit that person with a brick. Of course, her frame of mind had been in a much darker place back then.

Cooper had his own dark demons to deal with from childhood in the form of Eleanor. He hoped sitting down with Kinsey could remedy that. Although the strategy might fall short, it at least gave him the feeling he'd taken steps to make Eleanor stop. Proactive seemed a better approach than putting up with endless calls for the next twenty years.

They both found living in a small town had a surprising list of things to do as a couple. After work and on weekends they could go to any number of events.

June meant movie nights in the park. The first Thursday night, they'd taken a pass on *The Penguins of Madagascar*. But at some point they'd set aside time to see the summer's other offerings like *Guardians of the Galaxy* and *Ghostbusters*.

It was all about priorities. And right now the number one thing was committing to spending time with one another, getting to know each other better, and developing a trusting rapport.

But near the middle of June Eastlyn broke from that. At Cooper's urging she decided to take a Sunday afternoon and seek out the AA meeting at the Community Church. If there was a problem brewing she wanted to head it off.

According to Cord, the group used one of the Sunday school classrooms for their weekly get-together.

The simple building, a whitewashed stone and wood structure, might've been any little church somewhere in small town USA. It had ornate stained glass windows front and sides. The largest window was above the front door and depicted Jesus with his arms outstretched reaching out to his flock. At the very top, where the roof formed an "A" shape, there was a white wooden cross. A sign out front noted how many people had been in attendance for the morning services.

Running five minutes late, Eastlyn scooted through the wooden double doors as quickly as her leg allowed, past the empty auditorium, and into the hallway in the back that led to the classrooms.

She found the one room where she heard mumbled conversations coming from inside and opened the door. Among the meager attendees her eyes landed on four familiar faces—seven in all, not counting her.

Cord looked up from his stance at the podium, nodded toward her with a brief grin of acknowledgement before turning his attention back to the other six people in the audience.

"You already know my name's Cord and I'm an alcoholic. This is the Sunday afternoon meeting of our united group effort to beat alcohol and/or drug addiction and stay clean and sober. I'd like to welcome our newest visitor who just came in."

Without waiting for Eastlyn to reply, he went on, "If you want, it's okay by us if you take a seat for now and introduce yourself at the very end of the meeting. In a town this size, we all know each other anyway so anonymity is pretty much out the window. But I remind everyone that what we say here, stays here, no exceptions."

Eastlyn found a chair and slid in next to Margie Rosterman, who sat next to Max, the cook. In front of them sat Pete Alden, a man she'd met at the Fanning Rescue Center. She was also surprised to see the former veterinarian, Bran Sullivan. That left two men in their early forties who weren't at all familiar to her.

They all listened as Cord continued talking, reciting his way through the twelve steps. She wasn't sure if they did this each time they met or if it was for her benefit. Either way, she was a quick study and took mental notes. Cord's version was a condensed form of what she'd already found on the Internet.

Cord finished his turn with his summation, putting his own spin on the refrain. "Alcoholism and drug addiction are progressive illnesses. There are no cures. Abstinence is the only thing that works for me. Each day I wake up, it's up to me to decide that I have to take responsibility for not taking a drink. I've been sober three years and six months now. So I guess that's it for me today."

From that point on, Eastlyn watched as the attendees took turns introducing themselves and explaining what their particular problem had been.

Margie and Max were former addicts. Bran, like her, had found himself addicted to prescription painkillers after a back injury. During the exchange, she learned the names of the two men, Archer and Greg. Both guys gave practically an identical speech. Each man had gone through bad marriages that had turned into messy divorces. They'd used alcohol as their crutch to get through the stressful times.

When it was her turn to speak all eyes fell on her. She picked up the chorus everyone else had used. "Hi, I'm Eastlyn and I have a tendency to abuse pills, mostly Vicodin, but if I could talk a doctor into prescribing OxyContin I'd settle for that. For the past couple of years, I always found an excuse and a clever way to get more pills. Lately, I'm in a good place but...there are some days I feel that same old urge wanting to creep in, mostly during a stressful day when I have trouble with a task due to limited mobility, that sort of thing. The thing is I don't want to slide back into where I was before. I've been off the pills for four months, ten days and I don't want to mess up my life anymore than I already have."

"Who's your sponsor?" Pete asked.

She cut her eyes toward Cord. "He is."

"That's fine," Margie said. "But Cord's a busy man. You should know you can call any of us in this room, day or night, and we'll be there for you."

"Thanks for that. Let's hope I'm able to stay on the straight and narrow without resorting to making phone calls in the middle of the night."

The eight of them managed to talk for a while and wrap up the meeting in under two hours.

Outside in the parking lot she walked to her Bronco and spotted Brent Cody parked in the spot next to hers, leaning up against his Tahoe.

Hope for her friend bubbled up in her throat. "Did you find Durke?"

Brent shook his head. "No word yet from anyone. Do you know where our town cemetery is?"

She gave him an odd look. "Uh, yeah. Eternal Gardens, north of town, can't miss it heading toward Promise Cove on the right."

"Good. When you get a minute, meet me there."

"Why?"

"There's something I need to run by you."

Before she had time to reply, Brent had scuttled back into his truck.

"I have something to do first," she said, walking up to the car window. "It might be another hour."

"Take your time. But stay clear of the police station. Do we understand each other?"

Eastlyn had her suspicions. "Sure. We're meeting someplace out of town where we won't readily be seen together."

"That's right. Here's my phone number. Text me when you're ready to head out and I'll meet you there."

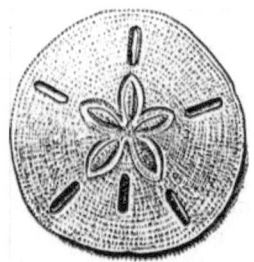

Nineteen

Eastlyn found it odd that Brent wanted to meet this far out of town.

Making the turn into Eternal Gardens, she noticed the place was deserted. Even in broad daylight, she felt a heightened sense of creepy. Relieved when she spotted Brent sitting in his SUV at the entrance, she got out of the Bronco and went over to his vehicle.

He didn't see her at first because his shoulders were hunched, his eyes glued to an iPad. He was pecking away at the digital screen when she walked up next to his car.

She tapped on the glass and watched as he jumped out of his skin.

"Sorry about that. What's up? Where do you want to do this?"

Brent stretched his back, rolled his head around on his shoulders to work out the kinks. "Let's take a walk."

They strolled through an iron gate that led into the first sea of headstones. They were several yards into the park before he finally stopped and looked around.

The word covert popped into her head.

Brent ran a hand through his raven hair, paced several steps away, and then back again until he stood in front of her, face to face. "I've thought about this situation nine ways to Sunday. I'm considering taking you up on your offer as long as you agree to two of my conditions."

"And they are?"

"We're doing this in two stages. First, you go out there to do recon, gain intel, take pictures if possible of the lay of the land. Second, you try to make a buy. When you go in to make contact, you have to wear a wire. Any time you set foot inside that compound, you wear a wire. That part is non-negotiable."

"Okay. What else?"

"You go in as a member of law enforcement. When I took this job the town council gave me the authority to hire a police officer down the road. This is down the road. It wouldn't be permanent, just until this mission is completed and we get clear answers as to what's going on at the Thorwald place. Is that agreeable to you?"

"So, I'd be a temporary police officer until we wrap this up?"

"That's the idea. If you don't have a sidearm, I'll take care of that."

"Okay. So what's the plan?"

Brent eyed her for several long seconds. "Just like that? You don't want to think about it?"

"This was my idea. Remember? I'm in."

"Okay. Since you arrived in town there've been rumors floating around about your major drug problem. We're going to exploit that."

Fascinated, Eastlyn plopped down on a concrete bench at the edge of the grass. "So I'm starring in my own sleazy movie for the summer and didn't even realize I'm the main attraction? Bummer. *And* you want me to make it look as though I'm strung out, looking to pick up any work I can get to raise the money I need for a dime bag? Is that where you're going with this?"

"You're perceptive. Everyone knows you hold down three jobs as it is. The ruse that you need the money for drugs should work."

Eastlyn rolled her eyes. "Well, you already know I was at the AA meeting this afternoon. Nothing happens in this town you don't know about. Will that be a problem?"

"No, in fact it goes along with the idea that you're desperate for help. And I resent the idea that I know everything that happens here. I don't make a habit of sticking my nose into people's personal lives unless they break the law."

"Oh, please. That may work for some people but it's like you have built-in radar or something. Otherwise, how would you know where I was this afternoon?"

"Like any good cop on patrol, I saw you pull up at the church. Pete Alden founded those AA meetings there on Sunday afternoons. Those meetings go back two decades. It's not exactly top secret they take place every Sunday."

"Hmm, likely story. I'm still in though. I'll let everyone think I'm still struggling with the pills. Also I might as well pretend I'm strung out enough to pick up any job I can find. But I draw the line at working the weedy lots around town collecting aluminum cans to recycle and turn in for cash. I'd like to keep a little of my dignity intact, if you don't mind."

Brent finally smiled. "It won't come to that. I promise."

"Famous last words."

"Just remember, we're going after a very bad guy, dangerous, who we suspect is the area's major supplier of crystal meth."

"Frankly, I never understood the draw to the stuff. I knew a guy in the army who had a problem with that crap before they kicked him out. It's a nasty habit. But I can certainly play the part with a little help from ivory pancake makeup and a few dark circles under my eyes. Dab a few imperfections here and there on my face, a few splotches to make it look real and I'm certain I'll look the part."

Brent parked his butt on the opposite end of the bench, cast her a quizzical frown. "We're not to that point yet. The first time you go out there it's for recon, not a dress up role-playing scenario or a fake buy, not yet anyway. We're going to do this my way or not at all. What do you know about the synthetic-made drug known as gravel?"

"Just what I've read on the Internet. It looks like pebbles, or rock candy. It can be snorted, smoked, or injected, and it's deadly stuff."

"It causes delirium, paranoia, and violent behavior. That's before the body temperature spikes as high as a hundred and five and then the kidneys begin to shut down."

"You think the Thorwalds are cooking gravel?"

"I do. Bran and Joy Sullivan have reported problems near the spread they bought for their horses."

"I wondered if you'd bring that up. I'm thinking the Thorwalds or their friends are likely the culprits trying to intimidate Joy and Bran. Did you know they tried to get help from the county?"

"I'm aware of it. I've reported it in an official capacity to the sheriff's office." Brent pulled out a map from his back pocket and pointed to the area between Pelican Pointe and the nearby town of San Sebastian.

"The Sullivans live here and the compound is a short two klicks from their house. Bran's complaint described high traffic in and around this region. According to Bran, people come and go at all hours of the day and night."

He chewed the inside of his jaw. "There's something else. There were five cases last winter within a two-month time period at San Sebastian High School that involved gravel. My suspicion grows when Bran tells me traffic on the road leading to the compound is high school kids. That leads me to believe Judd Thorwald is the gravel supplier. I think Judd picked up where Harley Edgecombe left off. I think Thorwald's taken over Harley's thriving meth trade with a few upgrades."

"Just tell me when you want me to go in."

"You understand this is a recon mission? I want you to scope out the area. That's it for now, nothing more than gathering data we use to formulate a plan for down the road. Understood?"

"I got it."

"Slip in, slip out, without drawing any attention to yourself. Promise me that, or the deal's off."

"That's the goal. When do you want it to happen?"

"Friday night. You'll have to make your way through the woods to get as close as you can to the compound. I've drawn you a detailed map to use and noted markers to follow along the way. Under no circumstances should you try to breach the perimeter. Gain intel by taking photos of any license plates in the area and make notes of any pertinent information we could use to make a case in court. And that's it, Eastlyn. No going in to approach any individual, or make a buy or make contact with any of the Edgecombes or Thorwalds. Are we clear?"

"Yes, I got it. And if they should catch me, I pretend I'm a druggie looking for a score. How many times do I have to tell you? I'm not that dense. I got it. Now stop worrying about me. I was in the army for goodness sakes. I know how to do recon."

Brent ran a hand through his black hair. "Then why am I already regretting this? Look, I don't care what time you get in Friday night, I want you to call me. If I don't hear from you I'm coming in after you. I won't sleep until I know you're safe."

"Yes, Dad, I'll be sure to do that."

Brent stood up, pointed to the map he had spread out on his lap. "Let's go over the plan one more time just to make sure you have the lay of the land."

Eastlyn whooshed out a loud sigh. "With all your thoroughness, you and my unit commander might be twins—the way you think and strategize reminds me a lot of him."

"That's because when it comes to warfare—and make no mistake this is similar to a combat operation—there's no such thing as being over-prepared."

"Funny, that was his mindset, too."

"And under no circumstances do you tell anyone about this. It gets out you're working for me undercover and your safety could be compromised."

"Undercover sounds so official." She practically whispered the statement. It ran through her head at that moment just how upset Cooper would be if he found out. The word betrayal popped into her head. She had to remind herself that this was a job now. It never occurred to her to break her promise to Brent and confide in Cooper about the operation.

Determined to keep this to herself, she'd have to practice discretion and tap-dance around the subject if it came up again.

Brent must have seen the hesitation or maybe the measure of doubt in her eyes because when she looked up at him, Eastlyn saw his inquisitive stare.

"It isn't too late to back out. If you want to change your mind, now's the time to speak up."

She shook her head. "No, not at all, I'm committed."

But after Brent left her alone, guilt took over. She felt like a traitor to Cooper, especially knowing how he felt about her even mentioning the compound.

Under a layer of hazy clouds, she set out to wander among the headstones looking for one in particular.

She'd almost given up when she came across the right one. Bending down to read the inscription, she noted its simple words and unassuming style.

David Scott Phillips
Beloved Husband and Father
Died In Service to His Country

Like the plaque at the park in town, this modest marker stood as a reminder that life was too damned hard, too damned short, and sometimes too damned unfair.

Scott stood over to the side watching Eastlyn's eyes. "Going around once is why you want to make sure you make it count."

Eastlyn fought for a stoic front. "That's the truth of it. You'll get no argument out of me."

"Wow, that's a first. What's the matter, Parker, getting soft?"

"Maybe. I feel like a heel."

"Yeah, you're making a mistake by not telling Cooper. Keeping the new job a secret will cause problems down the road. But you already know that."

"It's undercover," she pointed out in defiance. "Brent said…"

"You keep telling yourself that. You're following Brent's instructions to the letter. You keep reminding yourself of that."

"Then why do I feel bad about it?"

"You'll have to figure that one out on your own."

"Straight answers aren't your forte, are they? I'd get better results dialing up 1-800-Psychic."

"You want to know what the future holds? Go get a pack of tarot cards. All I know for certain is that any type of dishonesty in a relationship comes back to bite you in the ass, eventually. But you're gonna do what you want anyway. You don't need me to tell you what's right or wrong."

Eastlyn sent him a glare. "You're a piece of work, you know that?"

"Right back atcha."

Twenty

The same Friday night Eastlyn had agreed to go out to the compound, she and Cooper had been invited to a party at Julianne and Ryder's place. The couple had opened up the house dubbed Sandcastle Cottage to friends and family with the lure that a big announcement was coming.

Eastlyn had done her best to get out of going. But what excuse could she use when Cooper would've wanted to know why?

So at seven-thirty she stood ready and waiting for Cooper to swing by and pick her up.

When she opened the door, she saw the stunned look on his face at the outfit she'd chosen.

Cooper eyed the vision as she stood radiant and regal in a sleeveless lace dress the color of soft lilac embroidery. The empire bodice set off her waist while the flare of the skirt showed off her lanky frame.

"You just get more beautiful every time I lay eyes on you," Cooper declared and meant it.

"The other day I spent some time with Julianne in her little shop. I had a good run. She has the most amazing inventory of outfits and jewelry to my liking and taste. You just don't find that any ol' place."

"You look good in that color."

"I do have a tendency to gravitate to shades of lavender, don't I?" She glanced at her watch. "I didn't hear your car."

"That's because I walked over. It's such a nice night for it. I figure if we have a drink or two at Ryder's there'd be no worries about getting home. So do you mind if we walk?"

She grinned and held up her foot. "No problem. See, I'm getting the hang of these heels like a supermodel."

"I noticed." He took her hand, kissed the tips of her fingers.

Outside the light waned. The half moon hung in the southern sky. Crickets sang their evening song. They made their way toward Ocean Street in silence until Cooper asked, "Is there a reason you left so early this morning?"

She wondered if there was ever a good reason to lie and then slid into that role. "I had to meet Silas and Ben at the lighthouse." It wasn't quite the truth. Brent had wanted to go over the plan a second time so she'd had to sneak out without telling Coop the real reason.

By the time they reached Sandcastle Cottage, the wind had changed direction. It felt as if a storm brewed somewhere off the coast.

They saw festive lights hung around the porch and heard the swell of guitar riffs and piano chords coming from inside.

Cooper took Eastlyn's hand and led her through a jammed living room where the musicians, Malachi and Ross, had set up to play.

Bumping into neighbors along the way to the kitchen where the bar was, they learned that since Memorial Day the two men had taken to jamming together to form a band of sorts.

"When did Malachi and Ross decide to make a run at Simon and Garfunkel?" Cooper asked.

Jill Campbell, her tawny face breaking into a grin, gave her husband a loving look. "Since the two found out they love to play the same kind of music. Besides, Malachi believes he needs to stay closer to home on the weekends. Better to keep an eye on his teenage girls. My Ross just needs to be able to play music now and again. Not many people know this but that man put himself through school playing the blues at a dive in downtown Chicago. There are probably still YouTube videos out there somewhere of his band."

"What would that be under?" Eastlyn asked, taking out her cell phone and using it to search the website.

Jill grinned. "Hand that thing over here. I'll find it faster than you ever will."

Eastlyn handed Jill the phone all the while tapping her right foot to a rendition of *Layla*. "They're good."

"What are they calling themselves?" Cooper asked.

Jill handed the phone back to Eastlyn with the display sending out Ross's sound waves of cool jazz. "No name yet. They're working on it though, sat up last night until midnight trying to think up one that works for both of them."

Bree and Troy came in, hands linked, all smiles.

"Do you know what this party's about?" Eastlyn wanted to know.

Kinsey stood to the side eating a canapé. "Rumor has it Julianne's pregnant."

Troy smiled knowingly as if he already knew. "I guess we'll all have to wait for the surprise announcement."

Good music, good food, good friends put Eastlyn in mind of another time when she'd enjoyed the companionship of others in like social settings. She didn't realize how much she'd missed that kind of fun until coming to Pelican Pointe.

When Brent and River came through the door her good mood headed south, a reminder of what she still had to do later that night.

Brent sent her a polite but distant look.

Eastlyn ignored the cop, focusing instead on Cooper's face—glad someone was enjoying the party as much as she was.

Determined not to spoil the celebration, whatever it turned out to be, she elbowed Cooper in the ribs and nodded her head toward Abby Anderson who was flirting with Caleb. "It looks like you've lost the competition *and* the affections of a fan."

"I don't know what you're talking about," Cooper claimed. "I don't think is was me she was interested in at all but Caleb. She's followed him around the room tonight—twice. I don't think Abby was ever taken with me."

"Aww," Eastlyn said, ruffling his hair like a kid. "Is that an ego buster? Obviously Abby came into your shop all those times to gain valuable intel on your brother through you."

"You think?"

"Abby's a Ph.D, a smart cookie. She knows how to scope out the goods to get to her intended target."

Wasn't that what she meant to do at the compound tonight, scope out the goods? How did she intend to take care of that without Cooper finding out? Would she have to lie to prevent him from knowing where she planned to go?

"Troy and I would like your undivided attention for a minute," Ryder began.

Ryder's voice brought Eastlyn back to a cold reality. After all the conning she'd done to get Vicodin, deception didn't come easy. At least, not when you were lying to someone you truly cared about.

"Gather 'round, grab your champagne or drink of choice and prepare to be blown away," Troy said, his voice rising in excitement.

Eastlyn watched as Ryder gathered Julianne close and raised a glass of bubbly in the air. Those two something special together. Eastlyn doubted Julianne would ever lie to Ryder.

While her thoughts drifted toward dishonesty, Ryder went on, "We invited you here tonight because we have good news. We thought it was the best way to tell you all at one time. Plus, it gives Julianne a good reason to throw a party."

"Get to it, Ryder," Julianne prompted with a smile. "Our guests are about to burst with curiosity. I've already dodged a dozen questions tonight that the party is about me being pregnant. I'm not, by the way."

Ryder grinned. "Okay, okay, I was trying to build up the suspense and draw it out as long as I could. As everyone probably knows by now, we're a man short down at Tradewinds Boatyard. Zach's having a rough time of it lately and Doc says it's better if the guy takes some much-needed time off. While he's getting better, Troy and I plan to carry on in his absence. In fact, just this past week, Tradewinds Boatyard landed a big endorsement from one of the yacht racing associations for outstanding craftsmanship."

The room broke into whoops of cheer.

"But that's not why we're here. Troy and I want to announce Tradewinds Boatyard will be featured in *Docks* magazine's August issue, a feat we think is pretty cool considering we've only been in business such a short time."

Everyone in the room toasted the good news as Troy stepped forward, beer held high. "And in the boatbuilding trade that's practically unheard of. To get that kind of notice means Tradewinds Boatyard might be considered the new kid on the block but the company's made an impression on our constituents."

"That's right," Ryder said. "From now on, Tradewinds Boatyard is on its way to bigger and better things."

Bree leaned in, whispered to Cooper, "I so wish I could've gotten Zach to show up tonight. But he refused to come."

Empathy ran through Cooper. "You're keeping an eye on him, right? It'll be a while before he feels like his old self again."

"I'm trying. It's a struggle every day. I have a new business to run just like Troy and Ryder. It's the tourist season out at the bed and breakfast. Because of that I may have to get someone to stop in at Zach's house every other day to make sure he's taking his meds. The thing is Zach's so temperamental, so easy to rile these days, he doesn't trust strangers."

"Just be careful that he doesn't slide further into mistrusting everyone around him," Cooper cautioned. "But above all, make sure he doesn't miss a dose of those meds."

Eastlyn and Cooper stayed another hour before calling it a night and heading home.

As soon as they got outside, they noticed the change in the weather. The smell of rain was evident and a wall of fog drifted in from the north.

On the walk down Ocean Street, Cooper took her hand. "What's bothering you?"

"Not a thing. It was a great evening. It's good to help friends celebrate something important in their lives."

Her denial struck a chord with him. He'd seen the way she'd reacted when Brent had come into the room back at the party. Not only that, but she hadn't wanted to go in the first place. "Whose place do we crash at tonight, yours or mine?"

A wedge of panic lodged in her belly. If they spent the night at her place, what excuse would she use to sneak out of her own bed? If they went to his, he'd surely wake up at some point and wonder why she wasn't there. If she intended to follow through with the plan, she had to change out of her dress and back into jeans. How could she do that without making the stop at her place? Maybe she should just pick a fight with him to get out of making the decision.

"I'm a little tired," she blurted out and came to a painful conclusion. "Besides, I saw how you went out of your way to flirt with Bree tonight. In fact, you did the same thing with Jill Campbell and Julianne."

Cooper sent her a dubious look. "What are you talking about? I didn't flirt with anyone. Bree and I talked about

Zach. You were standing two feet away when Jill and I had a conversation. Julianne hosted the party so I took a few minutes to tell her what a great job she'd done. Not only that, but all of them are happily married women. I don't mess around with another guy's woman. And if you think that, you don't know me very well. What's gotten into you tonight?"

"I know what I saw," Eastlyn insisted, knowing she sounded like a shrew. But she'd already dealt herself this hand and now would have to play it out. She'd just have to make it up to him later.

"Accusations like that are nothing but cheap shots and beneath you," Cooper fired back. "I think I'll leave you to your attitude." With that, he started off down the street without her.

"Yeah? Well…who needs a man who's a player? The kind who flirts with other women right in front of them is…a cad."

Cooper didn't say another word and never looked back as he kept on walking.

The next time she looked up, he'd already disappeared around the corner.

"That was a little too easy," Eastlyn muttered, a bad taste settling in her mouth over what she'd done. As she headed home to change her clothes, disappointment still lingered. "He didn't even try to get on my good side."

Still mumbling to herself about Cooper's unwillingness to put up much of a fight, she unlocked the door to her house. Once inside, she wiggled out of her dress, sat down on the bed to adjust the height of her prosthetic foot for boots. After changing into jeans and shirt, she glanced down at her watch and realized it was go-time.

On Sandy Pointe Drive, Cooper settled back into his easy chair with the lights off, a cold beer nearby, to watch

SportsCenter. But after trying to watch a few highlights, he found he had trouble focusing on baseball scores.

Instead, he replayed the scene with Eastlyn on the street. She'd showed him a nasty side to her, one he was glad to learn about now, rather than later.

But it wasn't the lonely darkness engulfing his living room that made him feel like a stranger in his own house. No, it was Eastlyn's abrupt change that bothered him.

Just like Nick had predicted that day at the bank, Cooper had sensed for a few days beforehand that Eastlyn had been pulling away from him on purpose. She'd acted weird that morning when she'd left the house before breakfast. And now, without a word of warning, she'd turned into someone he didn't even know.

"You're kidding, right?" Scott said from his seat on the couch. "You actually fell for that? Even though it was the worst acting I've ever seen, you bought that crap about flirting? Sometimes I wonder about you, Cooper."

Cooper eyed him with open disdain. "What are you talking about?"

"Eastlyn obviously needed to ditch you and picking a fight was the best option she had."

Cooper shot up out of the recliner. "I knew something was off."

"Off? You mean other than her pitiful performance?"

"Why did she need to ditch me?" He'd no sooner got the words out of his mouth than it suddenly dawned on him. "She's headed out to that damn compound, isn't she?"

"Wow, there's no getting anything past you," Scott noted, every word underscored with sarcasm.

"She knew how I felt and deliberately deceived me."

"There are times mystery in a relationship might be considered a turn-on. But deliberate deception like she showed tonight needs to be addressed. I don't think you should let her get away with it," Scott prompted.

Cooper sent him a go-to-hell look. "I have no intentions of letting her get away with it. What kind of head start does she have?"

"About ten minutes," Scott said with a grin. "The woman moves faster than you think."

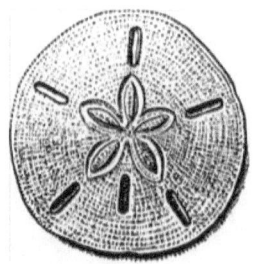

Twenty-One

By the time Eastlyn had changed clothes and got underway, Friday night had rolled into Saturday morning. The windy June night had turned misty and foggy. The weather made for slick roads and damp terrain.

It was headed toward one o'clock when Eastlyn parked her Bronco an estimated two miles from the designated destination.

Too remote and isolated, thought Eastlyn as she reached in the glove box for a flashlight. Before getting out to trek through the wooded, dark countryside, she decided to recheck Brent's map, making sure she had the correct coordinates.

After studying the checkpoints, satisfied she'd gotten as close to the compound as was safe, she grabbed her backpack. She'd stuffed it with two bottles of water and a power bar just in case she got stuck out here overnight without provisions. She also had her camera phone, a pair of binoculars, and the police issue M9 Beretta that Brent had supplied this morning.

She had a laundry list of things to do. First and foremost, find out where Judd Thorwald cooked his meth. Get documentation, hopefully clear shots of the place. Flesh out how secure Thorwald kept the area so that future surveillance could be done. Scope out any hindrances to making contact down the road for future buys.

She played sentinel for at least forty-five minutes scouting out the area. She discovered why Bran and Joy had seen high traffic here. Teenagers routinely used the secluded road for make out sessions. At the end of the now-empty lane, she found a slew of trash, beer and liquor bottles, used condoms, and a sea of fast food wrappers.

Other than her activity, she saw no other signs of life. There were no other cars on the road. No people standing guard at the fence line. The lack of both, she found odd. When she got closer to the perimeter the first thing that stood out was the inactivity near the compound. Of course, it was after two a.m. at this point, and everyone most likely had gone to bed. But there had to be a reason there were no guards posted.

She already thought she knew the answer. Traffickers often set up countermeasures and deterrents to make sure unwanted strangers steered clear of their turf. The devices were cheap to build and sent a strong message to any trespasser stupid enough to wander around in the dark. The devices were also difficult to detect. Using her flashlight, she took deliberate, measured steps through the terrain. The slow process cost her time but was well worth the extra precaution.

She went another twenty feet before spotting the first trap. Taking out her camera phone, she approached the area using tentative stages. These weren't the slapstick, Wile E. Coyote varieties meant for cartoons but rather sophisticated devices meant to bring harm to anyone who got this far on the property.

Not too far from that spot, she saw a clearing and a dilapidated shack. Heading that way, she was more convinced than ever that the region was full of booby traps. With every risky step, she took she noted someone had saturated the wooded landscape with a series of trip wires. From tree to tree, they occurred every few feet. She was by no means an expert, but even she understood that she'd just come across the basis for major criminal charges against the remaining Edgecombes or Thorwald himself.

Once she grew close enough to the decrepit cabin, she took pictures from a messy, littered front yard. But to look through the window, she decided that going around back might attract less attention. If someone happened to approach her, she had a backup plan. She'd go into her junkie act.

Peering through the glass, the inside of the place was a debris-ridden collection of old furniture—a dresser, a mattress, a series of folding tables with a cluttered display of bottles: camp fuel, bleach and other assorted ingredients used to cook crystal meth.

A twig snapped behind her. She cut the beam on the flashlight, made a point to hug against the exterior of the cabin, making herself as inconspicuous as possible.

Eastlyn got a whiff of demon Puerto Rican rum, a smell she knew well from her days in the army. Soldiers often came back to camp from taking leave stinking of the stuff.

Through the copse of silver maple, she caught sight of a disheveled man with days-old stubble on his chin. A twenty-gauge shotgun rested on his arm as he trudged his way toward the ramshackle cabin. It was at that moment she sensed someone had outflanked her and was headed around the corner.

"Get out of here," Scott whispered. "Now! I'll draw them over to the right. You circle back to the car from the opposite direction where you came in, better to keep them off balance."

"You got it," Eastlyn muttered, doing her best to hightail it out of there.

It took her three-quarters of an hour to get back to where she'd parked the car. She came up short when she saw Cooper leaning up against the door on the driver's side of the Bronco.

"I know you're angry but right now we need to haul ass out of here," she said in a hushed tone, pushing her way past him to reach the door handle. "Yell at me later. Get in your car! I'm not kidding. We need to get out of here. Now!"

"I'll follow you." By the time Coop ran back to the Mustang, Eastlyn had already turned the SUV around and headed south toward the cutoff.

Cooper shifted into gear, determined to trail the Ford and keep one eye on the rearview mirror at all times. Sure enough, he spotted another car approaching from a hundred yards or so behind them, closing in at a high rate of speed.

"Damn it, Eastlyn," he muttered as he hit the gas. "Right about now, I'd like to wring your sneaky neck."

There wasn't time to take his phone out to call or text. So he got as close to the Bronco's bumper as he could get and flashed his lights, hoping she'd know to speed up. When she accelerated, he kept eyeing the car in the rear as the distance between them grew. The headlights got smaller, indicating the vehicle had fallen back.

But Cooper didn't breathe any easier until the two cars had made the turn west and headed toward the Pacific Coast Highway.

At the city limits sign, he watched as Eastlyn slowed down and pulled her car to the side of the road. When she got out, so did he.

"So we're doing this in the middle of the 101. That's fine by me," Cooper shouted.

"Why?" she screamed when she got within earshot. "Why did you follow me? Don't you trust me at all?"

"Me? Don't turn this back on me. Don't do that shit. You deliberately picked a fight with me so I wouldn't catch you sneaking out here behind my back. Apparently trust and the fact that we now share a bed means nothing to you."

She stepped up toe to toe with him. "If you'd just listen…"

"To what, another bogus performance? You didn't clue me in about where you were going tonight because you knew I'd be upset. You did it behind my back. I never considered you so devious. Deny it."

"No, I did, but…"

"Why the hell did you go out there knowing how I feel about that place?"

"Nailing those bastards and catching them in the act is the right thing to do. And there's no need to yell at me."

"I'm yelling because right now I'm so furious with you I want to scream it out to the stars."

On impulse, she gripped his shirt, bunched it up in her hands and pulled him into her. Covering his mouth, she ate at his tongue. When she came up for air, she breathed out, "I'm sorry. I'll make it up to you."

"I'm not that easy," he stated. But even as the words left his mouth, he fused his lips to hers.

They broke apart once again and she fired back, "Sure you're easy, you just won't admit it."

To prove her words, she kissed him again, this time taking her time in slow, deliberate moves. Lingering at his mouth, she breathed, "Now are you finished being miffed?"

"Newsflash. I moved past miffed while sitting out there in the dark waiting for you to come back to the car worrying about whether you were safe or not, worrying that maybe they'd caught you and cracked open your skull or worse."

"Ouch. Okay, I'm guilty. I wasn't supposed to tell anyone. Brent swore me to secrecy."

"Don't give me that crap."

"He deputized me. But you're not supposed to know about it."

"Damn it! What was Brent thinking?"

"Maybe he was thinking that I could do this job. You know what? I heard Scott's voice telling me to get out of there right before I saw two men sneaking up on me."

Coop slung his arm around her shoulder. "We'll talk about ghosts at breakfast. Right now, we need sleep. I don't know about you, but my adrenaline rush is about to hit a wall."

She dug out her cell phone, turned back to get into the Bronco to make the call.

Cooper eyed her with suspicion. "What are you doing?"

"I have to touch base with Brent or he'll be pissed."

"More like he'll send out a statewide alert."

"That too."

"At least he didn't hang you out to dry."

"Don't start," she warned, putting her index finger to her lips so he'd shush long enough for her to talk into the phone. The last thing she needed right now was for Brent to know Cooper was now involved up to his eyelids.

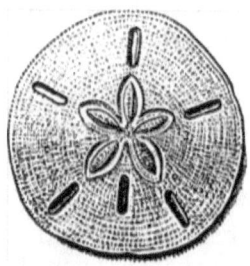

Twenty-Two

The next morning she dragged herself awake before Cooper and sat up in bed. She cut her eyes around the little bedroom inside her bungalow and realized last night hadn't been a dream. She still needed to give Brent a complete accounting of what had transpired.

She looked over at Coop's sleeping form and was tempted to run her hands under the sheets to make up. But he looked so peaceful she decided to let him sleep.

Instead of make-up sex, she hobbled into the shower to wash off the layer of grime from the trek through the mud.

By the time she got out of the bathroom, Cooper was no longer asleep. After getting dressed, she made her way into the kitchen where he sat stoic, drinking his first cup of coffee. The way he held his shoulders, rigid and unyielding, showed no signs their tiff was over. He barely said two words and then grunted through a bowl of corn flakes.

"I thought you wanted to clear the air," Eastlyn charged as she took down a bowl from the cabinet. "Not talking to me is clearly the way to keep the animosity going."

"Let's see. You're upset because I'm angry. The thing is I'm still trying to process the fact that you took a job as Brent's deputy and didn't bother to mention it. I'm just the guy you're hitting the sheets with and no one important enough to confide in about the important stuff."

"That's not fair."

"Sure it is," he grumbled. "My resentment is all I have. I don't particularly care for cunning women with their own agenda. I had enough of that as a kid watching my mother's manipulative games play out."

"Don't you dare compare me to your mother!" Eastlyn fumed. "I didn't manipulate you. I just didn't tell you about going to the compound because I knew you'd react this way. Well, maybe not this bad, but I knew you'd be pissed. So far I haven't been disappointed. This is the very scene I wanted to avoid."

"I see. So my reaction is not something you worried overly much about. Thanks for that."

"That's not what I meant at all. Don't you see? I had to make sure I could do this thing by myself, without help from anyone." She raked her fingers through her damp hair. "I wasn't sure but I thought maybe after everything I might've lost my nerve."

Cooper melted a little as he got to his feet to put his bowl in the sink. Without warning, he snaked his arm out, seized her around the waist. "You, lose your nerve? That'll be the day. You have a steel spine when it comes to formidable situations. It's in your DNA. Don't you know that about yourself by now?"

She laid her head on his shoulder. "I'm sorry I didn't tell you about going out to the compound."

"I'm sorry I yelled at you. But I really was worried you might not make it out of there without getting your head bashed in."

"If Scott hadn't showed up to run interference, I might not have."

"He's the one who told me where you'd gone."

She cocked a brow. "Oh really? The traitor. I should've known he couldn't keep his trap shut."

"Obviously Scott was worried too because he showed up out there right when things might've gone south."

"Hmm, I guess you're right. He did tell me the best way to make it back to the car."

"See, Scott was looking out for you."

"Yeah, just like River said he would." She ran her fingers up his chest. "Last night you mentioned an adrenaline rush. Was that for real? Could the bookworm become an adrenaline junkie?"

"Possibly. But only if my partner chooses to fully disclose what she's up to."

She held up a hand. "Scout's honor. No more lying."

His hands went around her shoulders. The look in his eyes said he wanted to make up.

The knock at the door stalled that.

Eastlyn flung it back to see Nick standing there.

"I know it's a Saturday but I tried to call before stopping by out of the blue like this. You didn't answer your cell," Nick pointed out.

She puffed out a laugh. "I probably cut it off last night and must've forgotten to turn it back on when I got up. Come on in."

"Hey, Coop, how's it going?"

Cooper looked over at Eastlyn. "Better every day. Want some coffee?"

"No thanks. I had to run to Ferguson's this morning to pick up paint. Our three-year-old went crazy yesterday with a batch of permanent markers trying to recreate the Mona Lisa, or something. Whatever it is, it takes up a swath across the living room wall." He turned to look at Eastlyn. "Anyway, I thought you'd like to know you're free to start work on the chopper. Paperwork's all taken care of. I also thought you'd like to know that I was able to trace the aircraft's ownership."

Her pulse picked up. "And?"

"It was originally bought by the Navy in 1953. The U.S. Coast Guard purchased it from the government for use in search and rescue. Cleef came across it at an army surplus auction over in Scott's Valley in 1988. There's some indication Cleef thought it had been used in the TV series *MASH* and had some value for resale. When that turned out not to be the case, he obviously couldn't find a buyer for it. I did come across an interesting side note to its history. That copter once participated in the manhunt for escaped Alcatraz prisoners in June, 1962. For roughly two weeks the crew flew over Angel Island looking for any signs of men or bodies."

Eastlyn pumped a fist in the air. "Yes, I knew it had a history. Every helicopter deserves an interesting backstory."

That afternoon, she drove to Eternal Gardens to meet with Brent again. During the face-to-face update, they sat on the same park bench as before.

"What you have out there is essentially a fully fortified hideaway. Thorwald or Edgecombe, somebody, has made sure that place is locked down tight and anyone who tries to breach the perimeter won't take the same wrong path twice." She went into detail about all the booby traps. "The two trap guns installed in front and behind the cabin were the last two things I found before company came calling."

"Those are illegal and dangerous," Brent stated, scrubbing a hand down his face. "What if you hadn't spotted them?"

"But I did."

"Did anyone see you?"

"They probably would have if not for... This will sound strange. But your wife would understand this a lot better than you."

"Understand what?"

She hesitated but then decided she might as well tell him all of it. "Scott Phillips warned me right before those two guys converged on my position."

With a bob of his head, Brent nodded. "I'm well aware Scott does things like that."

"You are? Well, so much for guarding a well-known secret ghost. Anyway, those mechanical devices alone are enough for you to make an arrest. That's the good news. You'd nail Thorwald for *something*. The bad news is you wouldn't get him for trafficking, which is really what you want."

"Thorwald must've set out all those traps to keep local hunters at bay, keep trespassers away from getting a look at that meth lab. He's gone to extreme measures to make sure his people living out there are left alone. Knowing all that, how do all these kids keep getting the meth? How are they gaining entry?"

"To the compound?" Eastlyn shook her head. "That's just it. I don't think kids are getting in. My guess is Thorwald handpicks a few dealers he can trust. Those dealers go in and bring the stuff out of the compound then distribute it to the various local sellers. Think about it. That would be the best way to ensure that no one like me goes in there for a simple buy. He'd feel that same way about a bunch of high school kids, who would surely blab. Then it would get out to the masses that Thorwald's a major supplier. Not good for business. But if Thorwald only deals with people he knows, people he trusts, he lessens the risk that his enterprise crumbles over loose lips or over the sale of a few dime bags sold to two-bit junkies, not on his land anyway."

"Makes sense. But what about all the traffic Bran and Joy reported seeing at all hours?"

"All I saw were evidence that kids were using the secluded road to make out." She took out her cell phone and held it up to him. "As you probably know by now, due to the party, I got there later than I'd planned. But I took pictures of the meth lab."

Brent took the phone, studied the shack. "Look at all the hazardous waste leaking into the environment. There must be fifty or sixty pounds of the stuff."

"Statistics show that for every ten pounds of meth that's the stuff left over."

"What else do you have there?"

"A picture of this guy. He was coming right toward me so it's a little dark and fuzzy."

"I'll say. You forgot to mention you're lousy at taking photos."

She chuckled. "Such a critic. It's not something I'm proud of. Do you recognize the guy?"

"Honestly, there's no way I could make out who that is if he walked right up to me this minute."

"Sorry for the bad quality. I'll do better next time."

"There won't be a next time."

"Why not?"

"Obviously, you can't enter the compound under the guise of needing a fix."

"But I can still use the second trip to gain valuable information."

"It's too risky, Eastlyn."

"Not as risky as it was the first time. Now I know my way to and from the cabin. This time, I'll get out there much earlier and stake out the area, maybe spread out and get pictures of the compound itself, the living quarters, write down plate numbers of the cars coming and going."

The look on his face said he wasn't convinced. "You want Thorwald bad enough, I'm the best shot you have."

Brent chewed the inside of his jaw. "Okay. But after you get back to town, I want full disclosure. Call me. We'll plan to meet in the alleyway behind the used car lot. You'll hand off any intel you gained then."

"Roger that."

There was another argument ramping up as she got dressed to go back to the compound.

"I'm going with you," Cooper insisted.

"No, you're not. It's better if one person makes that trek, not two. Besides, this is my assignment. I'm the person who has the military training to make it work. And if I should get caught, the ruse is still I'm there on the property because I'm a newcomer in town who heard this is the best place in the county to buy crack."

She finished applying the makeup to her face that gave her a gaunt appearance and added, "I look like a cracked-out addict while you, on the other hand, look like a choirboy and nothing like a strung-out junkie."

Insulted, the scowl he sent her said it all. Coop set his jaw, ready to do battle. "I do not look like a choirboy. My hair's longer than yours. That certainly plays better as a druggie than clean-cut. I'm sure not a wide-eyed innocent. For God's sakes, I've walked down alleyways in Brixton to get to the tube while gangs patrolled the streets nearby just so I could get the best shots of London's underground. So there's no point in arguing. I'm going with you, and that's that. You're just wasting your time."

"Look at you, you couldn't possibly pull off the drug addict role."

"Wanna bet? I can pretend to be as out of it as you. Give me that makeup kit and fifteen minutes and I'll prove it to you." When he saw the roll of her eyes, he stubbornly added, "I'm not letting you walk in there alone without backup and that's all there is to it. Certainly not if there's a chance you'll get caught. I didn't want to break it to you but you leave me no choice. You're not that great of an actress."

Offended, she huffed out, "I am so."

"You're not. There's no guarantee your pretend performance as a buyer will even work. Then what will you do? If we go together there's a greater likelihood that we'll look like two stumbling meth heads out to score. By yourself, I doubt Thorwald will buy into that story. You need me. It's non-negotiable. I'm disappointed Brent is willing to send you in there alone."

"That's unfair to Brent. He can't exactly stroll into the lion's den and expect the ruse to work when he'd be recognized in two seconds, now can he? Since Brent would give the whole thing away, there's no one else to go in there but me. I have a chance to pull this off and I'm taking it." She laid her hand on his arm. "Cooper, we had a really great day today, don't ruin it by doing this again."

"That might be true about Brent, but you just made my case for me. There's no one else who'd be willing to go with you. I'm it. You shouldn't go in there without backup and you know it. Keep in mind, I'm new in town, too, or have you forgotten? It's unlikely the Thorwalds would know me unless they somehow wandered into my shop. And even if one of the dealers has seen me around town, for all they know, I'm the newcomer from the Bay Area with a drug problem of my own."

"I'm not gonna be able to shake you, am I?"

"Not unless you possess the power of an eight-point earthquake, which you don't, you're not walking out that door without me."

"Then come on. Let's roll. Use the makeup to lighten up the area around your eyes. See, like I did." She showed off her Goth look. "It sells the sullen junkie. But if Brent finds out I let you come with me, he'll have my temporary badge."

"Big deal. So you'll find another job."

She grinned. "If I'm on borrowed time we might as well make this count. Grab your camera. Tonight you're the designated picture-taker."

It wasn't until they were sitting in the Bronco that Cooper handed her the keys. She angled in the seat to stare at him. "You actually confiscated these? That's low *and* sneaky. Just for that it gives me sheer satisfaction at seeing you have to put on makeup."

"I walked right into this, didn't I?" Cooper complained with an affable grin.

"Hey, you insisted on coming." She batted her eyes at him. "To protect the little woman. I'm grateful."

"Could've fooled me," he moaned as he began to smear on the light-colored pancake with a sponge.

She patted his knee and gunned the engine at the same time. "Oh, but I am. Not many guys would do this."

While Cooper made up his face, Eastlyn went over what she'd already discussed with Brent. "Just so you're up to speed, I'm thinking the only people who get into that compound are Thorwald's longtime sellers, people he knows personally and trusts."

"That's why you dropped the buyer ruse."

"Exactly. It won't work with him because he doesn't mess with smalltime drug users looking for a hit. Just follow me and watch out for booby traps."

"Booby traps?" Cooper swallowed hard in a show of fake fear. "I'm beginning to think this was a mistake. Why not just drop me off at the turnoff?"

"Very funny. That's what I love about you, your sense of humor. But if we get caught…that story about needing a fix is our fallback."

Cooper suddenly blurted out, "I've got it, a much better reason why we're in the area. It just occurred to me. We say we're out here taking photographs of the countryside."

"At night?"

"Sure. I brought my prime lens with me, a fixed-focal-length lens designed to take much better photos at night. If Thorwald doesn't believe us, I've got the equipment to show we're on the level."

"That's brilliant and so much better than this stupid Goth look we're sporting. But what am I doing out here with you, holding the camera?"

He began looking around for a napkin to use to get rid of the makeup on his face. "In a way. You're my assistant. All I need is to find the right angle, an elevated rise in the landscape where I can look down into the compound and focus on the out buildings, the meth lab, and the entry gate. You lead me to that kind of area and I'll get you the best shots."

"Brilliant," she repeated. "I love it. You're like that character, Robert Kincaid, in *The Bridges of Madison*

County. But instead of doing a photographic essay on old bridges, you're looking for old barns."

"Let's just hope we won't need either story."

Twenty minutes later, Eastlyn brought the Ford to a stop in an old asphalt parking lot.

"This is different than where I waited for you last night," Cooper noted.

"And should make our story more believable. If you check the map, you'll discover Cleef's old barn is about a half-mile from here. But we're going to take off walking in that direction." She pointed south and to the east.

Loading up the rucksack and camera case and the other supplies, they started out through the brush like pack mules. The dark woods beckoned ahead. Unlike the night before when it was foggy and misty, tonight the sky was clear with twinkling stars overhead.

Up the first gentle slope, to the tune of crickets and night peepers, Eastlyn whispered, "No more talking from this point forward."

"What do we do, use hand signals?" Cooper joked. To highlight the query, he pointed two fingers at his eyes and then turned them toward Eastlyn like he'd seen people do in the movies. The gesture meant, "I see you."

She cracked up with laughter and playfully tapped him on the shoulder. "Shhh, quit clowning around now or you'll give us away."

She took out a GPS, motioned for him to follow her down the incline. They hiked onto what looked like a well-worn trailhead, then deviated to a more obscure path, tangled with vines and underbrush.

They came to a shallow stream with pretty moss-covered rocks. Water birch and box elder were thickest here, along with trailing ivy and fan palm. They sloshed through the water where the creek tapered into a narrow inlet as it twisted and turned into thicker scrub.

They waded into a labyrinth of boulders until coming out on the other side. Eastlyn pointed to a hill and then made a gesture downward, indicating the compound was below the ridge.

Hugging the side of the slope, Cooper trailed after her as they both inched their way to the edge before it dropped off into a basin. The valley below was wide enough to hold the series of buildings and homes that made up the compound.

He peered over the crest, spotted the fence surrounding the property, the barbed wire keeping outsiders from breaching the border. He spotted activity below, a campfire, an assortment of cars and trucks parked within the circle of fence.

The encampment was massive in size and scope. Counting heads, Eastlyn decided it had to be home to at least fifteen families. Children ran around the fire as if it were the best summer camp experience of their young lives. It was hard to believe these kids had parents who'd taken to cooking meth as a source of income.

Cooper took out his Nikon, zoomed in, aiming his lens on the bivouacked inhabitants below. From this perspective Eastlyn could see what she'd missed last night. There were indeed guards stationed every forty feet or so along the inside perimeter. Their positions couldn't be seen from the cabin where she'd been last night.

But they could definitely have seen her.

After forty-five minutes, Eastlyn motioned for Coop to slide back down the hill.

As surveillance went, the endeavor had generated a disk full of pictures. But they still had to get off that ridge without anyone detecting their presence.

Before Cooper could pack up the gear, that proved to be tricky. Eastlyn caught sight of one of the guards staring up at them on the peak. Through the binoculars she studied the lookout while the lookout did the same to her. She signaled Cooper to remain perfectly still, and waited, trying to determine if they'd been spotted.

But when the guard didn't sound an alarm, she tapped Cooper on the shoulder and indicated for them to get out of there.

But then the dogs inside the compound started barking. It was as if the place lit up like a Christmas tree. The other side of the knoll was swathed in bright light. Gunshots rang out. A bullet whizzed past Eastlyn's ear.

Her military training kicked in. She reached for the small revolver she'd strapped to her ankle, just in case Thorwald's men charged.

They moved quickly down the hillside. Using the GPS, Eastlyn led the way back through the thick brush. She estimated it would take at least ten minutes for the guards to catch up with them, maybe longer. It gave them a scant head start. She used that time to scuttle through dense thickets in the dark, finally picking up the path they'd taken earlier.

They heard dogs in the distance, which meant they needed to keep up the pace.

Forging ahead, they came to the little stream again, and rushed across the water. From there, Eastlyn was able to locate the trailhead, which led them back to the Bronco.

Cooper started up the engine about the same time a rifle shot pinged off the pavement. He peeled out of the lot about the time two men emerged from the forest of trees.

Back home in Cooper's study, the adrenaline still pumped through their veins from the close call. While Cooper downloaded the pictures from his camera disk to his laptop, Eastlyn paced. The only time she stopped was to peer over his shoulder, impatient, to check his progress.

A time or two she stopped to appreciate the quality of his work. "Man, you got some good shots. You can even make out faces, license plates, and detail."

"I'm glad you approve of my work."

"Approve? You could pick up some extra bucks with that zoom lens as a member of the paparazzi."

The doorbell sang out and Eastlyn immediately thumped her head. "Uh-oh. I think in all the excitement I forgot to meet Brent like I promised."

Sure enough, when Cooper didn't answer fast enough whoever was out in the courtyard started pounding on the door.

Cooper flung it back to see Brent Cody agitated and pissed off. "Is Eastlyn here?"

Eastlyn stuck her head into the other room, immediately remorseful. "I'm sorry. Calling you completely slipped my mind. But we had a situation."

"So you're okay?"

"I am now."

Brent sent Cooper a long aggravated gaze. "What do you mean 'we' had a situation? You went with her, didn't you?" He turned his rage on Eastlyn. "You told him. So much for keeping your mouth shut."

"I didn't want her going out there alone. Besides, I'm a photographer, taking pictures is what I do for a living." To prove it, Cooper shoved the ones he'd already printed into Brent's chest. "These are good enough for you to get an idea what the inside of that compound looks like and who lives there."

"Now these are detailed. Let's have a look at the rest," Brent uttered, following Cooper into the other room and to the laptop set up on the desk. "Now we're talking."

"That's the beauty of the right filter and a zoom lens. Look at this one. If I'm not mistaken the camera caught this guy making a buy. Who knows how much meth is in those bags he's loading up in his truck?"

Brent's eyes bugged out. "It looks like he's counting out cash for the buy."

"Yeah, if I remember correctly I thought at the time it seemed close to three grand."

Eastlyn noticed Brent's jaw lock. "Do you recognize him?"

"Yeah, his name's Titus Driscoll. He lives in Pelican Pointe right around the corner from the elementary school."

"Our school? Then you just found your connection."

"You guys found it. I never thought Titus would stoop so low as to get himself mixed up with drugs."

"What's Driscoll's story?"

"He did serve time back in his early twenties for a couple of burglaries. I thought he'd put crime behind him. I guess not."

Eastlyn ran a hand through her mop of hair. "You know, I hate to point this out to you, but this Driscoll guy probably isn't limiting his activity to San Sebastian."

"That's why we need to find out all the places Titus frequents. I already know he hangs out quite a bit at McCready's."

"Maybe that should be your starting point. Although what sense does it make to go after Titus if you let Thorwald continue his operation?"

Brent frowned. "I have no intention of letting Thorwald continue."

"So this is it? I'm done in law enforcement? If so, my career will probably go down in some record book as having the shortest shelf life ever."

Brent patted her shoulder. "No need to worry. For now, you're my number one part-time officer."

"Hey, I'm you're only officer."

"That, too. Between the two of us, we'll keep an eye on Titus."

"What do I do?" Cooper asked.

Eastlyn ran a hand down his arm. "You show me how to take these kinds of pictures and I'll be forever grateful."

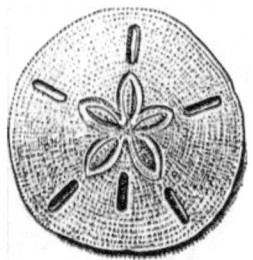

Twenty-Three

Children and lazy summer days seemed to go hand in hand. High on the list of things for them to do, hanging out at the beach ranked tops among their favorite.

That's why this Sunday parents had crammed the shoreline with their kids in tow. They stretched out on beach towels, blankets, and lawn chairs. They brought coolers packed with ice cold drinks and prepared for a day of swimming and surfing.

It was no secret that teenage girls, like Sonoma and Sonnet Rafferty, mostly preferred sunbathing to getting wet. They tended to migrate toward their respective cliques in packs and took up a lot of beach. They also had no trouble attracting teenage boys like gnats. All the girls had to do was show up wearing a skimpy bikini, slather sun tan lotion all over their bodies, lounge around on a stingy towel, and their male counterparts flocked around them in protective mode like guard dogs

It was the opposite thinking for energetic eight-year-old boys. They liked to stay in the water as long as possible. But even they had to come onshore eventually. It was impractical to expect to spend all day floating in the waves.

But rambunctious grade-schoolers on land didn't mix well with teen girls spread out and taking up valuable room on the ground. It seemed whenever the kids got around the teenagers, trouble brewed. The crowds around the girls made it almost impossible to find enough room to run around and play. For three energetic grade-schoolers like Jonah Delacourt, Tommy Gates, and Bobby Prather, war games and sand football were best played with a lot of space to roam.

Crowded space meant three active boys couldn't toss a football around without bumping into someone. Bumping into people, especially the teenage girls, brought complaints. If someone wanted to run a pass route or build a fort or even play combat with their army men and action figures, they had to put up with bitching and moaning just because their toys flew through the air and hit someone on the nose.

So after getting yelled at for the umpteenth time by several older teens, Jonah, Tommy, and Bobby decided to move on to someplace else.

"I'm bored with playing army anyway," Tommy grumbled.

"Me too," Jonah said in agreement. "If we can't sand bomb the troops without a bunch of girls squealing on us to their boyfriends, what's the point?"

"I wish the movie theater was open," Bobby moaned. "Since your mom and dad own the thing, we could spend the day in there."

"Nah," Jonah said. "They'd probably show some stupid love story movie that nobody but girls wants to see."

"Then what do we do now?" Tommy wanted to know with slumped shoulders. "I'm bored and tired of getting yelled at."

"I know what we can do," Jonah piped up. "Let's go see if Dr. Bennett will take us out on the *Moonlight Mile* and give us a tour of the bay."

The *Moonlight Mile* was a fifty-foot, renovated fishing trawler the Rescue Center used for a research vessel. The boat was kept docked on the south side of Smuggler's Bay directly behind the animal enclosure.

"That's not a bad idea, Delacourt," Bobby said, slapping his buddy on the back. "We could pretend to sail her out of the harbor like pirates."

"Let's do it," Jonah said eagerly.

"Shouldn't we tell our dads first?" Tommy suggested. "They're back there talking to Mr. Rafferty about selling the tourists more T-shirts."

Jonah scratched his bare belly, then his head. "Nah, all adults ever do is keep telling you not to interrupt them. Besides, we won't be gone that long. It's just around the bend on the other side of the bay."

Abandoning the football they'd been tossing around and all the other toys in the sand, the trio took off down the opposite end of the beach. They trailed past the fancy restaurant. They heard the sound of electrical saws and drills coming from the boatyard. By the time they reached the back end of the Fanning Rescue Center, they heard the din of the resident seals barking and carrying on.

But when they got to the dock area, the boat was nowhere in sight.

Bobby's shoulders slumped. "Just our lousy luck. I guess they had to go rescue something."

"So what do we do now?" Jonah asked.

"How about we go climb those rocks over there?"

Jonah's eyes bugged out. "Those rocks in the middle of the water? I'm not swimming out there. My dad says the current's too strong."

Disappointed, Bobby toed a rock. "Now what are we gonna do?"

Tommy picked at the scab on his elbow, turned to Bobby. "Remember that time you ran away from home? What did you do all that time you were gone?"

Bobby wasn't about to tell anyone how scared he'd been during that time. "Oh, man, it was great. I headed south of town, stuck to the highway, and just kept going. There's this overhang off the 101 that sticks out over the ocean. I crawled out over rocks to look at an owl's nest, thought about spending the night there. I'll show it to you if you want."

That sounded like a better Sunday adventure than the dumb old beach.

"Was it a family of owls, baby ones?" Jonah asked.

"Sure. The babies didn't even have their eyes open yet. There's a bunch of 'em. And they were fuzzy-looking and brown."

Jonah bobbed up and down. "Do you think they're still on the cliff? Let's go see 'em."

"I'll lead the way," Bobby said with confidence.

Beginning to have second thoughts about going that far without his dad, Tommy shifted his feet. "Maybe we should go home, get our bikes, and tell someone where we're going. It'll be pretty far on foot."

Eager to show off the spot he'd found on his own, Bobby dismissed that notion. "Nah. It's just down the road a little ways. Besides, if we go back now we'll probably get stuck with that horde of people on the beach. Who wants to spend the afternoon doing that if we can't play without getting into trouble?"

Jonah dipped his head in agreement. He'd already made up his mind what he wanted to do if it meant getting to see baby birds. "Then what are we waiting for? Let's go."

In the hope of doing something different for a change away from the watchful eyes of parents, the three boys trekked off in the direction of the cliffs south of town, on a quest to get to know screech owls up close and personal.

Back on the beach the boys' dads sat in camp chairs lined up in a row on the sand. Their debates ranged from raising active boys to dating after divorce to NFL football.

Forty-year-old Archer Gates had survived a tough year, maybe the toughest of his life. After going through an expensive and nasty divorce, Archer had moved out of the house in Fresno he'd shared with his cheating wife, and brought his son Tommy back home where he could raise him in a less hectic environment. His wife hadn't wanted custody, hadn't fought to see Tommy, nor had she asked for visitation. All she'd wanted was to get on with her life.

That was fine by Archer. He'd found a decent-paying job installing cable for a company over in San Sebastian and he was happy living back in Pelican Pointe.

Archer's situation had mirrored single-dad Greg Prather's. Both men were raising their sons alone just as Thane had been doing until meeting and marrying Isabella last year.

Archer rubbed his chin. "I've dated some since coming back, but let's face it, my date with Sydney Reed will be hard to top. We went over to Santa Cruz to see a movie, but instead of that we snuck into this little dive Ethan told me about and closed the place down dancing to a live band."

Greg shook his head. "Not me. I have no desire to date. Right now, I'm concentrating on doing right by Bobby."

"How'd Bobby do in school this year?" Thane asked. "Jonah says Bobby's not picking on other kids the way he used to."

"A lot better. Julianne said she's never seen a kid do such a one-eighty in temperament like Bobby has. All that bickering and fighting his mother and I did really took a toll on him. Now that his mother is no longer in the picture and he isn't witnessing a battle of wills every single day, it's like he's a different kid."

They shifted from that topic to the recent NFL draft and how well their respective teams had fared.

After picking apart the upcoming supplemental draft, Thane glanced over and looked around the beach. He stopped in mid-sentence. "Where's Jonah? I don't see that boy anywhere."

Archer Gates waved Thane off. "He's over there, playing with Tommy." Archer bobbed his head toward the water, expecting to see his son playing in the sand, and frowned when he didn't.

Greg Prather groused, "I hope Bobby's not bothering those girls again. God, I'm glad I don't have a daughter. Ever notice how teen girls spend most of their time shrieking and squealing? That would drive me up the wall. Then there's the way they dress. I wouldn't let a teenage girl of mine out of the house in a two-piece bathing suit like some of these other girls wear."

"Don't be so sure about that," Thane said, still trying to pick out Jonah in the sea of bodies. "Malachi does his best to keep tabs on his two, but says they're a handful and pretty much know all his buttons to push whenever his back's turned. Raising kids, boys or girls, is a challenge on the best of days."

Thane slicked his hair back, got to his feet to get a better view. "I don't see Jonah anywhere. I hope he isn't cannon-balling off the pier again."

He put his hand up over his eyes to block out the sun and scanned the bay, counted the surfers in the water. But he didn't spot Jonah.

Thane zigzagged his way through beachgoers to get to the edge, a ball of alarm hitting him in the gut when he didn't see his son swimming.

His heart pounded in his chest as he realized Jonah wasn't in the water. Thane began to yell out in alarm. "Jonah! Jonah! Where are you? Answer me!" He took off in the other direction, back toward the street. If he found Jonah playing between the cars, they'd go home right this minute.

But Jonah was nowhere in sight. Full-blown panic set in as he raced back to the pier. With each foot that hit the sand, fear swept through him. He spun toward Greg and Archer. "What if they got caught in the current under the wharf and were swept out into the bay?"

Archer took off in a run to see for himself with Greg following.

"Wouldn't someone have surely seen that?" Greg reasoned, a wall of terror building up.

Thane cupped his hands around his mouth and yelled as loud as he could, "Has anyone seen three boys? Did anyone see if they went into the water? Help us find our kids!"

Other than stirring everybody up, he didn't get the results he wanted. That's when realization hit him. The three boys were gone.

The blood drained from his face. His stomach felt sick.

Archer and Greg came running up. "The boy's action figures are still there on the sand. So is the football they were tossing around. Wherever they are, they must have gone together."

"Let's try looking down the beach where it curves around to the Fanning Rescue Center," Greg suggested. "They probably went to visit the animals. Bobby does that sometimes. He loves that place."

But after forty minutes of searching everywhere they could think to look, they didn't find the boys. Thane called Isabella to see if, by chance, Jonah had walked home with his friends. But she hadn't seen him either.

"I'll be right there," Isabella promised.

"I'm hanging up now to call Brent," Thane told her as he ended the call and punched in Brent's number.

Brent's phone rang inside his home across the street. Trying to calm Thane down was like trying to put out a raging wildfire with a water pistol.

"We'll find them, Thane. We have a system in place for this very thing. I'll mobilize a search right away utilizing our list of volunteers to get the word out."

While Brent made the jog across to the wharf, it went through his head that he'd been through this same scenario once before with Bobby Prather and it had turned out fine.

He reminded himself of that as he sprinted up to three worried fathers. "Did the boys get in trouble earlier? Were they angry about anything in particular that might have made them want to take off?"

Thane folded his arms across his chest, tucked his fingers under to keep his hands from shaking. "I didn't know it when I called you but some of the older boys got on to them about running around on the beach and annoying people. The teens told them to stop getting in their way and go find someplace else to play. I guess they did. No one has seen them since. I need to go get my truck and look for them. It'll be getting dark soon."

"Look at me, Thane. Look at me," Brent said again. "You're too upset to get behind the wheel. That's why the three of you should stay put here in case the boys circle back. Let me handle this. I'll call county and make sure they get Search and Rescue involved."

While Murphy handed out grid maps of the town sectioned off to start the hunt, Brent ordered everyone within earshot to begin canvassing the neighborhood.

After Brent gave his pep talk, the next thing he did was place a call to Eastlyn. "Are you ready to earn your deputy pay? We have three missing kids."

"I'll be right there."

By the time Eastlyn and Cooper pulled up at the pier, fifty people had already turned out within fifteen minutes of getting the call.

They hopped out of Eastlyn's Bronco and dashed down to the beach area where everyone had gathered.

Eastlyn bounded up to Brent and wanted to know, "Have you notified Search and Rescue?"

"I did, but they're dealing with a boat accident twenty miles out of Monterey Bay, several missing are feared drowned. They promised me they'd pull someone off that and head this way to patrol along the coast as soon as they can."

"So, in the meantime, it's up to us. Who's handling the grid? And where do you want me? North? South? East?"

Brent took out a map. "This is where I found Bobby the last time he did this, south of town at the San Sebastian cutoff."

"This happened before?"

"With Bobby. Last fall. I don't think this is a runaway situation with Jonah and Tommy or Bobby, for that matter. I think these kids went exploring." Brent circled an area behind the Rescue Center. "The dads already checked here and here. But my idea is three boys with time to kill on a Sunday afternoon would want some excitement."

"Okay, so where should we start?"

"South. We'll take two cars. You keep to the coast road."

"That two-lane job that hugs the cliffs?"

"That's the one. I'll take the 101 as it branches off and go back to where I found Bobby near the turnoff." He handed her a two-way radio. "Use this between us. If any of the dads call your cell phone, try to keep your voice level, the chatter upbeat."

"Got it." As she headed to the car, she thought of something and abruptly turned back. "Does this mean everyone will know I'm working for you and that it's no longer a secret?"

Brent shook his head. "Are you wearing a uniform? No. You don't officially have a badge yet either. Look around you at all the folks who turned out to help in the search. We're not giving anything away here. Right this minute, you're just another concerned citizen looking for three missing kids. Is that okay with you?"

"I guess it'll have to be."

It was well after dark when Eastlyn U-turned the Bronco around for her fourth trip up and down the narrow stretch of pavement barely wide enough for one car. She'd detoured here once before the day she'd gone to the barn alone and made a wrong turn. But that had been in broad daylight, not the pitch-black darkness she found herself in now. With only her headlights to guide the way, she could only imagine how three young boys might feel getting lost out here, scared, and this far from home.

As remote and isolated as it was, she was beginning to think Brent had deliberately stuck her way out here on purpose, for less interaction with the townspeople.

"Is it possible three kids on foot could even walk this far?" she muttered to herself, not expecting an answer. She should've known better.

"Never underestimate the curiosity of small boys," Scott said, looking out the window from the passenger seat. "They're out here somewhere."

Eastlyn rolled her eyes. "Could you narrow down 'somewhere' a little bit for me? This Bronco isn't exactly fuel-efficient. If I don't spot something soon, I'll have to head back to town for gas. What would they find to do out here anyway?"

"Bobby wanted the other two to see the owl's nest on the other side of this bluff. It got dark on them." Scott pointed to the other side of the road. "There, up ahead. See, on the shoulder. They're waving you down."

Eastlyn hit the high beams and sure enough, she spotted three filthy little urchins walking along the dirt track. They looked bone-tired and fed up with adventure. At some point, each one had shed tears because they had white streaks on their faces. But they were safe and that was the important thing.

Eastlyn pulled up alongside, wishing she had a badge to show the kids to put them at ease. "Is anyone hurt?"

"Will you take us home?" Tommy groaned. "We're hungry."

"You bet. I have a cell phone. Want to call your dads?"

But Bobby gaped at her. "You're the woman who talked to us at school about flying. She flies Black Hawk helicopters."

Eastlyn couldn't help it, she grinned. "That's right. I used to. So you guys want to call your dads or what? Who's first?" She held out the phone to Jonah because he looked like he needed to hear a friendly voice the most.

"My dad's gonna be so mad at me," Jonah mumbled. On the verge of tears, he hesitated to dial the number.

Tommy was in the same frame of mind. "You watch. Mine's gonna ground me for the rest of the summer. I won't get out of the house for months."

Eastlyn looked at Bobby, who had yet to offer a dire look into his future. "Did you find the owl's nest?"

They all started talking at once as they scurried into the backseat. They rattled on about birds and a ledge and how they almost fell off the side of the cliff.

"Okay, okay," Eastlyn finally said. "The whole town is out looking for you guys. Your dads are worried sick. Trust me on this one point, they'll be elated to hear from you."

Jonah wanted clarification. "Does that mean they won't be mad?"

"It means they'll be so glad to see you they won't lecture you until well after you eat when they put you to bed tonight."

That seemed to satisfy them all the way around.

She dug into the backpack she'd brought along and pulled out a bottle of water. She handed it off to Tommy. "Next time you guys decide to go exploring, make sure you bring supplies with you. And don't crawl out onto a cliff."

The boys took turns guzzling the water while Eastlyn picked up her radio to notify Brent. The whole time her passengers fought over who'd get to use the cell phone first.

Cooper had gone door to door from one end of Ocean Street to the other. After coming up empty, he stood on the boardwalk doing what he could to calm Thane and Isabella, Archer and Greg.

Small talk hadn't worked as he stood with them waiting for Search and Rescue to show up. So far, no chopper had appeared to search the water, or to fly along the coastline. The search dogs hadn't even made it there yet. "It's frustrating to wait this long for county help to get here."

"I was just thinking the same thing," Thane grumbled. "What's taking them so damn long?"

Isabella latched onto Thane's arm. "Brent said they're dealing with another emergency. But they should be here by now."

Cooper nodded. "It's a shame Eastlyn's just started work on the chopper. She was thinking about starting her own."

"Her own what?" Isabella asked, a confused look on her face.

"Her own search and rescue outfit for just this kind of crisis situation."

Thane cocked a brow. "How would she do that exactly?"

"Fixing up that old chopper rusting away out at Cleef's. I thought everyone in town knew about her plans to get it ready to fly. She wants to get her pilot's license back and start a rescue operation."

"I knew she wanted to fly again," Isabella noted. "But I had no idea her plans included something so vital to the community."

As if inspiration hit them at the same time, Thane and Isabella exchanged looks.

"You tell her to come see us first thing Monday morning," Thane said. "It's ridiculous to have to wait this long for the county to respond when our kids go missing. You tell Eastlyn we'll back whatever it is she needs to make it happen."

Thane had no sooner spoken the words than his cell phone rang. The number that came up was Eastlyn's. But Thane recognized the voice on the other end. "Jonah? Jonah, are you okay?

Cooper watched the man's face break into a grin.

"Eastlyn found the boys!" Thane shouted to Archer and Greg. His knees wanted to buckle in relief. "They're okay. They're fine. Thank God, they're okay."

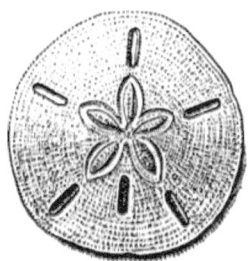

Twenty-Four

Eastlyn slapped the piece of paper down on the counter inside Layne's Trains and all but did a happy dance. "I just got notification I'm set to see the aviation doctor in Santa Cruz Friday. That's four more days from now. Do you know what this means?"

"That you can't party for the next ninety-six hours?" He came around his workspace and twirled her around.

"That, too. But it also means I'm getting closer to ShowTime with the FAA. My appointment is at nine a.m. I want you to go with me."

"Absolutely."

She threw her arms around his neck. "And just think what a good time celebrating we can have Friday night knowing I passed my physical."

His lips quirked, a lazy smile formed. "We don't have to abstain till Friday, do we?"

"Hardly. But I came in here for another reason. I'm planning to drag you to the meeting with Thane and Isabella. It seems like the right thing to do since the turn of events yesterday, and whatever you said to him prompted Thane to want to talk to me. I'm stoked at the prospect he might come through with the backing for my startup."

"When's the meeting? Where?"

"Thane said to stop by Longboard Pizza any time after the lunch crunch. You know what this means? If this becomes a reality, I'll have to give up at least one of my jobs."

He tossed out a laugh. "Thank God. I thought I'd have to hogtie you just to get to spend a few minutes of alone time."

"Come on. It isn't that bad. I don't work double shifts or anything and I'm always at home with you at night."

"So which one are you giving up? Landon will be disappointed if it's the garden center, but he'll understand."

"Good, because I don't think I can let go of the Lighthouse Project. It means too much to me since it was there that I first connected with so many people. Isabella's been a good friend to me. And since the plowing's done it means the job takes up the least amount of my time. All I do is make sure the volunteers show up to weed, make sure the irrigation system works, and keep the rabbits out of the lettuce."

Cooper cackled out another laugh. "Well, if that's all there is to it then no worries. Seriously, I think Landon gets that you aren't meant to spend the rest of your life operating a forklift for him. When will you let him know your decision?"

"It might as well be this afternoon. I won't leave him in the lurch, a two week notice should do it."

Friday morning Eastlyn was awake at four-thirty. It was still dark outside when she got out of bed leaving a still-sleeping Cooper curled into his pillow. She showered, got dressed and went into the kitchen to make coffee.

She was startled to see Scott sitting at her table.

"Don't screw this up."

The warning ticked her off a little. "How exactly do I screw up a physical? I've already completed my app online, answered all my medical history questions. And the last time I needed Band-Aids at Coastal Pharmacy, I sat down at one of those little self-checking blood pressure stations just to make sure it was normal. There's not one reason I should be worried about this part of the process. I have excellent height to weight ratio. I'm not allergic to anything. I have excellent vision."

"Who the hell are you out here talking to?" Cooper asked from the doorway, yawning, trying to wake up.

She turned to see an empty chair at the table. Letting out a deep sigh, she hit the button on the Mr. Coffee. "No one, no one at all, just muttering to myself. Good thing the physical doesn't cover stuff like that."

After getting the trip to the aviation doctor behind them, Cooper had just finished tapping together a frame for the latest photographs he called his "Lighthouse Series" when the shop door opened and in walked Caleb.

"I'm taking Abby Anderson out Saturday night."

An amused Cooper cracked a grin. "Aren't you supposed to be, I don't know, working or something, making deliveries right about now? You couldn't have just texted me with that update on your love life?"

Caleb sat down at the train table, started working the controls of the HO scale Santa Fe Flyer. "At least I keep you updated. Do I need to recite the rules of bros one more time so you'll understand the importance of full disclosure? You don't seem to get it."

Cooper detected a need in his younger brother for kinship. And then something else occurred to him. "You don't have a lot of friends in town, do you?"

Caleb visibly bristled. His shoulders slumped. But he kept his eyes glued to the train as it made its way around the track. "You escaped out of here. You left all the crap behind, only coming back for Christmases. Me? Some of the kids at school never forgot that I came from a nutcase."

Cooper went over to where Caleb sat. "It's true I ran out of here. I ran to escape, but I couldn't, not really. You can never truly escape your past. It's impossible to leave behind the memories. But you can learn to deal with them and understand how whatever Eleanor did, that's on her. Now I realize I've been a lousy brother to you over the years. And that's the last thing I ever wanted to be."

"No. You've always been the steady example to follow. That's why I was surprised, shocked really, when you decided to come back. For months, I wasn't sure you'd stay. Even after you bought your house, I still kept thinking I'd wake up and you'd be gone the next day."

Cooper slapped Caleb on the back. "I'm not going anywhere. My wandering days are over."

"Because of the hot pilot?"

Cooper grinned. "She's one reason. But you, Drea, Shelby, and Landon, are the other reasons. I tell you what, why don't you see if Abby's free later this evening and we all plan to meet over at McCready's for a round of beers and some stale nachos."

"You buying?"

"Sure. Eastlyn and I are celebrating. Aviation doc says she's physically fit to fly."

Caleb gave his brother a high-five. "Then we'll knock back a few and make it a party."

Once Eastlyn got into the habit of wearing dresses, she didn't seem to be able to resist making a weekly stop at Reclaimed Treasures just to go through the new inventory.

"I don't know how you manage to find such great stuff," Eastlyn told Julianne as she draped two tops and a skirt over her arm.

"During the school year, it's a challenge to find the time. But once summer gets here, I let loose and make trips back home to Santa Cruz, San Sebastian, you name it. I hit all my favorite places."

"Well, whatever it is you do, it works. Each time I come in here I find something new I want. And with your eye for color, I feel more at ease dressing for informal evenings around town."

Julianne grinned. "I'm glad you feel that way. It makes me think my little shop is as important as the bank."

"Oh, it is. My choices so far have gotten me a lot of compliments. I mean, I know I'll never be a fashionista but…"

"Who says you aren't?"

Eastlyn laughed. "It's okay. I don't really want to be a fashion guru. I just want to look my best when I'm out with Cooper."

Julianne pointed a finger. "Now you listen to me. Since the assembly, I've had three girls come up to me—from first grade to fifth—and tell me they wanted to become pilots because of you."

"Really?"

"You bet. You're much better than some fashion trendsetter, you're a role model."

"Hmm, come to think of it I don't mind doing a man's job driving a forklift or plowing, but I've discovered I like the look on Cooper's face when he sees me dressed up."

About that time her cell phone dinged with a text from him suggesting happy hour. She held up the message to Julianne. "See, I like the idea of putting on something other than jeans to mingle."

"It never hurts to show off our girlie side during downtime," Julianne said.

Pleased with that assessment of herself, Eastlyn bought several flattering outfits.

At home she showered, kept her curly hair sassy and wild looking. She changed into a white swing sleeveless tank that showed off her tan lean arms. She wrapped a flowing Mercado skirt around her hips, draped a turquoise necklace around her neck for color, and let little moons in sterling silver hang at her ears.

Walking into the drab, dark pool hall, Cooper decided she was the most beautiful thing there. But the stark change in her appearance did make a lot people do a double take, including several of the men at the bar.

Caleb and his date, Abby Anderson, waited for them at a table near the back.

Abby waved wildly at Cooper but almost didn't recognize Eastlyn. "You look awesome. What's gotten into you lately?"

Eastlyn lifted a shoulder in a casual sign that said she did this all the time. "What? A girl shouldn't dress up and make an event out of having a drink? These days, I do it all the time."

"She does," Cooper said with a grin. "She's the sort of woman who looks good in anything she wears, but mostly, mostly, she looks best wearing nothing at all."

Eastlyn felt her face flush. She elbowed Cooper playfully in the ribs as Abby, ever cheerful and spirited, simply went on with her glowing praise. "You look fantastic. Want to take a selfie with me to post on Facebook?"

Delighted with the idea, Eastlyn leaned over next to Abby's chair. "Sure. Let's do it."

Abby grabbed her camera phone, snagged the photo and then uploaded it to social media.

"What about taking a picture of all of us?" Caleb suggested, holding up his phone, capturing the image for all to see.

While they were goofing around, Eastlyn spotted a face she recognized. She leaned into Cooper's space. "There, at three o'clock, that's the same guy Brent ID'd as Titus

Driscoll, the one in several of your shots from the compound."

"The one making the buy. I remember. Driscoll seems to be friendly with a lot of the guys drinking at the bar."

Eastlyn kept her eyes on Driscoll as he joked with Flynn and several other men before heading off to the pool tables in the back. "Maybe I should go over and listen to their conversation."

When she started to get up, Cooper grabbed her hand. "Maybe now isn't such a good time to let him know you're on to him."

"Why do you have to be so logical?"

Cooper spotted Bree and Troy coming in and waved the couple over. "Hey, why not join us? We're ending the workweek with a happy hour to celebrate Eastlyn getting her aviation physical behind her."

Cooper noticed Troy didn't seem like his usual cheerful self. The guy didn't even acknowledge Eastlyn's achievement. "Sounds like a plan. Bree and I've had a rough week, what with Zach and all. I pulled Bree in here because I thought she needed to get her mind off things."

"How's Zach doing?" Eastlyn asked Troy.

Troy's eyes cut to Bree before he answered. "Haven't you heard? Zach's gone missing."

Everyone gaped but it was Cooper who asked, "What do you mean missing?"

Bree dabbed at her eyes. "Zach's gone. I stopped by his house before I headed to work to check on him two days ago, his truck was in the driveway, but he was nowhere around. I went to Brent right away. Brent issued what he called a BOLO or Be On the Lookout that same day. The BOLO went out to law enforcement, but still no word, no one's seen Zach. For the past forty-eight hours Troy and I have been worried sick about him."

Troy went on to explain, "We drove up and down the Coast Highway, north and south for miles, but couldn't find him anywhere. There's been no sign of him around town."

Bree's voice trembled. Her breath hitched. "I'm afraid he's wandered off without his medication. I found it sitting right there in the kitchen where he left it."

After ordering beers all around, Troy turned to Cooper and Caleb. "I just want you to know there are no hard feelings on our part about Drea breaking up with Zach. He's been…in a bad place now for months."

Cooper nodded. "We were concerned about Drea's safety, especially when Zach wouldn't leave her alone."

But Eastlyn was still having a problem processing the fact that Zach had simply wandered off. "I can't believe he'd up and leave like that without his truck. What did he do, walk wherever he went?"

Troy sipped his brew. "That's just it, we don't know for sure. We're afraid he's not in his right mind and might have tried to hurt himself."

Bree picked up her drink. "There are a dozen places he might go. Maybe he even headed back to Colorado. You know several years ago he took off for the Rockies. He didn't even let me know where he was for two days. He just packed up and left. When I think back to that time after our dad died, Zach's been acting strange for years."

Troy nodded. "It's those kinds of things in Zach's past that make us think life's pressures started getting to him. He just couldn't handle things."

Zach's disappearance still didn't make sense to Eastlyn. "But on foot? How far could he really get on foot? Think about it."

"But if he got a decent head start…" Caleb proffered. "He could be in Scott's Valley by now."

Eastlyn glanced over at Caleb and stared. "That's the point. Scott's Valley is less than thirty minutes from here."

"You don't think it's too late for a search?" Bree asked, her voice filled with hope. "It's been two days."

"In my book, it's never too late to look. A search is definitely doable," Eastlyn concluded. "Even with a two-day head start we could fan out, beginning at Zach's house. Did anyone think to look in the immediate vicinity of the house?"

Troy and Bree eyed each other. "You mean go up and down the street, door to door, search the field behind the house, that sort of thing?" Troy asked. "We didn't do that."

Eastlyn put her hand on Bree's arm. "That's a shame. That's what should've been done initially to eliminate the possibility that something happened to him in the house or nearby so you could move on to other theories."

"Is it too late to do that tonight?" Bree wanted to know.

Eastlyn shook her head and looked around the table. "Not for me."

"Then what are we waiting for," Cooper said as he drained his beer. "Let's go see if we can eliminate that area around his house before it gets dark."

Bree used her key to the house on Cape May and let Eastlyn inside to look around just as she'd done with Brent, two days earlier. The place was orderly. Dishes put away. Zach's clothes were still hanging in the closet along with his suitcase sitting beneath. And just as Brent had decided for himself then, Eastlyn saw nothing out of the ordinary that would indicate foul play. It looked as though Zach had simply disappeared.

After locking up, the six of them spread out along Cape May to the smell of newly mowed summer grass lingering on the evening air. The fragrant aroma drew them along as they looked behind every shrub, in between the houses, and covered every inch of alleyway.

From there, they combed the gully behind the house, then wandered through a tract of undeveloped pastureland that opened into an adjacent field where the terrain was overgrown with weeds and wildflowers.

The sun began to sink over the bay as they brought out flashlights and spaced themselves out to cover more ground. It was near a line of yaupon holly and a nest of sandpipers that Cooper spotted a pair of men's work boots sticking out from underneath the base of a large cypress.

"Over here. I found him!" Cooper shouted, signaling his location with his flashlight. Cooper kneeled down, checked to see if Zach showed any sign of life. He soon realized Zach was breathing but it was very shallow. He picked up a wrist, found a weak pulse.

"He's alive," Cooper shouted to Eastlyn. To Bree, he yelled, "Call Doc, tell him we're bringing Zach in."

Eastlyn dropped to one knee, did a quick assessment. "No visible sign of a wound, which doesn't explain his condition." She touched Zach's forehead, found it cool to the touch.

"Should we move him?" Cooper asked Eastlyn.

She ran her hands up and down Zach's arms, did the same with his legs. "Even though I don't feel any broken bones, or see any signs of trauma anywhere, it doesn't mean there isn't any. And look at this rash on the side of his neck."

"Those could be ant bites," Cooper said.

"Could be. But let's err on the cautious side. If you ask me, this looks more like a reaction to medication than an injury. It looks as though Zach dropped right where he stood for whatever reason."

"How do we get him out of this field?" Troy asked.

Eastlyn had an idea. "We could use a surfboard and strap him to it, carry him out that way, slide him into my Bronco with the seats folded down."

Caleb piped up. "My garage is just through that easement. I'll run back and get my surfboard."

"Make it quick," Cooper said, leaning over Zach's right ear. "Come on, Zach, stay with us. We're getting you some help."

Doc Prescott confirmed Eastlyn's field diagnosis. "I strongly suspect Zach suffered a reaction to his medication. It sent him into an unconscious, almost catatonic-like state. I've given him epinephrine to relax his muscles, aiding him to breathe, and saline to flush out his system. I'd like to watch him overnight. But if he doesn't lose consciousness again, he should be able to go home tomorrow."

Doc turned to look at Bree. "I know you're anxious to talk to him so go in, reassure him everything's okay now."

Bree covered her face with her hands. "I feel so awful. Troy and I just assumed that he…that he took off. If I'd known he was so close I'd never have left him out in that field for so long."

Eastlyn broke in, hoping to find answers. "Doc, did Zach happen to say why he went out to that field in the first place?"

"He hasn't been that verbal. It could be simple. He decided to take a walk after taking his medication and then had the reaction right there. So far, he barely remembers his name."

Doc sent Bree a sympathetic gaze. "You realize Zach will need to be looked after, at least until he becomes more accepting of his depression. I've looked over his file and based on his insurance plan, I'll suggest a few good facilities within a fifty-mile radius, relatively close by."

Troy blanched. "You mean long-term care? I'm not sure Zach will go for that."

"Not necessarily. His stay doesn't have to be but a few weeks at most in order to find a medication that works best for him without this reoccurring. Reactions to antidepressants are rare, but they do happen."

Doc patted Bree's arm. "Don't worry. For now, Zach needs some assurance from his sister that you're here for him. Even though he didn't say much, he's much more alert than when you brought him in. He'll be glad to see you."

After Bree and Troy left the waiting room, Doc turned to the others. "That young man is very lucky you guys found him when you did. Otherwise, I doubt he would have made it another night."

Twenty-Five

Restoring the chopper was sweaty work.

This far inland the dog days of summer turned the barn into a furnace. Add in using sanders to take off rust and blowtorches to weld new metal to old, and the place easily hit a hundred degrees in the heat of the day.

Behind protective eye goggles, Eastlyn kept her eyes on the task at hand. Sparks flew all around her as she sanded off decades of corroded metal.

She worked until her arms ached, stopping only to take a water break and eat her sandwich around noon. She and Cooper had texted back and forth a couple of times, making plans to get together for supper.

She'd just fired up the sander again when she heard the barn door squeak open. She looked up and saw two men standing in the doorway, backwashed in sunlight. One had a wiry build and held a pistol. The other was stockier and gripped an AK-47 in his fist.

The wiry-built guy spit tobacco juice and asked, "That Bronco outside belong to you?"

Eastlyn weighed her options while still gripping the power tool. Nervous, but determined not to show it, she inched toward her cell phone she'd left out on the table, tapped the screen to begin the recording process. Eyeing the men, she decided bravado might go a long way. "No. I borrowed it from the town cop. Why? What's it to you?"

Mr. Wiry went on to explain, "We think you already know the answer to that. You paid us an unwelcome visit the other night, trespassed on our property. We're here to find out the reason you were out snooping around."

"I don't know what you're talking about."

Mr. Stocky gestured with the assault weapon for effect. "Sure you do. You were snooping around. We want to know who sent you?"

She stuck to the fallback story. "The only place I've been recently is when my boyfriend, who's a photographer, dragged me on a hike in the countryside near here to take a few pictures of old barns. Similar to this one. What's your beef anyway? You bring guns in here to ask me about trespassing on your property? That's nuts. Why didn't you just call the cops to run us off? We'd have skedaddled along if someone had told us your place was off limits."

Mr. Wiry exchanged looks with Mr. Stocky, sending glaring shards back at her. But before either one could intimidate her further, the barn door opened behind them.

Cooper and Thane stood looming in the background.

"Is there a problem here?" Cooper asked.

Eastlyn cast a grateful look toward Coop. "That's the boyfriend in question. I was just telling these nice gentlemen that you took me on an odyssey into the woods around here to get pictures for the book you're doing. These men claim we wandered onto their property. They're apparently bent out of shape about it."

Cooper eyed the two men. "I see that, enough to bring guns to welcome us to the neighborhood."

"We just want to make sure you know to stay away from our place."

"Which place would that be?" Thane asked.

Mr. Wiry ignored the question. "We'll leave you to your work." After staring down Thane and Cooper, the two goons disappeared back out the doorway.

"Boy, am I glad to see you guys," Eastlyn said, holding up her phone. "Luckily, I recorded that entire conversation. Talk about intense."

Cooper stepped to the barn door to make sure the men were leaving.

"What was that all about?" Thane grunted. "Where did those guys come from? They have sleaze written all over them."

"A misunderstanding," Cooper answered before Eastlyn could. "I guess when we were out taking pictures the other day we crossed over into someone's turf. They must've taken exception to our presence." Coop eyed Eastlyn. "But after that kind of encounter, I don't think you should work out here alone."

"I was about to suggest the same thing," Thane added. "Plus, I'd put in a call to Brent, make sure he knows they were packing guns when they threatened you."

"Count on it," Cooper said before the talk turned to showing Thane the work that needed doing on the chopper.

"I like what I see," Thane said later. "If you and Wally need any help putting in the engine, I do have some experience, tinkering. My dad and I restored the old Range Rover I drive."

Eastlyn nodded. "I've never taken on such a big job before on my own. That's why you won't see me turning down help when it comes to installing anything mechanical, especially the motor or the instrumentation panel. I might be able to handle the rest though."

Thane tossed a look at Cooper. "I can get her more help." He ticked off a list. "I'll start by initiating a town hall meeting where the mayor and city council know our grievances about the slow response from the county. When I called Santa Cruz to ask why, they blamed it on being understaffed on a weekend due to budget cuts. My answer to that was bullshit. When it's your kid that goes missing, you need action, not excuses. I want everyone in town to know where I stand on this issue. As a parent, no one wants to wait for two hours without help showing up in an official capacity from the county. We pay our taxes as much as the people elsewhere do. Next time, a crisis situation here in town may not have the same positive outcome."

Eastlyn had seen the joy on Thane's face when she'd driven up with the boys in the car. "That's why the town needs its own. Ever since coming here I've heard the same thing over and over again. I'm beginning to believe that we actually take care of our own. Which means, I'm determined to make this work."

When it came time for the men to leave the barn and head back, Cooper convinced Eastlyn it was best to abandon her work for the day and follow them to town. While he'd dropped Thane off at his house, Eastlyn had headed to the lighthouse.

But that had been hours ago.

As the daylight inched toward dusk, Cooper found her on her knees near the cliff, weeding the beds of lavender. She wore gloves that were filthy with dirt and mulch, along with an edgy attitude, apparent in the lines that filled her forehead.

"Have you talked to Brent yet?"

"Not yet. I'm still trying to figure out how to get him to let me finish what I started. I have to get my ducks in a row before setting up a meeting. In the event I encounter a brick wall, I want to make him understand that I want more out of this than trailing after Titus. I want to make it permanent."

"Then you will."

She looked up into Coop's face, the sunlight causing his sapphire eyes to dazzle like glitzy gems. "Just look at this place." She stared out at the people whose turn it had been that day to show up and tend the crops—Abby Anderson, Jordan with her kids, Malachi and his daughters, Lilly Pierce and her two children.

"I had major doubts that a community farm would even work. But look at them. Dedicated to its success, determined to make a go of it despite water problems, pesky insects, a constant drain on time, you name it, the list goes on of what could get in the way till harvest time."

"And what about your part in it? You made this happen, too."

"I plowed a field and agreed to oversee things."

"Don't do that. Don't diminish the impact you've made here."

She sent him a sweet smile. "I like it that you can do that."

"What?"

"Redirect my mood when I'm ticked off or cheer me up when I'm down."

"Hey, I'm just as pissed off about those guys showing up and threatening you. Maybe we should do something about it."

She got to her feet. "Like what?"

"Between you and Brent, you'll think of something."

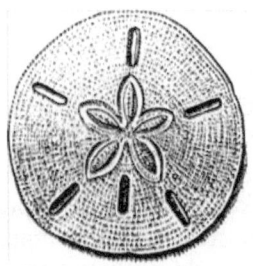

Twenty-Six

After calling Brent to ask where they should meet, Eastlyn was surprised when she was told to simply stop by the station.

An hour later she wandered in to see Brent plopped on the floor of the outer office surrounded by an elaborate fort built out of boxes. Luke deliberately crashed into it bringing the cardboard structure down in a heap.

"Am I interrupting?" she asked.

"Nope. Just smashing things up," Brent said, getting to his feet. "Nice job on finding Zach Dennison by the way."

Eastlyn waved him off. "Cooper's actually the one who located him. I need to talk to you about something else that happened earlier today at the barn." She sat down, took out her cell phone, played the detailed account aloud that described the encounter with the two men.

Brent didn't like what he was hearing. "These guys came out to the barn to intimidate you? That was stupid, tipping their hand like that."

Eastlyn pushed her hair back. "Maybe. But it was effective. I really want to nail these guys more than ever now. Did Thane mention he's backing my search and rescue idea?"

"That and then some. He's on a mission to show the county we don't need 'em."

Eastlyn's lips curved up. "Which is probably not the best approach to take."

"I'm glad you see the folly of thinking like that. We do pay a considerable amount of taxes to the county for their services. The thing is I don't think Sunday's lack of response was on purpose or personal in any way. It was a busy weekend for them. They were swamped."

"But still another reason we need to be self-sufficient. Where does the investigation stand with Thorwald?"

"I gave the sheriff's department all the evidence you and Cooper collected." When he saw the disappointment settle on her face, he added, "These things take time. And you knew going in that I didn't have the jurisdiction to touch Thorwald as long as he and his thugs stay in that part of the county. That's the frustrating part. The only hope is to somehow link Thorwald's operation to Pelican Pointe and go after the connection here, which is Titus Driscoll."

"Then we'll get more evidence," Eastlyn said.

Brent pointed a finger at her. "You got confirmation the compound has a meth lab on it. Your job is essentially done out there. We've already talked about the only way to go from here is to keep tabs on Driscoll. He's the only link we have. You can do that from right here."

Eastlyn puffed out a breath.

"Let me finish. I'm not risking an incident at the barn either. Don't work out there alone. When this took place today, did you have the Beretta with you?"

She laughed. "No, I'd left it at home. I didn't think I'd need it there. Turns out, my cell phone was the only weapon I had on hand."

"Play that threat again for me. Is there any way to transfer this to an audio for the file?"

"I have no idea. Cooper would probably know." She played the recording again but this time stood up to pace while the voices played out. Hearing that menacing tone one more time caused chills to run up her spine.

After listening to the recording, Brent's eyes grew wide. "I want you to keep your weapon with you at all times along with this." He reached into a drawer, pulled out a brass shield and slid the tin across the desk. "Here. You've earned it."

Overwhelmed, Eastlyn rocked back on her heels. "Really? Cool. What's next? Some kind of special training to be a member of the force?"

Brent smiled. "Maybe down the road. For now though, I think you've proved you can handle yourself. Besides, I like the idea that one of my officers is able to fly a chopper *and* head a search and rescue outfit."

"Do I get to wear a uniform?"

Brent couldn't remember the last time he'd witnessed this much excitement coming from a coworker. It certainly hadn't been that way with his brother. "Funny, Ethan never showed this kind of eagerness to wearing khaki."

"Khaki, huh? Well, I suppose it's too late to hope for dark blue. Khaki and camouflage aren't that much different from the army getup I wore. When do I get it?"

"I'll place the order this afternoon. You'll want to keep this to yourself until I make the announcement."

"Which is when?"

"When I take you off the undercover assignment I gave you originally. I'd like to keep this as quiet as possible."

"Does the town council know that I've been working…?"

"Undercover? Just Murphy. I went to him this morning, told him what I'd done. He gave me the go-ahead to make it official."

"Without talking to the council?"

"What can I tell you? He's the mayor. But until we make some headway with our case, I think we'll keep this under wraps for your own safety. It wouldn't do for Thorwald's thugs to get wind of your new employment, especially after what happened today."

"But I have to tell Cooper."

Brent grinned. "Yeah, I figured that one out already. Just make sure he doesn't spread it around."

That evening she flew to Cooper's to tell him the news. As soon as she walked into the atrium she saw him hunched over the kitchen counter, a piece of paper in his hand.

When he crushed the letter in his fist she stepped to put her arms around him. "Are you okay?"

"Why does she keep doing this? How does Eleanor even get my address? She somehow managed to get Caleb's phone number. How? Why does she bother with us now? It's like an obsession. What could she possibly have to say to any of us that we'd want to hear? An apology is never going to cut it."

She leaned over his shoulder to read Eleanor's words. "What is this bit about someone else's involvement in the murders?"

"Eleanor's always tried to pass the blame. Nothing's ever her fault. If a third party had been involved, don't you think her attorneys would've brought that up to the prosecution? They would've used that to say she wasn't the one who pulled the trigger that night on the beach. But no one did. There's always been a theory that she was having an affair of her own. But her affair doesn't mean another party did anything at all, except use poor judgment in hooking up with her."

"You really don't have a very high opinion of your mother, do you?"

"No, I don't. You don't know her. You don't know what she was like back then. I've always believed she reached a point where she wanted my father gone. Then she deliberately took extreme measures to do something about it. End of story."

"But your father wanted a divorce so he could be with Brooke?"

"That's the kicker."

"So why would she kill your father and Brooke if she was having an affair of her own?"

"Simple. No one leaves Eleanor Jennings unless Eleanor is ready for them to leave. No one. Not even her kids."

Eastlyn could see the distress on his face and hear it in his voice. She took a deep breath. "Maybe hanging onto this rage you have for her is a bad plan. Maybe getting rid of it is the only way to give you the peace of mind you need to move past the traumatic event that happened to you in childhood. You can either let Eleanor keep winning, tugging forever on that hold she has on you, or let go of it and refuse to give her the leverage she demands. There is a third option. You could go out to Chowchilla and have it out with her face to face, hear what she has to say."

He turned to stare into her green eyes. "How'd you get so smart?"

She combed her fingers through his hair. "Easy. I've lived with my own demons too long. I've survived most of them. And you will too."

"Honestly, I'm not sure I could look at her long enough to listen to her talk."

"You'll have to make that decision. Either find a way to put up with her harassment from jail without it upsetting you every time like it does, or have it out with her."

"What are you doing home so early anyway?"

"I have good news." She took out the badge from her pocket. "Brent made it official."

He grinned. "Then we should celebrate."

She ran a hand down his cheek, stood behind him to rub his shoulders. "We will. First, you need to get rid of all this tension."

He spun around and took her mouth. The kiss sent her pulse racing. Her mind went blank. "Back rubs are good and all. And you have exceptional fingers." To prove it, he kissed each one. "But I have a much better idea."

"Does it include getting naked?"

"Oh yeah."

With that, he lifted her up and onto the table, slid his hands under her cotton top. As he explored all the curves and angles, she moved her hands down his back, urging him on with a rush of need.

They eventually found their way to the bedroom where they stayed wrapped up in each other the rest of the night, closed off from the world, settling into their own private bubble—or tried to.

Just when they thought they'd pushed the world away, the issue with Eleanor reared up again. Kinsey called to tell Cooper she'd verified that the warden definitely had taken Eleanor's phone privileges away.

"It didn't make much of a difference," Cooper relayed to Kinsey. "Eleanor's taken to writing me letters, four in all, more like notes really, telling me she has something major to share and keeps begging me to talk to her."

"Persistent mother you have there, Cooper," Kinsey noted.

"Don't I know it."

"I'll do what I can to let the prison officials know she's becoming a pest. But, in truth, I'm not sure what else we can do other than file formal complaints."

"I know you've done all you can." Cooper left it like that and hung up the phone. He turned to Eastlyn. "If I were to agree to meet with Eleanor at the prison, would you go with me?"

"Absolutely. But why would you? Don't fall into letting her blackmail you. It's fine to go see her. But do it because it's what *you* want to do and not because she's using a lure to get you there."

"You're right. I'll give it a few days before making my decision."

Eastlyn's cell phone rang. She gave Cooper an apologetic look. "I didn't turn it off because I thought

Brent might need me for something, like what happened on Sunday, an emergency."

"It's okay. Who is it?"

Looking at the display, Eastlyn frowned and wondered if one of the animals at the clinic had taken a turn for the worse. She slid the bar over to take the call. "Hi Cord. What's up?"

"I hate to bother you this late but there's a guy hanging around the guest cottage. He looks disheveled, like a homeless person. When I asked him if he was supposed to be there he said he was trying to find you. He refused to give me his name. But, Eastlyn, he seems really out of it."

She went with her first thought. "Do you know what Titus Driscoll looks like?"

"Sure. Why? It's not Titus."

"Oh, okay. I'll be there in a sec." She looked at Cooper as she grabbed her prosthetic and clothes. "I have to go. Someone's hanging around the house. Cord didn't recognize who it is."

"It might be one of Thorwald's men snooping around your place. I'm going with you."

She drove the Bronco from Sandy Pointe to the cottage. Cautious in her approach, she slowly pulled up in the driveway she shared with the clinic.

Cooper got out of the passenger seat first before Eastlyn. But she caught up with him in time to spot Cord standing between the buildings, waiting. "There he is. The man said he was looking for you, Eastlyn. That's why I called so late. Do you recognize who he is?"

Eastlyn couldn't believe her eyes as she rounded the corner. "Yeah, I do."

She saw a gaunt man with hair as black as a raven's and big dark eyes to match. An exhausted Durke Pedasco leaned up against the railing of her little stoop looking as though he might pass out any minute.

She ran up to him, wrapped her arms around his shoulders in a hug and noticed he had a limp.

"Durke, how on earth did you find me?"

Durke let himself be hugged and then leaned his head on her shoulders. "I borrowed a guy's cell phone at the bus station three days ago in Salinas. I sent a text message to my mom. She told me you were here. No one's looking for me here."

Durke's forehead felt hot to the touch and she immediately saw that he was holding his side. "Is that blood on your shirt?"

"One of those sleazebags shot me. It's healing up though. At least I hope it is. It bleeds every now and then. I don't feel so good though. Could I sit down for a minute?"

Eastlyn turned to Cooper and Cord. "Let's get him into the house."

Cord spoke up. "I have a better idea. Take your friend into the clinic. I might be a veterinarian but I can still look at that side in a pinch until Doc takes a look at him tomorrow."

Cooper dashed up the step to help Durke stand. With Eastlyn on the other side, they dragged the injured man up the steps and into the clinic.

Once Cord got him on the table, he took charge of the patient. He went to work ripping open the man's shirt, saw a nasty, bulging wound where a bullet had entered a chunk of fatty tissue in the abdomen.

"This has been festering for weeks. It's infected now," Cord said as he unlocked a medicine cabinet. He took out a syringe and a surgical tray, and started an IV drip.

Durke began to murmur in short spurts, delirium setting in. "I cleaned the wound a couple times with peroxide, tried to dig out the bullet myself. Never could quite get it out."

"Lie still now. I'll take care of it," Cord assured him. "Cooper, do me a favor. Go ahead and give Doc a call. This might be the worst wound I've seen lately."

Cooper nodded and stepped into the other room to make the call.

Meanwhile, Cord turned to Eastlyn. "If you have any questions for your friend here, you'd better make it quick because I'm about to knock him out so I can dig out that bullet. If Doc's not here by then, I'll stitch up his gash and hope that we pump him with enough antibiotics to quash the bacterial infection."

Eastlyn stepped over, took Durke's hand. "What gives? Where've you been all this time? It's been weeks. With this kind of injury why didn't you get yourself to a hospital?"

"Whoa. Slow down there. Could I get some water? I'm really thirsty."

"Sure, as long as you start talking." Eastlyn took a paper cup from the water dispenser, filled it halfway full before holding it up to Durke's lips.

Cord slapped on gloves, glanced over and shook his head. "Even though he's dehydrated, just give him enough to wet his lips. No more than that. The IV drip will replenish what he's lost."

Eastlyn did as she was told. But as Cord began to get ready for the surgical procedure, the smell of blood mixed with the disinfectant odor brought her back to another time and place. Hit by a wave of images, like the ones she'd witnessed from the seat of a cockpit as her crew had helped the wounded, she felt woozy. The memory of her own injury suddenly made her feel like she wanted to throw up.

Cord took one look at her face and asked, "If you feel like you're about to faint, let me know now."

After a few long seconds, she shook off the lightheadedness. "The sight of blood usually doesn't get to me like that."

Cooper came back into the room just in time to overhear her comment. "It's likely a flashback from that day you took your own hit. That's my guess anyway."

Cord bobbed his head in agreement. "Perceptive man you have here, Eastlyn. Combat does strange things to the psyche."

She gave Cooper an unassuming smile and decided to change the focus off her and back to where it belonged. "Will Durke be okay?"

Like any good doctor dealing with an emergency situation who was unsure of the outcome, Cord sidestepped the question. "Like I said before, if you want answers from him, either ask them now or wait until he's out of surgery. Your choice."

Eastlyn leaned down to where Durke could hear. "People back in Bakersfield told the cops you were a drug informant. The Feds denied it but no one was sure what to believe."

"What? No. Not even close. How'd that rumor get started?"

"No idea. What happened that you thought you had to disappear the way you did?"

Durke licked his lips and closed his eyes. "It happened a few days after you got out of rehab. I'd closed up the bar, took the trash to the Dumpster for the night, set the empties outside just like I always do. I turned to go back inside and the next thing I know I hear this sound like someone's beating the hell out of someone else. I look across the alley and down toward Nathan's Donut Shop. I see these two dudes beating up Rona Simmons. You remember Rona."

Eastlyn's brows knitted together. "You mean Rodney? Sure. We went to high school with him. He's transgender, right? Has been for most of his life. Wears those red dresses and black stockings everywhere no matter the event, looks pretty good in them, too."

"Rona. She likes to be called Rona these days, Eastlyn. And she's always been eccentric like that, but Rona's always had a big heart. You know that."

Eastlyn exchanged looks with Cord knowing the morphine would soon kick in. So she prompted Durke to get to the end of his story before that happened. "I do. Okay, Rona. You saw Rona getting beat up. What did you do then?"

"These two guys beat her up so bad it looked like they were killing her, so I ran back into the bar to call the cops. While I'm on the 911 call, I hear two more gun shots, then two more. I go back outside and realize these two guys have shot Rona. There was no need to do that to her, you know? They'd beaten her so that it was hard to tell what her face looked like. Anyway, while I'm standing there, one of them points their gun at me and the next thing I know, I feel this burning sensation in my side. They shot me just like they did Rona. So I charge out of there and take off running back to my car."

"Did you recognize the two guys?"

He lifted his head off the table. "Sure. They'd just spent three hours in the bar giving Rona a hard time. It was Angus and Dolan Hardaway. At first I headed to the hospital, but they followed me there. So I took a few side streets toward home, but they showed up there, too, about five minutes after I got home. That's when I ducked out the bedroom window with just the clothes on my back. I panicked, Eastlyn, plain and simple. I didn't know what to do except take off, lay low, and hope the cops would put two and two together and arrest those two. But after four long months, mom says the brothers are still out there walking around free."

"So where've you been all this time?"

"I thought Angus and Dolan might find me at the cabin so I headed east for a bit, realized that was a mistake and changed direction. This time I went north, ducked into the Sequoia National Forest, camped out for a while and then headed north again. I hitched a ride with a family headed to Merced and ended up in Yosemite. Then after talking to my mom, I decided to come here. It took all my energy to make it west."

Durke closed his eyes again as the drug took over. "I don't feel so good."

And with that, Durke passed out for real.

For most of the night, Eastlyn and Cooper sat in the outer office at the clinic, waiting for news on how the surgery went. After Cord had removed the bullet, Doc had shown up to supervise Cord's stitches. That's all they knew until Cord, still dressed in scrubs, appeared in the doorway.

"Your friend's condition is good, even though the infection spread to his stomach, which is the reason he'll be on massive doses of antibiotics for probably two weeks. In about six hours Doc will assess his condition and make the determination then whether or not to move him over to his place, or not."

Eastlyn stood up. "You did a remarkable job with him, Cord. Thank you. I don't think he could've made it back home to Bakersfield."

Cord turned to go, but stopped. "If he'd tried that, he'd be dead by now. By the way, if you're curious I took out a .22 slug, kept it as evidence."

"Good. I'll give Brent a call at first light."

Eastlyn angled her head to look at Cooper. "You look so tired. Why don't you go take a nap for a few hours?"

"Only if you come with me." He looked at his watch. "It's four a.m. We could get three solid hours in."

She grinned. "Okay. But we sleep. No funny business."

Coop held up his hands. "Who, me? It's you who has such a hard time keeping your hands off me. I'm the one who should worry. So yeah, no funny business."

It wasn't until nine o'clock that they met with Brent inside his office. After Eastlyn's initial call, Brent had spent the morning on the phone with the Bakersfield police department. After learning more about the case there, Brent had decided every word of Durke's story checked out.

But Eastlyn still had questions. "Why didn't they mention Rona's murder to you back when they were probing into the missing person angle? I'm surprised the police didn't think Durke was somehow involved in Rona's death since it took place right outside the bar."

Cooper added, "It stands to reason the cops would look at Durke as the one who killed Rona because he took off."

Brent nodded. "That, and the first people the detectives spoke to ended up being Angus and Dolan Hardaway. The two brothers showed up at the police station and happily tried to point the finger at Durke right off the bat. The only thing that hung up their story was that the detectives couldn't find a .22—which is the murder weapon that killed Rona and now seems to match the slug that showed up in Durke."

"Ah. It's all beginning to make more sense. We now know who started the rumor about Durke being a drug informant and that he'd gotten in trouble with a local gang of dealers."

"It was Angus and Dolan who did their damnedest to make it look like Rona's death was tied to drugs and then link it back to Durke. Funny thing is the police couldn't make ninety percent of Hardaway's story stick. It had so many holes in it, the detectives weren't sure what to think."

"If the cops couldn't make the story stick then why didn't they just arrest the Hardaway brothers back when it happened?" Cooper asked.

Brent leaned back in his chair. "Because it doesn't work that way. Evidence didn't point to anyone at that point. And besides, the Hardaways aren't complete morons. The brothers likely got rid of the gun…somewhere. The fact is your friend witnessed a murder. This morning the authorities back in Bakersfield took what they had to the DA. He decided to finally issue a warrant for the Hardaway brothers. But it's my guess that unless Angus and Dolan plead guilty, Durke will very likely be the only key witness and will have to go back and testify to what he saw. So how's the guy doing?"

"Doc says Durke should be fine in a week or two. Until he's ready to travel he'll stay with me at the cottage until he feels well enough to go back home to Bakersfield."

After finishing up, Eastlyn walked Cooper across the street to the Hilltop Diner to have breakfast.

"Something's bothering you," Cooper said. "If it's about letting Durke stay with you, I'm fine with it."

"That's what I love about you—" A mortified look crossed her face when she realized what she'd almost admitted.

But Cooper downplayed the slip of the tongue the only way he knew how. He swung her into his arms and circled her waist, twirled her along the sidewalk in a dance. "That's what I love about you too—your generosity of spirit. You didn't hesitate to offer Durke a place to crash."

"There are some things you don't have to second-guess—being there for a friend is one of them. But that's not why I'm stressing. How can I put this? I'm beginning to wonder how I'm supposed to get everything done. I'm starting to feel like I'm taking on too much. The pressure is building up. Now I have a houseguest, or will have as soon as Durke gets released. Thane is on this mission to make the ugly-duckling H-13 airborne in record time with help from the townspeople. And Brent says I'm supposed to remain undercover all the while I have the FAA requirements to deal with, and I still have all my other jobs. I'm beginning to feel everything closing in around me. In all those books you've read, have you come across an effective way for me to clone myself? Maybe if there were two of me I'd be able to work on the helicopter and still do everything else."

Cooper led her to the curb in front of the diner. "Let's take things point by point. Durke won't need round-the-clock care so he'll essentially look out for himself. You said yourself your job at the lighthouse doesn't take that much time away from everything else. Landon will be shorthanded for a time but he'll get along fine without you. If the town pitches in on the chopper, which they will, that's one less thing you have to worry about. No matter what happens, you'll make time for the FAA. That's priority one. You'll slide into the role of officer recruit like you were meant to do. I admit you have a lot on your plate. But you aren't taking on the world alone anymore in any of this."

She tightened her hold around his neck. "You make me feel as though I can do it all."

"That's because you can."

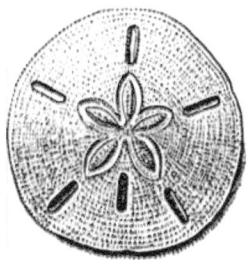

Twenty-Seven

In the past whenever the council needed a place to hold a town hall meeting they'd appropriate a classroom at the church. But since reopening the elementary school, they used the much larger auditorium.

Tonight the place filled up due to Thane's dogged efforts. He and Isabella had wasted no time getting the word out. They'd worked tirelessly over the past few days with Brent and Nick to line up enough people to voice their list of grievances over the lack of response from the county and what they intended to do about it.

According to Nick and Murphy, holding a meeting, voicing complaints in public, gave legitimacy to the forum.

If the town's participation in the Lighthouse Project had impressed Eastlyn, the driving forces behind the rescue outfit blew her away. Already the idea of taking a washed out old chopper and making it the basis for something grand had caught on, evidenced by the crowd. An indomitable spirit prevailed. Everyone seemed to like the idea that once completed, the chopper would belong to the entire town.

Murphy stepped to the microphone first to take care of town business before turning the platform over to Thane.

Thane led a rousing PowerPoint presentation that included photos of the model in its prime. "Our solution is the Bell H-13 Sioux chopper found in Cleef's barn. It's old but once it's refurbished it will look like this."

From the projected finish, Thane went into the history, segued into how the same aircraft had been used in the TV show *MASH* and rattled off its specs.

"This is the chopper we want to fix up to use for search and rescue. Recently, Eastlyn Parker bought it and began restoration. But that's a ton of work for one person. I'm proposing that the entire town pitch in and help her out, get it in shape, and ultimately make it airborne again. Because Eastlyn will be the pilot who flies it." Thane promptly offered Eastlyn's backstory.

She heard the applause but didn't trust her ears. She leaned in, whispered to Cooper, "It's hard to believe this is really happening."

"You've been in town how long now?"

"Four months."

"Then you ought to know the people here love a challenge. They're also willing to come together for the good of the town. By morning, Thane and Isabella will have a long list of people willing to help. Watch and see. I bet we have a slew of talented individuals around here you don't even realize could play a vital role in restoration."

"Nothing like piling on a load of pressure," Eastlyn grunted. "The FAA hasn't even weighed in yet. What if…?"

Cooper put a finger to her lips. "Tonight's for positive vibes. Look around at all the energy in this room. Besides, you've handled the FAA scrutiny before, you can do it again."

Resigned to the feel-good atmosphere, Eastlyn let go of the worry. "Hey, if they're willing to put in the sweat to get the town a chopper and if they're willing to take a chance on me to fly it, then who am I to argue with such an incredible break. Win-win for me."

"Hey, the aviation examiner already gave you a clean bill of health. That's the first hurdle in the battle."

On a roll, Cooper looked around the auditorium at the enthusiasm. "Would a dozen or so recommendations from prominent citizens go a long way in helping sway the FAA?"

Eastlyn's lips curved, her green eyes flashed. She lifted a shoulder. "Who knows? I suppose it couldn't hurt."

She started the next day inside Logan Donnelly's studio hoping to talk to him about his expertise at working with metal. But she was a little intimidated about approaching the renowned artist.

Flattery, she decided, would go a long way. "I love the dolphin sculpture in front of the school and the pieces you have displayed inside the Chumash Museum. I guess that makes me a big fan of your work, although to be honest, I haven't seen anything else of yours, except the work you did at the lighthouse."

Logan peered at the leggy woman with the golden wheat hair. "Thanks. But I happened to be a big fan of people like you, soldiers who saw combat, and came back stateside to overcome the odds. I'd say that's a success no matter how you look at it."

"I've had my share of issues in the past," she confessed.

"Haven't we all? What brings you here today? If it's a donation, Thane's already tapped me for my share and I'm happy to give it. I have kids of my own. I've always thought the county considers us an afterthought here in Pelican Pointe. For twenty years they did very little to catch the serial killer who killed my sister."

Eastlyn nodded knowingly. "I'm so sorry about that. They haven't yet identified that set of remains I found."

"I'm aware," he said, his tone dripping with bitterness. "And one more reason I believe the victims and their families are left to an inept trail of misdirection. They haven't ID'd the bones yet because it isn't a priority. They have the killer locked up and for the authorities that's it. Processes seem to drag on from the coroner's office right down to the cops, all the while there's a family out there without answers." He looked at her and shook his head. "Sorry for the rant. I've had a lot longer than Thane to build up my animosity toward the county and for reasons of my own."

"Why do you stay?"

"Because this is my home. I've never lived anywhere else that makes me feel a sense of community more than I do here."

Eastlyn nodded. "I'm beginning to understand. Thanks for the donation, but what I could really use at the moment is your expertise in working with metal. I'd like for you to show me in ten easy steps how best to deal with the rust. Not only that, I'd like to get the chopper out of the barn and into a better place in town to work on it."

"I can do that. There's any number of warehouses you could use. We'll get a flatbed and haul it over here so you won't have to make that trip every day. Will Saturday morning work for you?"

"That's perfect. And thank you."

"Not a problem. We help our own here."

Durke Pedasco also found that statement to be true. After a week spent recuperating he decided Pelican Pointe was nothing at all like Bakersfield.

For his first outing, Durke had been invited to tag along with Eastlyn and Cooper to a pre-Fourth of July barbeque at Promise Cove.

Durke sat at a table in the outdoor courtyard taking in the crowd. Sipping on a glass of iced tea, he listened to the guy who'd taken the bullet out of him tell the story of how Eastlyn had come to live here.

Cord became more animated each time he recounted the faces Eastlyn had made while storming into the boarding house that day, clomping around her room as she threw her stuff into boxes.

Durke laughed so hard he thought he'd crack open his stitches. "So let me get this straight? These guys actually drag you back here and you don't put up much of a fight other than stomping around like a petulant child? That description so nails the way you were acting back then."

Eastlyn punched Durke in the arm as she'd done since she was eight years old. "Oh, really? Should I walk down memory lane and share with them how you used to pitch a fit when you lost to me at basketball?"

"That was third grade and you were a giant even then. I never was much for sports."

Eastlyn sent her childhood friend a sly smile. "Excuses, excuses." Over Durke's shoulder, she caught sight of Cooper on his cell phone, noted his stiff shoulders and the set to his jaw. She rose out of her chair and went over to him.

"What's wrong? Was that Eleanor again?"

Cooper seemed agitated. "I don't know how she does it, but yeah. Another call I didn't take. But I've made a decision. First thing tomorrow morning I'm making arrangements to drive out to see her. I don't think she'll leave me alone until I do."

Twenty-Eight

Cooper had picked a Saturday to make the three-hour drive to Chowchilla Correctional Facility for Women. He'd scheduled his visitation well ahead of time, arranged to have Caleb keep an eye on the shop, and promised Drea he would do his best to get Eleanor to understand that her children wanted her to stop bothering them.

Cooper gave Eastlyn the keys to the Mustang and let her drive because he'd been edgy and anxious for two days prior to the trip.

In the months she'd known him, Eastlyn had never seen Cooper the sullen mess he was now. He'd barely slept all week, which made him short-tempered and exhausted.

"Why don't you put your head back and take a nap?"

Cooper cut his eyes over to the woman behind the wheel. "Maybe if I weren't so keyed up I could do that but I feel like I might be carsick."

"Let me know if you want me to pull over."

The closer they got to the Central Valley, Madera County in particular, the more Cooper's stomach churned.

When they blew past flat farmland where the CCFW sat on six hundred and forty acres, Cooper began to have serious doubts he could go through with the visit.

Eastlyn pulled the car to the shoulder of the road, threw the gear in Park. She angled in her seat and saw how distressed he looked. "Say the word and I'll turn the car around now."

Cooper buried his face in his hands. "What would you do?"

"I'd go in, face her, listen to whatever she has to say, then judge whether or not she's playing me and be done with it."

"For real?"

"For real. You've lived with this hanging over your head for so long it's time to end it one way or another and move on. You either decide if it's worth keeping her in your life or getting rid of the negativity she always seems to stir up. Either way, as I see it, it ends today."

"You're right. Let's get this over with."

Eastlyn located the visitor's parking lot, and found a space.

While they waited to board the prison bus that would take them to the processing center, Cooper looked around at all the buildings. "I checked this place out. This is where Susan Atkins was housed until her death from brain cancer."

"Manson family Susan Atkins?"

"One and the same. Eleanor shares these walls with other notable neighbors. Nancy Garrido lives here."

Eastlyn lifted a brow. "The woman who helped Phillip Garrido kidnap Jaycee Dugard?"

"That's the one. This is where they sent Kristin Rossum for poisoning her husband. Maybe that's why the place is full up, overcapacity by more than fifteen hundred inmates."

"Geez, now I'm getting a little nervous at the prospect of going inside."

But when the van pulled up, they reluctantly boarded but sat in silence while the bus took them to another building.

At the processing center they filled in all the necessary information to get a pass and got the first good news of the day for Cooper. He discovered the visit would be noncontact. That meant he would have a glass partition between him and his mother.

They went through security, which included a pat down and search. Cooper cleared the metal detector but the guard had to use a handheld wand on Eastlyn because of her prosthesis. Everywhere they looked there were surveillance cameras. After clearing all that, the guard stamped their hands and they were led down a hallway to one of the visiting rooms to wait.

It seemed like forever before another guard brought out Eleanor Jennings Richmond through a door at the rear of the room and removed her handcuffs. Cooper's mother sat down and immediately began looking around for her son.

Eastlyn could hear Cooper's intake of breath next to her as she stood back, rooted to the linoleum floor, and watched as he approached the glass partition. Her heart broke for him. She'd never felt the depth of sorrow for anyone before in her life more than she did for Cooper at that moment.

Eastlyn's first impression of Eleanor wasn't all that flattering. It wasn't the woman's unkempt appearance, although that was a shock. The mass of black hair tipping gray at the temples that fell down around her shoulders in a wild tangle would certainly put anyone off. But it wasn't Eleanor's wooly mane that concerned Eastlyn, more like the soulless eyes, the distant smile, the phony display of emotions that bordered on theatrical staging.

Cooper sat down on the stool and picked up the phone on his side, watched Eleanor do the same on hers.

He realized then that it wasn't his mother he saw on the other side of the glass, but rather the monster that had taken his father. All the rage at what this woman had put him through over the years, all that she represented, simmered to the surface. Even though his chest felt tight, his heart flipped icy cold. He gripped the phone so hard his knuckles turned white. "You look old."

"And you look exactly like the whiny mousy little bookworm I remember. Always with your nose in some book or complaining about something or other."

"If I was so whiny then why didn't you clean up your own mess that night? Why rely on a kid to do your dirty work for you?"

"Because you owed me."

"How do you figure that? Oh, wait a minute. I forget how special you always thought you were. The rules never applied to Eleanor Jennings, did they? As I recall, you even tried to make a cash deal to sell your kids once. Mother of the year material right there, weren't you?"

"You'll sing a different tune when I tell you the truth about that night."

"The truth? I'd be shocked if you recognized what it looked like. You've spent decades lying about everything, unable to show remorse about anything, unable to take responsibility. Brent Cody believes you killed your own father, made it look like suicide. Landon believes it, too. And when you couldn't sell your kids, you decided to abandon them in the middle of the night surrounded by water. What were you hoping for then, Eleanor? That we'd all drown and you'd be rid of us for good? That you'd add three little kids to your tally of murder victims?"

Cooper knew she'd dodge that issue so he wasn't disappointed when she fired off a sample of why she'd summoned him. "I didn't kill your father that night. I didn't kill his girlfriend. I've never killed anyone before in my life, no matter what Brent Cody or Landon believes. Even when he was younger Landon was nothing but a stupid boy who just accepted the fact our father had made us poor with all his bad business decisions."

"Aw, Eleanor disapproves of failure, especially when it comes to money. She was no longer the princess who got to tell people what to do. When things don't go well for Eleanor, she reverts back to what she does best. She either gets rid of people or takes off. Isn't that right? Just like you took off in the middle of the night because you didn't want to be a mother anymore. That's it, isn't it?"

He sat across the glass staring at evil. Knowing she wouldn't budge off her mission, he finally said, "Okay, I'll bite. If you didn't kill Layne and Brooke, then who did?"

"Flynn McCready."

"Aw, come on, surely you can do better than that. I sat in a car for three hours on the way here to listen to this bullshit. I don't think so."

"It's not bullshit. I saw him do it. We were having an affair. He wanted your father dead. Brooke just showed up at the wrong time."

"Eleanor, if all that's true, then why would you, of all people, go home and wake up your nine-year-old son to help you dispose of the bodies? I mean, you, who didn't want to break a nail opening up a can of chili to feed her kids, couldn't talk big, strong Flynn into cleaning up the mess on the beach that night? It's hard to believe that you'd be the one to pick up a shovel and attempt to dig a hole in the backyard to save Flynn from a murder rap? Not likely. After all, he'd just murdered your husband."

Cooper saw her flinch as she refused to make eye contact. Instead, she studied the wall on her side of the glass. "Look at me, Eleanor. I'm the person who knows you better than anyone else in the world. I know the real Eleanor and what you're capable of, not the one you want other people to see but the flawed woman who, for some reason, had three kids she never really wanted. I remember that night like yesterday. I think it's possible I'll take those images to my grave, no matter how long I live. I'll always see my father's face, gray and ashen, dead. He'd been sickly before that night because you'd spent six months trying to poison him to death. The medical examiner found the arsenic, found the evidence in his hair. So if you want to sit there and try to bullshit someone about how innocent you are, I'm the last person it would work on, the very last. I'll tell you the one thing I know for absolute certainty. You're one sorry excuse for a human being."

"What do you remember about anything?" Eleanor spat out. "You were just a boy, an immature boy who could never do anything right the first time."

"Yeah, well, not as immature as you might think. Why would the most selfish woman I've ever known step up that night to protect Flynn? Why didn't Flynn stick around to help you dig the grave if he was so enamored with you? I'll tell you why. It didn't happen that way."

Insulted, Eleanor stuck to her cagey ways. "I can't tell you all that now. Everyone's listening."

Cooper rolled his eyes and stood up. "I'm done. Please don't ever call me again. Don't call Drea or Caleb. Leave us alone. If we have to we'll change our phone numbers. I'll see you put away in solitary confinement before I take one of your phone calls. We've been through enough of your twisted manipulation to last a lifetime and it's over. Since you're serving life behind bars with no possibility of parole and this is only year-two of that sentence, I figure you can wait for me to come back here when hell freezes over."

From her chair in the back near the vending machines, Eastlyn saw a lively, angry debate going back and forth. She wasn't prepared to see Cooper push up, get to his feet, and slam down the phone he'd used to talk to his mother.

When he stormed past Eastlyn into the hallway, she flew after him.

"What happened? What did Eleanor say?"

"She made up this bullshit story about having an affair with Flynn McCready. She claims he's the one who pulled the trigger that night."

"My God, do you believe she's telling the truth?"

"Absolutely not." He changed direction to head for the exit. "Let's get the hell out of this place. The sad thing is, we just wasted six plus hours on this ridiculous odyssey that we'll never be able to get back."

Once they got back to the car, Eastlyn was able to calm him down somewhat. She spent the trip back coaxing out a plan to at least tell Brent about Eleanor's claims.

Even though it was almost dinnertime when they got back to town, Cooper placed the call to Brent and suggested they meet at the station.

Without preamble, Cooper laid out the allegation. "Eleanor's accusing Flynn McCready of murder."

Eastlyn studied Brent's reaction. "Cooper's convinced it isn't possible. He's certain Eleanor acted alone that night. What about you? You've had a long association with Flynn over the years, most people in town have. What's your gut tell you about Flynn?"

"That if it's true the man kept his mouth shut for an awfully long time."

Cooper ran both hands through his mop of hair. "You aren't buying this bullshit, are you?" He ticked off the same reasons he'd given Eleanor that it couldn't be true. "If Flynn had been at the pier that night, then why didn't Eleanor rely on him to help her with the bodies instead of her little boy?"

"That's a good point," Brent said with a nod.

Cooper roamed the room, his fury rising. "Let's say it's true Eleanor and Flynn were an item. Let's say Flynn knew about the murders and kept quiet all these years. There's one thing Eleanor can never lie about, and she can lie about a lot. She can't lie about the gun. She had it with her that night. She was holding it in her hand when she woke me up. And later, I saw it out on the kitchen counter where she'd left it."

Eastlyn sat up straighter. "So the idea that Flynn would've handed over the murder weapon to Eleanor is a little too over the top."

"So, are we done here?" Cooper asked, impatient to get home.

Brent swiveled in his chair. "For now. But I intend to dig deeper into Eleanor's blame game. When she was arrested during her incarceration and subsequent extradition back to California, she said nothing about anyone else being involved in the murders."

"I know. That's what I'm saying. If Eleanor's lips are moving, she's lying."

Brent came around to the corner of his desk. "Look guys, do me a favor. Until we sort through this further, I want you both to keep a lid on your conversation with Eleanor. The Flynn thing doesn't leave this room." He eyed Eastlyn. "In the meantime, you and I keep closer tabs on Titus. Before making a move on him, we have to flesh out his other contacts, the people he sells to. We know he has them."

Eastlyn rocked back on her heels. "Then one way or another, we'll find out who they are."

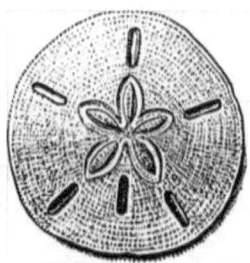

Twenty-Nine

The envelope from the FAA came a week later. Eastlyn was so nervous to open it she left Durke on her couch watching TV and jumped in the car to drive to Cooper's house so he would be with her no matter what the news turned out to be.

But when she reached his house, he wasn't home from work yet. Taking a seat in the courtyard to wait for him, she found patience difficult and overrated.

She drummed her fingers on the tabletop itching to open the envelope and get to the news inside. To her, the contents felt heavier than a rejection letter, which meant it could be more paperwork to fill out. So she was likely building up suspense for nothing.

Sitting there, she looked around for something to do to keep her mind off ripping open the paper. So when she noticed Cooper's bright red zinnias and gerbera daisies needed a drink, she turned on the outside faucet, used the garden hose to give the plants a good soaking.

As she went from blossom to bud, she spotted a folded piece of white paper stuck to the bottom of one of the flowerpots. She bent down, picked it up. Since it wasn't sealed, she flipped the single sheet open. The handwritten words stared back at her:

A son should listen to his mother.

Despite the warm and sunny afternoon, a chill ran up her spine. By the water stains and dirt on the paper, it looked as though the message had been left to the elements for at least a week. That would've been about the same time Cooper had gone to the prison to see Eleanor.

The implications were there, along with the threat. Someone in town had to be working with Eleanor in order to leave the note on Cooper's front porch. There was no other way, unless the inmate possessed superpowers that allowed her to come and go as she pleased under lock and key.

Eastlyn was about to text Cooper when she heard the muffler on the Mustang pulling into the driveway at the side of his house.

She met him at the gate, the envelope from the FAA in one hand, Eleanor's note in the other.

Cooper saw her standing in the yard and asked, "What's this?"

In that split second, Eastlyn realized she'd been thinking about hiding the note from him, keeping him in the dark about Eleanor's accomplice, whoever it was. But the look on his face made her think twice about any further deception. He needed to know.

"I have a dilemma." She fanned her face with the envelope. "It came. See, it's from the FAA. I need you to open it for me. If it's bad news we'll hear it together."

He grabbed it out of her hand, tore open the paper without warning and kept eyeing what was inside without saying a word.

"Well? What does it say?" Eastlyn prompted. "Do I have more paperwork to do? Another application to fill out?"

"It's not a letter."

Her shoulders slumped. "It's not? What is it?"

He grinned. "I'm no expert but it looks like a pilot's license to me. Your middle name is Elizabeth? I never knew that."

"Lemme see." She snatched it away and studied the blue-green background, the image of the jet, the hologram in the right corner, the FAA seal, the signature of the acting director. She eyed her name and date of birth. It looked like the genuine article to her.

She jumped. She high-fived. She turned in a circle. "Woohoo! Oh my God, that's my name on there. It says Eastlyn Elizabeth Parker has been found to be properly qualified for transport pilot."

"Why transport pilot?"

"Because that's what I was before. It's also what I need for search and rescue. It looks like the FAA simply reinstated my license. It must've been all those recommendation letters that did the trick."

"Let's celebrate."

Hearing that, Eastlyn came back down to earth. She held out Eleanor's note to him, watched as he read the words. "I found it when I was watering the plants. Someone in town has to be doing this for her."

Cooper rubbed his temple, felt a tension headache building. "Why would anyone want to do Eleanor's bidding after all this time? Why would someone do this kind of thing for her now? She never had a lot of friends back then so how could she possibly talk a sane person into helping her stalk her own kids?"

Eastlyn chewed her bottom lip. "At least no friends you knew anything about. Let me ask you something that's bothered me since I first heard the story that Eleanor took her kids out on the boat that night and left you guys there. Where did Eleanor go when she jumped into the water? What was her immediate destination? I mean, did she swim back through the bay to get to Pelican Pointe? I don't think so. She was leaving town, so that hardly seems like the thing she'd do. How far did she have to swim that night? Was she a good swimmer?"

Cooper's eyes grew wide. "You think someone was out there waiting for her that night?"

"Yeah, I do. It's the only thing that makes sense. I think they were sitting in another boat not far from where you kids were. They saw the whole thing play out because, they probably helped her get away."

"Another lover she's covering for?"

"Maybe. We'll have to…"

Cooper pulled Eastlyn close. "Right now, we need to set this aside. Eleanor doesn't get to ruin this for either one of us. You've waited too long to get your license back to have the news take a backseat. I say we should celebrate, the sooner, the better."

"Good idea. I'll call Durke, Thane and Isabella. Oh, my God, I need to let Kaeden know that I'm a pilot again. I need a computer. We need to throw a party, a big one. Now all I need is something to fly."

"Good thing we're working on that," Cooper said as he scooped her off her feet and whirled her in a circle.

Thanks to Drea and Caleb, Shelby and Landon and a slew of others, they got the word out. Less than twenty-four hours later Thane and Isabella had pulled off the impossible by setting up a huge Sunday barbeque at the lighthouse to mark the occasion.

Drea organized the potluck portion. Folding tables with brightly colored tablecloths held an assortment of covered dishes, desserts, and bags of chips.

Thane, Nick, Logan, and Troy manned the four grills set up brimming with hamburger patties, hot dogs and sausage links.

Even Zach tried to enjoy himself by taking turns throwing a Frisbee back and forth to Bree.

Hayden and Ethan set up a net for volleyball while Keegan and Cord introduced several of the kids to a litter of puppies and bunny rabbits.

Jordan and River dealt with fussy toddlers who needed naps.

Durke looked out over the carnival-like atmosphere and said, "I'm beginning to think you guys will use any excuse to throw a party."

"Hey, this is a big deal for me. Well, not just for me, but the whole town. Today they know the search and rescue idea is one step closer to becoming a reality." Eastlyn was in the middle of that explanation when she gazed over and caught sight of Scott standing near the scenic overhang, knee-high in lavender. He had his hands stuffed down in the pockets of his shorts, his shoulders tense and stiff.

She followed the track of Scott's eyes and realized he was watching Jordan tend to the children. The forlorn look on his face said it all.

Because she'd never seen Scott so sad, she wandered over. When she got within two feet, she reached down and snapped off a fragrant purple bud. "This is your legacy."

"What is? A bunch of flowers?"

"In a way. This entire town is your legacy and the people in it. If not for you, Nick would be back in LA miserable instead of helping Jordan run the B & B. Jordan would be living life back in San Francisco with so much sorrow packed inside her heart she'd still be trying to get past your death. If not for you, Cord wouldn't even be alive. If not for you, River wouldn't have her son back."

"What do you know about it anyway? That was all before you got here. Don't make it sound like you have a crystal ball where you know how it all would've ended up."

She smiled at his bristly attitude. "Surly today, aren't we? Well, I suppose a ghost is entitled to get pissed off now and again."

"Aren't you afraid people will see you out here and see that you're talking to yourself?"

She stuck her hands in the pockets of her shorts, mimicked his stance, content to watch him squirm for a change. "Haven't you heard? These days I don't much care what people think of me."

She glanced over at Cooper helping Jonah and Tommy get their kites in the air. Her heart lurched at the sight. Some places just felt more at home than others. "There's one more thing I know for certain. If not for you, I wouldn't have this second chance at doing what I love. I'd probably still be back in Bakersfield with a chip on my shoulder and a pill habit I didn't want to shake."

She cut her eyes again toward Cooper. "Thanks for giving me that once-in a-lifetime chance at being with someone who cares about me—ugly scars and all."

"I just brought you to town, the rest was up to you."

Eastlyn looked out over the crowd again, spread her arms out wide. "No, this is your doing, all of it. This is all on you. You'll just have to learn to live with the knowledge that all these people are gathered 'round in community spirit because you made it so."

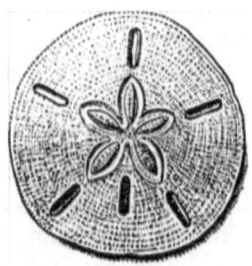

Thirty

When a logical man like Cooper Richmond couldn't find the key to a problem, he had to consider the alternative. But thinking outside the box for answers didn't seem to be working. After spending days trying to run down leads on who in town could be helping Eleanor, he'd followed dead end after dead end.

He'd circled back several times to all the people who he thought might remember any tidbit about Eleanor's life only to hit a brick wall. That is, until he realized that one man knew her even better than he did.

It took Cooper several days before he built up his courage enough to seek out his uncle.

When he did it was almost sunset. That perfect moment in time when the sky holds onto its dazzling shades of deep pink and golden reds like a revered overhead cathedral.

Cooper made his way past Landon's garden and into the greenhouse where he found Landon crouched on his knees fiddling with one of his hybrid tulips, an orange-tipped variety.

"What do you remember about the night Eleanor left?"

Landon stood up, as if weary of dealing with any further questions about Eleanor. "Why can't you ever just let it go, Cooper? Why can't you be more like Drea and Caleb and completely leave that night in the past?"

"I'm sorry I'm not who you want me to be. Apparently I never have been. I'm not Drea or Caleb. They didn't help bury their own father that night. For them, it's just a vague memory. While for me, it altered who I was and how I thought. But regardless of that insignificant event for you, I deserve to know if it was you waiting on the water that night to whisk Eleanor somewhere else?"

"Is that what you think? Is that what you're doing here?" He slapped his garden gloves on his thigh, went over and cleared off two crates. He set them upright, plopped his butt down. "Have a seat."

"I'd rather stand."

Landon took out a handkerchief from his back pocket, dabbed at his forehead. "Suit yourself. I did not help Eleanor leave her children on the water that night. But I have my suspicions about who did. It's been a long time. How blunt do you want me to be?"

Cooper studied his uncle. "As long as it's the truth. Brutal."

"All right, have it your way. Back when Eleanor was a teen she pretty much screwed anyone in pants. This behavior didn't change when she got married. Mostly her affairs occurred behind Layne's back, discreet hookups, he never even suspected. But there were a few she flaunted. One was with Kent Springer, the other one was with Flynn McCready."

Cooper decided he felt like sitting after all. He parked himself on the wooden box and let his forearms rest on his thighs. "Which one helped her leave her kids?"

"I have no way of knowing for certain. But my guess has always been one of those two. My money's on Springer." He lifted his arm around Cooper's shoulders. "How could you possibly think I could've helped Eleanor leave her kids out in the water like that?"

"I don't know. I have no excuse other than I've felt desperate for definitive answers after going to see her."

"Why did you do that?"

Cooper blew out a breath. "Because she refused to leave me alone. She told me about Flynn McCready. She also said he was the one who shot Dad and Miss Caldwell."

"You know she's lying, right?"

Cooper sent Landon a sly smile. "I brought that up. But someone left a note on my doorstep. Eleanor couldn't have done that. I thought if I discovered her liaisons they might shed some light on who did."

"What did the note say?"

"Brief, and to the point, listen to your mother. I figure if she implicates Flynn, he certainly wouldn't be the one who wants me to listen to her. He might end up in prison if she should ever get anyone to believe her story. So it can't be Flynn helping her now."

Landon bobbed his head. "Well, it can't be Kent. He's been dead for quite some time now."

"Another dead end."

"Maybe not." Landon let out a loud sigh and turned to stare at his nephew. "I never wanted you to know about this. But I've always suspected that you may have a brother." With that statement, Landon went on to explain how.

After his talk with Landon, Cooper had spent a busy forty-eight hours. When he did finally get a chance to unwind, it was in Eastlyn's bed. Durke had left to go back to Bakersfield and they had the little bungalow to themselves.

As they stretched out on the bed, Cooper went into what he'd discovered. "It seems teenage Kent Springer got Eleanor pregnant when she was fifteen. Typical reaction back then was to ship the unwed mother out of town as fast as possible under cover of darkness so no one knew the mother-to-be had sinned in such a major way. So my grandfather sends her away to a home in Santa Barbara for unwed mothers. She gives birth to a boy, gives the baby up for adoption. That makes the mysterious brother almost seven years older than I am."

Eastlyn adjusted her pillow. "At some point this brother had to find out the truth about his parentage and must've gotten in touch with Eleanor. We should track him down."

"Way ahead of you. Already done."

Eastlyn's eyes bugged. "You've already gone to see him. So what's his story?"

"His name's Jonathan Matthews, adopted by an Air Force doctor and his wife, who ended up settling down in the Denver area after his military stint. According to Jonathan's blog, which he posts to frequently, he's been trying to find his birth parents since he turned eighteen. He's known their names for almost two years. But by that time Kent was dead and he had no idea where Eleanor was. But when Eleanor's trial made headlines, Jonathan saw the news articles, wrote her a letter, started visiting her in jail and began a very emotional association with her. Of course, Eleanor did what she always does. She took charge of the relationship. She's been manipulating him from jail in the hopes that he would become what amounts to, my stalker. That note was just the beginning of what he had planned.

"Or what Eleanor had planned."

"No, I think Jonathan discovered he liked all the covert activities and planned a few on his own. When he discovered Eleanor didn't have a good relationship with her children, he decided she didn't need Drea, Caleb, or me. I think he was jealous because she kept bugging us to come visit her in prison. I don't think he really wanted that to happen. He didn't like the fact all Eleanor talked about were the kids who wouldn't have anything to do with her."

"That had to hurt. So why deliver the note?"

"A halfhearted attempt at best to fulfill Eleanor's wishes."

"Want me to go arrest this guy?"

This time it was Cooper who grinned. "Last time I checked it isn't against the law to leave a note. I told him as long as it stops, I wouldn't pursue legal recourse."

"Do you think it'll work? The threat through legal channels?"

"Let's hope so. I did ask him to move. Ever since Christmas, at the behest of Eleanor, Jonathan's rented a house from Logan and lives two streets over from mine."

"Oh my God, that's creepy."

"That's because Jonathan's a creepy kind of guy. I asked him to move. I suggested he find someplace near Chowchilla to be closer to Eleanor."

Eastlyn started laughing and snuggled into Cooper's chest. "At least she'll have one son nearby. What if this Jonathan doesn't move?"

"Then I plan to ask Logan to have a serious talk with his renter."

Eastlyn had a list of her own problems.

For two weeks Titus Driscoll had become her hobby. If she wasn't handling a drill or a sander working on the chopper on weekends or tending to the crops at the lighthouse, she spent her time trailing Driscoll around town.

She'd learned quite a bit about his activities. Even though he routinely knocked back a few at McCready's, he could be found most of the time out on the bay in his boat, a rusted seventeen-footer he used to fish.

Or at least that's what it looked like at a glance. Looking deeper, she discovered that fishing usually required some type of bait, even a tackle box. But Titus rarely carried one back and forth to the boat. Nor did he ever go inside the bait shop. Which meant if he wasn't fishing, what was he doing taking the boat out every day, rain or shine?

One thing she knew for certain, Titus didn't seem to have a regular job, at least one that encompassed a nine to five schedule.

A time or two she'd followed him out of town. He'd taken the San Sebastian cutoff, and from there had headed straight down the road to Thorwald's compound where she'd watched him from a distance.

Driscoll seemed to have his routine down. He did the same things at the same time almost daily.

There was no question in her mind that Titus was the key to bringing down Thorwald.

Thirty-year-old Judd Thorwald sat down to a breakfast of eggs and bacon, toast and jam in the house he shared with his mother. Judd had never married. Instead of marriage, he kept two girlfriends on the side, young ones barely out of high school. Between the two women, Judd could proudly boast that he was a father to four kids, two boys, two girls, all under the age of five.

The girlfriends knew about each other because Judd had long ago laid down the law. He wouldn't put up with animosity between females, no scratching each other's eyes out, no arguing, no disgruntled feuding. They would either learn to get along with one another or hit the road. Whatever the women decided to do, it didn't matter much to Judd. As long as they knew if they left, they'd be leaving the compound without their kids.

Judd pretty much ruled his domestic domain the same way he ruled the compound. Nothing went on that he didn't know about. When Judd had taken over it was right after Harley had been arrested. The man had been like a father to Judd during his teen years. So following in the man's footsteps seemed like a natural progression when they'd lost their leader.

Because Judd had grown up best friends with Harley's youngest, Bruno, it seemed someone needed to step up and fill the void. After Brent Cody had arrested the people he considered his family, Judd vowed to keep the enterprise going no matter what.

That's why he wasn't one bit happy about the turn the operation had taken in recent weeks. For years he'd run a successful meth trafficking enterprise without any intervention from law enforcement, or breaches in his security. Now he'd been told a couple of shmucks out for a stroll with a camera had put everything at risk.

"The woman actually denied she was working undercover for the Feds?" Judd asked his two henchmen. Judd stared at his stooges waiting for an answer from Mr. Wiry and Mr. Stocky. Both men refused to admit they hadn't gotten that far in the interrogation at the barn. But they were both determined to let the boss think otherwise.

"That's what she said."

"And I'm supposed to believe her? Based on what? Her word? Do I look that stupid to you? If she isn't working for the Feds, what does that leave? Now that Wild Brent Cody is out of office as the sheriff, we have an arrangement with the county, a nice one, one that is mutually beneficial. Because of that little agreement we know the snooping isn't coming from anyone there. Surely that piss ant Cody wouldn't have the nerve to send some stupid woman and inept toy store owner out here to spy on me?"

"Maybe her story is legit," Mr. Wiry added.

Judd eyed his henchmen. "Maybe. Just make sure you tighten up security around here by putting more men around that lab. And make sure that ridge stays clear from now on. Patrol night and day with the dogs if you have to."

After leaving Thorwald's place Eastlyn followed Driscoll back to Pelican Pointe where he promptly got back into his boat. This time Eastlyn was ready for his trip out to sea. She boarded the sleek twenty-two foot boat she'd borrowed from Isabella and cranked up the engine. Guiding the craft out of the bay, she took a slow cruise behind Driscoll.

She took out the camera Cooper had shown her how to use, adjusted its zoom lens and started snapping pictures. Despite the rocky waves and sway of the boat, she did her best to take the clearest shots she could get.

It took Driscoll just under three hours to finish his transactions before he decided to turn the boat toward the pier.

Keeping a safe distance back, Eastlyn guided Isabella's boat back into its slot, watched as Driscoll got out of his own and headed down the boardwalk.

She grabbed the camera bag and followed him until he disappeared inside the back door at McCready's. The time was just after two p.m. It was a little early to quench a thirst, but Eastlyn decided boating must've left Driscoll yearning for a refreshing beverage.

She pushed open the back door and slid into the little storage room immediately to the left where she had a view of the main room and the two men. Driscoll handed Flynn a brown envelope, which Flynn opened, and then counted the bills inside.

When Flynn had finished with his tally, he stuffed the cash under the counter at the bar and picked up a mug. He pulled the tap to fill it up with Guinness and slid it across the bar to Driscoll.

While Driscoll and Flynn were deep in conversation, as quietly as she could, Eastlyn left the confines of the little nook, slipped out the door and back outside into the alleyway.

Eastlyn made her way the four blocks to Layne's Trains, faster than a tailwind could blow her through the front door.

She took the Nikon out of the bag and placed it on the counter, sent a pleading look toward Cooper. "I need you to download what's on the disk and print out the pictures using your fancy printer. Then email me the pictures ASAP."

"What's up?"

"Can't talk now. Just work your tech magic and I'll see you in an hour."

"Hey, wait a minute. This isn't Fotomat."

"I know. But it's an emergency."

Cooper tilted his head to study her demeanor. "How can anyone have a photo emergency?"

"Just do your thing with the pictures and you'll see what I mean."

Before he could argue with that, he watched her rush out the door, hurry down the sidewalk and dash across the street. It occurred to him that for a woman with a prosthetic, she could really move that cute ass when she needed to.

Eastlyn arrived in Brent's office winded but pumped up on adrenaline. "I'm not sure how to tell you this, but I'm pretty certain that our first work as a team needs to include staking out McCready's."

"If this has anything to do with Eleanor's claim—"

"It doesn't. Give Cooper an hour and we'll have all the evidence you'll need to make an arrest. How do you get a warrant in these parts?"

Brent went over the procedure while she took notes for future reference. After he'd finished, she encouraged him to start the process. She told him what she'd witnessed between Driscoll and Flynn, explained what they were waiting for from Cooper.

Brent lifted a brow. "For a rookie, you're on a roll."

"I could carry this off because, let's face it, you would stick out like a sore thumb following people around town, not to mention following a boat out on the water."

Every so often she checked her email via cell phone until finally the notification popped up. She double-clicked the attachments, brought the images up on screen.

"What do you think now?"

Brent flipped through the camera roll. "I think when it comes time, you're due a stellar ninety-day review, maybe even a raise."

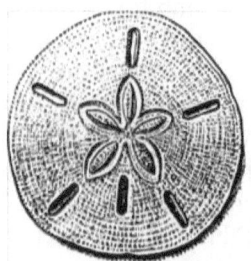

Thirty-One

The next morning it was as official as it would get. No more sneaking around working undercover for Eastlyn Parker.

Dressed in her uniform—khaki shirt, a badge displayed over the left pocket, a pair of dark brown, crisp trouser pants, a two-way radio, a Pelican Pointe police force patch on both sleeves, and a gun strapped to her waist—she looked like she meant business.

Cooper thought so, too. "You look…hot, really hot."

She grinned at him. "Is it the weapon? It's the Beretta, isn't it?"

Cooper shook his head. "Honestly, I think it's the badge. Or maybe it's all that khaki. Who knew, I'd love a woman in uniform. Although I think what I love the most is your dark green eyes."

She punched his arm before she realized what he'd said. "Love? Are you just kidding around?"

"How could I kid around when I'm looking at the best thing that's ever happened to me in my whole life?"

She took his head in both hands. "I feel exactly the same way about you."

"Then do me a favor. Try not to get shot up on your first day in uniform."

"I'll do my best."

"I have something for you." Cooper handed her a box, gift-wrapped in soft shades of purple paper.

"What's this?"

"You won't know until you open it."

Gingerly she worked the pretty ribbon off, began to thumb past the Scotch tape. After peeling back the paper, she removed the lid.

The box held a frame with a montage of pictures he'd taken beginning with the photo that day at the cliff, the one of the lavender in its infant stages with tiny buds just beginning to sprout. With each mosaic he'd captured its progress from seedling to a flowering bush laden with huge purple blossoms.

She clutched the picture to her chest. "Oh, Cooper, you couldn't have given me anything that I cherish more. This is amazing. I can't wait to see how it looks hanging on my living room wall. I know just where it should go. Which reminds me, I wonder if Cord and Keegan would consider selling me this little house?"

"I have a better idea, how about you move in with me?"

She grinned. "I like the idea of living in a hacienda."

"Then let's do it."

She placed a tender kiss on his lips. "I love the practical side to you, Mr. Richmond. By the way, are you sure you have that nutcase stalker of yours under control? Are you sure he'll pack up and leave like he promised? Because that kind rarely keeps his word about anything."

Cooper nodded. "I think Matthews will eventually move to be closer to Eleanor."

"You'll let me know if that isn't the case. I gotta get to work now. We'll discuss the move-in plans in greater detail later."

He grabbed her in a hug. "Be careful out there, Officer Parker."

"You bet I will. See you tonight."

She met Brent before eight a.m. at the station, eager and ready to go to work.

"Who do we bust first? Driscoll or Flynn?"

"Because we know he keeps to his schedule we nail Driscoll after he gets into the city limits with the supply of meth. We take down Titus after he's done the heavy lifting as quietly as possible. We don't want to tip our hand to Flynn since our upstanding businessman gets to bat clean-up."

"Okay, then where do we take Flynn down, home or at the bar?"

"Definitely when he's at work."

"Good thinking. So do we make a statement at a busy time when the place is packed or first thing right after he opens up?"

Brent turned to look at his enthusiastic recruit. "For what I have in mind we get Flynn alone. That means as soon as he unlocks the door at two p.m. this afternoon we're in his face." He studied her demeanor. "Who says you need special training for this job? You're pretty savvy when it comes to tactics."

"Thank the army."

"Let's hope that includes at least a marksman's badge."

She made a tsk sound to show her disapproval. "I think I can do a little better than that. Sharpshooter, thirty-one out of thirty-five, but I'm better with a handgun than a rifle."

Brent grinned for the first time that morning. "I knew I liked you for some reason. Are you nervous?"

"A little. I guess that's why I'm so chatty. Let's say we take down Driscoll and Flynn without incident. Does that insure Thorwald goes to jail as well?"

"I still have friends inside the sheriff's department. We pick up Driscoll and Flynn and I bet one of them starts talking. That should be enough to get a warrant for Thorwald's compound and bring down the operation."

"So when do we roll?"

He checked his watch. "Now's go time."

Driscoll drove a silver Toyota Tundra that was less than a year old. The truck had a Tonneau cover so no one could see the load of crystal meth he carried in its bed.

As soon as the pickup came into view, Brent let it pass at a steady clip doing forty-five even though at that speed it was going ten miles over the limit.

Brent sat back, watched Driscoll make the turn into the pier and put the Toyota in Park. He let the man get out and go to the back of his pickup.

From inside Brent's SUV, he and Eastlyn watched from the corner as Titus began to go through the bed of the truck, eventually unloading six smallish white trash bags.

Brent gunned the engine on the Tahoe and veered toward the pier. He pulled up behind the Tundra, quickly blocking the vehicle and preventing it from backing up.

With the Toyota now boxed in, Brent hit the Tahoe's red, white, and blue lights visible on the grill about the same time Titus Driscoll took a step toward the dock to load his boat.

Brent got out on one side, Eastlyn the other. They walked to where Titus stood near the wharf. Eastlyn stationed herself next to Brent, her hand resting on her weapon.

"What'd I do wrong?" Driscoll wanted to know as he started to get edgy. "What's this all about?"

"Whatcha got there, Titus?" Brent asked. "What's in the bags?"

"This?" Titus held up the white plastic trash sacks he carried in both hands, shifted his feet. "This is just a bunch of old batteries I had, I was taking them out to dump in the water."

"Hmm, do you believe that, Chief? That's a violation right there," Eastlyn said.

Titus started to look relieved. It even allowed him a brief attempt at humor. "Chief, that's funny. You know, because you're Indian, uh, Native American. You're also the Chief of Police, so it, you know, it's funny that she'd call you Chief."

Brent's face didn't show he thought it humorous or ironic. "Officer Parker, you want to get a look at what Mr. Driscoll is holding in his trash bags."

"Yes, sir." Eastlyn stepped forward and relieved Titus of one of the sacks. She stood back, untwisted the tie to peer inside. She saw sandwich-sized Baggies containing an off-white crystal substance, doled out in smaller quantities. Eastlyn unzipped one and sniffed the contents. "The odor's a dead giveaway. I'd say what we have here is medium-quality gravel."

Eastlyn took out her handcuffs. "Mr. Driscoll, I'm afraid we have good news and bad news."

"What do you mean?" Titus asked, ever hopeful it was all a big joke. Even as he felt the metal wrap around his wrists, he still looked dumbfounded that he'd been caught.

Eastlyn smiled at the dealer. "You were speeding through town. But this is your lucky day. We're gonna waive that speeding ticket for you. That's the good news. The bad news is we're charging you with violating California penal code HS 1-1-3-7-8, felony possession of methamphetamines with intent to distribute."

Titus looked stricken. "But... I go out on my boat every single day. I don't sell anything in town. I sell it out on the water."

Brent's face went hard, his eyes narrowed into slits. "You think that makes it okay? I've ID'd your contacts, Titus. And with your record, you're going away for a long time. Read him his rights. I really don't want to look at him any longer than I have to."

"Yes sir," Eastlyn said as she led Titus to the Tahoe.

"But what did I do wrong?" Titus asked Eastlyn. "I never sold the stuff in town. Judd explained it to me. He said it was okay as long I used my boat. He said I wouldn't be breaking any laws that way."

As Eastlyn stuffed him into the backseat, she shook her head and let out a laugh. "This is just a guess on my part, Mr. Driscoll. But I think all this time, Judd might've been lying to you."

At two p.m. on the dot, they repeated the teamwork as they moved through McCready's. Brent went through the door first while Eastlyn followed him inside as backup.

Eastlyn watched a somber Brent stand at the end of the long mahogany bar waiting for Flynn to notice his presence. Brent stood shoulders back, draped his thumbs through the loops of his jeans and stared down the owner.

"How's it going there, Flynn? You've met my new officer, Eastlyn Parker, haven't you?"

Flynn's eyes darted about and he started to act nervous. "Not officially, no."

"Hmm, maybe that's because you have a bad habit of staying away from town hall meetings. I wonder why that is?"

Flynn's face twitched with unease. "I run a business where I'm open seven days a week. The times you guys decide to get together usually coincide with me full up with customers."

"Fair enough. I think I can fix that for you. Mind telling me how long your bar has been part of Judd Thorwald's crystal meth business? Maybe you could tell me why you thought you could do it practically under my nose since my house is right across the street? How long have you been using this place as a front for Thorwald's Pelican Pointe connection?"

Taken aback by the accusation, Flynn put his hands on the wooden counter. "Now wait a minute. I don't know what you're talking about. I swear I don't. I've had your back a time or two, Brent Cody. You've known me a long time to make that kind of accusation."

"It's because of those two things—the times you've had my back and the fact that I took my first drink in here—that I'm standing here giving you a chance to tell me the truth, man to man. So don't come at me with a bunch of BS."

"I am telling you the truth."

Brent sighed. "So that's the way you want to play it. Okay. You were seen taking money from Titus Driscoll. We both know Titus is one of Thorwald's longtime drug runners. You've let Titus use your bar to set up drug dealers for Judd. They come in here to play pool, end up recruited by Titus to be one of Thorwald's distributors. The question is for how long? How long have you been doing this? I already know Titus Driscoll takes his boat out on the bay daily where he meets up offshore with the dealers. He distributes the meth from his boat, takes the money and brings it back onshore. That's when Titus makes his first stop in here right after he docks the boat. Why does Titus take the time to do that? Titus comes in to drop off your share before heading out to Thorwald's compound where Titus takes his share, leaving the bigger cut for Thorwald. If you aren't part of the whole mix then why take drug money from Titus Driscoll?"

Eastlyn saw Flynn swallow hard.

Without warning, Brent came around the other side of the bar and slapped the handcuffs on Flynn himself. "You're under arrest for knowing and aiding in the manufacture of methamphetamines and for helping Driscoll move it through my town."

He dragged Flynn around the front of the bar and plopped his butt down to sit in a chair. "You listen to me and listen good. There are children living within Thorwald's compound, not fifty feet from where his lab cooks the meth. You ever witnessed what a lab does when it explodes? It's a hellish nightmare. Just one wrong mix of chemicals and you get a massive fire that puts those kids at risk every day it's in operation."

Brent took a seat in one of the other chairs to meet Flynn at eye level. "There's something else. Did you ever have an affair with Eleanor Jennings Richmond?"

"What? No."

"Are you sure about that? Is that the answer you want to stick to? Because Eleanor tells a very different story about the night Layne Richmond and Brooke Caldwell died. She says you two were not only having a hot and heavy affair, but it was your idea to kill her husband. It was just Brooke's bad luck that she was at the pier that night. In fact, Eleanor says you're the one who pulled the trigger. Brooke was simply at the wrong place at the wrong time, sort of like collateral damage."

Flynn went pale. His chest began to heave hard. His breathing became labored. "No way did I have anything to do with those murders. Eleanor was acting all crazy back then. We did have a fling going on at the time but that's all it was to me, a fling. I did not have anything to do with Layne's or Brooke's death. I swear it."

"Like you swore just now you didn't know anything about Thorwald's meth operation. You mean like that? Is it possible two months after the fact that you watched as Eleanor abandoned her kids in the middle of the bay?"

Flynn's eyes grew wide. "What? No. I had nothing to do with that. By then our affair was over. She wasn't even talking to me then."

Sensing he might have the advantage, Brent played his trump card. "Okay, so maybe now you'll tell me everything you know about Thorwald's operation. Start at the beginning."

"Okay, okay. I got paid to turn the other way while Titus used the bar as a place to make contact with new buyers. You have that right."

Brent looked at his recruit. "Eastlyn, what's the penalty in this state for willingly knowing about and assisting in the operation of a meth lab the size Thorwald runs?"

"I think we can arrange for Flynn to spend up to five years in Tehachapi."

"Hear that, Flynn. Up to five years in one of the worst prisons that California has to offer. Would you be willing to testify to what you know in order to put Thorwald and Titus away?"

"If it'll get me out of the mess I've made? Absolutely."
"Good. Officer Parker?"
"Yes, sir."
"Read our friend here his Miranda rights."

Business had picked up inside Layne's Trains. For a summer day it seemed to Cooper that the steady stream through the door was mostly curious kids. Not a problem for him since he loved answering the questions they asked about the different train sets.

While a few were there to buy various pieces to add to their collection, most just wanted to browse and pass the time. There were older ones who begged for a look at the radio-controlled cars he kept in stock. To a kid, you were never too old and it was never too early to start their Christmas wish list.

That's why the holidays were on his mind when Cooper looked up and saw Jonathan Matthews standing inside the doorway. His first thought was the man looked out of place among all the kids. There was something about his demeanor though that signaled a more sinister problem. Matthews gripped a small silver pistol in his left hand.

Cooper's first thought was to get the kids out of the store. But how? He reached under the counter where he kept the store phone, dialed 911.

"What are you doing in my store, Jonathan? There's nothing for you here. I told you that already."

"You won't listen to your mother. Eleanor keeps trying to tell you the truth about what happened. But you won't listen. I'm here to make sure you listen."

Cooper realized trying to reason with this man and use any kind of logic would be a waste of time. After all, he'd tried once before and believed he'd gotten through only to realize now the man probably needed psychiatric care.

Cooper eyed the little gun and saw Jonathan's hands shaking, watched as his eyes darted in skittish fashion around the store. "How do you intend to make me listen?"

Matthews jerked the gun around. "You're coming with me to see our mother. Now."

Through the plate-glass window Cooper saw Eastlyn and then Brent make their way to the front door and stand on either side of it.

Eastlyn motioned that she wanted Cooper to lead Matthews outside onto the sidewalk just before she ducked to the right out of sight. That meant she had that side covered while Brent waited to the left of the door.

Cooper held up his hands. "Okay. I'll go with you but don't hurt the kids."

"I don't want to hurt anybody. I just want you to go with me so you can finally know the truth."

"The truth, huh? Are you driving? Where are you parked?" Cooper asked and started toward the front door. But Matthews had other ideas.

"I'm parked around back."

Cooper panicked a little, but hoped like hell either Eastlyn or Brent had thought to cover the alleyway. He changed direction, drifted through the store to the rear. Turning the knob, he flung the door back and took a couple of steps outside in front of Matthews. Out of the corner of his eye, he caught a shadow to his right.

"Come on, move," Matthews demanded as he shoved Cooper forward. "My car's the blue BMW parked by the dumpster. Now move!"

"I don't think so," Eastlyn said quietly as she held the Beretta to the back of Matthews' head. "Drop the weapon. Now. Because I have no problem shooting you, none at all."

Matthews tossed the silver .22 and it clanked on the concrete.

For the second time that day, Eastlyn took out her handcuffs. "And to think I thought this was a peaceful little town. Is it always like this?"

She looked directly at Cooper. "Whatever happened to me thinking this was Mayberry?"

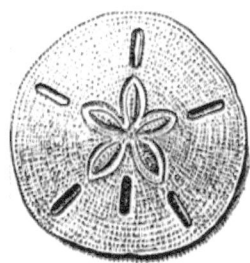

Thirty-Two

There was something warm and settling that moved through the soul at knowing the one you loved was waiting for you at the end of the day.

It was a new kind of feeling for both of them.

They walked hand in hand along the beach, the sun blocked from view as it made its drop somewhere over the horizon. The sky, hazy with low-hanging clouds, spit misty drops that made little splats on the jackets they wore.

Eastlyn shivered and burrowed closer into Coop. "With the wind, it sure doesn't feel like summer."

"I'm from the Bay Area you get used to the chilly summer nights there. You know what Mark Twain said about San Francisco, don't you? 'The coldest winter I ever spent was a summer in San Francisco.' That about sums up why you never wore shorts to a ballgame at the old Candlestick Park."

"You're just full of information."

"Did I tell you how amazing you were yesterday?"

"About a dozen times. I'm just glad you called 911 when you did and didn't try to take him on with all the kids in the shop."

"Do I look stupid to you?"

"You look windblown," she said jabbing him in the ribs with a finger.

"What will happen to Flynn?"

She toed a small rock considering that. "He's already started singing like a baby sparrow. More than likely he'll take a plea deal and serve six months in county."

"What will happen to the bar?"

"Beats me. For now, it's closed up tight."

"You know, happy hour should move to The Pointe. I've told Perry if he'd just drop his prices a tad he could make it all up in volume."

Eastlyn chuckled with laughter. "Perry should listen to you. You've probably already run the numbers for him."

"Come on, we'd better start back. Looks like the rain's coming down harder," Cooper suggested.

But new plant growth, sprouting through the sandy soil, caught her eye. She went over to inspect the crop, kneeled down to brush her hand over the tops of the purple lavender that had found its way through the dirt. "Cooper, look at this. The lavender's taken over what used to be River's archaeological site. Some of the seeds I planted from the cliff must've drifted down here to the beach and taken root. By fall it'll be all over this stretch."

He pulled her into his arms. "You did this, Eastlyn. Look around you. You've created your own lavender beach. What was it you suggested, for the town to hold its first annual lavender festival? I think there's a good chance you could pull it off."

"I'd certainly have enough people who'd volunteer to help. The question is do you think the town can withstand one more carnival-like atmosphere next August? Because that's when I figure the plants will be ready for a major harvest."

"I think you should go for it. Wally called the house before you got home. He's located an engine in San Jose. He and Thane plan to pick it up this weekend. I plan to ask Caleb to watch the store and go with them. Too bad you have to work."

"Don't rub it in." She finally stopped walking in the rain and turned to face him with rain dripping down her face. "Can you live with a pilot, Cooper? Can you live with me being a cop? Because I've got the life back that I want, the one I think I was meant to have all along. Then there's the fact that I'm in love with you. I think I was meant to have you in my life. And to tell you the truth, I don't want to mess this up anymore. Because I love you."

"It'll take some time for me to get that image out of my head, the one where you're holding a gun to that guy's head. Would you really have blown him away?"

"You bet I would have."

His face mirrored hers. "Then each day I'll be grateful you took him down without firing a shot. I'll learn to live with you strapping on a gun. And married to a pilot? Are you kidding? I want that ride over Pelican Pointe that you promised me."

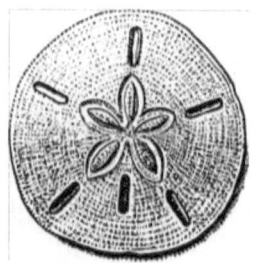

Epilogue

Four months later
North of Pelican Pointe

Eastlyn sat at the controls of the upgraded, renovated Bell copter and checked the brand-new vertical instrumentation panel. She glanced out the window onto the tarmac of the helipad Thane and Logan had built north of town. Even though nightfall loomed, it would be a clear November night for flying.

Since the aircraft would make plenty of flights over water, it carried flotation gear, in addition to medical kits, and survival equipment for search and rescue operations. If necessary two litters could also be installed for transporting injured passengers to a hospital.

"Sioux one-niner to Sky Park requesting takeoff," Eastlyn said into her headset as she waited for ground clearance.

"Sioux one-niner cleared for takeoff via direct to Smuggler's Bay. Climb and maintain four thousand feet."

"Roger that. Sioux one-niner straight out departure for mini run to Smuggler's Bay," Eastlyn repeated. She revved the engine, lifted off. As the polished blue and white bird climbed into the sky, she yelled out, "This is for you, Pop, wherever you are!"

"This is so cool," Cooper hollered over the blade noise. He watched her in the pilot's seat, saw the absolute joy on her face as she took a southern route along the coast. "You're absolutely knock-out beautiful right now."

"You need glasses," she said with a grin.

"I got a text from Drea before we took off. She says half the town is lined up back at the pier waiting for you to give them a ride."

"We should do that for a fundraiser, you know, down the road. I could take them up and out over the water. The bubble canopy makes a perfect observation deck." To prove her point, she glanced up at the night sky. "Look at that view. With you sitting next to me it seems like we're dancing with the moon right now."

Cooper stared at the huge illuminated sphere, so close it looked as though he could reach out and hold it in his hand. "What a perfect shot."

He grabbed his camera case so he could capture the moment with his Nikon, pulled out his telephoto lens, attached it to the front, and aimed. But when he looked through the viewfinder, he saw words instead of the waxing image he expected to see. He tried again. Same words. This time he took the bottom of his shirttail and attempted to wipe off any smudges on the lens to get a clearer shot.

"What gives?" Cooper said to Eastlyn.

"With what?"

"I mean, each time I try to focus, I keep seeing these same words through my viewfinder."

"What words? Don't tell me you're cracking up after everything we've been through."

He held the camera up to take a photo of her at the controls. Again, the same message appeared in the shot.

"Maybe I am cracking up," he finally admitted.

"What are you talking about? You're starting to get a weird look on your face."

"Each time I try to take the picture I see the same phrase through my viewfinder."

"What's the phrase?"

"You'll think it's corny."

"Maybe not."

Cooper repeated what he saw. "'You've captured a true warrior's heart, treat it with kindness.'"

"That's the phrase. That's downright romantic." She weaved to the left and saw the lighthouse come into view. "We're almost over the bay. Drea's right, look at the crowd below."

A throng of people stood on the dock, their arms waving in the air. There was so much enthusiasm she felt as though she'd landed in the middle of a hero's welcome.

"What's going on?" she asked.

Cooper looked at her and grinned. "I think this is Scott's way of telling us that we've both finally made it home."

Dear Reader:

If you enjoyed *Lavender Beach*, please take the time to leave a review.
A review shows others how you feel about my work.
By recommending it to your friends and family it helps spread the word.
If you have the time let me know via Facebook or my website.
I'd love to hear from you!

For a complete list of my other books visit my website.
www.vickiemckeehan.com

Want to connect with me to leave a comment?
Go to Facebook
www.facebook.com/VickieMcKeehan

Don't miss these other exciting titles by bestselling author

Vickie McKeehan

The Pelican Pointe Series
PROMISE COVE
HIDDEN MOON BAY
DANCING TIDES
LIGHTHOUSE REEF
STARLIGHT DUNES
LAST CHANCE HARBOR
SEA GLASS COTTAGE
LAVENDER BEACH
SANDCASTLES UNDER THE CHRISTMAS MOON
BENEATH WINTER SAND
KEEPING CAPE SUMMER (2018)

The Evil Secrets Trilogy
JUST EVIL Book One
DEEPER EVIL Book Two
ENDING EVIL Book Three
EVIL SECRETS TRILOGY BOXED SET

The Skye Cree Novels
THE BONES OF OTHERS
THE BONES WILL TELL
THE BOX OF BONES
HIS GARDEN OF BONES
TRUTH IN THE BONES
SEA OF BONES (2018)

The Indigo Brothers Trilogy
INDIGO FIRE
INDIGO HEAT
INDIGO JUSTICE
INDIGO BROTHERS TRILOGY BOXED SET

Coyote Wells Mysteries
MYSTIC FALLS
SHADOW CANYON
SPIRIT LAKE (2018)

ABOUT THE AUTHOR

Vickie McKeehan's novels have consistently appeared on Amazon's Top 100 lists in Contemporary Romance, Romantic Suspense and Mystery / Thriller. She writes what she loves to read—heartwarming romance laced with suspense, heart-pounding thrillers, and riveting mysteries. Vickie loves to write about compelling and down-to-earth characters in settings that stay with her readers long after they've finished her books. She makes her home in Southern California.

Find Vickie online at
https://www.facebook.com/VickieMcKeehan
http://www.vickiemckeehan.com/
https://vickiemckeehan.wordpress.com